FATIMA BALA

Broken

First edition

ISBN: 9798398234855

This book was professionally typeset on Reedsy.
Find out more at reedsy.com

To the girls who read Gibran, Rumi, and Darwish.

"If you put shame in a petri dish, it needs three ingredients to grow exponentially: secrecy, silence, and judgment."

Dr. Brené Brown

Acknowledgement

To my husband Kabir, when I started writing this story, it was supposed to stay on an online platform, and I was going to be an anonymous writer because I did not want anyone to know that I wrote a story about Muslim characters who were not perfect. *What would people say?* I asked him, and he wondered why I was bothered about what people think. He shows up for me always and always encourages me to write; He takes time out of his busy schedule to read my drafts, correct my mistakes and give his opinion. For the bike rides and my helmet, all of which made it into this story. I love you.

I am a better writer today than when I started this story three years ago, and that is because of my editor now turned friend, Khadija Yusra Sanusi. Her unwavering commitment to ensuring that Arewa stories remain authentic in a literary world that loves to brush us in a single color has helped my stories come to life. For the many emails, multiple edits, countless voice notes, and constant encouragement even when I fell out of love with the story, I am incredibly grateful.

To Fatima Mana Babangida, for her subtle threats carefully embedded in loving messages reminding me to fix what I broke in separating the main characters and why redemption is the only way the story could end. I love you.

To Grace Eke, Judith Kallaghe, Angelina Acheampong, Sa'ada Abdulmalik, and Mofe Popo, ours is a friendship that has made me better, and your belief in my capabilities has strengthened me, and I hope I do the same for you all. My support system.

To my brother, Ya Adamu Kabir, for always being the best brother, the most dependable, and the most caring, I am extremely blessed to have you.

To Ummita - my mother (Hajiya Hauwa Mohammed), every time I send you my stories to make sure the context is right, to ensure that I have captured the nuances of our complex culture, and every time you call back with a page full of notes to address, it only makes me want to be the writer you think that I am. Thank you for instilling the love of stories in me.

To my children, yes, mummy writes books that don't have pictures, and I know you think that makes them less interesting, but I think you understand how much mummy loves doing what she does, and Alhamdulillah for you always.

To the family of readers online who have told me how much they love Ahmad and Fa'iza's rollercoaster journey. I cannot name you all, but I appreciate you always.

I

Part One

Letting go of something nameless should be easy.
It's the web we've created that's difficult to untangle.
It takes a lifetime to scratch out the oaths,
to unlearn the imaginary traces of fingertips on skin.

Chapter 1

Abuja, September 2016

"So, do you want to talk about it?"

I really didn't want to talk about it, but I could feel his stare piercing the back of my head. We were in the living room in my parents' house, one of the three living rooms in the house that I grew up in. I didn't turn around because I could not stand to look him in the face, and even as I walked further away from his voice, all I could do in that moment was take a deep breath and in an attempt to distance myself from his gaze, I opened the fridge and took out a bottle of milk. Within seconds, the bottle fell on the floor, spilling milk on the cold, grey-marbled tiles of the dining room, missing the brown carpet by inches.

"*Ugh,*" I looked around for something to clean up the mess, angry at my clumsiness.

"Are you seriously not gonna answer me?" he asked again.

I could hear the hint of frustration in his voice, even though he maintained his distance. He was always good at taking a step back and giving me space – far enough for me to not feel suffocated, yet close enough for him to hover over me whenever he felt the need to. The strong scent of his *oud* perfume reminded me of happier times, and in a moment of weakness, it almost propelled me to turn around and look at his face. But I was determined not to. I could feel tears moistening my eyes, so I focused my sight on the marble tiles and the spilled milk that was refusing to get soaked by the paper towels I found on the dining table.

I heard the door in the outer hallway door close with a slight bang, and just as I was rounding up my cleaning, his voice dropped like a cannonball: "Someone is here." Crouched on the floor, I sighed as I heard him walking away from the dining room and towards the living room. Let the charade begin.

"Umma, *ina wuni.* Good evening," I heard him from the dining room and imagined him dropping to the customary crouch as he greeted my mother.

I could hear my mum walking into the living room that led her towards us. I looked up to find her regally dressed as though she were the mother of a bride, in a heavy cream-colored burgundy brocade gown and a maroon veil wrapped over her head with her gold bracelets clanking together by the slow, deliberate movements she made as she looked around the room.

She adjusted her veil over her head as she answered him: "Ahmad, How are you? When did you come back?"

"I came back last night, Umma," he answered.

"Oh yes, that's right. Your mum mentioned that you would be coming back this week." She smiled at him as he stood next to her by the door. *"An gama Masters din dai?* Have you finished the Masters?"

"Ph.D., *ne*," he smiled as he corrected her with the learned fake humility we perfect quite early in northern Nigeria.

"That's true; it's Ph.D," my mother corrected herself. "I suppose you came to see your friend, Amin?" She asked to confirm that he was at the house to see my older brother, his oldest friend.

He looked around the room for the first time since he arrived to give the impression that he had just come indoors himself. "Yes," he said, "I thought I would find him here."

She looked at me, our eyes met, and I watched a silent chuckle escape her, and then, in the most casual tone, she asked as she looked back at him,

"*Ya shirin bikin*? How are your wedding preparations going?"

He opened his mouth, then swallowed back his words. "*Um*... Alham.. Alhamdulillah." The always articulate, ever-charming Ahmad Babangida, who always had a witty comeback for everything, was struggling to find words other than "Thank God." For the first time since I've known him, he fumbled when asked about his upcoming wedding.

Ahmad Babangida was getting married. I blinked rapidly to force back the tears that threatened to spill down my cheeks when I heard Atine, our househelp's voice. In my determination to keep my eyes glued to the spill I was cleaning, I hadn't seen her walk into the dining room.

"Aunty Fa'iza let me clean it," she said in Hausa.

"I have told you to stop calling me aunty." I said to her under my breath as I stood up, grabbed my car keys and travel mug from the dining table. "Umma, I'm going to work. I'll be back by Zuhr *Insha'Allah,* God willing."

"Have a good day at work."

I walked out of the house without acknowledging the man standing next to her; I couldn't be bothered to feign courtesy or familiarity. I got into my car, slammed the doors, and it was only when I was well past the gates, past two traffic lights, that I parked the car on the curb and started hitting the steering wheel with my fists, losing the battle with my self-control as the tears streamed down my face uncontrollably.

Chapter 2

Abuja, September 2010

I looked around my room one last time – at my queen-sized bed and pink pillows, my half-empty closet, and my bookshelf as my fingers absent-mindedly scrolled over rows of novels and textbooks. I turned around, and my eyes fell on the family portrait that sat above the bed's headboard, which I got from Umma's room when she redecorated a few years ago and had kept in my room ever since then. It was a portrait of our family – my father, whom we all call Abba, my mother, Umma, my brothers (Ya Amin and Abubakar) and me, the youngest – taken on my parents' 15th wedding anniversary. The picture was taken almost a decade ago when I was just eight years old. Looking at it, my legs felt heavy, and my heart was filled with immense sadness.

"Fa'iza, have you prayed?" Abubakar's voice interrupted my thoughts. I turned around to respond but only caught a glimpse of the back of his black shirt as he rushed into his room without waiting for my answer. In our household, questions like this were rhetorical; they served as reminders.

I nodded to myself. After praying *Isha,* the last prayer of the day, I had spent about 30 minutes on my praying mat after reading my Qur'an and alternating from praying for a safe flight and strength to not break down and cry as this was the first time I would be away from my parents.

With a sigh, I closed my door for what would be the last time in a while and walked to the other side of the house towards my parents' living room. As I moved down the hallway that connected my father's section to the children's section, I was met with the scent of *turaren wuta*, local incense. I followed the scent into my father's living room and found Abba, a grey-haired man in his fifties, with a lean stature and a greying moustache sitting in his usual deep brown leather armchair facing the television that was on a news channel, but he had a newspaper open. His bespectacled face frowned at the news as he listened to the newscaster relay news regarding a political party, PCP. Politics was of no interest to me, even though my family had a significant stake in it. "Assalamu alaikum," I said, announcing my presence as I walked into the living room.

"Wa alaikumus salam," he responded, dragging his words slowly the way he always did. He folded the newspaper and put it away as he removed his glasses and looked up at me with a smile. "*Kin shirya*? Are you ready?"

"Yes, Abba," I sat on the Persian carpet next to him, ready for the *nasiha*, advice that I knew was the reason he sent for me.

"Fa'iza, you have always made me proud," he started. "Your first year in university is as important as any; the path you take right now can be the difference between a first class and a second class, so make sure you take your studies very seriously," he paused. "*Kina ji ko*? Are you listening?"

I nodded silently with tears coming down my eyes. Even with my determination not to cry, I couldn't help the tears as he spoke, as I imagined being so far from him for so long, as I imagined starting a new life in Canada.

"*Ba kuka zaki yi ba*. There's no reason to cry," my mother said as she walked into the room. She was wearing a white lace boubou, her long dark hair in a single plait reaching the middle of her back, half-covered with a long white veil. She inherited her looks from her half-Lebanese mother – her long hair, light brown skin, almond-shaped eyes and a dainty pointed nose. "Pay attention to your studies and surround yourself with the right people. Most importantly, *kar ki ba mu kunya*. Do not embarrass us." Umma liked to say she brought us up with iron fists, but I think she reserved that for just me. With me, she was quite the disciplinarian; my brothers, however, got away with almost anything, things that I never dared to do, like staying out late or having people my parents didn't know over.

"Okay, Umma. *Insha Allah*," I heard myself answer as I thought about the phrase, "do not embarrass us." Growing up, phrases like that and "what will people think?" governed our every single decision and action as a family and how I lived my life.

"You're not forgetting anything, are you?" she asked.

I shook my head to say no.

"If you have any issues at all, reach out to Mami and make sure that you visit her on the weekends when you can," Umma said. Aunty Mami was my mother's oldest friend; they had grown up together in Kano. Her husband, the current Nigerian Ambassador to Canada, also had a good relationship with my father; they went to university together and had remained inseparable ever since. The fact that they lived in the same city my University was situated was what finally convinced my father to agree to send me all the way to Canada.

"Okay, Umma."

"Make sure you call me on your layover in Paris," Abba handed me an envelope. He always made sure I had spare change in different currencies whenever I was traveling. For the sake of emergency, he would always say.

"*Insha Allah*," I stood up to hug him, from the corner of my eye, I saw Abubakar coming into the living room and I knew it was time to leave.

"*Allah ya kai ku lafiya*. Have a safe flight," my father said to us both.

To this day, Abubakar teases me about how much I cried when I was leaving home for university. I do not remember much after saying goodbye to my parents, but I remember the ride to Abuja airport feeling unusually long. So long, in fact, that I almost told the driver to make a U-turn and head back home. Maybe Baze University wasn't such a bad idea. At least I wouldn't have to leave home. Abuja has always been home for me – all through my primary and secondary school years, the comfort of having family and friends a few minutes away and attending family fairs and weddings with my cousins. Looking back now, I'm happy I left because if I hadn't left, I would never have met him – the one who turned my whole world upside down – Ahmad Babangida.

* * *

Hours later, the pilot's announcement woke me up. I had forgotten to remove my headphones from my hand luggage, and now that it was in the overhead bin, I didn't want to discomfort the people around me, so I decided not to play an in-flight movie, and I slept all the way from Abuja to Paris.

We arrived at Charles de Gaulle airport in the morning, and as Abubakar and I made our way out of the plane, he turned to me, "there's a prayer room in the transit area. Let's pray first, then head to the business lounge to rest before our next flight." He was used to this route, as he always transited in Paris on the way to and from his university in the United States.

I nodded and we walked silently to the escalators and then to the restrooms by the prayer room to perform our ablutions. I made a right to the ladies', and he turned left and disappeared down the corridor. Once inside, I opened my hand luggage and grabbed my travel-sized toiletries, brushed my teeth, washed my face, and performed *wudhu*, ablution. After that, I looked at my reflection in the mirror and readjusted my scarf to cover my hair before going out of the restroom. Abubakar was waiting for me outside. "I'm hungry," he said absentmindedly as he scrolled through his phone. "The meat in the lounge is hardly ever *halal* in this airport, so let's stick to the vegetarian options."

After praying, we walked towards the lounge, and I saw a bookstore and headed towards it. "I'm going to go and check if they have the second book of the Brandon Sanderson series," I told my brother, who looked around, pointed to the Starbucks coffee shop opposite and replied, "Okay, I'll wait there. Want anything to drink?"

"Grande caramel macchiato."

"Alright," he said as he walked away.

I went into the bookstore and browsed their recent releases. I didn't find what I was looking for, but I picked up *50 Shades of Grey,* curious to see what all the fuss has been about. After I paid at the counter, I turned around, and a guy bumped into me, his bottle of water spilling all over my sweater. He looked about six feet tall, with light brown skin and a muscular frame.

"Watch where you're going, miss," he said with a British accent as he pulled his phone from his ear.

"Excuse *you?*" I replied, getting angry.

"You bumped into me," he said like he was expecting an apology.

"No," I said, gesturing to his phone. "You weren't watching where you were going!"

He scoffed, shook his head and walked away.

I disliked that haughty attitude in men; it irked me. I hissed and walked out of the store towards Starbucks.

"Who pissed you off?" Abubakar asked as I walked towards him with a scowl on my face.

"Nobody," I answered, not wanting to linger on the topic. "We need to call Abba and Umma."

"*Dama, ke nike jira.* I was waiting for you."

* * *

"You have until 12 midnight to submit your assignment, if you have any questions, shoot me an email," the professor said as he turned off the projector in the lecture hall at Ryerson University.

I hurriedly scribbled 12 midnight in my notebook and underlined it, so I wouldn't forget, then closed my MacBook and put it in my backpack with my notebook and pens. It had only been a few months in Canada, and although my classes were going well, I was already sick of the snow. It was always so cold, and everyone kept saying it would get colder. Abubakar had left for the United States a few days after getting me settled into the University Residence for his Masters' degree in Economics. He was studying at Columbia University in New York, the same university our eldest brother, Ya Amin, graduated from earlier that year.

"So, what plans do you have for the weekend?" My friend, Sara, asked. Sara is Pakistani, and being the only two *Hijabis* in our class, our friendship was almost automatic. From the first lecture we had together at the beginning of the semester, we sat next to each other and exchanged stories about finding halal stores and mistakenly ordering items that had bacon in the cafeteria.

"I'm going to my Aunt's house. My cousin's coming to pick me up later this evening," I said as we walked out of class. "What about you?"

"I am going to Montreal. Have you been?" she was applying lip gloss to her already-painted lips.

I shook my head no.

"You should come with us! I'll be filming content for my channel, and we can go sight-seeing." Sara had about 20 thousand subscribers on her YouTube Lifestyle channel. A weekend out of Toronto sounded fun, but I couldn't just go off to Montreal without informing Aunty Mami, who was my guardian here in Toronto.

"Sounds great, but I can't. Maybe in the summer, when I can actually enjoy going out?" I laughed.

"Girrllllll, it's not even that cold," as we walked out of campus, her phone rang, and she let it ring out without answering. Her ringtone was a song from an Indian film I'd watched back home in Nigeria. She gave me a quick hug as we said our goodbyes, and I started walking briskly towards the residence, a 20-storey building that housed hundreds of mostly-international students. It had a gym on the 2nd floor, a movie theatre and a cafeteria on the ground floor. Local students lived in apartments in the city, but the residence was the closest place to Campus, so it was an easy and safe choice. It was my parents' choice.

I was freezing as I walked, despite the layers of clothing I had on. I tucked my hands further into the pockets of my jacket and cursed myself silently for forgetting my gloves. I had rushed out of my room that morning because I didn't want to be late for my lectures.

When I walked into the lobby of the residence, I was relieved to find it warm. My phone buzzed as I got out of the elevator and onto my floor. It was a text message from Afreen. I called Afreen my cousin because for as long as I could remember, I have called her mother my aunt even though in reality, we were not related. Afreen's text read: *On my way.*

Oh, damn it! I thought she said she would come in the evening. I texted back*: OK. See you soon.*

I hurried to my room, used my card to let myself in and put my phone to charge. I already had my weekend bag packed; I just had to pack everything I needed to complete the assignment due at midnight. I walked past the kitchenette I shared with my roommate to our shared bathroom and grabbed my toiletries. I was trying to recall if there was anything else I needed when my roommate Claire walked into the kitchenette in her pyjamas.

"Fa'iza, I used some of your cheese. I didn't realize that I had none left," she said, as she rubbed her eyes like she had just woken up.

"That's okay," I said absent-mindedly.

"I'll replace it when I get my groceries," she said as she opened the fridge, about to make a snack.

"That's okay. It's just cheese," I said again. My phone buzzed, and I went to check. It was Afreen again: *I'm downstairs.*

I stuffed my bag of toiletries into my backpack and carried my hand luggage. I was walking out of the room when I texted back*: Coming down.* "Claire, I'll see you on Sunday," I said.

"Have a good weekend!" I heard her say as I closed the door and walked down the hallway toward the elevator

Chapter 3

I found myself out in the cold again, the chilly wind seeping into my insulated winter jacket. Glancing at the parked cars in the visitor's parking lot, I saw a girl a little bit taller than me; I recognized her wide smile and high cheekbones from her WhatsApp display picture; she had on a white Canada goose parka jacket with black boots perched outside the passenger side of a white Porsche Cayenne. Her hair was wrapped with a white pashmina in a turban-like style, which shifted a little as she waved excitedly. It was Afreen.

I smiled and waved back. "Afreeeeen!!" I managed to say. My lips were so frozen and numb that I could barely feel them.

"*Yadai*, Fa'iza?" she greeted me with a quick hug as I approached the car. The car trunk popped open, and she helped put my luggage in the trunk. I was removing my backpack when I lost my balance in the wet snow and almost fell on my back. She caught me, steadying me as she held my hand and helped me open the door to the backseat. "*Ki shiga*. Get in. Let's get you warm," she said.

I got into the car, relieved at how warm it was. It smelled like home: leather and *oud*. I rubbed my hands together as I inhaled deeply. I heard her door close gently as she got into the passenger seat. It was only then that I noticed the gentleman wearing a white T-shirt and denim trousers in the driver's seat. He looked like he was in his late twenties, dark-skinned with a trimmed beard.

"Fa'iza, meet Zafar. Zafar, this is Fa'iza, my cousin that I've been telling you about," she smiled as she introduced us, then started buckling her seatbelt.

"Yadai, Fa'iza? How are you doing?" he pressed the ignition button, and the car started with a gentle hum. "*Ya sanyi*? How's the cold?"

"*Akwai sanyi fa*. It's really cold," I said, and they both laughed.

"This isn't your first time in Canada though, right?" He kept his eyes on the road as he asked me.

"No, we were here in the summer," I replied, thinking back to when Umma and I came on a campus tour. It was in June last year, and it was much warmer then.

"Are you hungry?" Afreen asked me, but before I could reply, she added: "Let's get some food. I'm hungry."

"What do you wanna eat, babe?" Zafar asked her with a low voice as we were driving slowly through the University gates. Her left hand grabbed his right hand, and he squeezed her fingers. *This – affection, or is it love? Whatever it is, it must be nice*; I thought to myself as I looked out the window at the white flurries falling so lightly. It was beginning to snow again.

"Let's go to Miku." Her reply, too, was almost a whisper.

I tried to pay attention to the music playing lightly. It was a Nasheed, an old favorite of mine, with Maher Zain thanking Allah for his partner and the beautiful thing their love was.

"Do you like sushi, Fa'ee?" She asked.

I looked away from the window and shrugged, "sure."

"Alright, let's do it!" she beamed at me with a slight twinkle in her eye. It felt good being with Afreen, especially when she introduced me to everyone as her cousin, even though we were not actually related. After sushi, we drove past a Golf and Country club to a gated community in the suburbs, and Zafar parked in the driveway and helped us get my luggage out of the car. We bade him goodbye, and we walked up the stone stairs and into Afreen's house. A two-storey building with two double attached garages.

"Don't tell me this is filled with books," she teased as I dragged my luggage up.

"I packed all of my textbooks." I joked. She opened the door, and we muttered salams under our breaths as we entered the house. White walls and a black grand piano on the main floor that was brightly lit by the light from the suspended multi-globe pendant chandelier. In front of me, two curved staircases led to the upper level. This was my first time at the house. I looked around at the luxury wallpaper, high pillars and gold accents. It was elegant.

"What do you want to do tonight?" she asked. "We can watch a movie." I noticed that when she asked questions, she answered them herself. It reminded me of my mother and made me miss her.

"There you are!" Aunty Mami's voice broke our quiet chatter. I looked up and saw her leaning on the silver railing of the stairs. A tall Fulani woman with a graceful demeanor, her smooth and even-toned skin glowed from the lights above her. She was wearing a *boubou* made out of pink Swiss voile, and she looked exactly the same way she usually did in Abuja – with her signature headtie style, which showed a hint of her hair and framed her face perfectly. It was a headtie style many women tried to replicate; you could tell by the comments on Instagram and articles in *Arewa* magazine columns. She held out her hands as I walked up the stairs to hug her.

"Aunty, *ina wuni*. Good evening," I greeted her.

"Fa'iza, wow. Look how beautiful you are!" she widened her eyes as she looked at me, "you look more and more like your Umma every time I see you, *masha Allah*."

Growing up, I picked up a strange rule – that one didn't respond to praises about his or her appearance; it was considered tactless in our culture to do so. In such circumstances, all one did was smile and hope the conversation would move to another topic. If it didn't, one tried to change it as subtly as possible. In my culture, subtlety was always key in everything we did.

"Umma sent something for you," I said as I brought out the gold-and-red wrapped package I had brought from Nigeria.

"*Oh ikon Allah*. My goodness. She went through all this trouble?" Aunty Mami asked as she held up the heavy square package. "Your mum always spoils me with the best gifts."

Gift exchanging was *Sunnah,* a Prophetic tradition. In Islam, the prophet encouraged it, and our mothers were constantly trying to outdo one another with the act. It was not about how expensive it was; it was the thoughtfulness that mattered. Umma never visited anyone empty-handed, and she made sure my first visit to Aunty Mami's house in Canada would be the same.

"*Nan gidan ki ne.* Feel at home here," she smiled at me. "Afreen's dad is still in Ottawa, but he will be back tomorrow, *insha Allah.*" I hadn't seen the ambassador in years since one of his visits to our house in Abuja. Like most of my parent's guests, I only caught a glimpse of him as he arrived at the house through the windows of our section in the compound, away from the entrance he used to enter my father's section.

Afreen was dragging my considerably light box to the guest room on the ground floor. When I got there, she was going through TV channels with the remote in her hand. "My room is next door," she announced, still looking at the TV screen. I nodded despite her being too distracted to notice. I looked around the brightly lit room with a queen-sized bed with plush pillows with a screen door that opened to a garden outside. She didn't look away from the screen until her phone started ringing, and a picture of Zafar flashed on the phone screen. To give her some privacy, I walked into the bathroom to perform my ablution, as it was time to pray *Maghrib,* the fourth prayer of the day, even though I could still hear her as I washed my hands. "Did I forget it?" Pause. "I can get it tomorrow then." Long pause, and then, "can't come today–" Just as the door closed shut.

After I prayed and freshened up, I decided to go to Afreen's room to work on my assignment, checking my text messages on my phone as I left the guest room. The first message was from my cousin, Aisha Batagarawa, asking me to like and comment on the picture she had just posted to her Instagram feed. I went to her profile and typed multiple love-struck emojis while knocking on the door across the hallway.

"Salam Alaikum," I opened the door opposite mine. The dark curtains prevented any amount of light from entering the room, so I could barely see the figure on the bed. "Afreen…?" I asked as I approached the bed. "Are you up?"

"Wrong room!" a gruff voice said as the bedside lamp came on, flooding the room with a dull yellow glow. There was somebody on the bed, and by the state of the room and the look on his face, I had just woken him from his sleep, and he didn't seem too pleased about it. I found my apologies stumbling out of my mouth in an incoherent monologue filled with embarrassment when I realized he was shirtless. I stumbled out of the room and closed the door a little louder than I intended.

"Fa'ee?"

I turned around and found Afreen standing in the doorway. *Next door* to the room I was in, not opposite. I had walked into someone else's room, and he was half naked; all he had on was a pair of boxers. I felt so stupid and embarrassed, but she looked like she was about to burst out laughing.

"My goodness!" she laughed. "You look like you've just seen a ghost."

"I –um, I thought you said. Sorry, I –"

"Don't apologize," she laughed it off as she led me into her room. After she closed the door, she asked: "He wasn't sleeping half-naked, was he? He does that a lot."

I didn't answer her. I was trying to remember where I'd seen his face. I knew that I'd seen that face somewhere, and then it hit me. How could I forget that face? It was the guy on his phone at the bookstore who bumped into me at CDG Airport during my layover. Oh, the horror!

Rihanna's *We found love* was playing in the background as I walked further into her room. The walls were covered with pale green wallpaper. In the middle of the room was a Queen sized bed that was covered in a cream and burgundy duvet, flanked by floating bedside tables, one of which had a burning scented candle that filled the room with the scent of jasmine and lily. Opposite the bed was a vanity table and a tufted stool on a white shaggy rug. Her pashmina scarf was draped on the ottoman by the foot of the bed, and her unfolded hijab was still on her mat where she had just prayed.

I got under the duvet covers, propped my laptop open on the pillows and was bringing out my notebook when Afreen asked: "Are you studying?"

"I have an assignment due at midnight."

"*Wana* course *ne*? Which course is it?" she picked up my notebook and started going through it without waiting for a response.

"LS103," I started explaining, "Res –"

"Research methods in Law, right?"

I nodded.

"Who's the lecturer?" she asked.

"McCain."

I can't believe I still remember that name. He had a thing for midnight deadlines."

"I didn't know you studied Law," I said, genuinely surprised. To be honest, I didn't know much about Aunty Mami's children, as they'd always lived outside Nigeria.

"No, I didn't. Ahmad did, and he was always complaining about it."

"Who's Ahmad?" I asked.

"My older brother – the one in the other room," she walked to her prayer mat and folded her hijab. "Is the music bothering you? I can turn it off."

"No, it's okay. I can study with music," I said as I thought of my two unfortunate encounters with the guy next door – her brother. I let it sink in while I worked on my essay. Once I started typing, I allowed myself to get consumed by it, forgetting everything else about my personal life – about missing my home, my parents, unanswered Instagram DMs, my upcoming quizzes and the shirtless guy in the next room who happened to be the good-looking, well-dressed but rude man at the bookstore and Aunty Mami's son. It was only when I finished that I started thinking of ways to avoid him this weekend until I returned to the residence on Sunday. How I was going to achieve that became my biggest dilemma for the weekend.

* * *

Chapter 3

The next morning, the breakfast table had a spread of delicacies – quiche, croissants, and everything one would expect for breakfast in a Nigerian home: yam, scrambled eggs, *akara*, pap, *masa*, and tea. Now, I understood why Aunty Mami insisted on taking her chef from Nigeria to every country they got assigned to. I had missed *masa* so much! I had a little bit of everything before I got full. As much as I wanted to eat more, I simply couldn't.

"Are you okay?" I asked Afreen. Her phone had kept buzzing throughout breakfast, and she was replying non-stop, leaving her plate untouched.

Before she could answer, the door opened, and Ahmad walked in. Our eyes met, and I couldn't look away from his chiseled face, strong angular jawline, and beard that was kept short. He looked like a man who worked out, with broad shoulders and muscular forearms that were covered in a crisp white shirt and dark blue pants with brown Oxford shoes that matched his brown belt. Quite similar to how he was dressed in Paris, the only thing missing was the brown trench coat. He caught my stare, and his thick eyebrows furrowed over deep brown eyes as they narrowed.

Afreen turned around as soon as he walked in. "Good, you're awake. Can I borrow your car? Just for an hour."

"No, take yours," he said as he held my gaze and slowly buttoned up his cuffs. The deep baritone of his voice was just like I remembered – confident, and his British accent made even the simplest of sentences sound arrogant. I quickly looked away as I brought an empty cup to my lips in an attempt to seem occupied.

"I haven't switched to winter tyres yet," she whined. It almost sounded like conversations I would have with my older brothers back home whenever I needed their help with something. If there was any wisdom I could pass on to Afreen, it was that whining never helped with older brothers.

"Then you should," he made himself some coffee. She saw him looking in my direction and pouted.

"Oh, this is Fa'iza," she introduced us. "She's staying with us for the weekend."

"Hi," he nodded in my direction as he sat opposite me before addressing his sister: "Call the dealership and make an appointment to have your tyres changed."

Afreen raised her hands in defeat, "I know, I know. I've just been occupied. But I really need to borrow your car, pretty pleaseeeee."

"No, I have an interview today and after that, I'm meeting with the boys," he said as he looked at his watch.

"What kind of interview takes place on a saturday?" Afreen asked.

"It's my company. I schedule interviews whenever the hell I want." He chuckled as he took a sip of his black coffee. *Aha – there it was!* I thought to myself. The self-righteous superiority was not a figment of my imagination. He never apologized for spilling water on me at the airport, never even acknowledged that he did it. And here he was with the attitude again.

He stood up, and his eyes caught mine again. To avoid eye contact, I quickly picked up my phone and started opening random apps – *anything* to seem occupied. I didn't look up until I heard the door close.

"Fa'iza, *lafiya*? Is everything okay?" Afreen was looking at me.

"I'm fine." I gestured to her plate. "You haven't touched your breakfast."

She sighed. "Tomorrow is Zafar's birthday."

Oh, Zafar. I guess we're talking about boyfriends now. Is this what having a sister would feel like? I wondered. Out loud, I said: "Nice. What are you planning for him?"

"Well, he'll be busy tomorrow, so we kinda have to celebrate today," she said, scratching the back of her hand nervously.

"Aww," I said awkwardly, unsure of what to say. I was not used to this kind of conversation. My brothers never talked about the girls they dated with me. They never discussed anything personal with me.

She looked at the wall clock, then continued. "I got him a cake and a few things. He's coming to pick me up later, but I need to go pick up the cake before he gets here so that I can surprise him."

"Why don't you take a taxi to the bakery?" I suggested hesitantly. I was not sure if she wanted advice or if she just wanted to confide in me.

She looked at me as she considered it. "Will you come with me?" she finally asked, and I nodded without thinking. "You will? Oh, you're the sweetest, Fa'iza. Thank you!"

"I don't mind," I said.

We were out within an hour. In the Taxi to the bakery, I couldn't stop thinking about Afreen telling Aunty Mami we were going to the Central Library to return a book. Why would she lie?

Chapter 4

It was just after 6 pm, and I was sitting on the ottoman in Afreen's room watching her apply lip gloss to her red lips. She was wearing a rose-colored jacquard off-shoulder midi dress, and small pearl earrings, with her hair in a tight bun.

"Oh, but you have to come." Afreen gushed as she looked at herself in the mirror. She turned around and held my hand, still pleading. "I feel bad leaving you here by yourself when we should be watching movies together like we said we would do this weekend."

"*Walahi*, it's fine. I swear. I don't want to be a third wheel," I smiled.

"He doesn't mind," she said, looking at herself in the mirror. She looked absolutely stunning.

"No, I'm going to rewatch old episodes of *Gossip girl*," I was relieved that I didn't have to dress up to do that. "Go, please. Have fun. Don't worry about me."

"Okay, babe," she said, giving me a hug. "Oh, and by the way, thank you for keeping my secret and for coming with me to get the cake." She smiled at me, and I smiled back. It was easy to keep the secret because Aunty Mami had gone to pick up the Ambassador from the Airport, and they were going to meet with a Tanzanian Diplomat before coming home.

Zafar called to say he was outside, and I helped Afreen carry the wrapped present in a paper bag and her clutch as we walked out of her room and towards the front door. I was utterly amazed at how she walked graciously in the highest stilettos I'd ever seen while carrying a box of cake. Zafar was leaning on his car, wearing a brown shirt tucked into dark trousers when we came out and when he saw her, his eyes glistened.

"Surprise," her voice was quiet, but the twinkle in her eye was hard to miss.

"Bobette and Belle," he sounded surprised as he helped her with the cake box. "But babe, you didn't have to."

"Of course, I did," Afreen smiled, "It's your favorite bakery!" The admiration between these two was so evident from the way they looked at each other, and it was amazing just watching them.

"Happy birthday," I said, passing the brown paper bag to Afreen to give to him.

"Thank you, Fa'iza," he said, opening the door for her.

Afreen blew me a kiss as they drove off. When the car was safely out of the driveway, I walked back into the house, into the living room on the ground floor and turned on the television. Netflix on a big screen was luxurious after weeks of watching all my favorite shows on my laptop. Looking back, this was the highlight of that first weekend – Netflixing alone in the quiet house, a break from student accommodation and uptight educationists. I was in a comfortable position on one of the white leather sectionals when the door flung open, and my eyes met Ahmad's.

"Hey," he said. And although the greeting was perfectly polite, the manner in which he said it seemed rude. *Hey.* Like I was some inconsequential extra human being in their house. He did not even wait for a reply as he walked into the room.

I pretended to be deeply engrossed in the fight between Serena and Blair on the 75-inch television mounted above the glass-walled electric fireplace in front of me, but I was suddenly conscious of the grey slacks and grey hoodie I'd changed into after praying *Asr.* I wished I was wearing something nicer. *Why do I care about what I was wearing?* I thought to myself.

He cleared his throat, "Are you alone?" He asked as he looked around the room. Where's Afreen?" From the corner of my eye, I saw that he'd changed into a white T-shirt and blue denim.

I glanced up briefly and tried to keep my expression neutral, "She just went out." I hated how timid my voice sounded.

He sat down on one of the white leather couches – not close to me, but I was painfully aware of his presence. I found myself trying to identify his perfume as he typed into his phone, and from the corner of my eye, I could see he raised the phone to his ear. A few seconds later, Afreen's unmistakable chipper, *hello, what's up?* could be faintly heard.

"Ya kika bar kawar ki a gida, ta zauna ita kadai, kaman wata marainiya?" he chuckled to himself, looking away from me as he asked 'Why did you leave your friend at home, sitting all alone, like a deserted orphan?' I could feel my toes digging into the soft green carpet and my eyes falling to the white orchid arrangement on the glass centre table. He was talking about me like I was not right there. I looked up at him, and from the smile on his face as he spoke into the phone, I immediately understood that he did not know that I understood Hausa. At the University, sometimes, people of other ethnicities mistook me for Somali or Eritrean, but Nigerians can always recognize other Nigerians in any space – except this one.

"Tana nan –" I heard him say into the phone again. "She's here –" I watched the smile fade slowly from his face, I had no doubt that at the end of the line, she was telling him that I understood everything he'd just said. I waited for him to end the call before getting up to leave the living room.

"Um – wait… what's your name again?" he asked in Hausa as he tried to stop me.

I let myself out.

"Fa'iza?" I heard him call out behind the closed door.

I made my way to Afreen's room and decided to watch my show there instead, but I couldn't concentrate. I didn't want to go back to the guestroom just yet because I didn't want to risk running into him again.

Kaman wata marainiya, he'd said. *Like a poor little orphan.* He didn't even remember my name.

* * *

Chapter 4

The following day, I went upstairs to the upper level which was divided into two bedrooms, a reading nook, an indoor office and another living room. The white walls had huge portraits of the family, and the carpeted floors were lined with big green plants and begonia flowers in white pots.

"You have to come back every weekend, Fa'iza," Aunty Mami said when I told her I was leaving for the residence. She was sitting next to Uncle on the black leather couch. They had a medical kit on the glossy white side table next to them.

"Absolutely. This is home," Uncle agreed, checking his blood sugar while Aunty Mami helped him with the level reading. "Our door is open for you anytime."

"That's a beautiful scarf," Aunty referred to the purple *Kate Spade* scarf wrapped around my head; it matched my purple turtleneck sweater that I was wearing over black denim pants.

"Thank you, Aunty."

"*Ina* Afreen? Where's Afreen?" Uncle asked, looking behind me. "She's taking you back, right?"

"She took her car to the dealership. I'll drop her." It was Ahmad's voice. I turned around to see him zipping up the brown leather jacket he was wearing over a T-shirt and black jeans.

"Oh, perfect," Aunty gushed. "It's a good thing you're home now."

His dad looked up at him. "Ahmad, you should be helping Afreen with things like oil changes, winter tyres and everything else."

"Dad, she needs to learn to be self-sufficient," he leaned down to give his mom a kiss on the cheeks.

"Well, you're here now. At least before you leave again, she should feel like her big brother is around."

When we said our goodbyes and went down the stairs, I put on my winter jacket, his phone rang and he answered the call while gesturing for me to go ahead and sit in the black Audi. He opened the door that led to one of the two-car garage, and as I approached his car, the lights blinked as the doors opened. I huffed as I sat alone in the passenger's seat, watching him in a heated conversation. A few seconds later, he joined me, and the scent of his oud filled the car.

"Sorry. That was work," he said, his hands on the gearshift. He put the car in reverse, and even though there was a backup camera, he didn't look at the screen. Instead, he put his hand over my headrest as he reversed. I was so uncomfortable with our close proximity, suddenly aware of how small I was next to him.

A few seconds later, we were on the road with a French song I'd never heard before playing softly through the speakers. "So about yesterday –" he started.

"Don't worry about it."

His eyes glanced at me and then back at the road, "no. You need to know that what I said to Afreen was just curiosity; I was just wondering why you were alone."

I said nothing.

"Wrong choice of words on my part, I admit," he glanced back at me and smiled. His right hand was resting on the gearshift. As he moved it, it came closer to my thigh.

I swallowed.

"I just didn't know that you were Hausa. My sister's friends from school come over fairly often and none of them is Hausa."

"So, you just assumed I was Canadian?"

"I thought you were East African," he said as the car slowed down. We were stuck in traffic now.

How long was this ride going to take? I thought to myself. The car was quiet except for Wizkid's song now playing.

"I should've taken another route. I completely forgot about how bad northbound traffic is on Sunday evenings."

It sounded to me like he was trying to fill the uncomfortable silence with filler talk. The car hadn't moved for a whole minute. I knew because I was counting my breath. Sitting this close to him, I could see the faint waves in his hair and his full lips; he also had Aunty Mami's straight nose and perfect dentition.

"So, how's school?" Before I could answer, I caught him looking at me again with his eyes squinted like he was trying hard to remember something. "Wait. I've seen you somewhere before."

Uh oh. This is not the time to go down memory lane, sir.

He made a fist with his left hand and put it over his mouth, shaking his head slightly from side to side, "Wait a minute, was it Paris?" He asked. "I've been trying so hard to recall since I saw you at breakfast yesterday."

"You bumped into me." My accusatory tone was hard to miss.

"So, it was you?" His eyes widened. "*You're* the 50 shades girl."

Hold up. What did he just call me? "What?"

"You were reading the blurb at the back of that 50 shades book when *you* bumped into me," he laughed. "Wow, what a small world."

So maybe I didn't mention that I was reading the back of the book in the bookstore when the infamous bump occurred, but, in my defense, Mr. Darcy here was also on his phone.

"Well, you were also on your phone," I was defensive.

"No. When you bumped into me, you spilled my bottle of water *on* my phone," he explained gently.

"I remember it quite differently," I said stubbornly, even though I could feel a smile forming at the corners of my lips.

"I bet you do. So, how was the book?" he smiled, then shook his head. He glanced back at me, and our eyes met. "Was it worth it?" The words rolled off his tongue slowly, deliberately. Maybe I imagined it, but it felt like his eyes were piercing into mine. I swallowed my words and looked back at the road, not understanding why it suddenly felt hard to breathe. Luckily, the traffic started moving just then.

* * *

A few days after my eighteenth birthday in March, I was in the student laundry room sorting out my whites from my colored clothes while talking on the phone with Umma. She was already asking about my summer plans. "Will you be flying back through Lagos or Abuja?"

"Umma, I won't be coming home this summer, I want to take a bridge semester." I explained to her that taking two courses in the summer would reduce my course load for the fall semester. I was getting my laundry out of the drying machine and almost gasped out loud when I realized my favorite white top had shrunk two sizes smaller.

"*Ko* for a few weeks?" She didn't sound too pleased. There was a short pause on the other end, then, "well, you can meet us in Milan in June. We're going for Kaltume's wedding." Kaltume was the daughter of a family friend and a childhood friend of mine.

"*Toh,* Umma."

After I hung up the call, I headed back to my room, where Claire was warming up a pop tart in the microwave above the kitchen sink. She was sitting on the counter, looking at the empty box as she bit into an apple. "I should probably stop eating these," she said, reading the nutrition fact label.

"I remember you saying the same thing last week," I laughed.

"170 calories!" she exclaimed. "And look at all that sugar! This is bad. This is so bad."

I rolled my eyes as I grabbed a glass of water. Claire was the skinniest girl I knew. She ate like a junkie, and when she wasn't eating, she was complaining about how unhealthy everything was.

"You haven't touched half of the fruits we got over the weekend," I said, looking at all the berries we had in the fridge. I grabbed an apple too.

"Do you know that 28 percent of berries have pesticide residue?"

I didn't know this and resorted to mulling over it as I ate my apple, our loud chewing filling the silent dormitory room. Needless to say, these were the kind of conversations that occupied my mind those days. Between my super health-conscious roommate, who was on a new diet every other week, there was also Sara and Ada; the three of us made up the most efficient study group. We met four times a week at 4 pm to work on essays and review notes.

Later that evening, I made my way to the second floor of the University to the study room we had reserved for our meet-ups.

"Okay, here's Fa'iza. Let's hear what she thinks," I heard them say as I walked closer to our study table. It looked like I was walking into an argument.

"Let's ask her then," Sara was saying. She was wearing a beautiful pink scarf, and her face was contoured so perfectly. "Musk or Besos – who do you think will rule the next decade?"

"Oh, that's a tough one," I said as I sat down and brought out my books.

"Not just *Tesla*. Think of *SpaceX*, too. Technology for the future," Ada was saying. She was a smart, fast-witted, natural-hair-wearing Nigerian who was so easy to hang out with. Our little study group was fast becoming my favorite part of school because of her.

"I agree with that," I said, "Elon Musk is a force to be reckoned with, but Jeff Besos has dominates not just ebook platforms, but also online shopping, TV, music and film," I said, counting on my fingers as I spoke.

"Exactly!" Sara said, as if somehow my opinion validated hers.

Two hours, five mugs of coffee and three chapters of public and constitutional law later, we were all hungry. "I'm gonna order us pizza," I said, pulling up the delivery app on my phone. We always took turns ordering dinner. It was a little pact of sorts that we never really talked about, yet we handled it with an almost precise rotation.

"*Wallahi,* I am sick of eating out of boxes," Sara groaned. "Let's go to a restaurant. It's Friday."

"We can check out that Italian place we walked by the other day," Ada suggested. A new restaurant had opened up in the shopping square across from the University. It was only a five-minute walk, and with the weather getting nicer and warmer, I didn't mind at all.

"Ah yes. *Terroni*," I said. "Let's go."

We packed up our notes and laptops, and in half an hour, we were seated in the beautiful upscale restaurant glancing through the menu. I ordered seafood pasta and was halfway through when Ada, who was sitting opposite me, said: "Fa'iza, don't look up, but there's a gentleman on the table behind you who's been staring at you since we came in." I wiped the tasty Alfredo sauce from the corner of my mouth.

"Wow," whispered Sara, "He is handsome, *Masha Allah*." She bit into her mozzarella stick in a naughty manner, and we all laughed.

"He's probably looking at one of you," I said just as the waiter dropped by our table to refill our cups with water.

When we were done with dinner, just after 7 pm, we split the bill and said our goodbyes outside the restaurant, and I started walking back to the residence. It was such a beautiful evening. The cool breeze was better than the winter chill, that's for sure.

"Fa'iza." I heard a familiar voice call out.

Ahmad?

"I thought it was you," I heard him say as I turned around. I wasn't prepared for the sight that met my eyes when I did – for how good he looked in the light of the setting sun. It had been a few months since he dropped me off at the residence and helped me with my luggage to the elevator. I didn't know what he had been up to since then, but whatever it was, it was working for him; he looked terrific.

"Um, what's your name, again?" I asked, and he burst out laughing. We had inside jokes now.

"*Touché*," he put his hands in the pocket of the trousers. He wore a tan blazer over a cotton buttoned-up shirt. "*Ya kike?* How are you?"

Not to sound like a brat, but I honestly hate it when people say *ya kike*, instead of *yadai*. Sure, they mean the same thing, but I think *ya kike* should be reserved for kids. Wait, he doesn't think I'm a kid, does he? I shook my head to dispel the thoughts from my head as I answered, "I'm okay."

He mock-frowned, "Are you, really? Because you're saying you are, but you're shaking your head. Which one is it?"

"I'm okay. Just a little tired," I chuckled, suddenly pleased with myself that I had my green Ted Baker trench coat on. I was also glad I'd put some makeup on, albeit minimal, but at least I didn't look like a homeless girl standing next to someone who looked so well put together.

I figured he was the "handsome" man seated at the table next to ours and turned back to glance at his party. Through the huge glass windows of the brightly lit restaurant, two other men and some blonde ladies were laughing at a shared joke. It looked like an outing with a group of friends. As I looked, one of the ladies looked in our direction, her hand going through her shoulder-length bob as she tried to get his attention. She had the kind of face that I was used to seeing on the cover of magazines – light-colored eyes and pale skin. *Was she his girlfriend? Wait, why did I feel a pang of uneasiness at the thought of her being his girlfriend?* Her attention went back to the table when a group of waiters carrying a cake moved towards them, singing a birthday song.

I looked back at him. "What's the occasion?" *Was it his girlfriend's birthday?*

"Nothing major," he shrugged, looking away from the window and back at me. "It's really good to see you. I, *um–* " He cleared his throat, "I never got your number."

You never asked, I thought to myself but instead, said: "*Oh haka fa*. That's right."

"So, what are you doing tonight?"

"Heading back to my room, pray *Isha,* watch a movie, have some tea, then go to sleep," I said without thinking. That was my daily evening routine.

"In that order? You follow a schedule?" He looked amused.

"I like being organized, that's all."

He nodded, his eyes searching mine." How about we go watch a movie?"

"Which movie?" My reply sounded cool – nonchalant even, as if my heart didn't just skip a beat.

He brought his phone out of his pocket, typed on the screen and handed it to me. It was the Cineplex app displaying a list of movies showing in nearby theatres. "I'm sure there's a movie you would like that's showing tonight," he said as I scrolled through the choices.

There were many choices I really didn't care to watch as I scrolled. The two I was interested in – *The Vow* and *Jump Street* – were movies I'd already watched with Claire. *Fast and Furious 5* it is. "Oh, there's *Fast 5*," I finally said.

He leaned closer to look at the phone screen. "Yeah, we can watch that, if you want." He was standing so close to me I could smell his perfume around his neck: Creed Aventus. I could tell because years of living with my brothers had gotten me unnecessarily well-versed in male cologne. *Why did he always smell so damn good? More importantly, why did I like this attention he was giving me?*

Without thinking about it, I took a step backwards. "*Um* – I need to pray Isha," I handed his phone back to him.

"Of course," he said, putting the phone back into his pocket. "We can go after you pray. I'll drop you at your residence and wait for you while you do."

"Don't you need to pray as well?" I wasn't sure if there was a mosque around the shopping square. The closest one I knew was the one at the University, in the Student Affairs building.

"I will, whenever I get home," he shrugged.

I was getting worried that going to watch a movie at this time might not be a wise idea, so like I always did when I had second thoughts, I readjusted my scarf and tightened the ends around my neck while he looked at me with a half-smile on his face like he knew I was about to come up with an excuse.

"It's getting late," I swallowed. *Why is my swallow sound so loud? Did he hear it?* "By the time I pray and we drive all the way there, it would be dark." Since I got to Canada, this is the latest I have been outdoors, and it was only a few minutes to seven.

"Oh, yeah. I guess you're right," he smiled, looking at his watch. "It *is* getting late. "How about tomorrow afternoon, instead?"

I nodded.

"Can I walk you to your residence?"

I nodded again, and we started walking down the deserted stony pedestrian pathway in the shopping square and towards the looming brick-walled 20-storey building with the word 'residence' spelled out in red. The walk was quiet for the most part, but he eventually broke the silence with small talk. "So, how do you like it here?" his eyes lingered on mine for a second.

"I like it a lot," I answered truthfully. It was my first time living away from home, and the experience had been scary yet exciting so far.

"I never really liked school dorms, never stayed in one." We were at the junction now, waiting for the pedestrian sign to turn green.

"*Ya gida*? How's home?" I asked. I inwardly rolled my eyes, disappointed at what I could come up with to keep the conversation going.

"Fine, I guess. Haven't you spoken to Afreen?" The light turned green, and we crossed the road.

"We talk almost every day." We send each other funny memes or screenshots of bizarre tweets. Not much of a conversation, but he didn't need to know that.

His head turned as he watched a car drive past us so I couldn't see his expression and wondered how he felt about my friendship with his little sister. "You didn't say goodbye to your friends," I finally said.

"So?" he answered like it wasn't rude to leave without saying bye. "They'll understand."

Or you just lack basic manners. At the entrance of the residence, we watched as a loud group of friends walked past us, slightly inebriated. Then he asked: "What time can I pick you up tomorrow?" He was looking at me, and I could tell he expected me to come up with another excuse.

"After Asr."

"So, can I get your phone number?" he smiled.

I nodded, and he handed me his phone. I dialed the number so I could have his, too. "Thanks for walking me back," I said, giving him back the phone.

"Enjoy your tea," he said and walked away.

Was that a wink, or did I imagine it?

Chapter 5

I held up a white linen shirt against myself as I looked in the full-size, jewel-encrusted mirror propped up in the corner of my dorm room and shook my head. *No, white is too basic.* I held up the red top I got on an impromptu shopping spree with Afreen a few weeks before. Great color, but it showed too much cleavage. I sighed. My bed was scattered with outfit options I hadn't yet tried on. I just couldn't decide what to wear for our date. Not a date. Just a movie. Movie date. Nope, not a date. Just watching a movie together. Why couldn't I get it together? Just looking at the mess I'd made was giving me a headache. *How long would it take to fold all of that and have them back neatly in the closet?*

I picked up my phone and tapped on the screen to check the weather forecast. It was 19 degrees Celsius – not bad, warmer than I expected. Just then, the soulful call to *Asr* prayer filled my room from the Muslim Pro app on my phone. I walked into the washroom to perform my ablution as I heard the Arabic words, but my head automatically translated the words into English*: Come to Prayer. Come to Salvation.*

After my four *raka'ats*, the series of movements during prayer, I seemed to have gotten more clarity on my outfit choice. I walked to the closet and brought out a pair of grey jeggings I'd never worn before. I paired it with a black bodysuit off my bed, and added small golden hoop earrings. My hair was tied into a bun at the nape of my neck and was wrapped in a blue jersey scarf. I was tying the laces of my high-top Converse when my phone started ringing, and because I hadn't saved his number – even after he'd called to "check up on me" last night and earlier today to ask if I was "still good for later?" – I hesitated a bit before picking up.

"Yeah, hello?" I said into the phone.

"Hey," his voice in my ear gave me butterflies in my tummy. *Stop it, Fa'iza. That's the devil tickling you*. I thought about what my Quran recitation tutor used to say when we were growing up to my older cousins who said Brad Pitt in Mr. and Mrs. Smith gave them 'butterflies in their tummy.' "I'm in the lobby," he said. *Was I losing it completely, or could I actually hear the smile in his voice?*

"Oh, okay. Coming down," I replied, wondering why my heart was beating faster than normal.

I glanced at my reflection in the mirror. This bodysuit accentuated my tiny waist. *Not bad, miss,* I thought to myself. I looked more confident than I felt, and in typical Fa'iza fashion, I grabbed an oversized denim jacket to feel more comfortable. Still, I couldn't stop looking into the elevator mirror, wondering if I looked good. When the elevator door opened on the ground floor, my eyes scanned the lobby, past the front desk and the brightly colored armchairs in front of the fireplace, and I saw Ahmad standing by the bar stools just behind the pool table, with an expression I could not quite read coloring his face. It disappeared almost as quickly as it arrived, and he started smiling more broadly as we closed the distance between us.

"You look good," he said. He was wearing a taupe leather jacket with a black shirt underneath.

"Thanks."

There was a twinkle in his eye. "You ready? I am parked right outside," he asked, and I nodded. "After you," he opened the door for me and waited as I walked past him. *Oh, how chivalrous, Ahmad Babangida. Who would have thought?*

Outside, he walked ahead of me, and I noticed black leather gloves sticking out of his back pocket. I didn't think much of it until he stopped, climbed a huge black power bike and passed me a black and silver helmet. My mouth slowly hung open as my eyes darted from the helmet to his face. "Are – are you mad?" I stuttered. I couldn't get over how magnificent and dangerous the bike looked, and with him sitting on it, it was a scene straight out of a James Bond movie.

"What?" He asked, failing to hide his amusement.

"I'm not getting on this –" I clenched my fingers into a fist as I searched for the right word to show my disdain, "– on this *thing.*"

"Well, it's the fastest way to get there. You know how the traffic gets during the weekend."

I didn't know and honestly, it didn't matter. I would rather arrive late than in pieces. I shook my head no. "I don't care," looking at the silver headlight cover as it gleamed in the sunlight. "This is too dangerous."

"You can trust me," he looked from my eyes to my lips and back into my eyes again. "I'll be very careful. I promise."

I looked away as I sighed out loudly, and finally took the helmet he was holding out to me. I strapped on the helmet and fastened it tightly. He watched me; then he put on his matte black helmet as I got on the bike, delicately balancing my feet on the silver foot pegs.

"Are you okay?" He asked as he wore his leather gloves. His voice was slightly muffled under the helmet.

"Yeah," I said. I was nervous, but I couldn't deny that I was beginning to get excited.

"Hold on tight," he cautioned. I felt the blood drain from my face, and it suddenly dawned on me that the passenger had to hold onto the rider. I held onto his shoulders as he leaned forward, and the bike came on. Within seconds, we zoomed off through the streets. I leaned in as we swerved, making low right turns and moving fast in traffic. I watched the buses and cars we passed, and it felt like I was seeing the city through a different lens like I was a first-time visitor. The buildings were beautiful, and the art sculptures and food trucks made it feel like a moving portrait, and we made the most beautiful painting.

Chapter 5

* * *

We shared a large bag of popcorn while we watched the movie, and after, as we dumped the 3D glasses in the recycle bin, we decided to get dinner. He told me about an excellent restaurant a few blocks away. As we approached his Kawasaki bike, I grumbled jokingly about being on the bike.

"Well, you're dressed for it," he teased as he handed me my helmet. "And I *know* you enjoyed the ride." He was right. Once I got over the initial feeling of being scared, I did enjoy the ride.

When the bike slowed down and gradually came to a halt in front of a red brick building, the outdoor patio was unoccupied and above the entrance to the restaurant was a placard that had the name *Casa Madera* in cursive black letters. My ears were buzzing from the wind, and I felt slightly lightheaded as I took my hands off his back and gingerly got off the black bike. He removed his helmet, set it on his bike and alighted in one easy movement.

"Here. Let me help you with that," he said as I struggled to unclip the helmet's harness from around my neck. His fingers went over mine, and with a soft click, he unfastened my helmet. I removed it and handed it to him, watching as he clipped it in place next to his.

"How long have you had a bike?" I asked as we walked towards the restaurant.

"I got my first bike when I was seventeen," his hands went into the pockets of his faded denim trousers, his grey timberland boots crunching the gravel entrance as we entered the restaurant. "So, you've never actually been on a bike?"

I shook my head.

"Really? Even in Abuja?" he seemed surprised. Powerbike races and car drifting were big things in Abuja. My friends from school often invited me, but I knew my mother too well to even ask for permission to go with them. She didn't think any responsible girl from a good home should be found in such rowdy places. My brothers, of course, didn't even need to ask permission; they went to the driving range, smoked *shisha*, and screamed along with everyone else and their upbringing was never questioned.

"Good to see you again, Ahmad," a tall, tanned man with a Mexican accent welcomed us into the restaurant. As he spoke, I was distracted by the waterfall simulation behind him.

"Hello, Javier," Ahmad said. I could sense a familiarity between them and wondered if they'd known each other for long.

"I don't know why you bother making a reservation, when you can just walk in and have your favorite table," Javier said with a smile, looking at the white monitor in front of him.

"It's a restaurant, not McDonald's," Ahmad laughed.

Javier laughed with him as he led the way into the brown-walled restaurant with life-size paintings of surrealistic figures on the wall. We removed our jackets as we got settled into the plush velvet seats. As I looked around the sparse restaurant, Javier was telling Ahmad: "Your waitress will be with you shortly."

We were quiet for a few seconds, and then, "so, full disclosure," Ahmad started as he leaned forward, his hands on the table. "That was my second time watching that movie."

My eyes widened as I fiddled with the neckline of my top as I looked at him. "What do you mean?"

"I saw it as soon as it was released," he explained, his eyes moving from my hands on my neck and back to my face. "I just wanted to spend time with you."

"Hello, guys. My name is Paige, and I'll be your waitress today." We were interrupted by a red-haired girl about my age, wearing a black dress and heels, who handed us the menus, filled our glasses with water and notified us of the Chef's special.

I pretended to be reading the menu, but my mind was going over what Ahmad had said*: I just wanted to spend time with you.* It was such a simple sentence, but there was something about the way his voice dropped when he said it and the intensity in his eyes when they met mine. And that godforsaken accent made it sound like so much more than a platonic get-together. I had almost forgotten about the waitress's presence when I heard her voice again: "would you like a few minutes with the menu before placing your orders?"

Ahmad looked at me from behind his menu.

"Yes, please," I said, looking up at her.

"Of course," she smiled. "Any drinks to get you started?"

"Water's fine," I said.

"I'm good with water, too. Thanks, Paige," Ahmad closed the menu and placed it on the table.

I kept my eyes on the menu, trying to figure out what to eat, pretending not to feel his stare. It was always hard trying to filter out the *halal* food options. Everything that looked good had bacon bits or ham in it, or it was sauteed in lard.

I looked up at him, "Why is your menu closed?"

"I know what I want," he said, looking at me. It was quiet in the restaurant except for the faint clink of cutlery and soothing jazz over the hidden speakers. *I know what I want* rang in my ear. It could mean two different things. He explained, "I always get the same thing when I come here."

Okay, so I imagined it. He was talking about the food. Just the food. Paige came back with a notepad and a pen in her hand, ready to take our orders.

"Is your meat *halal*?" The steaks looked good, but I needed to know if it was permissible for me to eat according to Islamic standards.

"*Um* – I don't believe it is. But I can confirm with the chef, if you'd like," she said and started heading towards the kitchen.

"No, don't worry about it," I stopped her, opening the menu again, "I'll have the Butternut Squash ravioli, then." Muslims always have backup orders when eating out.

"That's a good vegetarian option," she quipped as she scribbled it down, then turning to look at Ahmad: "And for you, sir?"

"I'll have medium-rare Steak and Prawns," he said, handing her the menu.

"You want mashed potatoes and grilled asparagus to come with it?"

"Always," he looked down as his phone lit up, but he ignored it.

"You don't care that the meat isn't *halal*?" I asked once she was out of sight

He shook his head. "It's beef. I say *bismillah* like we're supposed to before eating. Doesn't that make it halal?"

I thought about it. Yes, we start every activity with the name of God, even eating. "I guess. But we're supposed to look for *halal* whenever we can."

"So you only eat where it explicitly says halal?"

"Yup," I had never even considered the alternative. "When I'm not sure if the meat is *halal*, I go for vegetarian or seafood options." It was one of the things I noticed Umma did when we traveled together.

"Interesting," he said, taking a cup of water to his lips. "What are you studying?" He leaned back, but his eyes followed every movement I made.

"*Um* – Law," I said, suddenly aware of my hands clasping and unclasping on my thighs.

"Why Law?" his voice dropped again.

Why Law? I asked myself. No one had ever asked me that. Ever since I was in secondary school, my family always joked about how I would take after my father. I think I just subconsciously imbibed that, and I went with it without too much thought. "I guess I've always been interested in protecting rights," I replied. I knew immediately that sounded lame but he nodded slowly, like he was trying to understand.

Our food arrived. It looked delicious and tasted even better. "You studied law too, right?" I asked, remembering my conversation with Afreen.

"I dropped out in my first year," he cut into his steak, "switched to Interaction Design at Cambridge. I just finished my Masters."

I wondered what my parents would think if I decided to switch majors. Not that I wanted to, because it had grown on me, but I wondered nevertheless. By the time we made it out of the restaurant, it was already dark outside.

"Uh oh, I have bad news for you," he said as he zipped up his jacket.

"What is it?" I looked around the empty parking lot.

"It looks like it's going to rain," looking up at the full moon illuminating the skyline.

And he was right. We were on the bike for barely thirty seconds when it started drizzling. Little at first, but then it got heavier. We were soon completely drenched. The raindrops had formed multiple stings of water falling off my helmet, and I could barely see. At the traffic lights, he raised the glass visor of his helmet to talk to me, even though I could barely make out the words he was saying with the wind howling. "It's dangerous to keep riding," he wiped the visor with gloved hands, "the roads are too wet."

I nodded, my grip getting tighter on his shoulder.

"We're a minute from my place," he continued. With the wind blowing so hard, it was getting harder and harder to hear him. "Let's go there until the rain subsides."

"Okay," I said, shouting so he could hear me. I hadn't realized that they lived so close to this part of town. I knew Aunty Mami was in Nigeria, but it will be nice to surprise Afreen.

We rode carefully until we made a left at the tallest skyscraper I'd seen in this part of town. As we approached the doors to its underground parking, they rolled upwards. We rode through the brightly lit multi-storey parkade and stopped at an empty stall. He powered down the bike and we got off.

"Where's this place?" I asked, looking around. My voice was low, but the slight tremor was noticeable.

"I live here," he said as he removed his helmet. He stopped when he saw the confused expression on my face.

"What? You said we were going home."

"No, I said *my* place."

"I thought home –" my words failed me. I had assumed that we were going to his parent's house.

"Fa'iza, I don't live with my parents."

"But your room – the room –" I was stuttering, remembering when I walked into his room when he was asleep.

"Oh, the weekend you saw me there?" He ran his hands through his damp hair, "I had just come back from the UK the night before, so I went to spend the weekend with them."

"Oh." Most people don't move out of their parent's house in northern

Nigeria until they got married, so it was a surprise for me.

"You're shivering. Let's get you out of these wet clothes before you catch a cold." He said with concern in his eyes. "Fa'iza?" he called out to me softly when I didn't answer; his voice was almost a whisper.

"I – *um*, I –" I swallowed. "I just want to go back to the r–residence," my voice cracked as I was shivering so much from the cold.

"Okay, I'll drop you back at the residence," he said reassuringly, maintaining the distance I had put between us. "But if you stay in these wet clothes any longer, you *will* catch a cold."

"I dunno – I –" my voice trailed off. There was a pause – a heavy one. I heard my teeth chattering.

"Fa'iza?" he asked again, his voice low. "Look at me."

I peeled my gaze from the exhaust pipes on his bike and looked up at him. There he was in his drenched shirt under his jacket, his face wet from when he had his visor open. "You're safe with me, Fa'iza. *Wallahi*. I swear." It was so quiet down here and my heart was thumping wildly in my chest. He sighed and ran his left hand through his hair again. "Trust me."

I reluctantly met his eyes. He's Aunty Mami's son. Of course, I was safe with him. It was just that there were many stories I'd heard growing up that led to questions like *why was she alone with him?* No one ever asks *why did he do that to her?* That was the sad reality in conservative societies like ours – the girl was always expected to know better, to be the responsible one, and to not put herself in compromising situations.

I nodded, and we walked together into the elevator. Ahmad called it to his floor and a green light blinked beside it as the gentle whir of the elevator going upwards filled the silence. As the elevator stopped, an automated female voice announced: "Penthouse." The doors opened, and we walked out. The floor was dimly lit, and the army green carpet we walked on stopped the sounds of our footsteps from echoing until we reached a brown door with *PH* 2 written in silver letters at the top of the silver door knocker. Ahmad fumbled with the keys, and when the door opened, he stood aside so I could walk in first.

Even though the apartment was warm, I was still shivering as I sat on the black ottoman by the entrance to remove my shoes. Ahmad walked past me, and the motion sensor lights came on as he walked further into the apartment, illuminating the high ceilings, hardwood floors and walls lined with abstract artwork with colors that matched the deep brown and black leather of the furniture I could see in the living room. Moments later, he was out with a couple of towels. "First door on your right," he said, wrapping one around my shoulders. "You can go in there and change."

I walked down the hallway, opened the door and closed it behind me. The first door on my right led to a bedroom, and I made my way to the bathroom and placed the towels on the white marble countertop that held two sink basins with black faucets. There was a walk-in-steam shower beside a freestanding bathtub, and I made sure the door was locked as I removed my scarf while I stared at my reflection in the mirror, allowing my bun to unravel. My long, wet hair fell down my shoulders and stuck to the sides of my face. Then I removed my jacket and dropped it to the floor, peeled off the jeggings I had on and removed my bodysuit in one quick movement. I grabbed one of the plush Terry cloth towels and wrapped myself, patting myself dry while rubbing my feet on the heated floors until I stopped shivering.

When I was no longer shivering, I looked at the pile Ahmad had handed to me. There was a white *Calvin Klein* shirt, a pair of sweatpants, and a white robe. I removed my wet bra and slipped into the white T-shirt and sweatpants. Not quite warm enough, I wore the robe and tied the belt around my waist. It came flowing down to my ankles. I wrapped the other towel around my head in an easy turban and put all the wet clothes in the sink. I put my ear to the door, and when I couldn't hear a sound, I unlocked the washroom door and walked out into the empty bedroom, looking around for the first time. The king-sized platform bed had black upholstered headboards that reached the ceilings and blended in with the dark wallpaper, grey sheets, duvet, and dark paneled walls. Yet somehow, the white pillows and the abstract art pieces caught the light that the hidden light bulbs behind wall fixtures reflected, bathing the massive room in a luxurious glow.

My feet sank deeper into the soft carpet as I walked towards the large glass sliding doors that revealed a walk-in closet at one end, where I could see his clothes hanging and another abstract art piece that covered the entire wall in there. I was looking at the piece when I heard the knock. "Fa'iza?"

"*Na'am*? Yes?"

"Can I come in?" He asked.

"Yeah."

He didn't come in; he opened the door just enough to poke his head in. "Where are your wet clothes?" He asked, "I want to put them in the dryer."

"Okay."

"I'll be in the living room," I heard him say as I walked towards the bathroom to pick up the pile of wet clothes. I was halfway through the room when I realized I hadn't removed my wet bra from the pile. I folded it and slipped it into the pocket of the robe I wore. When I got to the living room, he was standing while watching a basketball match on the large flat-screen television. He'd also changed into dry clothes – black slacks and a red hoodie. I didn't hear him come into his room, so he probably had clothes in another part of the apartment – perhaps the laundry room. He turned around as I walked in.

"You okay?" He asked as he took my wet clothes.

I nodded with a slight smile.

He walked down the hallway, and I looked out of the ceiling to floor glass panes as I heard buttons beeping and the sound of the dryer came on. I could see the city below us as it rained and if I hadn't fallen in love with it before that time, I did then. I walked around the living room and realized he had a theme going on – dark luxury. The dark paneled walls continued here, flanked by a black leather sectional and two brown leather accent chairs. The low centre table was more of an art piece than a functional table; it was an intricate shape carved out of a stone, which balanced an ivory sculpture of a human bust. I walked towards the dining area with four minimalist black chairs around an oval dining table with an elegant pendant chandelier overhead. It was separated from the kitchen by a wall covered in another large abstract piece. Its splash of color and smudges in green and burgundy were the only bright colors in this entire space.

"Would you like some tea?"

I looked up and saw that he was in the kitchen.

"Yes, please," I answered.

"There's green tea, chamomile…" he started listing.

"Green's fine."

"Oh, there's peppermint here too." He said, raising the green box.

"Eww," I said before I could stop myself.

"Exactly! It's like drinking toothpaste," he laughed as he walked towards me with two steaming mugs of tea.

"So, why do you have it?"

"This one time I had a flu and I thought it would help. Couldn't even keep it down," he chuckled as I scowled after taking a sip of the unsweetened tea.

"I take mine plain," he explained, "but there's honey and sugar in the kitchen if you want."

I stood up and walked past the bar stools by the kitchen island into the kitchen with stainless steel and black appliances. "Where's the honey?"

"By the coffee maker," he answered, already sitting down, his feet stretched on the center table as he turned down the volume of the television.

Right by the Nespresso machine was a mason jar of organic honey. I stirred a teaspoon full into my tea and walked back to the living room.

"Are you warm enough?" he asked when I sat down. "I can turn up the heat, if you want."

"No, this is perfect," I replied.

We drank our tea quietly while he watched the game. A few minutes later, the dryer beeped. He got my dry clothes and handed them back to me. I went back into the room, locked myself in the toilet and changed back into my clothes and put his shirt, robe and towels in the laundry basket, ignoring the feel of the slightly damp bra against my skin. When the rain subsided, we walked to the underground parkade, and towards his Audi.

"I know the last thing you'd want is to get on the bike again tonight," he smiled at me, and I couldn't help but smile back. He was breathtakingly handsome; there was something about the way he carried himself and how safe I suddenly felt around him. We got into the warm car, and as though he'd forgotten he'd already asked, he wanted to know if I was warm enough. I nodded yes, as *Adorn* by *Miguel* played softly through his speakers. As the car started moving, he reached out and held my hand with his right hand and his fingers lightly caressing mine. His eyes were fixated on the road as we drove silently back to the residence.

* * *

I was dreaming of him when I heard the loud bang. I wasn't sure if it was from the dream or if someone across the hallway had closed their door with a bang. Whatever it was, I was snapped out of my sleep. *What was the dream about?* I couldn't remember much except that he was in it – him and his bike. I threw the covers off as I slid my feet into my fluffy bunny slippers and headed towards the kitchenette in pink shorts and a white Victoria's Secret sweater. The door to Claire's room was closed, but I could hear the white noise from her sound machine.

I drank some water and went back to the room, but no matter how hard I tried, I just could not get comfortable. I sighed as I reached for my phone on the reading desk next to my bed, ignoring my *Twitter* and *Instagram* notifications. I opened my messages: *Sleep tight,* Ahmad had sent at 11:15 pm, a few hours after he'd dropped me off. When I returned to the residence, I took a hot shower, prayed my missed prayers, and fell straight into bed. I didn't even have tea.

I typed back: *You too, Ahmad :-)* then I deleted the smiley face. Maybe I should just say thanks? I pressed the send button before I could delete more words from my three-worded reply before getting up to make some tea. The kettle hadn't even whistled when my phone beeped. I couldn't stop the smile that formed on my face as I read his reply: *You are awake...*

Slept for a few hours, just woke up. I leaned back against the counter as

I replied. I hit send and watched the bubbles form as he started typing immediately.

Bad dream?

I chuckled as I poured water into my cup. How did he know? I couldn't remember the dream in its entirety, but something about it woke me up. The bang? Was that even from the dream? I replied immediately: *You could say that. Why are YOU awake?* I hit send as I walked back to my room, mug in hand.

His reply came as I was getting under the covers, propping up the pillows against my back. *I work better at night... Can I call you?*

My heart started beating faster. It was 2:59 am and I was not sleepy at all. I typed a simple *Yes* and hit send. Seconds later, my phone started vibrating, and I cleared my throat before answering the call. "Yea, hello?" I said into the receiver.

"Hey, you." There was something about the low baritone of his voice I found alluring. I could hear the sound of his keyboard in the background. "I'm just trying to connect to my headphones."

"That's alright," I said as I took a sip of my tea.

"Wouldn't have pegged you as an insomniac," he said. The typing in the background stopped.

"Definitely not an insomniac," I said, getting defensive.

"Well, it is 3 am, and you're awake," he said.

I could listen to him talk in this accent all day. "Um, you're awake too. Mine was a bad dream. What's your excuse?"

I heard him laugh, and I smiled as I imagined it. "Work." The typing in the background had resumed. "Half my team is in Japan, so it works out with the time difference."

"What are you working on?" I asked.

"Nothing major. Just finishing the touches to an app I recently built."

"You code?" I asked. I was impressed.

"Yes. Do you?" The cockiness in his voice was back. Or maybe I imagined it? Hard to tell with the damn accent.

"No," I took another sip. "What's your app for?"

"Well, the complete version should help doctors record visitations easier and have all the insurance directly billed instead of filling out the details manually for each patient," he explained. I heard the air sound of an email being sent on the other end, and then "Anyway, how bad was your dream?"

I tried to recall the dream unsuccessfully. I only remember running before the bang. I was running from something. What or who was I running from? "Did I say it was bad?"

"If it's keeping you up, it had to be a bad one, no?" he sounded a bit concerned. I didn't answer, and the silence stretched for a few seconds before he broke it: "It was nice hanging out earlier – before, you know, the rain."

"Yeah, it was. I had a nice time, thank you," I responded. I felt like he knew what I was talking about – for the tea, dry clothes and things I could not quite put into words.

"I'm leaving for New York in the afternoon for an investor briefing on Monday."

"Oh, okay," I said, hoping the disappointment in my voice wasn't too obvious.

"I'll see you when I get back?"

I didn't want to have to wait a while before seeing him again, but I also didn't want to seem too eager. I listened to his breathing at the end of the line, and I couldn't resist teasing him.

"If I can remember your name."

"Wooooow. Really? You'll never let me live that down, will you?" I could hear a smile in his voice. I loved the fact that I could tell he was smiling, even though I couldn't see him.

"Never," I promised.

Chapter 6

Claire and I started shopping for our groceries together recently, and we dedicated Sundays to it. Like most first-year students in the residence, we had a meal plan for the cafeteria, but we also enjoyed snacks and since none of us had a car, we would take a cab to and from the store once a week. I was in the refrigerated section picking out halal turkey bacon when I saw Zafar and started walking towards him him, happy to see a familiar face. As I moved closer, I noticed a small boy a little over a year old, who looked like a younger version of his – dark skin, clear bright eyes and dimples – running towards him.

"Daddy, Chase and Marshal," he said as he pointed to the fridge.

"Okay, let's get your *Paw Patrol* yogurt," he replied.

"Zafar, *Indillah*. Let's go," a female voice said in Fulfulde.

I stood still. A beautiful lady with a button nose and dimples was walking towards him. She was wearing a black abaya, her hair and ears covered with a black chiffon scarf wrapped around her head.

"*Mi do wara*, Maryam," he replied. "I'm coming."

"Mummy, Chase." The little boy was still pointing at the refrigerator, and I watched as Zafar grabbed a small case of a dozen yogurt pouches. Before I could turn away, he looked up, and our eyes met. I looked away immediately and started walking away as fast as I could, my head buzzing with questions. *Afreen's Zafar is married? And he has a kid? Oh, poor Afreen, she doesn't deserve this.* I met Claire picking out gluten-free bread and we used self-checkout to pay for our groceries. As we bagged them, I silently prayed not to run into Zafar and his family before leaving the store.

"Is tofu halal?" Claire asked as we walked out of the grocery store, pushing our carts full of organic juice, fruits, and boxed dinners.

"It's soybean," I answered, distracted. "All grains are halal."

"Right," she said as she pondered over my reply. "So, you can't even have a tiny piece of bacon, right?"

"Right."

"You aren't missing much. It is too greasy, anyway," she said.

Being roommates has introduced Claire to Islam. I appreciated that she asked for clarification whenever she stumbled upon information she didn't quite understand. The other day, I was washing my lunch plates when she came back from lectures with a scowl on her face as she showed me her phone. "It says here that Muslim men can have more than one wife."

I dried my hands on the kitchen towel as I answered. "Polygamy existed before Islam," I explained to her. "Men could be with as many women as they wished and these women had no financial security for themselves or their children when they weren't on good terms with the man" I dropped the towel, and turned around to look at her. "When Islam came, it put a cap on the number of women a man can marry and ensured that the women are properly cared for."

"Patriarchy is messed up," she said, processing the new information. "But do all Muslim men have to marry more than one wife?"

"Oh no." I answered truthfully. "Polygamy exists, but there are a lot of monogamous marriages in Islam." I did not add that sentiments around polygamy differed culturally around the world, some of my friends whose parents were in polygamous marriages vowed never to marry into one.

On the taxi ride back to the residence, my mind was jumbled with thoughts of Zafar and Afreen. I had never been in that kind of situation before – one where I stumbled upon sensitive information that could hurt my friend.

"Claire, if your boyfriend had another –" I hesitated. "If your boyfriend had another woman in his life and your friend knew about it, would you want to know?"

She looked up from her phone and tried to make sense of the question. "So, like, if my hypothetical boyfriend was cheating?" She made air quotes when she said boyfriend.

Married, actually. "Yeah, something like that."

"Would I expect my friend to tell me? Of course, Fa'iza; that's what a good friend would do," her attention went back to her phone. "*Heck*, I would cut ties with the friend who knew and didn't tell me," she muttered under her breath as she continued swiping.

I sighed as I looked out the window. I didn't want to be the bearer of bad news, but I didn't seem to have a choice. I got my phone out and typed: *Hey, Afreen. Are you home?* Later that evening, I took a cab to the ambassador's house, and as I rang the doorbell, I remembered how in love they seemed to me – how happy she was to introduce me to him, their holding hands as he drove, the way they looked at each other. And on his birthday, too – the joy on his face when he saw her and the cake from his favorite bakery. *Should I tell her?*

Afreen squealed as she opened the door for me. *"Fa'iza am"* – "my Fa'iza" – a term of endearment. She was wearing a big purple hijab that covered her body all the way to her feet. "Did you see the funny Harlem shake videos I sent you?" She'd sent me about five videos on the viral Harlem shake challenge that was flooding the internet, and I never replied. I nodded yes as I came into the house and started removing my shoes, before giving her a quick hug.

"*Hmm*, you smell nice," she said, closing the door. "Have you had dinner? Let's eat, there's jollof rice," she answered her questions as usual, and I smiled sadly. Afreen was such a ray of sunshine, I didn't want to break her heart with the news I'd brought.

"No, I'm not hungry," I said, my voice dropping down a notch. "I really wanna talk to you about something."

"Is everything okay, Fa'ee?"

I shook my head. I felt horrible to be the one to do this to her. She suddenly looked serious, a solemn look settling on her face. "Let's go to my room," she said, moving towards it. I followed behind, my head beginning to hurt. When we got to the room, she removed the hijab, tossed it on her bed, revealing the knee-length pink silk robe with black trimmings she wore underneath, and sat on the tufted chair in front of her vanity facing her mirror. I closed the door and sat on the ottoman at the foot of her bed. I looked at her black hair, which fell to the middle of her back, and she watched me through the mirror.

"I don't know how to say this, Afreen," I started. As I spoke, she grabbed a facial serum tube and slowly applied it to her face. The room felt cold and uncomfortable. *I just have to rip the band-aid off. There's no easy way to go about this,* I thought. "I saw Zafar at the grocery store today," I said slowly. Her eyes were on mine through the mirror. She grabbed her moisturizer and started applying it. Her movements were slow. Judging by the number of tubes in front of her, I figured she was in the middle of her five-step bedtime facial routine. "I think he's married, Afreen," I blurted out, "I'm sorry."

She looked away and closed the serum in front of her, avoiding my eyes. The room was silent; the gentle hum of the air conditioner was all I could hear. I suddenly started remembering her words from months ago: *"his birthday is tomorrow... but we have to celebrate today", "Mum, we are going to the central library... I have a book to return", "Thank you for keeping my secret..."* Her eyes met mine reluctantly, and then it hit me.

"You already knew," I gasped quietly.

She averted her eyes from mine. Of course, she knew! He was spending his birthday with his family – that's why they had to go out the night before. If her parents were anything like mine, they wouldn't want their daughter to be a second wife. That's why she couldn't tell her mum about him. It all made sense now.

"Fa'iza, it's more complicated than you think," she said quietly as she finally looked at me.

"You knew why I was here." It wasn't a question.

"Yes," she glanced at her phone. "He texted me from the store."

I nodded slowly, then sighed. It was weird, but I was strangely relieved that she wasn't heartbroken and crying right now. "Well, *um* – good to know you weren't being played, or something." I brought out my phone and started looking for the Uber app to request a ride.

"Fa'iza, I've known him since I was fourteen," she tried to explain.

"You really don't owe me an explanation," I said, glancing at my phone. My ride was two minutes away.

"I feel like I do," she looked up at me, a sad smile crossing her face. "You're the only one who knows about us."

"Don't worry," I said curtly. "Your secret is still safe with me."

Chapter 7

After what felt like the longest weekend in my life, Monday finally arrived. I was in class twelve minutes early for my 8 am class with a Venti Starbucks cup to give me a false sense of productivity. I was snacking on almonds when my phone buzzed. I knew who it was from even before I opened the message. *Did you make it to class on time, Insomniac?* It was from Ahmad. We were on the phone until 4:30 this morning. Time didn't seem to exist when we talked on the phone, and we never ran out of things to talk about – the worst meals we've had, places we wanted to visit, or our hobbies. He loved books as much as I did. We'd even read the same authors – Brandon Sanderson, Khalid Hossein, Margaret Atwood and John Grisham. Like me, he wanted to ask Chimamanda what happened to Kainene in *Half of a Yellow Sun.* We argued about Gatsby's obsession with Daisy Buchanan; I argued that it was true love, but Ahmad believed Gatsby just loved the idea of being in love with her. I didn't understand his thought process sometimes. Like, why would anyone choose DC over Marvel? Apart from Batman, what else was holding up that franchise?

I replied back, with a smile on my face. *I will have you know I was the first person to come to class.* I hit send just as our teaching assistant, Mike, walked in. I watched as he settled in, connecting his laptop to the projector.

Nerd. Another buzz. *I'll call you after my meeting. Wish me luck.*

I replied: *Break a leg!*

After our lecture, the class gradually emptied. Sara went to the cafeteria to get coffee, and I was left alone in the brightly-lit class. Suddenly, my phone started buzzing. He was calling on Facetime. I looked at my reflection, suddenly aware of the fact that I wasn't wearing any makeup, not even lip balm. I wanted to hear about his meeting though, so I answered. His face filled my screen, and a smile spread across it when he saw me.

"So, how did it go?" I asked.

"Better than I expected," he beamed. He seemed better looking than the last time I saw him. Or maybe it was the camera?

"That's good. Where are you?"

"Grabbing a bite," he answered. "How was class?"

"Went well. The next one is –" I looked at my wristwatch, " – in 45 minutes."

There was a look on his face I couldn't quite place, the same one he had when he picked me up for the movie. Like that time, it disappeared quickly. "What time are you done with lectures today?"

"After my next one. I've got Torts at 3:45, and will be done at 4:30."

He nodded. "And after that?"

"Back to my room," I said. I'd planned on going to the gym for yoga afterwards, but I didn't mention it.

He smiled as he nodded. "Can I come see you?"

I felt a grin trying to form on my face, but I suppressed it. "Oh, are you coming back today?"

"That wasn't the plan, but the biggest hurdle is over. My team will handle the rest."

"Oh, okay." I heard the door open and saw Sara walk back with a Tim Hortons coffee cup. She was on her phone, looking distracted as she usually did when replying to her YouTube comments.

"Is that an answer?" He probed.

"Yeah, sure," I answered, smiling now.

"Great, see you later, insomniac," he laughed.

"Definitely not an insomniac," I corrected him.

"Gotta change your name on my phone to –" he pretended to think for a second. "Insom," he laughed.

"Insom?" I exclaimed, "isn't that a Calabar name?"

"Hey! People from Calabar are the most selfless friends you can find. My best bud Edet? Upstanding man, I tell you."

"*Kai ka sani,* na you know," I mused. "You and this Edet."

Much like our banter from the night before, our conversation was effortless. It was hard to believe that this was the same guy I thought had an attitude just a few months before. After my last lecture for the day, I went back to the residence, prayed, and half an hour later, I was trying to hold a pose at yoga, but the muscles in my right calf were beginning to sting. My outstretched hands were straight and tense as I tried to balance myself on one knee, and my other outstretched leg was wobbling dangerously close to the ground. I slowly inhaled and exhaled, aware of the sting that was beginning to turn into pain.

"Hold – and release," the yogi instructed as the whole room let out a collective sigh as we gently moved into child's pose.

I took a sip of water from my bottle and tucked my knees under my chest, then I brought my head flat to the ground, with my forehead and the tip of my nose touching my yoga mat. It almost felt as peaceful as *sujood,* when we Muslims put our foreheads to the ground in prayer.

"Breathe in and out slowly," her voice urged in the dim room.

I cleared my mind and focused on my breathing. It was finally getting quiet in my head – no overbearing thoughts and inner monologues. I exhaled, basking in the quiet and darkness for seconds that stretched into a minute or two.

"Thank you all for coming, ladies," the yogi said. The lights flickered as they came back on. I sat on my mat, stretching my neck to the left. "Don't forget to sign up for Friday's class," she reminded us, pointing at the sheet of paper taped to the door of the residence's yoga studio.

I folded my mat, grabbed my purple water bottle, and walked out of the studio, leaving about a dozen other girls in the room. I went past the elevators, and as I walked up the stairs, I dialed Abba's number and put the phone to my ear as it started to ring.

"Assalamu alaikum," he said after three rings. "Mama?" His gentle voice filled my heart with serenity. Sometimes, he called me Mama because I was named after his mother, my grandmother.

"Na'am, Abba," I said, the biggest grin filling my face. *"Ina wuni.* Good evening." I could hear Sudais, a renowned Quranic reciter, reading *Suratul Baqarah,* one of the longest chapters in the Qur'an, in the background. "Hope I'm not interrupting?"

"Not at all, my dear," he answered, and I found myself trying to calculate the time back home. It was late, probably past 9 pm, and I knew he read the Quran before settling in for the night. It was a time he accepted no interruptions, yet he had picked up my call. "How's school?" he asked gently. I could hear the slight worry in his voice. "How was your midterm?"

"Aced it, Abba," I couldn't help but brag. "Everything's fine, *wallahi.* I just wanted to say goodnight," I reassured him.

"Na gode. Thank you. *Allah ya miki albarka,* Mama. May Allah bless you."

"Amin, Abba," I said, "Goodnight." I felt my chest tightening. I missed him. I missed home.

"Allah ya tashe mu da rai da lafiya," he said as he ended the call. In the Hausa language, "goodnight" was always followed with a prayer like the one my father said – may God wake us up in good health. *Ameen,* I thought to myself as I held the phone against my chest and opened the door that led to my floor. I missed Abuja so very much and since I couldn't go home, I started looking forward to seeing my mom at Kaltume's wedding, which was taking place in a month's time.

My phone vibrated and I checked to see a message from Ahmad: *Touchdown. See you in a bit.* I started typing a reply as I moved closer to my room but stopped dead in my tracks when I saw someone waiting outside my door. She was wearing an oversized brown wool coat over blue denim jeans and brown leather brogues and was fumbling with her phone. As I approached the door, she looked up, and our eyes met.

"Afreen?"

"Hi," her eyes traveled over my purple Lululemon capris and long sleeve top before glancing at the door behind her. "Your roommate said you were at yoga."

I nodded.

"My phone died when I got here," she held up the phone without even a smile on her usually cheerful face.

"Oh," I forced a smile and fumbled with my fob before opening the door for her. "After you."

She had no expression on her face as she went into the shared common space and looked around. The door to Claire's room was closed; she probably left for her evening lectures already. I looked back at Afreen, who avoided my eyes, I honestly hated how painfully awkward it had gotten between Afreen and me in just a few days. Since I left her house that evening, we have not even exchanged one text message or funny screenshot. As I closed the door, I dropped my keys and water bottle on the small table in the shared kitchenette.

"Water?" I asked, moving towards the fridge.

"No, thank you," she answered, placing a gift bag on the table. "Mum brought this back from Abuja for you."

Shoot me. This was a nightmare. She was looking at everywhere else but my face.

"Thank you," I said, making a mental note to call Aunty Mami tomorrow to thank her. We stood there for a moment, saying nothing. Then she turned around to leave. "Listen," I started, hoping she could hear the sincerity in my voice as I spoke. "I had no right to judge you. I'm sorry."

She stopped at the door and slowly turned around, and we stared at each other in silence. Suddenly, her eyes started getting misty and she looked away as a single tear fell down her cheek. "Fa'iza, it's just so hard – the creeping around, the secrets, the lying," she managed to say in between sobs.

I rushed to her side and gave her a hug.

"I didn't plan for this," she was crying uncontrollably now.

I passed her a box of tissue from the counter and she nodded gratefully.

"Oh gosh, I'm such a mess. Everything is a mess! And now, with Adnan in the mix –"

"Adnan?" I asked, as I pulled out a chair at the table for her, led her to it and sat down next to her.

"His son," she said, looking up at me. I put my palms over hers as she continued. Maryam doesn't deserve this." I remembered that Maryam was the name the called the the lady I saw at the store with him. "None of us deserve this."

"You know her?" I asked.

"Yeah, she's his cousin," she sniffed. "About three years ago, he came to ask for my hand in marriage," she said, dabbing her eyes with the tissue.

I raised my eyebrows, trying to connect the dots together.

"Yes, in Abuja. Dad and some uncles turned him down. *Wai* he was too young, that he didn't have enough to start a family, I needed to finish school..." I could see the pain in her eyes as she listed the reasons and felt bad for her. "His mum felt insulted and that same year, retaliated by getting him married off to Maryam."

"What about his dad?"

"He passed away when Zafar was young," her eyes were beginning to well up with tears again. She took a deep breath and confessed: "Sometimes, I feel like they rejected him because he isn't from a well-known family."

I held my breath and slowly exhaled. I could understand her anger and helplessness. Our religion advocates for marriage when a girl finds a suitor, and our culture advocates for the best suitor, not just *anyone*. Depending on the girl's family, the best suitor had to have a lot of things – wealth, lineage, family status, and so on. How well marriages in that family had fared were also issues that were usually considered, as opposed to love and definitely not wishes, hopes and promises.

"Then he got the PTDF scholarship to come here for his Masters," she continued. "Fa'iza, *wallahi* we tried to fight it. But we – we –" her voice trailed off.

I opened the fridge, got the bottle of water she'd rejected earlier and placed it in front of her, avoiding eye contact. I was in no position to have an opinion and I was afraid my eyes would betray me. I could understand her anger, but I was raised to believe that adults knew best. And until that moment, I had never realized how dangerous that rationale was.

"Thanks," she smiled, then started laughing in between her sobs. "If someone had told me when I was younger that I would be head over heels in love with a married man, I would've smacked them right in the face."

I nodded, realizing that she was right; it was quite complicated. She was barely a year older than me, and this was the card she was dealt. This was a love story destined to burn right from the beginning. I sighed, "Afreen, if this relationship isn't heading anywhere... what are you doing in it?" I sat down opposite her and held her hands in mine. "I don't want you to get hurt."

"The heart wants what it wants. Love is..." she paused as she thought of the right word, squeezed my hands and smiled, "stupid." We both burst out laughing as she wiped a tear from the corner of her eye. "Who knows? Maybe when Ahmad finally gets married – and I'm *still* single – my parents will get tired of me being in their house and allow Zafar and I to get married."

My heart did this weird tingle thing when she said Ahmad. I wondered if he was already on his way.

She exhaled out loud, "it feels good finally talking to someone about this."

"Thanks for telling me," I said, and we sat in silence for a minute. "I'm gonna make some tea. Would you like some?"

She looked at her wristwatch, and her eyes widened, "No, no, no, no, no," she said, getting up, "Mum's back now. I can't be outdoors after *Isha*." She smiled as she reached for the door. "You should come over for the weekend."

"I have my study group meeting Friday evening." I said. "Maybe Saturday?"

"We're having a birthday dinner for Ahmad on Friday," she explained. "His birthday was last week Friday, but he was busy, so we're celebrating this week."

"Oh."

"I can come pick you up after your study group," she offered.

"It's okay. I can Uber." I said, giving her a hug. She held on to me longer than usual, and with a smile, she was gone.

* * *

"I can't believe you didn't tell me it was your birthday!" I said as soon as I saw him. He was standing in the lobby, wearing a light blue buttoned-down shirt with the sleeves rolled up. He had this subtle smile that only touched a corner of his lip that added to his charm and appeal, he didn't look like he was tired or like he just drove straight from the airport after a long day.

I saw his eyes travel down my body and quickly back to my eyes. He smiled as I covered the distance between us, but he remained quiet.

"There was a birthday cake that day at Terroni!" I had to keep talking to distract myself from his eyes and the way he was looking at me. I couldn't believe he left his own birthday dinner to walk me back to the residence.

"You seem all riled up for someone who just got out of yoga," he laughed.

"How did –" I looked down, then realized that I was still in my yoga clothes. I hadn't even taken a shower. I pulled the top of my headscarf suddenly feeling a little self-conscious.

"I'm guessing Afreen told you about this dinner that I'm being forced to attend on Friday."

I nodded. "But why did you not tell me? I would have gotten you a gift, or something."

He shrugged. "Eh, birthdays are overrated. Oh, by the way, look what I found." He pointed towards a brown parcel on the barstool next to the fireplace, picked it up and gave it to me. "Open it," he said with a twinkle in his eye.

I slowly moved towards it, aware of his eyes on my every movement as I opened it. When I finally unwrapped it, I gasped: "Mistborn!" I couldn't believe I finally had this book in my hands. "I was looking for this in Paris," I was almost squealing in delight. Brandon Sanderson had a way with world-building that no one else had, and I was so excited to finally read this book.

"You mentioned," he said. Every time someone passed the lobby, they glanced at us. I saw them linger for a second or two at him but if he was aware of the stares he was getting, he did not show it. I smiled at the thought that he must be used to the attention. "What are you doing tomorrow?" He asked after I'd calmed down from my excitement.

"I just have one lecture at 11 am," I said, as my fingers ran over the burnt orange and yellow glossy cover of the book, "and then I am diving into this."

He looked around us and back at me, like there was something on his mind, but he was holding himself back. It was so weird standing with him in this lobby because apart from Afreen, I never had visitors; yet, I felt like I could stand here talking to him for hours. I wondered if he felt the same, if bringing me the book was just an excuse to see me or if this was just a stop on his way home.

"Um –" he started, and right at that moment, my *athan* went off.

"Isha," I mumbled, gesturing to the phone.

He nodded. "I should let you go," his voice sounded like he didn't really want that, and I felt the same way. "Goodnight."

"Goodnight," I said, holding the book to my chest as I walked into the elevator, wishing our little rendezvous did not have to end.

The next day, I had just gotten out of bed when his message came in: *Insom.*

It would help if you'd stop calling me that, I typed back.

Do you hate it?

I wouldn't say I like it.

Because you're not an insomniac or because it sounds like you're from Calabar?

Both.

Oh my. Edet will be displeased.

Smh.

And he was just beginning to like you.

I was in the middle of brushing my teeth when I read that, and I paused. I spat out into the sink. Was he talking to his friend about me? I texted back: *Too bad.*

You good?

Not really.

Why? What happened?

Class got canceled.

So?

I hate it when things don't go according to schedule.

Wow, control freak much?

Just organized, that's all.

His call came in as soon as my last message got delivered. I rinsed my mouth and walked out of the bathroom as I answered. "You're probably the first person in the history of students who gets upset about a canceled class," he said. I could hear Kanye West playing in the background.

"I was supposed to go to the library after class," I said, laying flat on my bed, looking up at the ceiling, "and now because the class is canceled, Sara isn't coming to campus, so there's no study group, either."

"Well, come study at mine." There was a pause as the invite hung heavy between us.

"Okay," I said, hoping that I didn't sound too eager.

"Great. I'll come get you in 5 minutes."

"Wait, what? No, come in like 30 minutes," I was still in my pyjamas.

"Cool," he said, and I hung up.

I thought about what to wear while I showered and decided on black tights and an oversized fuzzy sweater; the combo gave me the look I wanted – like I wasn't trying too hard. As I got dressed. I lazily draped my scarf over my head, lined my eyes with dark kohl, then dabbed my favorite perfume – which was *Rosabotanica* by Balenciaga – on my neck and wrists. I packed my backpack and was finishing my spinach and feta wrap when my phone buzzed. I grabbed my chai latte and went downstairs.

"Good morning," I said as I walked out of the elevator. There was something about the way I was dressed that made me feel immensely powerful today. I would be lying if I said I didn't like how his eyes lingered as he looked up from his phone appreciatively.

"Is that Starbucks?" He asked about my two-tailed mermaid cup when we got into the car.

I nodded. "Want some?"

He looked at me and for a moment, I thought he was going to take my cup to his lips, but instead, he laughed and said: "Not unless it's a double-double."

"What's a double-double?"

"A double-double from Tim Hortons." He watched me shake my head slowly to admit I didn't know what he was talking about, and he raised his dark and full eyebrows in disbelief. "You've never had a double-double?"

"No," I wondered what the big deal was. I knew Tim Horton's was Canada's answer to Starbucks, but I just never tried it.

"Oh, we have to change that. It's a matter of national pride."

"The Starbucks on the residence is a lot easier to get to than the Tim Hortons in the food court at school," I said, suddenly feeling the need to explain why I'd never tried it. He swerved as he changed lanes and made a sharp right, obviously taking a detour.

I glanced at the car behind us and back at him, "Where are we going?"

The car slowed down at a brown and red building, and we drove into its drive-through. "Welcome to Tim Hortons. May I take your order?" A voice asked through the static.

"Hello. Can I get two medium double-doubles and a box of twenty Timbits?" he asked. I had never heard that combination of words being used in a single sentence before.

"Assorted?" They were talking in English, and I understood nothing.

"Yes, please," he said, laughing at the look on my face.

"What are Timbits?" I asked as we started driving towards the pick-up window and stopped behind a black sedan. "Donut holes," he explained.

"Why don't they just sell donuts?" I asked, still confused.

"There shall be no Timmies slander around me," he said and with that accent, it was hard not to laugh. He paid when we got our order, and we drove to his apartment.

When we got there, he had set up a study station for me in his home office.

I got settled in quickly while he went into his room to take calls. I had never been more comfortable during a study session; I had snacks, coffee and natural light. I even Facetimed Sara, and we discussed and reviewed our notes and had a mini-review session with Ada. It was honestly the most productive morning I'd had in weeks.

When I got tired of sitting, I would take a walk around to look at the books on the shelves. The religious texts were all arranged according to *Mushaf* or collections. He read authors from every corner of the globe – Rabindranath Tagore, Adeline Yen Ma, Salman Rushdie, Steve Biko. I took out some books and realized he'd written notes on the margins and highlighted specific chapters. He didn't just read these books; he studied them and kept them as part of a growing collection. I was going through the notes he'd made on the pages of 'The Age of Reason' by Thomas Paine, scribbling about skepticism of miracles in holy scriptures to the concept of free will and arguments against the idea of written destiny when he came into the study.

"*Ya karatun*? How's the studying?" he asked, and I immediately closed the book with a snap. Reading his thoughts about religious institutions being societal constructs and their constraints on spirituality on the pages felt like I was eavesdropping on a private conversation. If he'd noticed my abrupt action, he spared me the embarrassment by not acknowledging it. His eyes fell on my open books and laptop on his desk. "I got us some lunch," he said as he looked at my schedule. "What's this?"

"My planner," I answered. My neon-green yearly planner had lots of stickers and colored pens circling words I found important. It almost looked like a scrap journal.

"I can see that," he pointed at the line I'd written in purple gel pen. "11 am to 1 pm: Study, 1 pm to 1:30 pm: lunch, 1:30 pm to 3:00 pm: watch something." It amused him, but I cringed as he read out loud from the open page. "You schedule a time to watch TV?" He laughed, looking up at me. "Seriously?"

"I just like being organized, that's all."

"Right, you've said that before," he suddenly looked serious, "so do you set an alarm or a timer?"

"Sometimes," I admitted.

"So if your alarm goes off mid-episode, do you finish the episode or do you stop watching immediately?" His facade cracked as a chuckle escaped him.

"It's not funny," my lips formed a thin line on my face.

He dropped my planner on the table and put his hands up: "Okay, I'll stop." But he didn't stop laughing as he watched me unplug my laptop and walk out of the door.

On his kitchen island were two brown paper bags. I hadn't realized I was hungry until I got closer to the bags; the aroma wafting in from them was tantalizing. He opened the cabinet as he brought out plates, his white T-shirt lifted up and I could see the black band of his *Calvin Klein* boxers just below his taut six-pack. I quickly looked away as he turned around.

"Can you get us cutlery?" he asked, pointing to the drawer on my right. I nodded as I dropped my laptop on the island and moved towards it, silently praying he didn't catch me ogling earlier. That would have been embarrassing.

"Are you okay?" he asked, interrupting my thoughts. I looked up, and there was a concerned look on his face.

"Y –Yes."

"It's *halal*, if you're wondering," he said, bringing out a platter of rice and potatoes. The other bag had fresh pita, garlic sauce, shredded chicken and beef.

"So," he started as he fetched some tabouli salad, "what are you scheduled to watch today?"

"Gossip Girl," I answered unashamedly.

"Hell no," he walked to the front of the TV in the living room in protest. "There shall be no Gossip Girl watching on this TV." He turned it on as he sat down, and the HBO logo came on the big screen. I was already sitting on the sofa when I realized that I'd forgotten my laptop, "Do you watch Game of Thrones?" He asked.

I shook my head.

"No way. You have to watch Game of Thrones," he said as he clicked buttons on the remote without looking at it. "Try it. If it's not for you, you'll know in the first episode."

I ended up watching half of the first season that day. I only got up to pray or to get more water to drink. Later in the evening, when I got cold, Ahmad turned on the fireplace and got me a blanket. I stayed there until after *Isha*, and then he drove me back to the residence, with Joe's *I wanna know* playing from the car speakers as he pulled into the last available empty parking spot in the Visitor's Parking area.

"You know, you can always come over, right?" he said as we sat quietly in the car. "I'm just a few minutes away, if you ever want a break from... *this*." He gestured towards the building in front of us.

I nodded as I looked straight ahead. "I just hope Ned gets back to his family." I was still thinking about the show I was now very invested in – the lies, the politics, and the incest.

"I'm not in the business of giving away spoilers," he laughed.

"A simple yes or no would suffice," I opened the door and let myself out of the car.

"Tough luck," he said, coming out and standing next to me. He was now by my side, and we walked side by side toward the residence. His hands were in his pocket, but our arms slightly brushed against each other as we walked. I was enjoying his company, and I didn't want the day to end.

He held the door open for me, and I entered the deserted lobby. As we waited by the elevators, Ahmad brought out his phone, sent a message and put it back in his pocket.

"Alright," I said, looking up at him as I heard the elevator nearing the lobby.

He was biting his lip distractedly like he wanted to say something but was thinking against it. "I just sent you the login details for my viewing account, so you can continue the show anytime you want," he said, looking into my eyes and gauging my facial expression. He had the most beautiful brown eyes I'd ever seen. "Or we could watch it at my place tomorrow? I can pick you up after class."

Without waiting for an answer, his hand reached for mine. As I looked up at him, his hand went to my lower back and he pulled me into him. The hug just lasted for 2 seconds, yet it got me so disorientated that I couldn't even place the name of his cologne, even though it smelt so familiar.

"Goodnight, beautiful," he winked and he began walking away, his hands back in his pocket.

I walked towards the elevator, with tiny little bells in my head ringing *Haram*!

Chapter 8

The week went by really fast – mostly because I started my Peer Mentorship program. I was matched with a final-year law student named Hodan Hubbard, who encouraged me to join the Students' Law Society. Sara and I joined her at the association's weekly meeting.

"Do you have any plans for the weekend?" Hodan asked as we entered the building; her black curls seemed to have a life of their own – the way they bounced over her shoulders almost on their own accord. Her skin was about a shade darker than mine; she had round cheeks and was always dressed in monochromatic colors. She was the kind of person who commanded respect just by being in a room. She had kind eyes and often spoke of her Somali heritage.

"I'm going to my aunt's place," I answered.

"Oh, you have family here?" she asked, surprised. "That's good. I saw 'International Student' in your mentee profile and assumed otherwise."

My phone started buzzing before I could answer. I glanced at it and turned it face down on the desk. After the meeting – which was mostly about community service projects and networking opportunities to connect with former alumni who are practicing attorneys, I walked out of the auditorium with Sara. "Are you avoiding someone?" she asked.

"No," I answered slowly. It was not true. "Why?"

"That was the third call you're ignoring today," she said as we walked into the courtyard.

"I just didn't want to have to excuse myself out of the meeting," I answered. I knew she didn't believe me, but I appreciated the fact that she didn't push it. We went to our usual designated spot for our study group and met Ada there; she'd been waiting for us. For the two hours we spent there trying to study, my mind kept wandering back to my conversation with Ahmad.

I can come get you on my way home, he'd texted.

No, it's ok. Thanks.

Are you okay?

Yes, I am.

I'd brushed away all his invitations to come and study at his place earlier this week. Actually, he only asked once. We didn't talk much on the phone either; I'd been avoiding his calls since the day he hugged me. To be honest, I was uneasy about seeing him that evening. I wished I could cancel, but I promised Aunty Mami when we spoke on the phone that I would be there. As I walked back to the residence, my phone rang. I looked at the screen. It was Afreen. "Hello," I said.

"Heyyyyy," she said on the other end, "I'm actually around your Uni. I'll come get you, so we can go home together." *There goes the quiet Uber ride I was looking forward to.*

"Are you sure?"

"Of course," she chirped away. "Besides, mom will be upset if I allow you come in an Uber."

"Okay, then. *Sai kin zo.* Till you come."

Back in my room, I carefully did my makeup and wore a burgundy jumpsuit. It was sleeveless, so I wore a blazer over it. I wore a gold statement piece around my neck, and as I tied my scarf around my head, I looked at my reflection, wondering if the necklace was too much. Before I had a chance to take it off, there was a knock at the door. It was Afreen, looking ethereal in a long white body-hugging dress with long sleeves and pearl studs earrings. She had a white silk scarf wrapped around her head with two tendrils of curly hair framing her face.

"Fa'iza, *mashaAllah,*" her eyes widened when she saw me. "You look stunning!"

"*Na gode*. Thank you," I answered. "You look great."

"And this necklace," she said as she put her fingers delicately on it.

"It's too much, isn't it?"

"No!" she exclaimed as she adjusted it for me. Then she took a step back to look at me more carefully. "It completes your look. I love it."

A few minutes later, we were walking down the hallway, heels clicking away, and laughing at jokes Afreen was making. There was a red Mini Cooper parked at the other end of the lot. "That's me," Afreen pointed her key in its direction and the car blinked. We got in, and *Enta eih* by *Nancy Ajram* started blasting through the speakers, and we sang along, laughing heartily at times when we didn't remember the lyrics. Her playlist only comprised of Arabic songs and as we pulled into the driveway, I thought about how this was definitely better than an Uber ride, even though she raced through two yellow lights.

"Thanks for coming to get me," I said, as we got out of the car.

"Oh please," she replied, as we walked into the house already bustling with guests.

When the door opened, I was bracing myself. I didn't know what to expect, but I was amazed to see how much the already-beautiful house had transformed. Past the foyer, the great room was decorated in gold and black. Under the Venetian crystal chandelier was a large table in the middle of the room with ten chairs circling it. In front of every chair were orchids, placemats, and name tents.

Aunty Mami and the ambassador were interacting with the few invited guests. Two waiters in white shirts and black bowties quietly moved around the room, offering *hors d'oeuvres* and drinks on golden trays. As I approached Aunty Mami, her eyes lit up, and she engulfed me in a warm hug.

"*Salam Alaikum* Aunty. Good evening," I let myself rest slightly in her arms. "I love what you've done with the room. It's so beautiful."

"*Wa alaikumus salam,* Fa'iza *am,*" she answered. She was dressed in a majestic green Senegalese boubou with a matching headgear. It had the most exquisite needlework I'd ever seen. The white gold around her neck, ears and wrists clinked lightly with every movement she made as she dismissed my compliment with a wave of her hand. "Ahmad never wants anything over the top," she explained with a laugh. "This is the most I could get away with."

"Good evening, Uncle," I greeted him.

"Fai'za," he smiled. He was wearing a black kaftan and as he moved his hand, I noticed airplane cufflinks. I'd seen a similar set at Ahmad's. "I was on the phone with Chief Justice earlier today," he said, referring to my father. "*Ya Makaranta*? How's school?"

"It's fine, *Alhamdulillah*," I managed to get out before Aunty chimed in, telling me to get something to drink before dinner started. She beckoned at a waiter and he walked towards us. Afreen, too, who was talking to other people, started walking towards me when she saw the waiter next to me, offering me a red dark liquid.

"It's *Zobo*," Afreen whispered, and I took a sip. "Or, like mum's friends here say, her "famous hibiscus cocktail," she said in an exaggerated accent, and we both burst out laughing.

"I was just talking to some of Ahmad's friends," she explained as we walked towards them. It was hard for me not to notice his absence. I didn't want it to look like I was searching for him, but the room only had five other people I didn't already know.

"Fa'iza – Brooke, Tumi, Hasaan and Edet," she said as she introduced them one after the other.

Oh, Edet. I thought to myself as I watched the gentleman wearing a brown short-sleeved shirt put a glass to his mouth. He looked like he was hiding a smile. He was light-skinned, with coarse textured hair and an athletic build.

"Guys, this is Fa'iza," she said.

"Fe-ehza. Am I pronouncing it right?" Brooke asked me, with a smile on her face. Her red hair was pulled into a loose ponytail. I instantly didn't like her.

"Fa-ee-za," I corrected her. It had three syllables – as easy as Arabic names got. Why would you have a hard time pronouncing it? In the day and age of Lupita Nyong'o, Chiwetel Ejiofor and Mia Wasikowska.

"Nice to meet you, Fa'iza," Tumi said.

"Likewise," I said with a smile and gave a slight nod to Hasaan.

"Finally!" Afreen's voice interrupted." That was one *long ass* phone call."

My heart slightly somersaulted as I turned around and saw Ahmad walking into the room in a black buttoned-up shirt tucked into black trousers.

"How did it go?" Edet asked him. "Did they agree to our terms?" He was the only person in the room who came close to Ahmad's height.

"No shop talk. It's Friday," Ahmad replied, and Tumi laughed. He turned around and acknowledged me by saying my name. For a second, it felt as if everybody in the room had disappeared as I looked at him.

I was brought back to earth by Aunty Mami's voice, trying to get everyone's attention. "Alright, everyone, dinner is served."

We all moved towards the table and looked for the placemat with our names on it. Uncle was at the head of the table, and Aunty was seated to his right. Their two guests were seated close to them. Next was Afreen and I, with Brooke seated opposite me. Tumi, Haasan and Edet were sitting closer to Ahmad, who sat at the other head of the table.

"I'd like to thank everyone for coming." Ahmad said, looking around, his face lit up as his gaze settled on Aunty Mami. "Mum, you're the best. I love you." She beamed with the light of a thousand stars and blew him a kiss. He looked towards his dad, "I appreciate you being in Toronto this weekend for this, dad. I know how busy Ottawa gets."

The ambassador raised a glass towards him, "I just came here to see my beautiful wife but sure, whatever makes you happy, Ahmad." The whole room burst into laughter.

"Afreen, thank you for insisting – even though this isn't my kind of thing," Ahmad continued, looking at his sister, who responded with a little curtsy while seated. "Seeing you all here," he looked around the table, his eyes settled on me, my breath hitched, and I looked at my plate, "makes me feel immensely grateful."

"Happy birthday to the best CEO ever!" Brooke said, raising her glass towards him.

"Thanks, Brooke," he smiled as he sat down.

As I looked around the room, indulging in small talk with Afreen and Tumi, watching the parents in deep conversation with their son's friends about the stock market and companies going public. I realized how different our families were. This family was more fluid and liberal than mine was, even though we shared the same identity – Muslim and Northern. My family was on the end of the spectrum from this one; my parents would never host a dinner for a birthday. And even if they did, they wouldn't attend it, talkless of sitting in it and participating in toasts. Neither tradition was wrong; this was just a new experience for me, and I was glad to be a part of it.

After dessert, the conversation turned to a topic I had no interest in or input on – American politics. They all looked like they had known each other for years, and I preferred watching them from a distance, so I walked to the garden in the backyard, sat on the swing by the fire pit with a slice of cake on a plate. As I looked at the stars in the sky, I kicked my shoes off and tucked my feet in the grass underneath the swing.

I thought about how handsome he looked that evening – the way his fingers went around the gold-plated cutlery, the luminescent gleam around the face of his Patek Philippe wristwatch every time his hands went to his mouth, the way his smile lit up the room whenever Aunty Mami spoke. I noticed the way everyone in the room looked toward him when they told a story or cracked a joke. It mattered to them that he was listening and that he found their stories amusing. I didn't think anybody noticed me stealing glances at him. Our eyes met a few times and every time they did, I looked away.

"Running away from the party?"

I turned my head to see Ahmad walking down the few patio stairs that led into the backyard. He'd rolled up his sleeves and unbuttoned a few buttons. In the moonlight, I could see his muscles ripple under his shirt. I swallowed as I looked away.

"Or just from me?" he asked as he sat next to me on the swing. He was not looking at me.

I opened my mouth to deny it, but closed it back.

"I like to think that I'm pretty discerning," he turned and our eyes met. "I'm sure I can tell when someone is avoiding me."

"No, I'm not actually," I lied. When I use 'actually' at the end of a sentence, there's a high chance I'm lying, but he didn't know that yet. "I've just had a busy week." *At least that part is true.*

He nodded. "How did your debate go?" he finally asked, remembering what I was studying for earlier in the week.

"It went well," I answered. "We lost marks on argumentative points, but our citations were solid."

"That's good," he said. "Maybe one day I can hear you argue a case."

I couldn't help but smile as I finished my cake. I sighed. I had misjudged him. I can say that now. Maybe the hug was a reflex, and maybe it was just a one-time thing.

"I finished season one," I said about Game of Thrones, unsure of what to say.

"Really?" the light was back in his eyes. "And, what's the verdict?"

"*Ai,* I am done with that show," I said, and he started laughing. "How can Ned Stark die? And then Khal Drago too? I prefer shows where the main characters don't die."

"Oh, c'mon. What's the fun in that?"

"No, seriously. I was shocked, and angry," I said, recalling how much I screamed at my laptop while watching that episode.

"Wait till you see the red wedding," he muttered under his breath.

"The what?" I asked.

"Never mind. Aren't you curious about the dragon eggs, at least?"

"I don't care much for the dragons, or the girl with white hair."

"Oh, that's a first," he said, leaning back and looking at the stars with me as we swayed gently. We were quiet for a few minutes, swaying in the cool night breeze with the sounds of laughter and chatter from the party in the far background. *This is nice,* I thought to myself. *Every time I'm with him, I feel content. Safe and content.*

"You look lovely tonight, Fa'iza," he said very quietly. "I'm glad you came."

* * *

I got Ahmad a birthday gift. It was *Dreams from my Father* by Barack Obama. I noticed it was missing in his library. He said he loved it, and he finished it really quickly; I even saw the notes he wrote on some pages. The frequency of our phone calls had increased. It felt like we spoke all day. My phone was constantly cradled between my neck and ear up until the late hours of the night.

I found myself in a football stadium on a Sunday afternoon two weeks later. Did I care for football? No, I did not, but Ahmad invited me to watch him play, so there I was. He called it soccer; I called it football.

I was seated on a bench in the sparsely-filled stadium where his team was playing a friendly match against another team from Vancouver. It was easy to spot him on the field because he had bright red soccer cleats on. As we drove there, he told me that he was a striker – whatever that meant. He tried explaining the different positions to me so that I could follow the game, but it was only when I was watching the game that I realized I understood one or two things. Before then, the only words that stuck with me while watching my brothers scream at the television were 'Offside' and 'Own goal.'

My attention shifted back to the game as I watched someone pass the ball to him and someone else fell down trying to get the ball from him. The stadium's momentum was getting louder as he got closer and closer to the other team's goalkeeper, and then the ball was suddenly in the net. He scored. The whole place erupted. I hadn't even realized that I'd stood up to clap until his head turned toward my direction. He'd picked out this seat for me, and knew where I was seated. Our eyes met, and I flashed him a smile, doing a little celebratory dance with my hands around my head when he formed a heart with his fingers and put his hands on his lips, without taking his eyes off mine even for a moment. His teammates suddenly bombarded him, and he was out of my sight.

I was also aware of the few glances I got; people had seen his gesture toward me. I raised my straw to my mouth to hide my embarrassment and finished my iced cappuccino from Tim Hortons in seconds. It was new to me, but I loved the attention. *SubhanAllah,* I loved the attention he gave me, and I loved the tiny little butterflies I felt when he did that. I felt the same way when he gave me a red jersey with his name on the back to wear over my top when he came to pick me up today. I was falling for him despite myself and didn't know how to stop it.

The rest of the match was a blur. When the final whistle was blown, the claps brought me back to reality. His team won. I adjusted my scarf around my head, suddenly aware of how hot it was. The air was hot and dusty and I stood up, brushing off as much dust as possible from my blue denim trousers. Then I saw him walking towards me and I went down the stairs to meet him halfway.

"Did you enjoy the game?" The sweat on his skin glistened, but I was carried away by his smile and the slight crinkle around his eyes as I looked up at him.

"It was a good game," I answered as I tossed the cup in the recycle bin. My mind kept replaying the goal he scored in the second half and everything else that followed. Thank God I was not lighter in complexion; I would have been blushing furiously.

"I want you to meet Edet," he gestured to the person next to him. I hadn't even noticed there was someone beside him. Edet was as tall as I remembered. Today, he had on the same-colored sweaty jersey as Ahmad, his cleats strung around his neck, and he was wearing flip-flops with his socks.

"Hi. I think we met at dinner," I said, embarrassed that I hadn't noticed a whole human being by Ahmad's side. Everyone seemed invisible when he was there.

"Yes, we did," he replied enthusiastically. "We didn't get a chance to chat, though. You kinda took off right after dessert that day." He was a good-looking guy. Now that we were having a conversation, I could tell that his accent was the same as Ahmad's, and I recalled that Ahmad told me they had schooled together in the UK.

"She was hiding from me, man," Ahmad said with a laugh, "can you believe it?" He made it sound like a joke.

"Not exactly," I interjected.

"I can't blame you, even *I* hide from him sometimes," Edet said with a big smile.

"Hey, don't you have somewhere to be?" Ahmad asked his friend. Edet winced and grabbed his arm as Ahmad threw him a light punch.

"Nice to finally meet you, Fa'iza, *properly*." he said to me as he shook hands with his friend as we said goodbye.

"Same here," I said, wondering if he knew about the Calabar banter I had with Ahmad. As we watched him leave, I realized we were the only ones left in the stadium. It was hard not to notice Ahmad's muscles because I was standing so close to him. It didn't help that he flexed his biceps as he pulled up the bottom edge of his shirt to wipe his face. My gaze fell upon his abs and the exposed band of his boxers under his shorts. I looked away immediately. I need to train my eyes to follow *sunnah,* the teachings of our prophet – to always lower my gaze around him.

"Come kick some with me," he said, nodding towards the football field.

"Huh?"

"Let's go," he said, grabbing my hand and pulling me towards the field like he knew I was going to protest.

"I can't play football," I said, but we were already on the field.

"That's okay. All you have to do is kick it." He was watching me as I rolled my eyes. This is child's play, I thought to myself. Why would he think I want to kick a ball? I had never been interested in football. We played badminton a lot at home, and I liked it. I didn't mind table tennis too. But football? Never even attempted.

He stared at me until I kicked it and in no time, we were running and trying to get the ball from each other. He dribbled me a few times until I had to bump into him to try and get the ball from between his legs. That happened a couple of times and I finally got the ball and started kicking it toward the goalpost until he got it from me and kicked it straight in. The only sounds that could be heard in the stadium were our laughter, and the lights had not come on yet, so it was a bit dark but I could see the rapid heaving of his chest as he looked at me. My chest was rising and falling rapidly, and I realized that my scarf had fallen off my head, no doubt revealing my messy bun. The mental alarms in my head went off as he closed the distance between us, and I felt his hand reach for mine, and his other hand came to my face. He cradled my chin between his thumb and finger.

"Ahmad –" I never got to finish my sentence before I felt his lips cover mine, and my mind went blank. I felt his hand making its way around my neck slowly. It felt warm against my cold, sweaty skin. His hard chest against the softness of mine, and underneath, my heart was thumping wildly. It felt like my chest would burst. When I placed my hands on his chest as I pulled away, his hands slowly fell to his side.

"Babe?"

Babe. He called me babe. I used to think that was corny as hell, but there was something about the way he said it – how his voice sounded – that made it sound like music to my ears. I swallowed. This was wrong. This was so wrong – religiously, culturally, everything-ly. "We can't do this," I answered, looking up at him.

His lips were slightly apart, and his eyes looked puzzled. "Okay," he finally said, stepping back. "I'm sorry, I thought –"

The lights came on. I looked around the empty stadium before announcing: "We should probably get going."

"Yeah," he said. We walked out of the stadium to the car parking lot. When we got to his car, he put his sports duffel bag into the trunk while I got in and put on my seatbelt. "Are you okay?" he asked when he got into the car and pressed the ignition key.

I nodded, and we drove silently. When we got to the residence, which was about a four-minute ride away, I opened the door, and he did too. We walked silently until we got to the lobby. I forced a smile and mumbled goodnight, so many thoughts racing through my mind.

"Fa'iza?" I stopped. He looked around us, hands in his pocket, and then his eyes came back to mine. "What did you mean by we can't?" His voice was almost a whisper.

I paused, looked at the doors behind him, and back at his face. He looked genuinely puzzled, which confused me because he *had to know* why we couldn't kiss. I raised my eyebrow at him, and he shook his head. "Because it's – it's *haram*. It's against our religion," I said, annoyed that I had to explain.

"Oh," he let out a breath before he started to chuckle. I frowned, and he stopped immediately. "Yes, of course. Of course," he said.

I immediately knew there was a disconnect. Was Ahmad one of those Muslim guys that touch women who were not their *mahram*, or family without thinking of the consequences?

"You do know that any form of touching is *haram*, right?" I asked, thinking about the few times our bodies touched – like when I was on his bike, and my hands were on his shoulder or in the car when he held my hand, or earlier that evening, when he pulled me by my hands to the field.

The smile was no longer on his face as he nodded in agreement. "Yeah, yeah, I know." We watched as someone pressed the button for the elevator and went in, then he looked back at me. "But c'mon, you want me to believe you've never kissed before?"

"No," I said pointedly. I didn't break eye contact with him. I had never kissed anyone. *Well, that changed about twenty minutes ago,* I thought to myself.

"Really? Never?" He seemed genuinely shocked.

I shook my head. I'd read about it and heard other girls talk about it, but I just had never done it before. I bit my bottom lip, remembering the feel of his lips against mine.

"Fa'iza, I –" he exhaled. "I like you a lot, and I love spending time with you." He stopped, watching the expression on my face. There it was – finally! Someone I liked telling me that he felt the same way. All my life, when guys told me they liked me, I almost felt sorry for them because I never felt the same way, and I always told them so. They all considered me to be some sort of prude. This was different. I liked Ahmad. I liked him a lot. Hearing him say this to me made me feel all fuzzy inside. I realized that he was still talking, and I looked up at him again. "…do you feel the same?"

I opened my mouth to respond, but I didn't trust my voice to speak. I was unsure of how things would go after admitting my feelings to him, but I didn't want to keep him wondering about how I felt. I nodded yes.

He nodded with me, the smile coming back to his face. He started leaning in for a hug, but I stopped him.

"But," I said with my hands against his chest for the second time that evening. "We can't be doing all these *haram* things."

"Not even a hug?" He asked, and I shook my head no.

He thought about it for a moment, then agreed with an okay. He stepped back, hands still in his pocket, and looked at me as he bit his lower lip. Just then, my athan went off. *Great timing,* I thought. *Saved by the bell.*

"*Maghrib,*" he said, and I nodded. "I'll call you when I get home." With that, he pressed the elevator button for me, flashed me a smile as I got in and turned around and left.

My hands went to my lips as soon as the doors closed, and I had the biggest smile on my face. *So, are we boyfriend and girlfriend now? How does this work?*

Chapter 9

June came, and it was suddenly Summer. Winter jackets and parkas gave way to cropped tops and shorts. As winter boots became sandals, lattes and cappuccinos became iced teas and slushies, you could smell a barbeque around every other block. Studying for my final exams was keeping me really busy, and I was still spending all my free time with Ahmad. He was teaching me to drive a manual, even though I knew I would never own one. Why would I ever get a car with a manual transmission when automatic cars were easier to drive and their safety features got better every year? I had gone on a few more bike rides, poetry slams and picnics with Ahmad, although I was very disappointed one evening as we drove back from Niagara Falls when he told me that he would not be traveling to Milan for Kaltume's wedding.

"Have you gotten your ticket?" Umma asked me on the phone one day. There was so much background chatter around her, with all the preparation for Kaltume's wedding.

"Yes, I got it," I replied. My dad's secretary had sent me an email earlier that day with the Milan itinerary for the weekend. Kaltume's mom and the ambassador were cousins, so I was going to be on the same flight with Aunty Mami and Afreen. Some years back, Kaltume's father was accused of embezzlement, and it was so bad that he was wanted by the Economic and

Financial Crimes Commission (EFCC) in Nigeria. So, he exiled with his family, moving between Milan and Paris. In short, he can't be in Nigeria without leaving the airport in handcuffs, but we're all pretending it's a destination wedding because nobody really talks about that.

"Good. Your *asoebi* arrived from the tailor this morning," she said, referring to my outfits for the two wedding events. "You should see the jewelry I got you. You would love them." Umma always picked out the most exquisite pieces for me. She believed I was an extension of her, and my appearance at events such as this one mattered to her a great deal. "Be careful with this one, handle it with care. It's for the bride," Her voice had turned into the curt tone reserved for the domestic workers at home. "Can you imagine?" she was saying to me now. "They are mishandling a *Deola Sagoe* dress!" Weddings were such a big deal back home. Families on both sides were always competing to outdo the other in style, extravagance and elegance, even though the prophet advised that everything should be done in moderation. We always seem to conveniently forget that during weddings.

I had no lecture, as it was exam week. I had study sessions with Ada and Sara in the mornings, and after those sessions, Ahmad would usually come to hang out with me. Sometimes, we ended up back at his place. His study had become my sanctuary, and he never disturbed me while I was in there; he was always working in the next room. Most evenings ended with us on the couch, watching TV before I returned to the residence. The day I wrote my last exam, as Ada and I walked out, we found him waiting for me in the parking lot. He was wearing a white shirt over well-tailored grey dress pants, and he had sunglasses on.

"This is my friend Ada," I introduced them and she extended her hand toward him. "Ada, this is Ahmad."

"Hi, Ada," he said as he shook her hand, "how was your exam?" he asked, looking at me now. Next to him, Ada widened her eyes at me, her mouth quietly forming the word *wow*.

I shook my head at her, laughing as I answered him. "It was fine. I can't believe we are done – Finally!" It felt good to say that out loud.

"For real!" Ada said, looking at her phone and announcing her ride had arrived. She gave me a quick hug, and as she walked off, she turned around and added: "It was nice meeting you, Ahmad."

"Same here," he said with a smile, removing his sunglasses as we started walking towards the residence.

"So, I was hoping we could spend time together before you leave tomorrow," he said as I adjusted my tote on my shoulder.

"Sure, but you have to drop me at home before *Isha*," I said to him. I was spending the night at his parent's place because our flight was at 10 am the following day.

He glanced at his wristwatch, then slipped his hands into his pocket like he normally did. "I can work with that." The past few weeks had been great. Ahmad did anything to make me uncomfortable. There were times when his hands would almost reach for me, and then he would remember and stop himself.

"I can't believe you're not coming. Aren't you guys cousins?" I asked for the fourth time that week.

"You can't choose your family," he said.

"What does that even mean?" I got the feeling that he didn't want to talk about it, but I wanted to know, so I kept going at it.

"Just principle," he said.

"What principle?" my phone vibrated. I ignored it.

We were almost at the residence now. There were so many cars parked out in front of the building as people loaded trunks with their luggage, excited chatter filling the air.

"Let's just say that out of all my uncles, her dad is my least favorite." He opened the door for me as we walked into the lobby. "Do you need help with your luggage?"

I answered yes, and he followed me into the elevators filled with other students chatting and exchanging numbers. The luggage I'd spent the last two days packing was definitely too heavy for me to haul down the hallway and into the elevators by myself. In the elevator, we were quiet; he stood against the wall, and I stood in front of him. *This is going to be his first time in my room*, I thought, trying to remember the state I'd left my room this morning before running out for my exam.

The elevator stopped, people got off, and more people got on. As it got fuller, I moved closer toward him, my back leaning into his chest. When we got to my floor, I moved slowly in front of him as we moved toward my front door. When we finally got in, there was a note in Claire's handwriting on the table: *'Have a fantastic summer. See you in the fall.'* She must have left for Saskatchewan, where her mom and stepdad lived, while I was at my exam. The door to her room was wide open, her bed stripped of its cover. Her study table, which was usually cluttered, was now bare, devoid of all her colorful Post-it notes. I walked into my room, quickly scanning to make sure I had no underwear sticking out of my laundry basket. I laughed at how foolish I felt while Ahmad quietly inspected the Simpson magnets on our fridge in the kitchenette. I was disconnecting my chargers and folding my praying mat when he walked into my room and threw himself on my bed.

I closed my luggage and walked over to the window to pull the blinds, then turned to face him: "Ready?"

"I ordered us some food. Should be delivered by the time we get to my place," he said, wheeling my purple Rimowa suitcase. "Please don't tell me you're taking books with you to Milan?"

"Of course, I am! What am I going to do with all my free time since you're not coming? "

* * *

The seatbelt light came on almost at the same time as the pilot's announcement, interrupting the in-flight movie I was just beginning to get into. *"Ladies and gentlemen, we are now crossing a zone of turbulence. Please return your seats and keep your seat belts fastened. Thank you."* I removed my headphones and to my right, Afreen closed the book she was reading. I looked at the trip tracker on my screen; we were halfway to our destination. The first wave of turbulence hit the cabin a little harder than I had anticipated, and I felt my hands grab the glossy polished wood of the armrest.

"This is the longest flight ever. We should have taken a night flight," she complained, rolling her eyes as she fastened her seatbelt. If we had taken a night flight from Canada, we would have arrived at Milan in the evening and missed the first event of the wedding, but I didn't say anything because I knew that she knew this. "I'm excited about getting my face beat by Mamza!"

"Who?" I didn't hear the end of her sentence over the rumble of the cabin.

"Fati Mamza," she answered, applying lip balm. "She's flying in tomorrow and will be doing the bride's and the bridesmaids' makeup. She's –" She was interrupted by another wave of turbulence, her lip balm falling on the brown carpeted floor.

I silently muttered a prayer in my mind as I felt my seat shake slightly. The wedding had not officially started, but it was already gaining some traction on the internet. There was a hashtag, #SGKS, with the couple's initials that wedding vendors were tagging guest outfits with. The posts were getting a lot of likes. I tried to recall who'd tagged me on an Instagram post that had my name on it. With all the comments, it was hard to filter through. "I like Fati Mamza. She doesn't go crazy with the nose contour," I said when the plane finally seemed to have won its battle with the clouds.

"I know, right? It's like everyone steps out with a new nose at these events," she picked up her book and started flipping through the pages, trying to find her page.

After touchdown, we grabbed our hand luggage and went to Aunt Mami's seat. She was reading a message on her iPad, looking stately in her black Abaya. "The chauffeur, Matteo will be waiting for us at gate 6," she said as she looked up from her itinerary. She adjusted her glasses, picked up her handbag, and we got off the plane after her, making our way quickly through Milano Malpensa Airport Security and Immigration.

After we got our luggage, we walked towards the exit and saw a man in a white uniform holding a white placard with the wedding hashtag and

Toronto in block letters. "Welcome to Milan," he said as he helped with one trolley of luggage. He spoke English with a heavy Italian accent. "My name is Matteo. I will be your chauffeur for the day; or in this case, night."

"Thank you, Matteo," Aunty Mami answered, glancing at his nametag to confirm. "How far are we from the hotel?"

"About 30 minutes. No traffic at this time," he said as he put our luggage in the trunk of the Maserati that served as the hotel's complimentary airport shuttle, whistling as he did. It was dark outside, but the streets were brightly lit.

"We're staying at the Gallia," Aunty Mami was reading to us off her iPad as the car began to move. "Dinner at the Terrazza – oh, I'm glad the venue for the event is at the same hotel," she added to herself.

I offered Afreen and Aunty Mami mints. I always carried mints when I traveled. Same reason I don't talk to people after long flights without brushing.

"Na gode Fa'iza *am,"* Aunty smiled, as she popped the white circle in her mouth and continued reading, *"Kamu* is tomorrow evening, Nikkah on Monday morning and the reception in the evening," she pulled her rimless glasses down the bridge of her nose as she observed the buildings in the distance through the window.

"Shi kenan? Is that all?" Afreen asked. "That's fantastic. Lucky Kaltume – she doesn't have to sit through multiple events for one whole week."

"Or nine days," I added.

"Right?" Afreen concurred. We clearly felt the same about dragged-out wedding activities.

"That's the thing with destination weddings – with most people flying in for just a few days, we're working with a limited time frame," Aunty Mami was reading another email as she answered.

"Must be nice to pick and select what part of your culture to display," Afreen's voice had a hint of sarcasm to it.

If Aunty Mami heard her, she didn't dignify her daughter's statement with an answer. Instead, she looked at me and said, "Fa'iza *am*, Umma will be arriving in three hours."

I looked at my wristwatch, which was unhelpful as it still displayed Toronto time. I made a mental note to adjust it when we got to the hotel. "Yes, I tracked her flight while we were in the line for immigration," I answered. Her flight was arriving as scheduled. No delays, *Alhamdulillah*.

The car finally pulled up to an iconic stonewalled building, and while our luggage was wheeled in, we went to the lobby to check in. The historic-looking exterior and the contrast to its sleek modern interior captivated me as we walked through the revolving doors; the marbled architecture wrapped around my senses in hues of gold, black and white.

"Welcome to the Excelsior Hotel Gallia. My name is Monica. How can I assist you today?" a woman at the front desk beamed as we approached her.

"Checking in for three," Aunty Mami replied, and we all brought out our passports as identification.

"Oh great, you're with the SG Wedding party," she said as she looked up our names on the computer. "How was your flight in?"

"It was uneventful. Thank God," Aunt Mami answered as Monica made the keys and handed us hotel brochures.

"Uneventful is always good. The entire wedding party is on the fifth floor. The brochure has details about your dinner tonight at the Terrazza Gallia on the seventh floor." Monica summoned the porter who helped Matteo wheel our luggage towards the elevator with a slight nod. "Alfonzo will be helping you up to your rooms. If you have any inquiries, please dial 0 on your room phone to be connected to the concierge."

We followed the bellhop into the elevator, listening as he told us the floors that led to the gym, spa, golf course and all the available eateries in and around the hotel.

"Go and rest," Aunt Mami said as we got to the fifth floor, "*Bayan sallan asuba sai ku zo*. Come to my room after the morning prayer."

* * *

Afreen and I walked into our tastefully furnished room. The twin queen beds had flowers and chocolates with a note welcoming us to Milan. *Your presence is truly a gift – Kaltume.*

"I'm going to take a shower," I announced unnecessarily to Afreen, who had walked out to the terrace overlooking the city. When I came back out from the bathroom, she was removing outfits from her box, hanging them in the closet, then she went to the washroom. After praying the *sallah* I missed, I picked up my phone, connected to the hotel wifi, and messages came rushing through. I opened the first one. It was from Ahmad.

Safe flight?

I typed back: *We arrived about an hour ago.*

Almost immediately, he started calling.

"Hello," I said, as I felt a smile slowly creep up my face, "were you just sitting around waiting for my reply?" I teased.

"You would love that, wouldn't you?" his voice filled my ear, and I found myself reminiscing the previous evening – the quiet drive to his parent's house and sitting in the car for a while as he showed me some pictures he took of the sunrise that morning before we finally went indoors.

"So, how was your day?" I asked.

"Boring as heck. What time is it?"

I propped my head on the pillows as I looked at the digital alarm clock on the bedside table between the beds "4:56 am."

"Oh *haba*? You should get some rest, then."

"No, it's okay. I wanna talk to you," I answered. My wristwatch said it was 9:56 pm in Toronto. This time yesterday, all three of us were playing cards and watching TV at the ambassador's residence. Afreen had no idea what was going on between us. She assumed Ahmad brought me home because his mom asked him to; she didn't know he was going to even if she hadn't asked.

"Do you wanna know something?" his voice brought me back to earth. "You can't laugh, though."

"Tell me," I was already laughing.

"I almost came by the airport this morning, so that I could see you before you got on your flight."

I'm sure he could hear the sound of my breathing at the end of the line. I remembered how much he lingered around the house yesterday evening – so much that Aunty Mami asked if he was going to sleep over because of how late it had gotten.

"I wish you had come."

The bathroom door opened, and Afreen came out wearing a white robe and a toothbrush in her hand, "Fa'ee before we leave, let's try out the Shiseido spa" She turned around and exclaimed, "oh sorry! I didn't know you were on the phone."

"I guess I'll leave you ladies to it," he said.

"Talk to you later," I said and I hung up the phone, kind of disappointed that our phone call had come to an abrupt end.

As we made our way to Aunty Mami's after *Fajr,* Afreen's phone rang. "Zafar's calling," she announced. "Go ahead. I'll join you in a bit."

I nodded and knocked on the door as I watched Afreen go back into our room, closing the door quietly. The door opened and Aunty Mami was wearing a long light blue hijab and holding a *tasbeeh,* rosary, in her hand. I hadn't realized how much luggage she'd brought until I saw all five boxes open in her suite, which was bigger than ours, with a great view of the city.

"What can I help you with, Aunty?" I asked as she removed her hijab.

"So much to do, so little time," she murmured. "Where's Afreen?"

"She's coming," was all I could say as I knew Zafar was not yet common knowledge to the family.

"Help me with the souvenirs," she gestured toward a box filled with perfume boxes. We worked together silently until we heard a knock on the door. By the time Afreen came in, half of the souvenirs were packed in brightly colored paper bags. The bags lined the hallway in the hotel suite. Meanwhile, I kept glancing at my phone to check if the message I sent to Umma had been delivered.

"They're probably going through immigration now," Aunty Mami said. Like me, she was also checking her phone for a message or call from my mom.

Chapter 9

As I helped my aunt unpack, Afreen steamed the creases out of the dress her mother was wearing that evening. After a couple of hours – with all the souvenirs in bags, outfits hanging in the closet, shoes and bags for each outfit placed neatly on the carpet in the closet, presents for the couple wrapped and displayed on the center table, jewelry locked in the safe – we returned to our room.

Afreen was already asleep when the phone in our room rang. I reached over and picked up. "Good morning, Ms. Fa'iza. A guest who just checked in has requested to be connected with you," the lady announced.

"Go ahead," I said. I could barely contain my excitement.

"One moment," the voice said again, and within a minute, I heard the unmistakable voice of my mother. "Hello."

"Umma!!" I screamed into the phone. "What's your room number?"

"510."

As soon as I hung up, I grabbed my key and walked briskly down to the hallway and knocked on her door. Almost immediately, the door flung open, and I fell into my mother's arms, giving her the biggest hug I could.

"I kept waiting for my message to be delivered so that I could call you; I would've been in the lobby to receive you," I said without stopping to breathe.

"Oh, what nonsense," she said, stepping back to look at me. "You just got off a flight yourself."

I looked at my mum, and she looked just as beautiful as always; it was hard to believe that she'd just traveled across continents over the last 12 hours. I hadn't finished admiring her when her finger flew to my cheeks. I hadn't realized there were tears in my eyes.

Her suite was identical to Aunty Mami's, and multiple boxes filled the room, making it hard to navigate to the king-sized bed.

She saw me looking at all the boxes. "*Muna da aiki.* We have work to do," she said with a laugh. But before she could go on, there was a knock on her door, and she opened it. I heard Aunty Mami's voice: "As salamu Alaikum." They both started laughing.

"Wa Alaikumus salam." More laughter, then, "You got my text."

"It just came in." They hugged and laughed with the ease of a friendship that spanned over decades. Aunty Mami smiled when she saw me in the room, "Fa'iza, go and rest." Then she turned to my mum: "She's been helping me unpack my own boxes."

I opened my mouth to object, but Aunty Mami cut me off. "I'm here now. We can handle this without you."

"Let's start with the bride's accessories," Umma said, then turned towards me: "The box over there is for you and Afreen – your *asoebi* is in there. You can take it to your room." She pointed at a brown Louis Vuitton box as she spoke.

"I can help, so that we can finish faster," I offered.

"Don't worry. We'll have enough time to rest before tonight's event. Go."

"Okay," I gave her another quick hug before wheeling the box out of the room. This was going to be an interesting wedding. I was sure the fifth floor of the Gallia had never housed such a diverse bunch of people from different parts of the world. The bride and her family alone took up half the suites on the floor. Then there was the groom's family and then their friends who were also invited guests. Early breakfast was organized by the catering team at the hotel in the morning; there was so much chatter in the breakfast hall designated to the SG Wedding party filled with conversation in Hausa, English and some French.

When Afreen and I woke up from the much-needed morning rest later that morning, we went to Umma's room to help with the remaining souvenirs and gifts. After brunch, Umma and Aunty Mami took a nap before dinner, and we went to meet their bride in her suite. As soon as we entered the white-walled suite, the scent of *turaren wuta* took me back to many wedding events back in Nigeria. The room was bustling with all her female friends and cousins – trying on dresses, taking pictures, and at least three people were getting their hair braided.

"*Assalamu alaikum*," we entered the room. I felt at least a dozen eyes on me immediately, and I was sure Afreen did too.

"Afreen Babangida!" someone said, ever so lightly between a gasp and a whisper. It was the bride, Kaltume. She was wearing a black sleeveless tunic, sitting on pillows with her hands stretched out in an attempt to dry the beautiful *henna* drawings quicker. Her dark, short hair with brown highlights was in a cute bob and tucked behind her ears. "Fai'za Mohammad, I can *not* believe this!"

Kaltume Sherriff. How do I describe her? There was something elegant about her – her big dark almond-shaped eyes, the way her ebony skin shone in the morning light or the graceful manner in which she spoke? She had this beautiful way of making you feel like you mattered, like you were always welcomed into her space.

"Congratulations, couz," Afreen said in a sing-song manner as she gave Kaltume a quick hug, taking care not to get stained by henna.

"You look radiant," I added as I leaned in for a hug after Afreen. It was true. She looked like a princess with elaborate golden jewellery she wore on her earlobes and around her neck.

"I'm delighted you both made it here," she managed to say, before her attention got drawn elsewhere. Afreen and I took the opportunity to exchange pleasantries with her friends; she introduced me to the ones she knew, and the room was soon filled with chatter and laughter.

Time flew by really quickly, punctuated by visits from Aunties who dropped by to see the bride and room service who brought our various lunch orders. By the time we left her suite, she had started getting ready for dinner.

The whole floor was buzzing with photographers and their lighting assistants, videographers, mounted tripods, make-up artists, hairdressers and stylists. Doors to the many suites were opening and closing as people went from room to room, all following a schedule. Everything was planned to the most minute detail.

Afreen and I both got our hair and makeup done. I couldn't recall a time I had this amount of makeup on; the mink false lashes felt so heavy and it took a minute for me to get used to them. Afreen was already in her dress – an ink feather-embellished dress with a cinched waist that fell straight to her legs. She opted to leave her straightened hair out without a scarf and she looked spectacular with nude lips and smokey eyes. When she was done, she helped me zip up the tight, semi-sheer bodice on my navy-blue dress which gently flared towards my ankles with its illusion long sleeves stopping at my wrists. As I watched the silk scarf getting wrapped around my head in such an intricate style, I saw a younger version of Umma staring back at me in the mirror, from the widow's peak on the top of my head down to the cupid's bow on my upper lip.

"I daresay we look amazing tonight, Fa'ee," Afreen said, admiring herself in the mirrored elevator and smoothening her glossy hair as we made our way to the 7th floor. Before I could answer, my phone beeped, and I looked down to see two messages from Ahmad: *I hope Milan is treating you right?* and then *The days are longer without you here...*

Before I could reply, the elevators reached the 7th floor with a ding, and we were immediately ushered to a rose-walled wedding backdrop for pictures. As my eyes adjusted to all the lights flashing around, Afreen and I posed for pictures – both separately and together – knowing fully well the pictures would be posted on Instagram, with or without our explicit consent.

The Terrazza Gallia on the rooftop was breathtakingly decorated for this private event. Fairy lights glistened through mirrored panels that reflected the night sky. Pictures of the couple were printed on huge placards in the dinner area, flanked by blush-toned dahlias. We had the most beautiful panoramic view of the city, including the central railway station.

"I'm going to the bathroom. I promised Zafar a video call," Afreen whispered in my ear before disappearing.

I looked around at the room – a different white rose backdrop and at the faces of unfamiliar guests. My eyes found Umma, Aunty Mami, and their friends who were just arriving and posing for pictures. They all brought Nigerian high fashion to this event, with expensive laces, silks, and cashmere. It was gratifying to watch. I walked over to say hello to them as they took their seats. Aunty Mami squealed with delight when she saw me: "I can't wait for your wedding, Fa'iza *am*! We'll have the time of our lives," and everyone chorused, "Ameen."

I found it amazing how during weddings, mothers prayed for more weddings. I saw the quick pride that passed my mother's eyes when she saw all the aunties take in my subtle but classy and expensive jewelry, dress, and respectful gait as I greeted them around the table. It was a matter of utmost importance to her that they knew that her daughter of marriageable age was not only beautiful and well-spoken but also well-brought up.

I stood up and beckoned Afreen over as she came out of the bathroom, her eyes scanning the floor, looking for me. She came over and hugged Umma. "Aunty, you look great!" she said. They exchanged compliments, then Afreen went around the table, greeting everyone just as I had seconds earlier. She was just circling back to Umma when the DJ turned up the music, and the bride and her mother came in, dancing slowly toward the guests. The bride was dressed in a stunning champagne-colored V-neck mermaid dress with sequins beaded up all through its removable train. The videographers and camera crew were all over them. When they found their seats, we made montages of speeches describing the bride and wishing her well in her marital home.

The great food was secondary to the fun we were having. Later in the evening, as the mothers were on the dancefloor and we had all been properly acquainted with Kaltume's school friends and relatives, chatter flowed seamlessly across the bridesmaids' table.

"I was disappointed when I heard Ya Ahmad couldn't make it," a distant relative of the bride suddenly said.

"Oh yeah," Afreen said. "He's so busy. You know he shuttles between the States and Canada often."

"I read about him in the Forbes *Under 30* article. I was so proud!" Kaltume said. "He called me when he heard about the wedding. Oh, he's the sweetest," she added, putting her hand to her heart.

"Afreen, is he single?" one of the bridesmaids asked, and they all laughed.

"Is he *still* dating that Turkish girl?" Kaltume asked, wide-eyed. "Remember when we used to stalk her on Instagram whenever she posted their pictures?"

Afreen nodded frantically as they both giggled like teenage schoolgirls. "No, they broke up a while ago, but I think he's dating someone else now."

"*Wace ce*? Who's she? Do we know her? Please tell me she's Nigerian *this* time," Kaltume asked.

Afreen shrugged. "You know how he hates me being all up in his business, so I really don't know. But he's always on the phone with someone. Somto, or something like that. Can't remember her name, but she sounds like a Calabar babe.Or was it Insomto? I don't really –"

I choked on my drink. *So she knows about Insom!* I was startled, but luckily, nobody noticed; they were all consoling each other after hearing the news that their shared crush was taken – and by a Nigerian girl this time, who had a more probable chance of marrying him than his foreign exes. The look of disappointment on their faces as they heard the girl's name was hard to miss, even if I wanted to.

* * *

The next event, *Kamu,* which means 'catch the bride,' an event where the groom's family pay to see the bride's face, it was a staggering display of opulence – from the decor that brought the heritage and observance of regal *Arewa* from the days of yore, to the traditional music played on local instruments by a cultural musical troupe, to how modestly everyone was dressed as was expected of northern Nigerian events that our parents attended. Stepping into the decadent hall draped all around in multiple rows of curtains, carpeted in northern textile and piles of textured animal skin cushions, it was hard to believe we were miles away from home. One was immediately transported into northern royalty. The room had a cloud of its own from the incense that was burning from various burners. At the centre of it all – seated on a throne made of pillows and leather cushions, in white and gold *al-kebba* draped over her slim body and covering her hair – was Kaltume. In all her glory. All her friends were seated on the steps that led to her seat, chatting excitedly and taking pictures in their *asoebi*.

That was the first time I saw her husband-to-be. He was followed by male and female members of his family. The men were dressed in traditional

Hausa attire, kaftan and matching trousers, with some of them wearing *babban riga* on top. The festivities were dragged out, but thoroughly enjoyable. By the end of the evening, we were all exhausted.

Later that evening, back in our room on the fifth floor, I was on another call with Ahmad. "Ms. Mohammed, you looked dazzling today," his voice was sensual in my ear.

"Why thank you, Mr. Babangida," I answered with a laugh. I was in a white hotel robe in the bathroom, taking off my makeup in front of the mirror.

"No, I mean it. Afreen sent me pictures and…" he paused. "When's your flight back?"

"About that…" I started, turning on my Clarisonic facial brush, running it across my cheeks, "We're going to stay for a few days after the wedding." Umma and Aunty Mami had decided to extend our stay to explore Italy and enjoy the weather. Afreen and I didn't need convincing; we couldn't wait to shop elsewhere.

"Wait a minute," he said and hung up. A second later, his video call came in. I rinsed my face and patted it dry with a towel before I answered. He was wearing a white sleeveless shirt, and his head was buried in white pillows. "You're joking right?" he did not sound impressed, even though he was smiling as he looked at my face. "Babe, you're supposed to be back in two days."

"Two days, six days – what's the difference?" I liked teasing him.

"I haven't seen you in a week," his voice was low.

"Four days, you mean," I corrected.

"Well it feels longer than that."

* * *

The following day was the Nikkah, and Quranic recitations filled the bride's room. I was sitting with Kaltume when she got a call from an uncle who informed her of the proceedings at the Mosque – how much was paid as dowry: the gold coins and two properties, one in Abuja and the other, a Parisian apartment in the sixth arrondisement included in her *mahr*. A few minutes later, she got a call from her husband, Sani Garba.

The whole room erupted in congratulations. I watched her toy coyly with the thin belt on her brown abaya as she talked to her husband for the first time since becoming his wife. It was something special – how much new brides relished all the firsts; like the first phone call after the Nikkah, which, in our culture, women didn't attend, or the first hug, the first prayer as husband and wife, or their first meal alone together.

"Where's our *Amarya?*" Umma came into the room asking for the bride. She was followed by Aunty Mami, two of their friends and their own cloud of *turaren wuta*.

In the midst of all the sounds and distractions, Aunty Mami pulled Afreen to the side. "Senator Fatima is here and she wants you to meet her son, Babagana," her voice was low enough that no one else could hear her, but they were still within hearing distance that I could still hear them even without meaning to. "I don't want your usual excuses. You'll do the right thing and be polite." She left Afreen's side and went back to the big swarm of Aunties as more of them came into the room.

When we finished our make-up in the bride's suite, Afreen and I headed to our room to change into our outfits. This was the first time we would see the couple together as husband and wife, and all the guests from the bride and groom will be present; it was undoubtedly the biggest event of this wedding. Afreen and I wore our second coordinated outfit for this event – a pink beaded and sequined lace for all her friends. Mine was a *Hudayya*-crafted off-shoulder dress with sleeves that reached past my elbow. The lace material accentuated my tiny waist and flared at the hips, with stilettos making me appear taller. There was something about looking at my reflection that made me feel very confident.

My phone beeped as I was getting my fuscia pink headgear tied: *Hello, gorgeous.*

Hey, boo. I typed back.

I love the sound of that. What are you up to?

Getting ready for the reception. I looked at my wristwatch. *I think we're going to be late.*

Through the mirror, I glanced at Afreen in her peplum blouse and skirt. She looked beautiful, even though her demeanor had changed since the not-so-discreet conversation with her mother.

"Are you okay?" I asked.

She looked at me with a smile on her face. "I'll be fine," she shrugged. "You make that dress look great."

I looked back at my reflection. My dress was figure-hugging, but it was so easy to move in. With all the adrenaline pumping in my system due to all the excitement, I had forgotten about the discomfort from my heels. I squeezed her hand as we got into the elevators, and she sighed.

The reception was taking place in one of the banquet halls on the main floor, and as the elevator doors opened, I heard Afreen squeal, "you made it!" she rushed to hug a gentleman wearing a white kaftan and a dark brown and grey embroidered *Zanna Bukar* cap. There was something about the way the kaftan looked on him – the crisp embroidery etched across his chest, the color of the material against his skin and the well-balanced cap on that perfect head of his. As he hugged her, I saw a familiar smile on his face as his eyes slowly went over my body. I could not believe my eyes. It was Ahmad. My Ahmad.

As Afreen chippered soundlessly to her brother, I walked out of the elevator behind her. I stood still, watching them, until I realized the distance between us had become smaller. He was walking towards me with slow, deliberate steps, his eyes never leaving mine.

"I couldn't stay away," he said softly, and he chuckled at my expression. *Lord, this man is fine.*

Here I was – overly dressed under the yellow glow of the ceiling lights, trying unsuccessfully to hide the shy smile that was fast becoming a permanent feature. I couldn't believe he got on a plane to come to Milan! We spoke a few hours ago, and he didn't say anything about coming.

Afreen's voice broke the silence, telling us that this was the best possible surprise Aunty Mami could get. "I have to record this," she said as she fished for her phone from her pale pink sequined clutch, "Mum's face when she sees you – I can't miss it. I have to be there," she said, laughing.

"What's her room number?" he asked her, his eyes lingering on the henna pattern on my hands.

"It's okay, I'll lead the way, I have her keycard," she said as she got into the elevator and started recording. "Aren't you coming?" she asked me.

I shook my head reluctantly, taking my eyes away from his. "Just send me the video, I'll go save us seats." Aunty Mami and Umma were getting ready together. My mum would see through my expression or mannerisms around Ahmad and start asking questions I honestly didn't have answers to.

Ahmad got into the elevator with his sister, and she leaned across to push a button. As the doors closed, I watched as he winked at me, and my heart skipped a beat. *God help me! The butterflies again.*

I walked down the hall and into the banquet hall. Still dazed with excitement, I tried to keep my composure as I walked past aunts and uncles. It was easy to find where to sit, as the hall was divided into four *asoebi* colors. There were several tables assigned to the bridesmaids wearing the pink lace I was wearing, and they were all surrounded by Kaltume's friends. I rushed to the most sparse table and got Afreen and I seats with a good view of the bride. From there, I watched people come in and out of the hall while trying to look distracted when the camera crew began recording them. There was a rule to it – when the camera was recording you, you needed to make sure you were not drinking or eating anything; you wanted to seem unaware of the crew, but not in a way seems rehearsed; and you always avoided waving at the camera or making faces. That never aged well in wedding videos. A slight smile to someone across the room or a glance at the menu should be picturesque.

"Hello, beautiful," I felt someone's hands at the back of my chair. The familiar scent of oud wrapped my senses, and I knew it was Ahmad even before I turned to look at him. He took the chair next to me around the circular table.

"What happened to –" I paused as I struggled to come up with the best British accent. "Out of all my uncles, her dad is my least favorite?" I couldn't keep the smile off my face.

"I missed you," he simply said, his eyes dropping to the rest of my outfit and then back to my eyes. Some glances were being thrown in our direction – mostly at him. "I wasn't gonna wait another week."

Umma, Aunty Mami and their friends were now dancing in with the bride's mum. Afreen was behind them, and as soon as they walked in, she started making her way toward us.

"Are you okay with me being here?" Ahmad asked, leaning close to my ear so I could hear him over the music.

"Of course. I can't believe you're here. I almost hugged you!"

"So why didn't you?" he asked, still leaning towards me.

"You know why," I smiled, looking away.

"You know you can't sit here, right?" Afreen was here now. She plopped herself next to me and gave me her phone, pressing the play tab as she did.

"No?" he was feigning ignorance. "I'm representing you at this event. You can go sleep."

I increased the volume on the phone so I could hear the video above the music playing through the speakers. When Aunty Mami's door opened, Ahmad's back came into view as he walked into the suite. I liked the way he walked – tall and proud. Aunty Mami, who was fully dressed in her purple lace, was putting on her golden bangles when she turned and saw him. You could see the look of surprise on her face when she realized who it was, then a giant beam that rivaled that of the sun settled on her face as she stretched her arms towards him and gave him a hug, his face turning to give her a peck on her right cheek. I could hear Afreen giggling in the background as the mother hugged her son.

"I'm glad you changed your mind," she dusted something off his kaftan. The camera shook and turned around as Afreen captured someone coming out of the inner room. It was my mum. She was wearing the same purple lace covered in a raisin-colored laffaya. Ahmad couched down to greet her.

"Umma, good evening," he greeted her in Hausa.

"Ahmad! We were just talking about you! How was –" The video came to an end, and I turned to see Afreen and Ahmad in the middle of an intense discussion.

"...really don't want to," Afreen was saying.

He nodded as he listened intently. "So why didn't you just tell mum that?"

"I can't. Not everyone can get away with things when it comes to mum. We can't *all* be you."

"Listen, if you don't want to meet him, you don't have to."

"It's not that simple," she sighed and looked at me for support, urging me to say something. "I just can't back out. How would that make mum look? How would Aunty Fatima feel? She asked for her son and me to get acquainted and it would be a slap in the face if I refused – *especially* without meeting him."

I nodded. She was right. Pride and expectations were deeply ingrained in the atomic fibres of an unwritten culture in *Arewa*. This was particularly evident when it came to the rules of interaction and what someone could take offense to.

"And why should people's opinions matter so much?" Ahmad shook his head and looked from Afreen to me, then back to her. "It's your life we're talking about here, Afreen."

I looked up as the bride and groom made their way into the hall. They looked so happy, and while he was older than the bride by at least a decade, they complemented each other so well. I wondered what their story was – if they had met on their own or if they were introduced by someone in the family. It didn't matter because, at this moment, they looked like they were made for each other.

"I'll be right back," he said to me as Afreen took pictures of the couple after they had sat down. I nodded and watched as he walked towards the couple, stopping at a few tables to shake hands with other men he knew.

Afreen cleared her throat. I turned around, and she had a smile on her face as she looked at me teasingly.

"*Um,* Afreen," I started, "Ahmad and I –"

"Aha! I was wondering when you were going to tell me."

"You knew?"

"Well, today confirmed it. I noticed how quickly he followed you out to the garden after his birthday dinner, and you also looked uncomfortable when I was talking about him with Kaltume."

We looked up as Kaltume – wide-eyed and well-surprised – introduced him to her husband, and they chatted for a little while.

"Oh," I smiled, my voice shaking as I looked at the henna on my left hand. "I really like him, Afreen."

"And he has to be in love with you to come all the way here – because he really really hates Uncle Sheriff," she said, taking a sip of water. "I think I like you two together."

I laughed. I was glad I told her about it, but it did nothing to remove the uneasiness I felt at the bottom of my stomach. I was new to all this, still figuring it out, but most of all, I was uneasy about how very attracted I was to him.

"Our mothers must feel like they won a jackpot. They wouldn't have made a better match if they tried," Afreen said. I couldn't help but think of her and Zafar and how she was holding onto a glimmer of hope that someday they would accept him.

Hours later, when everybody was on the dancefloor, I found my way to the dessert bar to get a tiny cup of ice cream.

"Why aren't you dancing?" Afreen asked, bobbing her head to the music. I hadn't realized she was by my side.

"My feet are killing me!" I replied honestly, glancing at the white sneakers she had changed into before going to the dance floor.

"Doesn't that bother you?" she gestured towards the girls attempting to flirt with Ahmad, who was being pulled into a photo session by Kaltume's siblings.

"Is it supposed to?" I asked. "Aren't they your cousins?" The girls all had the same button nose that characterized their household. Or Kaltume's mom's side of the family, at least.

"Yeah, they are. But I remember how it was when Zafar and I first started dating. I was so possessive; I would freak out if any girl did as much as look at him," she said as she sighed and reclined in the chair. "It's so different now."

I didn't feel that possessive toward Ahmad. But to be fair, we hadn't really spent a lot of time around other people. As I finished my frozen yogurt, a man who looked in his mid-thirties approached us. He was chubby and dark, wearing a navy blue *babban riga* and a black cap. "Assalamu alaikum," he said to us both and then, "Afreen?"

"Wa alaikumus salam," I answered.

"Babagana," Afreen said with a mouthful of gelato. "*Yadai*? What's up?"

I did a double-take at the man in front of us; *so this was the Babagana?* "I am going to…" I scrambled for an excuse as a scowl formed between Afreen's brows like she was warning me not to leave her with him. "…I have to throw this away," I held up my empty cup as I left them together.

I tossed the cup in a recycle bin by the exit, made my way out of the banquet hall and made a left to the empty restroom. After the bride and groom left for the airport for their honeymoon, most of the older wedding guests did the same. The only people left in the hall still partying were younger family members and friends who were catching up before everyone checked out the following morning. I looked at my reflection in the mirror, ignored the incessant beeping on my phone and fixed my turban. When I got out, Ahmad was outside waiting for me, leaning on the wall, hands in his pockets. "I called when I saw you leaving the hall," he said, biting down on his lower lip like he was distracted.

I remembered the night he kissed me. I shook my head to dispel the thoughts. This wasn't the time to be thinking about that kiss. It was a one-time thing, a mistake.

"What's wrong?" his eyes had that look in them again – the one I'd seen a few times, but I still couldn't place it.

"I'm exhausted. It's been a really long week."

"Fair enough. I –" he was interrupted by three girls making their way to the elevators. "Ya Ahmad, goodnight," they said in unison, giggling to themselves as they saw us standing shoulder-to-shoulder.

"Goodnight. Have a safe flight, Anisa," he called after them, and I started making my way back into the hall, looking for Afreen.

"Is this gonna be a problem?"

"What is?"

"Something's off with you, and you are not talking about it." he looked past me into the hall and then back at me,

I sighed. It was not his fault that I barely knew anyone at this wedding and that he was flocked by so much attention from all angles all evening. I hadn't even realized that I was feeling some way. It was a new emotion for me, one I couldn't name. "There are things I don't know about you. Like your ex – the Turkish one." A frown settled on his face as he wondered where that came from. I explained: "I heard someone talking about her."

He nodded slowly. "Well, that's why we're in a relationship – to learn about each other. I'm not keeping anything away from you. It just never came up and you never asked."

"Fa'ee, I can't believe that you abandoned me in my time of need," Afreen was walking out of the banquet hall, heels in hand. "Oh, am I interrupting?"

I shook my head.

"Let me walk you guys to your floor," Ahmad said, and the three of us walked toward the elevator.

"What floor are you on?" Afreen asked as she pressed the elevator button to the fifth floor.

"I'm staying at the Armani," he said. "I never RSVP'd, so I made my own reservations."

"Kaltume was happy you made it – even if it was for just one event," Afreen said with a yawn.

"Yeah," he said as the elevator dinged to a stop.

Afreen swiped her key on the pad and pushed the door, saying goodnight as she entered the room. He acknowledged it with a nod, "You should get some sleep, but we have to talk about this tomorrow." I nodded and pushed the door open as he walked away.

The next morning, I woke up a few minutes to ten. The black-out curtains kept our room dark, but I could still hear the wheels of housekeeping carts as they made their way down the hallway to clean the now-vacant rooms.

As I moved my legs, I felt a familiar cramp in my tummy and stickiness between my legs. I groaned as I climbed out of bed and went into the bathroom, making a mental note to call the concierge for some pain relief medication. My menstrual cramps were bad on the first two days.

I stood in the shower, and as the water flowed down my back to my legs, I thought about how this explained my sudden mood swing last night during my conversation with Ahmad.

"*Uhh...* what time is it?" Afreen yawned as she looked around, disoriented. I must have closed the door a bit too loudly on my way out of the bathroom that I woke her up.

"Eleven-ish," I answered, sitting on my bed.

She covered her head with the white duvet and went back to sleep. My stomach cramps tightened, and I winced as I got back into bed. Umma also had a 'Do Not Disturb' sign outside her door to keep housekeeping out of her suite for most of the day. Aunty Mami didn't come out of her room either. We all slept in, our empty trays of food lining the hallway outside our doors.

The next morning, Afreen and I went to the Shiseido spa and, later in the day, met Ahmad at a café not too far from the hotel for brunch, easily recognizable by its colorful awning and elegant outdoor sitting area. I was wearing high-waisted black jeans, a graphic top, wedges and a scarf around my neck, and we found him sitting on a crowded patio under a canopy of lush greenery, decorated with potted plants and flowers, wearing a blue T-shirt, dark jeans, black Hermés slippers and sunglasses. He looked casual, yet, he always stood out in the crowd.

"Good morning," I said as I sat next to him on one of the comfortable chairs in front of the table with crisp white tablecloths, surrounded by the gentle hum of conversation and laughter in the background.

"*Buongiorno*," Afreen said with glee. "Wait, hope this isn't one of those places we have to order in Italian," she asked as she picked up the menu.

"I don't think so," he removed his sunglasses and turned towards my direction before dropping a red rose in front of me. "How did you sleep?"

"I slept okay," I smiled.

"I slept okay too, if anyone's interested," Afreen said, her eyes on the menu. "Can I order from the lunch menu?"

"Let's ask," Ahmad flagged down a waiter, who was promptly by our side.

"I don't want anything from the breakfast menu, but it says here that your lunch starts at two" Afreen looked at her wristwatch. "It's twelve-thirty. What can I do?"

The waiter looked at her blankly until Ahmad translated her request. He nodded and replied.

"*Grazie*," Ahmad said.

"I heard *si* so I guess I can," she said with a triumphant smile.

I flipped through the menu. It was filled with a variety of drinks: espresso, cappuccino, iced coffees, cocktails and wines. I flipped over another page and saw that they offered light bites and pastries, all beautifully presented, but there were many non-*halal* meat options on the breakfast menu that I was having a tough time deciding what to eat. "The gnocchi sounds good," I thought out loud.

A different waiter came to our table when we were ready to place our orders. He spoke English and nodded his head, and said *bene bene* when we pointed out our orders on the menu.

"What do you wanna do after lunch?" Ahmad asked.

"I wanted to go sightseeing, see Milan a bit," I said.

"We can go to the Galleria Vittorio and Duomo di Milano; they are less than a minute apart."

"Mum said we're going shopping tomorrow," Afreen said as the waiter placed her red-sauced pasta in front of her.

"Yeah, I'm driving us there, " Ahmad said as the waiter placed my creamy-sauced gnocchi in front of me and Ahmad's meat and cheese stuffed rigatoni before him. We ate in silence as we observed more people who came on the patio.

Afreen and I ate off each other's plates out of habit. "Oh, that's so good. I should have ordered that!" she said as she took another bite.

"Right? I love it. I have to recreate it back home."

"It can't be that hard; it's pasta," she said, grabbing the menu to look at the description of the meal.

"Afreen and *santi*," I teased. *Santi* was Hausa for that moment when someone is enjoying a meal so much that they say things that they normally wouldn't.

"*A sa ma ta weji*; put a wedge behind her," Ahmad completed the saying, and we laughed.

Afreen's face turned into a frown as she handed Ahmad her menu. He glanced at my plate as he squinted at the menu. looking at the food I ordered and reading the Italian description. "*Um*, Fa'iza?"

I stopped eating. He only called me by my name when he was about to get serious.

"*Bianco* is white, right? So *vino bianco* – that's white wine, *Formaggio* is cheese," Afreen spoke, almost to herself. "It''s a wine-based sauce."

Ahmad looked at me as I dropped my fork, "But alcohol evaporates when you cook with it, doesn't it?" he asked.

"Yeah, but alcohol is alcohol," Afreen looked at me as I gulped the water down like it would do anything to wash the wine off the tasty creamy sauce.

"Afreen!" he was beginning to get visibly irritated.

"What?"

"Don't go on about it. It's not like she *drank* alcohol."

"It matters to her," Afreen argued. "I eat out with her a lot. I know how much she checks these things. She doesn't even eat burgers with me when she's not sure the meat *halal*."

I felt like I was going to throw up. It had to be all in my mind. *If I concentrate on something else, I'll be fine.* I would be fine if they stopped talking about me like I wasn't there.

"I know that," Ahmad's voice interrupted my thoughts. "But what's done is done, so stop going on about it. We're judged by our intentions, and this wasn't intentional. That's it."

"I'm fine," I said as I pushed the almost empty plate away from me.

"Do you want something else?" Ahmad asked.

"No, I'm good. Thanks."

After lunch, we got into the car Ahmad had rented and made our way into town since we were only expected back to the hotel to have dinner with Umma and Aunty Mami. My mother's flight back to Abuja through Frankfurt was the following evening, so I spent time with her after dinner.

The following day, we spent hours shopping. I helped her pack her bags, and by 9 pm, we had checked out and were making our way back to the Airport. I was emotional when my mum boarded the plane to Frankfurt, so much so I couldn't stop the tears as we said our goodbyes. Afterwards, we checked in our luggage, sat in the lounge and waited for our boarding call to Toronto.

"Ahmad, when is your flight?" Aunty Mami asked in the middle of their conversation.

He looked at his wristwatch, "We start boarding an hour after yours leaves," he said. He'd told me the day before that he was going to Washington from Milan. His firm had secured a new project, and he was going to be there for a couple of days. That was right before he gave me a small Chanel box with a black ribbon tied around it. That box lay unopened in my handbag, along with the single red rose from the Café.

Chapter 10

"When are you going to take your driving test?" he asked as I drove us back from his football game. It was mid-summer in 'the 6ix'. That's what everyone called Toronto, and I was beginning to catch on. Apparently, it was given the nickname because six different boroughs came together to make the city. Looking back, my first summer here was one of the best moments of my life, like nothing I had ever experienced – my bike rides with Ahmad continued, we went to carnivals, concerts, loud music festivals with food trucks blocking the whole street, and bringing flavorful cuisines from different parts of the world, frozen popsicles at water parks numbing my lips, watching the fireworks on Canada day and most importantly, the Reviving the Islamic Spirit (RIS) convention where I watched Mufti Menk and Imam Zaid Shakir speak in person for the first time – it was all an experience.

"I think I'm nervous about taking it," I answered as I made a right turn into the underground parkade, the gold Chanel bracelet he'd bought me in Milan slipping further down my arm.

"Why? You aren't bad at all," he was in the passenger seat, watching me.

"What if I fail?" I asked, putting the car to a halt next to his power bike.

"Then you retake it. A lot of people flunk their first driving test, anyway."

I failed my first driving test, and the second one with just a few points to the passing grade. I was doing well at the University though, my summer classes started at noon. After classes, Ahmad would usually come to get me and we would go downtown to check out whatever festival was taking place that week. When we got back to his apartment, I went straight to the couch to get my laptop, which I'd left to charge when I picked him up. I opened it to reply to the class discussion on the topic of the week for my class in an attempt to earn more marks.

"I am going to take a shower. What are we watching today?" he asked as he went towards his room.

I was too distracted by the one single downvote to an earlier comment I made. "Your turn to choose," I answered as I typed away on the laptop, making sure to attach links to cases supporting my argument.

"Have you watched *Sinister*?" the scent of his aftershave announced his return about five minutes later; he sat next to me, he had changed into a sleeveless white shirt and black shorts.

I shook my head, preoccupied with the immediate reply to the comment I'd just posted. Out of the corner of my eye, I saw Ahmad scrolling through Netflix, and a few seconds later, a movie started playing. After I posted what I decided would be my last comment of the day, I closed my laptop and paid attention to the TV screen, to an eerie opening tune and a foggy forest. "Is this a scary movie?" I asked, even though I could already tell – because it didn't start with a happy family moving into a new house.

He leaned into the cushions as he nodded; a smile tugged the corners of his lips.

"You know I hate scary movies," I reminded him. As a child, I'd watched *Child's Play* and *Bride of Chucky* with my brothers and had been scarred ever since.

"So, let me get this straight," he looked down at my hands and back at my eyes, "You're afraid of moving figures in a small rectangular box and fake sounds?" he teased, trying hard not to laugh.

I tried to give him the meanest look, but my scrunched-up face must have seemed comedic instead because he burst out laughing. I took the brown cashmere blanket he always had out for me to cover my legs as I was beginning to get cold, and that was when I noticed black lines below his collarbone. "Wait, what's that?" I asked, pointing.

"This?" he asked as he pulled down the neckline of his shirt, revealing the Roman numerals on his skin: XII.XXIX

"A tattoo?" I asked, dazed.

"Yeah," he answered slowly, watching my expression.

I nodded slowly and looked back at the television, where a young girl and her brother were crouching behind a door, hiding from an unknown entity.

"Are you going to say something?"

"I just didn't know you had a tattoo. As a Muslim –" I left my sentence incomplete. I didn't have to say it; he knew that tattoos were *haram*. The body was a vessel, a loan from the Creator, and Muslims were supposed to return that vessel in the same state it was given to them – unmarked, unbotched.

"Oh, you wanna go there. Alright then, let's have this conversation."

"I'm not judging you," I said quietly.

"But you *are*, though." He didn't sound spiteful, just like he was stating facts. "Me having a tattoo makes me a lesser Muslim?"

"I never said that."

"You implied it," he stood up. "I'm going to make some tea. Would you like some?"

"Yeah, sure."

"So, our grandparents, or great-grandparents who had tribal marks on their face – are they condemned to hell, too?"

"Nobody said you were going to hell for a tattoo," I followed him into the kitchen.

"So, what is it then? Why can't a Muslim have a tattoo? How is that different from traditional body scarring and tribal marks?" He measured some rooibos loose-leaf tea, dumped it in the tea maker and poured hot water over it.

"I don't *make* the rules, I just know what I've been told," I rubbed my forehead, then turned around to get the mugs.

"It's never enough to just be told. You should never be afraid to question things," he said as we waited for the tea to steep.

"Question things? Ahmad there are rules we shouldn't question." As Muslims, there are things that we might not understand, but we still have to abide by them because they are tests of our *iman*, our faith.

"I disagree," he said, shaking his head slowly as he added honey to my tea; he knew exactly how I liked it. "why can't you question things you do not understand?"

"Because that's how it has always been." Our parents abided by these rules from the scriptures, and so did their parents and their parents before them.

"That is a very lazy approach to life, except if you are scared that something you believe in might crumble under scrutiny—"

"—of course not," we seem to be digressing from the matter at hand, "wait, why would you even say that? Are we still talking about your tattoo."

"Aren't we?" He never took his eyes off mine as he passed me my tea, and our fingers grazed lightly as I took the mug from him. "This tattoo means something very important to me. To the best of my knowledge, the ink isn't harmful to me."

"You don't have to explain all this to me."

He chuckled to himself and shrugged, "okay then."

I remained quiet, mulling the whole conversation in my head. When we went back to the couch, we'd missed one-third of the movie, so we restarted it. As much as I hated scary movies, I enjoyed trying to guess who was behind all the chaos. I tried to get invested in this movie even though I was watching it with one eye closed. The scariest thing about horror movies, for me, was the jarring theme music, and the loud unexpected sounds made them worse. If I were by myself, I would watch it muted. Halfway into the movie – with our argument about tattoos forgotten – our mugs were on the center table, empty. There I was flinching at everything that came on screen – my chin on my knees as I folded myself to take up as little space as I could out of unnecessary fear. My hands were on high alert to cover my eyes every time I felt something scary coming on the screen. But Ahmad was enjoying the movie – a little bit too much, I thought; laughing at my reactions made it an even better experience for him. At one particularly graphic scene that was totally unexpected and visceral, I screamed, and before I could stop myself, I buried my face in his shoulder. *Sauvage by Dior.*

I raised my head slowly and stared into his brown eyes. He held my gaze, not saying a word. My heart was beating fast at the feel of my arms against his skin and my cold feet by his warm legs. He bit his lower lip as his gaze fell to mine and slowly back to my eyes. I felt a flutter in my chest, then pulled away, cleared my throat and sat back to face the TV. I had just broken the "no touching" rule I'd imposed on the relationship months prior. Out of the corner of my eye, I could see frown lines on his forehead as he concentrated on the movie attentively till it finished. But he didn't say a word. I saw the movie, but I didn't watch it. All I knew was that I was deeply, madly and undeniably attracted to the human being next to me.

The *athan* went off just as the end credits rolled on the dark screen. "Gonna go pray," I muttered as I grabbed my phone and headed toward the restroom.

I need something to scream into, I thought to myself as I paced back and forth the cool marble floors in the restroom. *Why did I act like I had no home training*? I turned the tap on and off again and continued pacing the floor. I didn't even know how to navigate my feelings for him without changing a fundamental part of who I am – a Muslim. 'Why are you disappointed that he didn't hold you, when you put your head on him?' a voice in my head said. I shook off the thought as I began my ablution. 'If he had held onto you, you would've told him not to.'

"Stop it," I muttered to myself in the mirror. I slowly tapped the back of my head on the wall behind me with my eyes closed, trying to steady my breath. Through the closed door, I heard him start his prayer. It was the first time I was listening to his *Takbir*. He said *Allahu Akbar* in his deep baritone voice and if I wasn't in love with him already, this would have done the trick. I replayed the scenario in my head – how I screamed and buried my head in his neck, his eyes as he looked at me, the silence. I replayed it over and over, right down to my awkward withdrawal, his hands keeping to himself the entire time. *Just admit it to yourself,* the voice in my head came again. *You wanted more.*

No, I did *not*. I turned on the tap again and rolled up my sleeves as I rinsed my hands up to my wrists, the first step in my ablution. I rinsed my mouth and looked at my reflection in the mirror as I continued with my ablution.

Maybe this attraction you feel for him is one-sided.

It was the first time in my life I was aware of the voices in my head. *Is this what anxiety does to you?*

I jumped as I heard a soft knock on the door. "Babe, you okay?" There was concern in his voice.

"Yes," was all I managed to say, my voice shrill in an attempt to sound normal. I hadn't realized I'd locked myself in the restroom for a while.

"Okay, just checking."

I took a deep breath and opened the door, grabbed my hijab and unfolded the prayer mat. I found solace in prayer, all my thoughts evaporating as I took time to recite the verses from the Qur'an. I had always found peace in this routine and was grateful for it. I folded my white hijab and walked out of the room with it to put it in my tote on the dining table. Then I walked towards the couch to disconnect my laptop and pack it up to leave.

"I was thinking we could go for a concert before summer ends," he said absentmindedly as he scrolled through his phone. He was laying on his back on the black leather couch, one hand behind his head.

"Yeah, sure."

His phone started to ring, and he put it to his ear. I stood in front of the mirror in the foyer and wrapped my scarf around my head.

"Yeah, hello?" pause and then: "are you serious?" another pause: "how is this going to affect our timeline?" He stood up and walked into his study. I could hear him typing away on his keyboard from where I stood. "That's expected. We had mitigations in place. It shouldn't be a code red –" his voice trailed off.

I wondered what the urgency in his voice was about. I knew he was working hard on the projects he had going on. I knew the launch date of the health app he designed was fast approaching and how important it was to him that everything went exactly as planned. If one of his staff was calling him at this time on the weekend, there had to be a problem.

"Well, I'm with my girl right now," he said. "What time is Brooke scheduled to arrive?" silence. Then: "Alright, let's have a conference call in twenty."

My girl. I smiled at the thought, then quickly took it off my mind. "Is everything okay?" I asked.

I was sitting on the ottoman by the door and wearing my shoes when he came out and started walking towards me. He had a frown on his forehead yet, he managed to still look good. "What's it called when everything that could possibly go wrong starts going wrong?"

"Murphy's law?"

"Yeah, that's it."

"That sucks. I'm sorry."

"Nothing I can't fix," he said as we walked out. "Although now I'm just wondering what else I might have missed."

"It's gonna be fine, *insha Allah*," I said as we entered the elevator.

"Insha Allah," he agreed with a nod. "Thanks, babe."

* * *

It was another day of shopping with Afreen because she needed new things every time she was stressed, and since we got back from the wedding, it had become very often.

"He just said he was going to be in Toronto and was wondering if he could come and greet Mama!" Her whisper sounded less and less like one after every syllable.

"Just like that? I asked as I looked for my size among rows of lacy brassieres in the pink glow of the *La Senza* store.

"Just like that." She was holding out three racerback bras. "Despite all my attempts at acting like a spoilt brat, Babagana still wants to meet my mother. He doesn't take a hint," she powered through another row of strapless bras, and added three to her collection.

"Well, you must have left quite the impression on him that he thinks it's worth the trouble," I said as we made our way to the fitting rooms.

"And mum keeps mentioning Aunty Fatima in every single conversation these days," she rolled her eyes, then lowered her voice as she began imitating her mom. "Aunty Fatima said you should send her the number of your tailor in Abuja, oh I spoke to her this morning, she asked after you, you should call Aunty Fatima and congratulate her, she was nominated for-whatever-it-is," then back to her normal voice: "Aunty Fati this, Aunty Fati that." Afreen was waving a red bralette around in anger as she spoke. "I have no peace in that house. They're trying to get rid of me so badly. It's not even subtle anymore."

I took the bralette out of her hand and placed it on the counter. This would take a few more hours of shopping to resolve. "Okay, maybe we should check out Victoria's Secret for PJs after this."

"Good idea."

"We just need one changing room," I said to the nice lady behind the counter. "And what's your return policy?"

"14 days with the original receipt," she said as she led us into a changing room with neon pink cushioned benches outside the doors.

"Great. If it doesn't fit, I'll be back tomorrow," I said.

"That's not a problem. Let me know if there's anything else you ladies need," she offered.

Afreen was already trying on the bras in one of the changing rooms. I sat outside, staring at my reflection in the mirrored hallway as she spoke. "Zafar says maybe it's a good thing Babagana is coming," she said from behind the door.

"Oh, you told him?" I asked, staring at a pimple over my left eyebrow.

"Of course," she answered like she was confused by my question. "I tell him everything."

"Why does he think it's a good thing?" I asked, resisting the great urge to pop the pimple. My mother's voice was in my head, disapproving of my picking at anything on my face because it would be unladylike.

"He thinks we can come to an understanding," she opened the door. "Should I get this?" She was standing in front of me with her top crumpled around her waist over her jeans. She had on a matte black plunge bra. It was strapless and the sidebands wrapped around her like a second skin.

"It looks good," I said, "turn around," and she did. The back of the bra was halfway down her back and with clothes on, it would be perfectly invisible.

"But it's digging into my skin. Should I get a size up?"

"Yeah, probably," I said, and she closed the door and continued trying on the others. "What kind of understanding is Zafar thinking about?"

"We're just going to be honest with Babagana when he gets here," she said.

I couldn't imagine a scenario in which that would end well, but they say honesty is the best policy. So, maybe it is. I looked up and she was looking at me, trying to gauge my reaction. I nodded and let out a prayer: "*Allah ya sa shi yafi alheri*. May Allah make that the best decision."

After two hours of more shopping and a quick lunch at the food court, she was in a better mood. "Fa'ee *am*, you're so lucky," she paused as she sipped her bubble tea. "To be with someone that you *know* your parents will definitely approve of? That peace of mind is priceless, *wallahi*."

I always knew that I could never marry someone my parents didn't approve of, no matter how much I cared about him. When the time came, I knew there would be no objection from either side of the family regarding Ahmad and me. We had been in a relationship for a few months and while he talked about the future, he never really talked about *our* future. I wondered what that meant. Did he think about us being together in the future? Isn't that the whole point of a relationship?

That voice in my head was back: '*But Ahmad has had other girlfriends before you. He didn't marry them. Who's to say there isn't going to be another girlfriend after you?*' I shook my head, desperate to get the thoughts out of my head.

"When's he coming?" I asked, taking the straw to my lips, even though I could barely taste my watered-down drink because all the ice had melted while we talked.

"Next week," she sighed.

* * *

It's been two weeks since Ahmad had to leave unexpectedly for the US. As he got closer to finishing off his project, more issues kept popping up that he had to go be there in person. I was at my guardian's home for the long weekend. I always went to Aunty Mami's place when there was a public holiday. But I made sure to go to my room a little early, so I could work on assignments and talk to Ahmad before bed.

"Insom."

"I am not an insomniac," I said. I had just submitted a section of the group project I was working on.

"I miss you, babe," he sounded tired.

"Another long day?"

"Like you won't believe."

"Is that your dinner?" I asked when I heard something rustling in the background.

"Yeah, I got some Chinese. Oh, by the way, Tumi is coming on as a consultant. So happy about that; we honestly should have done that sooner."

I could remember Tumi from his birthday dinner – a soft-spoken guy with a big Afro. Ahmad told me about how he met the programmer in Japan at a conference a few years prior.

"That's good, right?" I asked him.

"Yeah, it should be."

"So, why don't you sound enthusiastic about it?" He had put so much into this project, and I could sense how complicated it was getting, especially with the amount of interest his idea was generating.

"Honestly, I should've gone with my instincts from the beginning. What's happening right now would have easily been avoided. The one time I decided to listen to other people... I should've known better." Ahmad prided himself on how well he controlled his life and how logical his decisions were, despite the popular opinion.

"Don't beat yourself over it."

"I should probably stop boring you with work," he said.

"No, it's okay. You can always talk to me about this," I said, and I meant it.

We were quiet for a few minutes. I was lying in bed with the phone to my ear. I imagined he was doing the same. He was probably still in a loose tie and rolled-up sleeves. I imagined a box of take-out somewhere on the bed next to him.

"Gosh, I miss you," he said again. I basked in it, his voice sounding like a lullaby in my ear.

"Well, who's to be blamed for that?"

"Me," he laughed. It was followed by silence and then, "I wish you were here."

I felt the same way. It had been weeks since I last saw him. Facetime calls and Skype were nice, but it didn't feel the same as having him in the same space as I was. He had given me the keys to his place, but I hadn't gone there since he left. Everything reminded me of him. The other day, Sara and I got coffee from Timmie's, and I remembered how much he loved coffee, and for the rest of the day, I lost my smile.

"Do you know when you're coming back?" I should have said I missed him too.

"Say the word, and I'll come back," he teased quietly, his voice suddenly sensual.

"Me? I don't have the right." I had to laugh it off to get rid of all the images of him my mind had started conjuring.

"But you do," and then he was suddenly serious: "You own me."

I opened my mouth, but no words came out. I couldn't find my voice; all I could hear was the ticking of the clock in the room and the gentle hum of the humidifier. I swallowed. "Less than 48 hours to launch day," I finally managed to say, a lame attempt to change the topic.

"How did you do in criminal law?"

"Grades aren't up yet," I answered. The conversation flowed into schoolwork and upcoming exams. I silently wondered why I didn't just tell him that I missed him too, that I couldn't wait to see him, that he owned me too.

It was a week later, on a Thursday afternoon, when I received the news. I'd just finished a study group session with Ada and Sara in the relatively quiet library when I got a link forwarded from Afreen. Before I could open it, Ada interrupted me: "So, how's your boyfriend?"

I saw Sara looking at me from the corner of my eye. "How come she has met him, and I haven't?"

"Chill, he came to get her the other day, and I just ran into him," said Ada. "It wasn't planned."

"He's alright," I said.

"So, it's serious then, *ay*?" Sara quipped. I didn't know why I felt like she was judging me. She probably wasn't, and I was only projecting my insecurities through her.

"They look soooooo cute together," Ada went on.

"Wait. His parents are your guardians, right?" Sara asked, trying to recall the little I'd said about Ahmad to them. "So, it's an arranged thing, yeah?"

"No, it's not an arranged thing," I answered. "Our parents don't even know yet."

"Really? Wow, that's weird."

"Weird? How is that weird?" That was Ada.

"Couldn't be me," she said as we walked out of the library.

I bit my tongue, trying not to snap back.

"Why not? Muslims don't date?" Ada propped.

"Well, it's not allowed," she continued. "We get marriage proposals, and then we choose a good match, and arrange a meeting – *at home* – to see if we're compatible."

"That's not entirely true, Sara," I knew I was being defensive, but I had to say something. "It's different across the world. In some countries, Muslims date for a little while before marriage."

"Well, not in Pakistan. It's not done," she answered with a laugh. "A girl should never be alone with a guy she's not married to, except a chaperone is present."

"Why?" Ada asked, "Y'all don't trust yourselves?"

So it wasn't in my head. I was being judged.

"When a guy and a girl are alone, there's always a third entity present."

It took every fibre in my being to resist rolling my eyes. I knew what Sara was saying, but I was angry at what she was insinuating.

"Yeah, a chaperone or the *Shaitan*," I completed.

"Say what now? The who?"

"The devil," I started. I hated having to explain my religion sometimes. People just didn't get it. "If a chaperone isn't present, then the devil is; and he can influence their thoughts and actions."

"Oh, okay, that actually makes sense," Ada nodded, then took a sip from her bottle of water, "that's why you girls wear this, right? So you do not tempt the boys," she gestured towards the scarves that covered my head and Sara's.

"Nope, that's a misconception," I said. "We cover ourselves in obedience to God's command."

"Yeah, not for the men," Sara added. " I'm sure it was a man who first said that."

"Oh, I always thought that was the reason." Ada laughed.

"But maybe it's different in Nigeria – like dating before marriage," Sara added.

"Well, at the shisha bar I work downtown, I see a few Pakistani guys come in with girls they're obviously not married to, so –" Ada shrugged.

I resisted the urge to laugh out loud. Instead, I brought out my phone and clicked on the link Afreen had sent. It was taking a while to load.

"Same time tomorrow?" Sara asked as we exited the building.

"Yeah," I answered absentmindedly as I read the words on my screen. "Bye, guys."

"Bye, Fa'iza," I heard them say as they walked towards the car park, and I headed back to the residence. The link was for a *Business Insider* page. As I scrolled down, I gasped. There was a picture of Ahmad and a detailed article about his newly-launched app. The journalist called it "a revolutionary concept." I opened another search bar and searched the name of his app. There were half a dozen articles in the past 12 hours. It was unbelievable. I replied to Afreen with dancing emojis and exclamation marks; then, I dialed his number. I got a busy tone, so I typed him a message instead. *So so proud of you <3*

By Maghrib, the number of articles had doubled, and I had read each article at least twice. It was inspiring reading the comments under the articles. I tried reaching him a few more times before heading to bed, but messages weren't being delivered, and calls weren't going through.

Chapter 11

It was just after 11 pm when the knock on the door woke me up. At first, I thought someone down the hallway had banged their door shut, which occurred regularly at the residence. I started drifting back into my slumber when I heard the unmistakable knock again.

I yawned and turned on the bedside lamp, got up and walked towards the door. *Did I sleep through a fire alarm? Is a Resident Advisor knocking to check up on me?* I thought as I looked through the peephole, sleep immediately disappearing from my eyes. It was him.

He was in a black sweater, his *Goyard* hand luggage by his side, leaning on the wall opposite my door with both hands in his pockets. *Did he come here straight from the airport?* He knocked softly again, and I slowly opened the door. As soon as I did, I suddenly became conscious of my silk maroon pyjamas. *I should have thrown on a robe before opening the door,* I thought to myself, but it was too late then.

He looked at me with a smile on his face. I had gone to bed angry that he hadn't replied to my messages, but now looking at him standing in front of me with the slight stubble on his jaw, the tired look in his eyes and that good-looking face, I couldn't stay mad at him.

"Hi," he whispered, biting down on his lip like he was trying to stop smiling.

"Hi," I whispered back, still holding the door. My hair was uncovered;

the scrunchie that held it must have fallen off while I slept, and my hair was now falling over my shoulders.

"Can I come in?" he asked quietly as his gaze held mine.

My heart fluttered. I stepped aside to let him in, and he dragged his black hand luggage into the dark kitchenette. The soft yellow glow from the bedside lamp in my room was the only source of light. I closed the door and turned to face him.

He looked at me and slowly pulled me into his arms, burying his face in my hair. His arms wrapped themselves around me, and I felt so tiny in them. As he held me, I felt his heartbeat against mine, and in that moment, it didn't feel wrong. It didn't feel *haram*. It just felt like the purest expression of our emotions.

"I missed you," he said softly as he pulled away, planting a kiss on my forehead.

I hadn't realized how much I needed that hug. It felt so right. It felt like home, and I wanted to hold on for so much longer. I wanted to pull him back in, feel his heartbeat against mine and have his arms wrapped around me, but instead, I linked my hands awkwardly together in front of my chest as I smiled up at him. "I tried sending you a message," I said, going to the fridge to get a bottle of water for him.

"Yeah, so many calls drained the battery and I didn't have my charger on the plane," he explained, taking the bottle from me and placing it on the table.

"Oh," I said. That made sense. "Congratulations. I'm so proud of you."

"Thank you," he nodded, putting his hands back in his pocket, his eyes locked on mine.

"Let me get your keys," I said as I walked into my room to get the set of keys he had given me – keys to his car and apartment.

"I have my keys with me," he called after me. "I made you an extra set. You can keep those."

"Oh," I said.

"Were you studying?" he asked, looking at my laptop through the opened bedroom door. I shook my head in response. "Did I wake you up?" His eyes lingered at my pyjamas for a few seconds; then, he quickly looked back into my eyes. I nodded. "Sorry, I would have called, but my phone was dead," he ran his hand through his hair as he explained, "and I had to see you."

The words hung between us like energy. *Had to see you.* Crackling static. He looked at me as though he was waiting for something, even though no question was asked. We looked at each other in silence, our quiet breathing filling the room. It felt surreal. "I missed you," I finally said.

A few hours later, at 1 am, Ahmad was laying in bed next to me. He was using my laptop to reply to emails while his phone charged on my desk. I was propped up on pillows listening to his story about his dad forwarding the *Business Insider* article to all his friends in Nigeria.

"You would think he was thrilled when I told him I wasn't going to study law anymore," Ahmad said.

"And now he's the proudest person," I added.

"No, mom will definitely beat him to that position," he laughed as he closed my laptop and put it on the bedside table. "She has always been my number one supporter - doesn't matter what it is, she's always had my back." His head sank into the pillows, and he turned on his side to face me. I stared at him. Being this close to him, I could see his eyelashes. I hadn't noticed how long they were before.

"I should call a cab," he murmured. I remained quiet. There was a cab dispatch station just around the university. A call would have one outside the residence before he even got off the elevators. "Or… I could stay and bore you to sleep with details of the numerous meetings I chaired this past week…?"

I closed my eyes and pretended to snore, and he burst out laughing. His laughter made me feel good. I liked this – being with him, having regular conversations in the middle of the night. In my room. On my bed. When he was just inches away from me. *I can touch him if I extend my arm,* I thought as we looked at each other quietly, my hands tucked under my head.

His hand reached over to me and gently touched the bracelet on my wrist. "You wear it to sleep?"

"I never take it off, " I said, trying to steady my breathing, which quickened when his fingers lightly grazed my wrist. It was the first gift I'd ever accepted from a guy who liked me. And I loved it.

His eyes darkened as he nodded, "that's perfect." He slowly pulled his hand from me and swallowed. The room was filled with silence once again and then he said: "I am gonna have to go."

He stood up and looked at my phone that was by my pillow. "Wait, why is my number on your call list?"

"What do you mean?" I asked as I threw the duvet off of me and climbed out of bed. I sank my feet into my fuzzy wool slippers.

"You never saved my number?" his eyebrows were raised in disbelief. He passed my unlocked phone to me and his number was the last on my call list. I didn't see what the problem was.

"Oh, that. It's a bad habit I have," I said. His number ended with 717. I always knew when it was him, so I never bothered to save it.

"We've been together for months and you haven't saved my number?" he laughed, "I don't know how I feel about this."

"Well, I almost saved it 'Ahmad-with-the-attitude', but I didn't," his laughter drowned out the rest of my sentence, "you're welcome."

"Well then?"

"Well then, what?"

"Save my number," he said, waiting to see what I would save his number as. I created a new contact and I typed a new name over his number and saved it.

"Happy?" I asked as I showed him my phone.

"It works for me," he said, a smile slowly forming on his face as he read what I'd saved his number as. "Together, we make sense, Insom."

"I knew it! So, I'm still "Insom"?" I grumbled.

"Forever," he kissed my forehead again. "Goodnight, babe."

I felt giddy as I watched him grab his hand luggage and leave my room. He turned at the door, and our eyes met. He winked and quietly closed the door behind him. I walked to the door and locked it. Leaning with my back to it, I sighed. I couldn't believe that this was my life – giddy over a boy planting a kiss on my forehead, feeling at home when my head is buried in his embrace, missing the feel of his body laying in bed next to me. And nothing about this felt wrong.

My phone buzzed. It was message from NIAC: *Insom + Niac. Together, we make sense.* Then another buzz: *We complete each other, Fa'iza.*

* * *

That weekend, Ahmad and I had our first fight. I had just finished getting ready for an art exhibition we were going to that evening and was scrolling through the opened tabs on safari to pass time when I realized that he hadn't logged out when he used my laptop to reply to emails that night he came over. I was going to log him out, but curiosity got the best of me when I saw an unread mail from an Ezgi.

Ezgi. He'd never mentioned that name to me. I knew the first names of all his friends and staff, and Ezgi was not one of them. My cursor hovered over the mail with the subject "WOW", as I contemplated whether or not to open it. I knew it was wrong and that I had no right to invade his privacy like this. So, I removed my finger from the trackpad, closed my laptop and left it on the bed. But I couldn't get it out of my head. Ezgi. It was a Turkish name. I'd watched enough Turkish shows to know a few phrases, and I can pick out unique Turk names from a bunch. I remembered the conversation between Kaltume and Afreen about his Turkish ex-girlfriend. Maybe this was her. I flipped my laptop open and opened the email.

Askim,

I read the news today, and you were in it. No surprise there, I always knew you could do it. From here on, the sky is the limit. It has been forever. I hope you're doing good? Thinking of you, always. Xx

I was flooded with guilt after reading the email. I shouldn't have invaded his privacy like that. I hurriedly marked it as unread and closed the laptop. *That must be her,* I thought to myself. There was a certain intimacy in the email; it couldn't have been any random friend. It was definitely his ex. Ezgi. She called him *Askim*. Isn't that 'lover' in Turkish?

By the time Ahmad came to get me, I'd gone over the email in my mind at least seven times.

"Hey babe," he said as I walked out of the residence. He was wearing a blazer over a brown shirt with black jeans, leaning on the railing of the few steps that led towards the visitor's parking in front of the building. He was putting on sunglasses, and put his phone into his pocket when I joined him. I wondered if he'd read the email.

"Hey," I wondered if he could see the guilt on my face.

"You look great," he said.

I was wearing a green wrap-around dress with a yellow scarf. As I got into his car, I saw that he had gotten us iced cappuccinos from Timmies, our daily dose of caffeine.

The drive to the art gallery was long, but it didn't feel long. We were chatting about the most recent book we read: *A Man Called Ove.* "I know you cried," he said as he made a right turn.

"I actually didn't," I started to deny, but there was no point. The book did make me cry a little.

"Hey, there's no shame in it," he started laughing. His eyes crinkled a bit when he laughed and it made him even more handsome, if that was possible. I finished my drink and peered up at him. He was in such a good mood. *Is he happy because he heard from Ezgi? Did he take her to art galleries too? Did she love Timmies as much as he did? What else did they do together?*

"Street parking is always hard to find around here," he said as we went around the building. Eventually, we were able to park in a spot where someone had just pulled out of.

"Are we late?"

"No, we're not," he reached for my hand. "This art has a particular niche."

"Oh, okay," I put my fingers through his as we walked into the building. It was beginning to get dark. He reached for tickets in his pocket and handed them to a redhead at a desk. I walked in and looked around. This rustic-boho gallery was quite different from the other white-walled ones I had been to – the brush strokes on the grey walls were still evident, like they were left there on purpose, the visible pipes that ran through the ceiling and a bar located in one corner of the L-shaped room. It worked quite well in invoking a suave urban feel.

There were a few people in the room, looking at the various art that adorned the walls, most of which were abstract, and others were oil paintings of famous people I really didn't care about the interpretation of abstract art. I was moved, instead, by a big, green and brown painting of Bob Marley that occupied a focal point in point in the gallery. I gravitated towards it and stared up at it, lost in my thoughts.

"Are you okay, babe?" Ahmad was by my side.

"Yes," I lied. "Why?"

"Your eyes. Are you sure you're okay?" He looked at me, concerned.

"I'm fine," I said. "Come, show me this piece you can't stop talking about."

"There's plenty of time for that," then he looked up at the painting in front of us. "What do you think about this one?"

I looked at the deliberate strokes that creased the corners of the Reggae king's eyes, the circles around them. The artist was intentional about drawing you in with the eyes, which were almost lifelike."It looks like he actually painted him from the flesh, not from a picture."

"How do you mean?" he said, moving behind me and looking at the painting like he was trying to understand it from my point of view.

"His eyes look… sad."

Ahmad's chest was leaning into my back, "The artist's actually Nigerian."

"Really?"

"Yup, Komi Olaf. He grew up in Kaduna, and lives here in the 6ix." Ahmad pointed to another painting a few feet away. "Come. I think you'll like his other pieces." Twenty minutes later, we had moved on to other artists, and we were standing in front of a pile of junk. A chair and a table turned upside down, some clocks, a shoe, a curtain draped over a pile of a broken air conditioner. I looked at the collection, trying to understand what I was looking at, wondering why it was left in the middle of the gallery. Compared to all the meaningful portraits and landscapes I had seen so far, this looked very out of place. Were these the artist's furniture? Was this supposed to give us a glimpse into his life?

"So, what do you think?" Ahmad asked.

"About the pile?" I asked.

"Yeah."

"What am I looking at exactly?"

"Exactly." He held my shoulders and steered me to the right of the painting."Now look at it from this angle." There was a bulb hanging above that cast a shadow on the wall behind the pile of items, and it displayed a woman wearing a wide-brimmed hat, looking into the far horizon. It was spectacular. The element of surprise made it even more beautiful. "Shadow art," Ahmad said, as he took in the awe on my face, "not everything is at it seems."

We looked around the room, looking at pieces and trying to understand the artist's message. We were looking at a landscape of the Canadian Rockies, leaning shoulder to shoulder, when a couple started moving towards us. One was an olive-skinned brunette wearing a silk shirt tucked in grey pants, and the man next to her couldn't seem to take his eyes off her even as she and Ahmad exchanged a brief hug.

"Zehra?" Ahmad asked, and she replied to him in French. From the little I remembered from IGCSE, he was surprised to see her. And as I stood there, I realized that there was still a lot I didn't know about him. They chatted, then noticing me for the first time, she turned back to him a question: "Ezgi?" *You've got to be kidding me.* Ezgi. The girl from the email. Or is it a French phrase?

"Zehra, meet Fa'iza," he looked at me, and I felt his hand reach for my waist as he moved closer to me. "Babe, Zehra and I interned in Montreal together."

"Nice to meet you," she said in a heavy French accent, a saccharine smile on her face. Her eyes went from my face and then to Ahmad, "Sorry, I thought it was your sister. How's she?"

"She's good. She's –" he was cut short by the guy next to her, who cleared his throat.

"Oh, where are my manners?" she gestured towards him. "This is Nikolai."

"Nice to meet you," he said in a Russian accent, nodding politely toward me and Ahmad.

Zehra immediately switched back to French but Ahmad, in respect to me, responded to her in English. I could sense that he was trying to end the conversation as graciously as he could, and when he eventually did, we said our goodbyes and left the couple.

"Do you wanna go to the basement and see the art supplies they have?" he asked me as we walked away from them.

"I think I'm ready to leave."

"Sure," he said as he reached for my hand. We walked out of the blinking neon lights bordering the exit door and quietly moved toward the car. When we got in, I brought out my phone and started replying to the messages I had on WhatsApp. Claire had sent a picture of her Burmese cat. I replied with an array of emojis, and she replied almost immediately, asking me how I was doing. We kept exchanging messages, and with fall just around the corner, I was glad I would get to see my roommate soon.

"Are you okay, babe?"

It was unlike me to be distracted by my phone when I was with him. The only time I multitasked was when I was doing schoolwork. "Yup," I answered.

The car came to a halt. I looked around and noticed that we were parked on the side of the road with few stores around us. The place looked strange and unfamiliar, and if I wasn't with Ahmad, I would have been scared.

"Where are we?" I asked as he turned off the ignition and leaned back in his seat. He looked at me, his face serious, and he said: "We can't keep doing this."

"Doing what?"

"If we have a problem, we have to talk about it," he turned down the music and looked at me. I had never seen him this serious. "We're not going to sweep things under the rug."

"We're going to talk about it *here*?"

"So, there's something to talk about then?"

I sighed and looked away from him. Out of the tinted windows, someone in their sixties, judging from the grey hair, was walking their dog, a big shaggy brown-haired Collie.

"Talk to me, babe."

I said nothing. How do you admit that you breached your partner's privacy, that you read an email they got from their ex? How do you admit that you spent more time than you cared to admit googling the name *Ezgi*, pouring through pages and pages of accounts on Instagram and Twitter that had the name Ezgi in their handle? How do you explain the guilt that kept eating at your heart as you kept going – because you knew that you shouldn't? How do you admit that you didn't stop until you found one account with a mutual friend? Edet. How do I tell him that I found her Instagram profile? That I zoomed in on her clear skin, her perfect smile and looked at all the 127 pictures she posted? That I had read her quotes on love and passion, saw pictures from her visits to East Africa and Asia? Pictures taken here in Toronto with friends and family, pictures of her with celebrities? How do I tell him I saw a candid picture of them at the beach, posted two years ago and was never deleted? What do I make of the caption "I will love you forever, *Askim*" and the one thousand and eighty-nine likes she got on the post? How do I explain the pain I felt in my heart when I saw how happy he looked with her – the smile on his face as she kissed his cheek in a lime green two-piece bikini, their feet buried in the white sands somewhere warm and tropical.

His fingers reach for mine and gently squeezed.

I turned to look at him and blurted, "Back there, the girl we met – did she ask about your ex?"

"Yes, she asked about Ezgi." He paused. "You knew her name?"

Oh shit. The silence in the car felt so loud I could hear the rush of blood in my ears. I had been caught. "At…at the wedding," I started to stutter. "*Uhm…* someone must have mentioned her name when they talked about her." It wasn't true, but it wasn't exactly a lie.

"This is the second time you're bringing her up," he said, his eyebrows raised like he was asking if I was aware that I'd spoken about her a few months prior.

"I need to know more."

"She's in the past."

I didn't respond.

"Okay. What do you want to know?"

"How long were you two together?" I sighed, ignoring the notification sounds on my phone.

"Two years."

"Why did you break up?"

"Does it matter?"

Maybe it shouldn't, I thought. But it did.

He looked at me quietly for a few seconds. "I moved out of the country and we wanted different things."

"Two years?" I tried to control the quiver in my voice as I asked. I thought about the picture, which seemed to have been taken on vacation together. "Were you guys... *intimate*?"

His eyes narrowed as he looked at me with a questioning look, and I stared back. It was already dark outside, and there were fewer cars on this part of the road at this hour so the street was empty, and the streetlamps illuminated our faces.

"Fa'iza, what are you doing?" There was a worried look on his face as he leaned towards me.

"I just – I just I need to know." I pulled my hand away before he could touch me. I was angry, mostly at myself – for being so jealous, for the inexplicable need to know details about his past. But above all, I was angry at an intimacy I assumed he'd shared with her.

He sighed loudly as he leaned back in his leather seat. After what felt like a long minute, he answered: "She was my girlfriend so yes, we were having sex."

I didn't know what I was expecting the answer to be, but I definitely didn't expect to feel like I'd been punched in the guts. All this was his past, yet his admission made me even more insecure.

"I just feel like – like –" I knew what I wanted to say, but I didn't have the words. He was still looking at me with a questioning look in his eye. "I feel like I don't know what we're doing."

"What do you mean?" He spoke softly, dragging out every syllable, looking at me very closely.

"I feel like you're – *um,* how do I put this?" I put my finger to my lip, "I feel like you're used to certain *things* in a relationship – things I can't quite give you."

"Give me?" He scoffed.

I nodded slowly.

"Sex isn't something you *give.*"

"You know what I mean."

"No, I don't, Fa'iza."

"Why are you even with me?" I whispered, like I was scared of the words that escaped my mouth. "You – you could have anyone you want. But you chose me. Why?"

He held my gaze, probably wondering where all this was coming from.

"I read a message in your inbox, an email she'd sent. But then I found her on Instagram and saw a picture of you two in the Bahamas or Barbados, or wherever that was. I don't know why I did all that. I know it's not right, and I'm sorry. I just wanted to know more than I already did." A single tear fell down my cheek. *Damn it!* I looked down at my hands, so he wouldn't see me cry.

His index finger immediately went to my cheek, wiping away the tears. I pulled my face away. "Look at me," he said softly. I shook my head, then turned to look out of my window, and into the darkness.

I heard him open his door and within seconds, he was outside mine. He opened it gently and crouched in front of me. His hands found mine on my laps and his thumb grazed the inside of my palm.

"Why you? Let's see. You're smart. You're kind. You're unintentionally funny. You're honest. You make me want to be a better person," his fingers squeezed mine gently. "For weeks, I couldn't get you out of my head. It felt like fate when I saw you again at that restaurant. I can't explain how I felt in that moment – how it felt then, how it feels now. I look for things I can move around on my schedule just to spend time with you. This feeling – what I feel for *you* – it's different from anything I've felt in the past," he paused, then sighed. "I would be lying if I said sex hadn't crossed my mind these past few months. I'm so fucking attracted to you – so much that I'm willing to be celibate, if that's what it takes to be with you. No, the irony isn't lost on me." I looked at him and he smiled. "Damn," he said after a moment of silence. "You got all that information on Instagram? The CIA has got nothing on you!" Despite myself, I started laughing , and he joined me. "This is what I like to see – your laughter, not your tears," he said, then kissed my hands after we'd stopped laughing.

When he got back into the car, he turned off the hazard lights and we got back on the road. Speeding on the highway on our way back to the residence – my hand in his – we couldn't stop laughing and stealing glances at each other.

Chapter 12

It was Sunday morning. I had been up since Fajr, which at that time of the year, was at 4:15 am. It was the last week of the summer holiday, and students who had gone home for the holidays would be coming back to the rez that week. Grades for all the classes I had taken during the break were already posted, and – not to brag, but – I aced them all. Things were already looking great for the fall semester. I just needed to find the perfect place to volunteer for twelve weeks, a requirement for my three-credit elective on green spaces.

I spent most of dawn rearranging my closet, taking out summer clothes and throwing them in an old bag I was going to donate to *The Salvation Army*, a non-profit organization that collected fairly-used clothes for people in need. When I was done, I moved to the shoe rack, making space for the new ankle boots I'd gotten from The Bay and throwing some sandals and flip-flops into the bag. I had just removed the second pair of ankle boots from the box when my phone rang and as I made my way to my desk to unplug it from the charger, I almost tripped over my open laundry basket and almost missed the call. "Hello," I smiled as I answered the call.

"Hello, Fa'iza?" It was my mum. I could barely hear her as there was so much noise in the background.

"*Ina kwana*, Umma. Good morning," I said.

"You called earlier?" I had called her twice after talking to my dad earlier, but couldn't reach her.

"Yes, twice."

"I didn't hear my phone; it was in my bag. We're at Farida's wedding," she screamed into the phone, her phone rising among others.

"Oh okay. How's it going?" I asked. Like Kaltume, Farida was another family friend my age getting married.

"Ah, *biki ya yi kyau*. It's going very well, *alhamdulillah*," I could hear the smile in her voice as she continued, "*ai bakatsine ta aura*. The groom's family is from Katsina."

I nodded and wondered why the information was necessary to share. "*Allah ya ba su zaman lafiya*," I responded. It was the customary thing to say when someone got married, a prayer for God to bless them with a peaceful marriage. In my culture, it was customary to pray at every celebration and adversity. At the birth of a baby, we said *Allah ya raya*; may God raise him/her. When someone was about to embark on a journey, we said *Allah ya tsare,* may God protect. When we heard bad news, we shook our heads, pulled on our *tasbeeh,* and we said: *Allah ya kiyaye,* may God protect. And when we heard good news, we celebrated and prayed: *Allah ya sanya alheri,* may God bless it.

"Ameen Ameen," she said, "Hold on." I heard her speaking to someone else and then: "Here's Hajiya Uwani, say hello to her." Before I could object, I heard my mother's friend's sing-song voice in my ear: "Helloooooo." I immediately pictured the robust and ever-jovial Aunty Uwani with her beautiful henna-stained hands. I couldn't quite remember when they became friends but in recent years, she had become an active and permanent part of our lives

"*Ina kwana,* Aunty Uwani," my voice had dropped an octave almost subconscious, as I greeted her. It was not my doing; my language demanded it. I absentmindedly scratched my head as I stared at my reflection in the mirror.

"*Lafiya lau,* Fa'iza. Everything's well," she responded with a laugh. "*Ya makaranta*? How's school?"

"*Alhamdulillah. Ya su* Aisha?" I asked after her oldest daughter, who was married with a kid and had moved abroad with her husband just a few months prior. I saw her regular updates on Instagram and knew exactly what she was up to, but asking after people to keep the conversation going was just another thing our culture demanded.

"*Tana can* UK. She's in the UK," she answered, then changed the subject: "*Allah ya nuna mana naki, mu sha biki*. May God let us see your wedding, oh how we'll jubilate!"

"Ameen," I said, the only acceptable answer.

"*Amma ban da bature*. But we don't want a white man," she cautioned with a laugh as she handed the phone to my mother.

I was relieved to hear my mother's voice on the other end of the line. "I'll call you when I get home," she said without acknowledging Hajiya Uwani's comment. She didn't have to; she trusted that her daughter knew what to do. Growing up, no one gave us the husband criteria, but we overheard and knew just what to do from conversations our mothers and aunties were having at social gatherings, conversations not meant for our ears. We would hear comments they made after weddings about the families of the bride or groom – what they praised, what they spoke about in hushed tones, what they deemed shameful. "*Ai suna da mako*. They are very stingy," they would say about men from a particular state in Nigeria, or "*ai ba su da hakuri; abu kadan saki*. Those ones are not patient; they divorce their wives anyhow." Of course, these rules were not set in stone, and they often changed depending on whether someone knew someone who had a different experience with men from that state. An outlier with prominence in the political scene was, however, always welcome. Growing up with comments like that allowed us filter through what our mothers thought was desirable and what wasn't.

Thinking about it now, that was why my mother made the "bakatsine" comment. Like us, he was from Katsina, and that was desirable. A good choice, a preferred choice – never mind the cousin I had whose *bakatsine* husband somehow managed to have a drinking problem. When she came home to complain about his drinking and his abandonment of *sallah*, she was met with "*Allah ya kiyaye*" and was advised to pray for him. The aunts gave her verses from the Qur'an to recite for him in the middle of the night. All but my mother. Umma told her to leave him. "If you were the one with a drinking problem, no mother or aunt would advise him to stay with you," she argued vehemently. And although no one could deny the truth in her words, the aunts bowed their heads in response and reminded her: "it's different for a woman." I remember my mother sighing in defeat. Nowhere in the Qur'an did it say that sins would be judged in accordance with one's gender. Yet, in our culture and tradition, many Muslim rules were only applicable to women. Society turned a blind eye to the wrongdoings of men – that's why they get away with almost everything. Women, however, were always expected to uphold standards to which men were never held accountable. I thought back at my conversation with Ahmad about his relationship with Ezgi, and I was not exactly surprised. If anything surprised me, it was the fact that he didn't hide that he was in a *haram* relationship.

Later that afternoon, I sat at the dining table at the ambassador's house, enjoying the *danwake* (bean dumplings garnished with vegetables) the chef had made. Aunty Mami had just gotten back from Nigeria, and had she sent me some Abayas earlier in the week, so I came by to say thanks. Afreen picked me up from the residence just after I finished my laundry that morning and had been talking about her internship at the Mayor's office since. It was only at dinner time that she asked what was going on with me.

I opened my mouth to bore her with school and the conversation I'd had with Sara about relationships in Islam. What came out, instead, was a story about my first fight with her brother.

"What?! He made you cry?" she asked.

"No, no, no. He didn't *make* me cry. I said I cried *during* the argument," I tried to explain.

"So, why did you cry?"

"We were talking about something – sorry, I can't tell you what exactly – and I was embarrassed – no, not embarrassed – but it just kinda got awkward, and I cried a little. But he didn't *make* me cry."

"Well, he had better not," she said, still looking at me oddly. I liked that she didn't press to know what the conversation was about.

"How about you – how's Zafar?"

She had barely spoken about him in the weeks that we'd been chatting and when I asked, she took a sip of water and sighed. "He's fine, just getting mad impatient."

I nodded slowly, waiting for her to give me more context, the sound of the vacuum going off in the next room making the silence less awkward.

"So, he says now is a good time for him to meet my parents again," she shook her head and avoided eye contact. "He feels things are a bit different for him now, so it might be better than the last time." I nodded, and she continued: "I think we should buy ourselves more time. I need time to get mum warmed up to the idea that the person I like is married."

"How do you think she would take it?" I asked.

"I think she wouldn't mind as much if he were a widower." Most of the issues people had with polygamy was that the man might not treat both women equitably as he was expected to. There are many stories about men having favorites among their wives, while the least favorites were left to fend for themselves.

I pursed my lips. I knew exactly what she meant. Even though Aunty Mami was actually the ambassador's second wife, the first wife had passed away years before they met. So, she would definitely prefer if Afreen were with someone without so much baggage and responsibilities – a wife and a child.

"*Allah ya zaban mana mafi alkhairi*. May God choose what's best for us," I said.

"Ameen. Fa'iza am," She perked up a little.

The weekend went by pretty quickly as we spent most of it in bed watching *Gossip Girl*. But on Sunday, we were having lunch at the dining table when Aunty Mami walked in dressed in a peach-colored lace sewn into a long gown. Her hair was plaited back and uncovered. Her stud earrings caught the light as she moved and the scent of *La vie est belle* filled the air with her entrance. "The *turaren wutan* smells burnt," she sniffed around as she moved further into the room and opened the windows. "You can't smell it?" She was referring to the incense on the electric burner that filled the room with the scent of sandalwood.

"Maybe it's the coal," I walked to her side and helped with the windows. It didn't smell bad, but the incense was beginning to burn.

"I might have gotten a bad batch."

"It doesn't smell bad to me," Afreen said with a shrug, standing up and taking the burner from her mom, and left the room to go empty it.

"*Toh,* Maybe it's my nose," Aunty Mami said with a laugh. Her jet-black hair had a strand or two of grey that I noticed for the first time.

"Fa'iza, I'll leave this here for the cleaners," she dropped a white envelope on the table. "Please tell them they don't need to come next week."

I nodded as I moved the envelope closer to me. Just then, the door opened, and we both looked up to see Ahmad walking in a navy-blue slim fit shirt and charcoal chinos. We'd been chatting all weekend and had agreed he would take me back to the residence when I was ready. But I didn't realize he would be arriving this early.

"Ahmad, do you smell *turaren wuta*? Does it smell burnt?" she asked, unrelenting in her quest to see if she'd gotten a bad batch.

He smiled as he moved towards her. "It smells great," he kissed her on the cheek and added, "You smell great."

"Maybe it's just my nose then," she said to herself as she walked out.

He took the chair opposite me, removed his sunglasses and kept them on the table. He ignored the food warmers and plates on the table and kept his eyes on me. "What are you eating?"

"Rice," I answered, "*Za ka ci*? Are you eating?"

"We're going to see Edet, remember?" He shook his head with a smile on his face.

"I thought that was tomorrow." Edet's longtime girlfriend was visiting from the UK and they had invited us for an early dinner at their place.

"Babeeeee," he raised his eyebrows. "I reminded you on Friday."

"So, do we have to leave now?"

"No, we've got time. We can leave after Asr."

* * *

Edet lived in one of the high-rise buildings downtown and in two hours, we were standing outside. He buzzed us into the expansive lobby with a fireplace burning, and we made our way into the elevators.

"How many people are going to be there?" I asked Ahmad.

"Why? Are you nervous? My friends don't bite." A smile slowly formed on his face, as he fixed the ends of my scarf over my shoulder. His hands lingered on my arm. "You look great." He always complimented me, even when I was wearing the simplest of things, like today – a red buttoned-down shirt over white jeans.

"Thanks. You too," I smiled.

The elevator door opened to a carpeted floor and Ahmad led us to Edet's apartment. The door was opened as soon as he knocked and Edet stood at the door in brown khaki trousers and a black shirt. He had a kitchen towel over his left shoulder.

"Fa'iza," he looked at me. "Good to see you again."

"Hi, Edet." I smiled at him, as he shook hands with Ahmad. Ahmad waited for me to I remove my shoes, and we walked into the eclectic-designed living room together. As Edet walked towards the kitchen, I looked around the space decorated with multiple minimalist frames on the white walls with two white couches flanked by green plants.

"Ahmaaaad," a stunning lady about my height walked out of the bedroom, wearing a short white romper. She had bright, expressive eyes, full lips, a slightly broad nose and high-arched brows. Her long box braids formed a big bun on the top of her head, and her caramel skin glowed.

"Joanne," he said as he hugged her. "Hope you're keeping my guy in check?"

They laughed. Her laughter was contagious; I found myself smiling. "He's behaving, he's behaving." Across the room, Edet shook his head, and she turned in my direction. "You must be Fa'iza. I've heard so much about you!"

"Good things, I hope?" I extended my arm to shake her.

"I am a hugger," she held my hand, then she pulled me into a hug. She turned towards Edet and gasped, "You didn't tell me she was a beaut!" Then she turned back to me: "You're gorgeous."

"And so are you," I said to her with a laugh, following hẹr to the sofa in the living room.

"We were just watching *Nigerian Idol*," she said, gesturing to the TV.

"Oh really? How do you guys get Nigerian channels?" Since I left Nigeria, I hadn't kept up with my regular TV shows, and the ones on YouTube had too many ads or were incomplete.

"He has a thing…" she turned towards the kitchen where Edet was busy"“‘, "Sugar, what's the name of your box thingy?"

"What box thing?" he asked.

"The TV channel box thing."

"Oh, World net," he answered. "Guys, let's eat," and we moved to the dining area. The table had already been set for four and was decorated with many dishes: jollof rice, fried plantain, mixed green salad, fried chicken and then a jar of freshly made juice.

"Let me warn you in advance," announced Edet with a laugh. "I made the Jollof."

"Noted. Okay, so avoid the rice." Ahmad joked as I unfolded the napkin and placed it on my lap.

"Fa'iza, don't worry. We made sure the chicken was *halal*," Joanne said.

"Oh, that's so kind," I looked from her to Edet, "That's so thoughtful of you guys, thank you."

"You should thank Ahmad. He kept insisting," Edet said. "How was your summer?"

"Can't believe it's September already! It's been incredible," I replied.

"How long are you around for?" Ahmad asked Joanne.

"I leave on Thursday," she said. "I have to get back to work."

"Still at Barclays?" he asked, and she nodded.

"Tell her the opportunities in Canada are just as great," Edet said. "She won't listen to me."

Ahmad chuckled. "You guys have to talk about the pros and cons of her moving here – like how it affects her career, her relationships… everything."

"This is why Ahmad is my favorite person! He's very objective," Joanne turned towards me, then took a sip of her wine, "I've been trying to get sugar to have the conversation, but he won't listen."

"Long-distance gets exhausting, no?" Ahmad looked up at them.

"Thank you," Edet thundered as if that was the validation he'd been waiting for. "Fa'iza, would you be in a long-distance relationship?"

They all looked at me expectantly, waiting for an answer. I appreciated their trying to include me in the conversation but I would have preferred if they had allowed me to finish the morsel of food in my mouth first before putting me on the spot. I swallowed, looked at Ahmad, and then Edet. "Well, I've never really thought about it, but it doesn't seem like the ideal situation," I glanced at Joanne, "But I can understand if that's the only possible way."

"Yeah, it's hard," Joanne nodded, "My sister's husband is in the army and she goes months without seeing him."

"I could never," said Ahmad shaking his head.

Edet laughed. "A bit of distance is good for every relationship. You prioritize more and fight less." A soft smile settled on his face as he looked at Joanne.

"Don't get me wrong. I understand that for others, it's a way of life. For me, I always want my woman by my side," Ahmad took a sip of water.

"So, it's a dealbreaker for you, then? Fair enough," Joanne said. "Everyone has something they know they can't handle."

"Exactly – as long as you're honest with yourself, and your partner," Edet agreed.

"What's your dealbreaker?" Joanne asked me.

"Cheating," I said. I didn't even have to think about it. Infidelity and dishonesty seemed to be the worst things in relationships, or at least, that's what Hollywood wants you to believe.

"Mine too," Joanne agreed. "Like, why cheat? Just break up instead of breaking someone's heart."

After dinner, Joanne made us some tea, and the conversation was moved to the couch. The sliding door to the balcony was open, and cool breeze wafted in, creating a relaxed ambience heightened by the 90s RnB playing on the soundbars.

"How long have you guys been together?" I asked them. They seemed like they were in love, like best friends. Even their movements mirrored each other.

"We went to Corona together," said Joanne.

"Corona in Lagos? No way – you've been together since secondary school?" I asked.

"No, we only started going out when we got to Oxford," Edet answered.

"Ahmad pretty much made it happen," Joanne said, laughing. "My guy here was shy."

"Did you go to Corona, too?" I asked Ahmad.

"Yes, I did my junior secondary there, and then we left for Australia," he replied. They had been friends forever. That explained the camaraderie they shared.

"You schooled in Abuja, *ko*?" He asked me.

I nodded, "Doveland." His hands lightly touched the back of my shoulders as silence hovered over the room. I guess this is what makes a relationship – learning tiny tidbits about someone over time until they became an open book to you, like Joanne and Edet.

As we left their apartment, Joanne pulled me into another hug. "It was so nice meeting you, Fa'iza. I understand why Ahmad is smitten."

Smitten, I thought to myself, as I looked up at him and he pretended not to hear her. I looked back at her: "Thanks for having us over. It was so fun."

As we entered the empty elevator and pressed the button for the lobby, Ahmad pulled me gently towards him, his hands on my waist. "Had a good time?"

"They're the best."

* * *

Chapter 12

September started with the golden glow of Autumn – with the falling leaves and reddish hues of dried ones on the pavements. I was barely a month into my second semester, but it was harder than the first. The coursework was heavier, the classes were more demanding, and I still had not finalized where I would be volunteering for my 3-credit elective. The deadline for us to submit the contracts with our chosen organization was fast approaching, and I hadn't found one.

Fall fashion was easily my favorite – the multiple layers, ankle boots and knitted sweaters. I was no longer a newbie in the 6ix; I knew my way around most libraries, art galleries and shopping malls. Claire had returned from Saskatchewan with a tan, a new hair color and two new minimalistic tattoos - one on her ribcage and the other by her ankle. The day she returned, we squealed so loudly we were sure some neighbors would come to our door to ask us to keep it down and were grateful that no one did.

The next day, we went down to the residence's cafeteria on the main floor to eat breakfast and she went on and on about her trip – how she went salmon fishing with friends from her hometown, hiking in Alberta and attended stampede, the biggest outdoor rodeo in North America, she said. "Enough about me," she finally said as she pushed her bleached blonde bangs out of her face. I glanced up at her blue eyes and thought about how lovely the color was against her pale skin. "How was your summer? I wanna hear everything," she took a sip of her black coffee.

I told her everything – about the food and music festivals we attended, my trip to Milan, my classes with Professor Blake, how lonely the dorm was without her to share avocados with, the pottery class I tried and failed at woefully. It was only when I was done that I realized Ahmad's name had kept coming up in most of the activities I spoke about because she had a huge grin on her face when she asked: "Do you have a picture of him?"

"I should have a few," I said, knowing for a fact that I did.

"Show me," the grin on her face got even bigger.

I swiped through my phone, looking for a picture I didn't mind sharing with her. I scrolled past a picture he sent me of an English Breakfast meal he'd made the previous week. He made a funny face as he took the selfie, his kitchen messy behind him. *Not this one,* I thought to myself. I scrolled past one I took of him at Nordstrom. He was trying on a black coat in front of a mirror. I shook my head. I finally found another that I'd taken of him in the car. It was in front of the residence on a particularly sunny day. He was wearing a red jersey and sunglasses. I passed the phone to her and continued eating my granola and oat bowl.

Her smile got wider as she looked at the picture. "I don't usually say this about men, but *damnnnn,*" she fluttered her lashes playfully, and I laughed, my chest swelled with pride.

"He's alright," I said dryly.

"Oh honey, he's more than *just* alright," she swiped to another picture and chuckled. "Aww, you guys are so cute, it's actually disgusting," she teased as she passed the phone back to me. I looked at the picture she'd swiped to. It was a picture of us from the previous week watching a movie on his couch. I was wearing a green hoodie I'd gotten from his closet, concentrating hard on the subtitles from the French movie when I saw from the corner of my eye, that he had his phone up in the air. I playfully scrunched up my face, and he stuck his tongue out as the flash went off. I was surprised it turned out to be a good picture.

After Claire and I went back to the room, we spent the rest of the morning on my bed talking about movies and shows. Later that afternoon, after my study sessions with Sara and Ada, I walked outside to meet Ahmad by the parking lot just beside the faculty building.

"Hola," he said as I got into the car. He'd changed his Audi to a newer version a few weeks prior. So far, the only differences I'd noticed were the white leather interior and some dashboard upgrades. He turned down the music as I got in, so that The Weeknd was now playing in the background.

"Hiya," I closed the door. He was wearing a white buttoned-down shirt and navy-blue pants. His company had recently gotten a new office downtown and he spent most of his time there these days.

"You good?" He asked as he glanced my way, a smile gradually filling his face.

"Do you have a bad angle?" I asked.

He suddenly put on his best Keith Urban impersonation. "Oh, I can be bad, if you want," he winked, then started driving out of the parking lot. It was a bad Australian impression accent, but it sounded so hot.

"Stop it," I lightly hit his arm, "you know that's not what I meant."

He glanced at me and feigned a lack of understanding as a frown settled on his forehead. "No? It's not?"

"Sorry to disappoint you, but no."

"When you change your mind, though, I'm gonna make it worth your while."

"What are you even talking about?" I asked, still laughing because his impression was horrible.

"What are *you* talking about?" He was still in character, even though he was the worst actor ever.

"I was looking for a bad photo of you to show Claire, but there wasn't a single one in my gallery."

"Oh, I'm sure you can get one when I'm asleep or something," he looked back at the road. "You know we aim to please." The mischievous grin was back on his face. I shook my head.

"I can't deal with you right now," I said, ending the conversation.

"What did I say?" He asked again.

"Nothing."

"I got these for you," he said as he picked up some pamphlets from his console and handed them to me. I removed my glasses and looked through them. They were volunteer opportunities *at Inn from the cold* and *The drop-in centre*. "I know you were specifically looking for places you could help women and kids, so I did some research for you."

"It says here that *Inn from the cold* is exclusively for displaced women with kids," I read the words on the yellow pamphlet out loud. "This is actually perfect!" I turned the page.

"Yeah?"

I looked up at him, and he smiled. My unresolved issue with volunteerism had been giving me sleepless nights, and I was always telling him about how much it bothered me that I hadn't gotten a spot. "This is really sweet of you," I said, "*Na gode*. Thank you."

"If you like that place, why don't we just go finalize it?"

"We can? I'd love that!" I grinned.

"Of course. Anything for you," and the mock accent was back. I groaned and he laughed, amusing himself.

Thirty minutes later, we were at *Inn from the cold*, a grey-walled building that still retained most of its Victorian feel from the outer architecture. Inside, however, was just like the walls of a university – white walls and clear window panes. I sat on a brown mahogany chair in an air-conditioned office with pictures of smiling women and children on the walls across from the director, who was going over the forms I'd filled out at the reception earlier. She made a photocopy of my student ID card and handed it back to me with a smile. She was an imposing woman with kind eyes. Her movements were quick and fluid like she was someone used to doing this regularly. "You can start as soon as you get a copy of your police report," she said, handing me a copy of her contact card. Her name was Jasmeet Kaur.

"Thank you very much, Jasmeet," I said as I stood up and left, making my way to the reception, where Ahmad was waiting for me.

"How did it go?" he asked when he saw me.

"I can start as soon as I get my police report." I said excitedly.

"Let's go get you one, then."

Chapter 13

Halfway into the semester, I broke a promise I made to myself. I didn't see it coming. It all started when I texted Ahmad while heading back to the rez from a study session with Ada and Sara. *How are you feeling, bae?* His reply took longer than usual. In fact, I didn't hear back from him until after I prayed Maghrib. It was a phone call. "Hello?" I answered, wearing a black abaya I'd changed into after taking a quick shower that evening.

"Bae?" he cleared his throat.

"How are you feeling?" I asked. He'd been down with the flu that had been going around. When we spoke earlier that morning, he'd been sure it would pass in a few hours.

"*Ugh*. Still bad."

"Have you taken your meds?"

"Not yet," he answered, barely audible.

I sighed, "I'm coming over."

"No, baby, it's okay. I'll take them later, I promise."

"On my way."

"Fa'iza, don't worry about it. I don't want you to get sick," he mumbled into the phone.

"I'm probably already sick. You've been drinking from my cup all week," I said, as I left my room and closed the door. We often found ourselves sharing cutlery as we tasted each other's food and drank from the same straw. If he had the flu, there was a big chance that I also had one coming.

I called for a taxi before getting into the elevator, and it was already outside the residence by the time I got out of the main doors. I gave the driver the address, and in no time, I was letting myself into the building with my fob.

As I opened the door to his apartment, he came out of his room in his black hoodie and slacks, looking surprised when he saw me. "Babe, I don't want you to fall sick," he groaned. I shrugged as if to say, "too late for that now," and he engulfed me into a tight hug, burying his head in the nook of my neck. I pulled away and looked at his face. The only tell-tale sign that he wasn't feeling great was that his eyes were a little reddened.

I looked at the unopened brown paper bags that laid untouched on the kitchen island. "You haven't eaten all day, have you?"

"I don't have an appetite," he walked to the living room and fell on the couch. I shook my head and opened the bags, put the bowl of stir-fried rice in the fridge and warmed up the bowl of chicken noodle soup in the microwave. Then I got a glass of water and set them on the table next to his medication.

"Bae," I called out. When he didn't answer, I walked towards the couch and found him asleep, his left arm across his face.

I touched it lightly. "Bae?"

He stirred, "hmm?"

"You have to eat," I gestured towards the dining table.

"Thanks, babe," he smiled lazily at me, then stood up and walked to the table. "Let's eat."

"I already had dinner," I said, pulling the chair next to him and sitting down. While he ate, I went through the bag that contained his medication. They were all unopened.

When he was done, I moved them toward him, and he narrowed his eyes. "I'm already better," he started to say, trying to avoid taking the bright blue tablets.

"Drink," I said, giving him the tablet and some water, and he did just that.

"Thanks for coming," he said after a short while. I smiled at him, I didn't have to say it, but I knew he would do the same for me.

After we prayed *Isha,* he removed his hoodie and was now wearing a white T-shirt. He looked considerably better. We were on the couch watching a cooking show on The Food Network when he moved closer and put his head on my thigh. I combed my fingers through his hair, and when I glanced down at him 15 minutes later, his eyes were closed, and his chest was heaving gently. He looked so peaceful. I didn't want to wake him up, so I turned down the sound of the television and watched the rest of the show with subtitles. Thirty minutes later, he opened his eyes and looked up at me. I was tapping away my phone. "What are you doing?" he asked quietly.

"I'm calling a cab," I wasn't going to allow him to drive me back to the rez in his current state. "How are you feeling?"

He inhaled as he stretched his neck to the side, "I feel better." He looked at the clock. It was a few minutes past nine.

"That's good," I said. I was glad to hear that.

"It's late," he sat up, his eyes settled on mine.

"Yeah, these shows take forever to get to the final challenge."

"Spend the night."

"What?"

"Spend the night," he said again, quietly, his eyes never leaving mine.

"*Um*... no," I paused tentatively. I couldn't. How could I? "No, I can't."

"You can't, or you don't want to?" he asked.

Can't, won't – does it matter? I thought to myself. "Ahmad, you *know* I can't."

"Why not?" he asked again, quietly. The cooking show was over now, and ads were playing noiselessly in the background, the light from the television shining on our faces.

"It's not appropriate..."

"You don't trust yourself to spend the night here?" he asked, "or you don't trust me?"

"I'll see you tomorrow," I said, getting up to leave.

"Fa'iza," he was serious now. "The meds are making me drowsy; I can't drive you back, and I don't want you in a cab alone at this time."

"It's not even a 5-minute ride," I said, "I'll call you as soon as I get back, so you know I'm safe."

"Please stay," he pleaded.

I opened my mouth and closed it. I had never spent the night with him. What if somebody found out? How would that look?

"I'll drop you back in the morning," he said. "You know you have nothing to worry about."

"I don't have my pyjamas," I said, although that was the least of my concerns, "or my toothbrush."

He answered almost immediately, "You can wear my shirt, and I'm sure I have an extra toothbrush somewhere."

I said nothing. I put my hand to my head and rubbed my eyebrows. *What can possibly go wrong? It's Ahmad. He has never given me a reason to be uncomfortable around him. Besides, I spend so much time in his apartment already,* I thought.

"What do you want me to say – that I'll sleep on the couch?" he leaned back into the couch and spread his arms out. "Is that what you would make you comfortable?"

"Where's the extra toothbrush?" I asked as I walked into the bedroom, "it's already way past my bedtime."

He followed me. I felt my heart pounding away as I collected the new toothbrush. "Help yourself," he said, gesturing to the neat rows of shirts hanging in his walk-in closet at the other end of the room. His phone started buzzing and he muttered, "I've gotta take this," as he walked towards the living room.

I sighed, grateful for the privacy. I looked around the dimly lit bedroom in the apartment with its black and brown decor. I'd been in here many times, but it felt different this time. I was acutely conscious of the faint scent of a Maison Francis Kurkdjian oud that enveloped me, the luxurious soft feel of the carpet underneath my bare feet, the gentle hum of the air conditioner, which was now the only audible sound in the room as I walked to the dark, spacious closet. The motion sensor activated the ceiling lights when I walked in, and multiple rows of perfectly folded white T-shirts revealed themselves. Then the colored ones – mostly blues and blacks. His silk ties and wristwatches were in a clear display unit just below them. Above the T-shirts hung dress shirts. I grabbed one that looked bigger than the rest. It was a long-sleeved white shirt with clear buttons and a stiff collar, and I carried it into the bathroom, the quiet night air interrupted by the sound of my brushing my teeth. When I was done, I took off my abaya and wore the shirt over my bra and underwear and retied the scarf around my head.

What if I toss and turn in my sleep, and my boobs peek out between the buttons? I would die of embarrassment, I thought. *What if I snore?* It was beginning to look like a long, sleepless night. I walked back into the empty room, pulling the shirt down. But it could only stop mid-thigh. It was an oversized shirt on me, and the sleeves went past my hands. I quickly got into bed and under the covers, looking at the ceiling with my fingers clasped over my chest.

Claire. I have to text her. Whenever she was not spending the night at the rez, she always made sure to text me so that I wouldn't worry. I got up from the bed, got my phone, and began typing her the text. *At my guardians...* That was a lie. I deleted it. *Staying over at Ahmad's,* I started to type but deleted it. Too much information. *Not coming back tonight, see you tomorrow.* Sent.

I dropped my phone and walked back to bed. It'd been a long day and when my head sank in the memory foam pillows, I could feel my eyes closing. But somehow, I willed myself to stay awake. Some minutes later – maybe 15 or 50 minutes (I'd lost track of time), I opened my eyes. The door to the room was opening slowly. Ahmad walked in, typing absentmindedly on his phone. Without looking up at the bed, he walked into the bathroom, closed the door and a few seconds later, the shower was turned on. After some minutes, he walked out with a white towel wrapped around his waist and was drying his hair with another. The black ink of the upper chest tattoo was now very visible. They were French words with Roman numerals etched across. I held my breath. *He looked good half-naked,* I thought, *maybe even better than the Nate Archibald from Gossip Girl.* His whole chest was glistening with wetness he didn't bother to dry off as he walked further into the room, and I found myself looking at his chest and going lower.

"Oh," he said quietly, "I thought you were asleep already?" He suddenly looked towards the bed. I shook my head. "The shower woke you up?" he asked with a puzzled look on his face. "I didn't know you were such a light sleeper." He went into the closet. I heard some rummaging, and then he came out with a pair of black boxers on. It made me remember the day I walked into his bedroom at his parent's house when he was sleeping in his boxers. *Is that a regular thing?* I thought as I watched him come closer to the bed. He picked up two pillows from the bed and smiled. "Go back to sleep, babe," he said when he caught me looking at him and started walking towards the door.

"Where are you going?" I blurted out despite myself.

"To the couch," he said with a smile on his face. He started to open the door.

"The couch is uncomfortable," I twiddled my thumbs underneath the covers. The black leather sectional in the living room was both stunning and aesthetically pleasing, but comfort was not one of its strong points – at least not for someone as tall as Ahmad. His neck would be badly cramped in a couple of hours.

"It's just for a night. I'll be fine," he was out of the door now, pulling it to a close.

"Ahmad." I heard myself call out.

"Yes?"

"The bed's big enough… if you want."

"Are you sure you're okay with that?"

I don't know, Maybe. "Yes," I said, "as long as you keep to your side of the bed."

He chuckled and started walking back into the dimly lit room. I turned over to my side, away from him, staring at the abstract art on the wall. He threw the pillows back on the bed, and my heart began pounding loudly in my ears as I felt the dip of the bed when he put his weight on it. I heard a click as he switched off the bedside lamp, and we were soon engulfed in darkness. "Goodnight, babe."

"Na-night," I replied, as I stared straight into the darkness.

* * *

I opened my eyes. It took a few seconds for them to adjust to the darkness, and when they did, they settled on the brown wall decals and the artwork I had fallen asleep looking at. I suddenly remembered that I was not in my bed and felt my body stiffen in defense. The only light in the room was a faint blue glow from a digital clock mounted on the wall. It was 2:59 am. I'd been asleep for a little while. I threw the covers off of me and tip-toed to the bathroom. Behind the closed doors, I thanked God for the faint glow of the night light on the wall that came on in the restroom; it wasn't bright enough to wake Ahmad up, but it also helped me find my way around without bumping into anything. I found my way to the toilet seat to pee, and as I washed my hands afterwards, I looked up at the mirror. My scarf was back in the bed, and my low ponytail was almost undone.

I turned off the faucet and made my way back into the room, the coolness from the air conditioning urging me to hurry back under the covers, and I did just that. I turned to my side and realized Ahmad was wide awake – shirtless, one hand behind his head on propped-up pillows. *That body.* I looked back at his face and could make out a half-smile in the darkness.

"Sorry I woke you up," I said as I pulled the covers up to my chest. There was a lot of space between us, yet it seemed like the room was not big enough for both of us.

"Don't apologize, I haven't been able to sleep."

"Have you taken your midnight dose?" I asked, and he nodded in response. "How do you feel?"

"I feel much better."

"So, why can't you sleep?" I asked.

"This is actually harder than I thought," he sighed.

"What is?"

He closed his eyes and turned around to face the ceiling, lost in thought as though he was considering his words. "Being this close to you and not being able to touch you."

Oh.

"Did that make you uncomfortable?" He asked, breaking the silence after what felt like forever.

"What?"

"That you turn me on *so* much?"

Part of the drapes was open, and a stream of moonlight flowed in. I could see him clearly, as I was sure he could see me. I shrugged, mostly because I didn't trust my voice to speak while trying hard to ignore my racing heart.

"Do I turn you on?" He asked slowly.

My breath hitched, and my eyes looked away from him and at the sheets we laid on. How did we get here? I opened my mouth to answer but closed it again. *What do I say in this circumstance – with us so close together on his bed alone, with the look in his eyes? Why is the look pulling me in?* Everything about him pulled me in – the way he looked at me, the muscles on his arms, his chest. "Tell me about your tattoo," I finally said.

He smiled like he was expecting me to change the topic and sat up. "Can you see what it says?"

I shook my head, and he stretched out his hand to turn on the bedside lamp. The room was flooded with a dim yellow glow again, and I stared at him, wondering how he managed to look even better in this light.

"Here," he moved closer to me. He was on my side of the bed now.

I looked at the numbers on his chest and tried to recall my Roman numerals. My breathing changed. Being this close to him – his thigh touching mine underneath the covers – I could feel his body heat.

"Two… nine…. Twelve? What's that?" my voice was barely a whisper as I read the numbers off his chest.

"It's a date: December 29th."

"What about it?" I asked as I slowly pulled my thigh away from his.

He put his head on the pillow next to mine. "We were traveling for a holiday, and we had an accident..." his voice caught. "Mom was... unresponsive ... and was in a coma for weeks. The doctors were going to take her off life support before the new year, and –" he heaved a big sigh, "she regained consciousness barely an hour before they pulled the plug. It was a miracle. "

"On the 29th?"

"Yes," his voice was thick at the painful memory. "I was told that no one thought she would make it. I was barely a toddler then," he paused. "Life is so fickle, you know; the tattoo – the story – it reminds me to never take the time I have with the people I cherish for granted." He looked sad, and without thinking about it, I reached out and stroked his arm. His gaze fell on my hands on him, and he reached and held it for a while. "You should go back to sleep, babe," he finally said quietly.

I stared at him without saying a word, unsure I would be able to go back to sleep that night.

"Can I hold you?" he asked after a while. I nodded. He reached over and switched off the light again, and he settled on the pillow next to mine, gathering me in his arms as he patted his chest for me to lay my head. I laid my head on his chest, and his hand draped lazily over my shoulder as he drew soft, tiny circles on my arm. I could hear the steady beating of his heart which was gentle against mine that was beating louder by the second. I stared at the blue light from the digital clock in the darkness for over an hour, and imagined him doing the same. I knew I was safe with him. I felt safe. But I was too conscious of the way my body was reacting to him. As I laid there on his chest, listening to his steady breathing, I wondered how long I would be able to hold out for.

I scratched my cheeks again. The right side of my face was tickling. I was hurrying to my exam, textbooks and study notes kept falling out of my hand and getting carried by the wind. It felt like I could not get there fast enough. I bumped into an open door, and everything I was holding toppled to the floor, including my pencils and pens. I thought I zipped my pencil case? Clearly not. When did I become such a klutz?

"The exam has been moved to H building," I heard Afreen say.

"What?" I was confused. Why was the exam moved last minute? Why did I not get an email about it? Most importantly, why is Afreen in my class?

"Ahmad said if we're late, he won't allow us to take the exam," she said, hurrying away.

Wait. What? My face was still tickling. Ahmad was my professor? Since when? Why is Afreen on campus? Why is my face tickling? Why won't it stop?

I opened my eyes. Somehow, we made it to morning with me fast asleep on his chest. Bright morning light streamed in through the windows of the high-rise penthouse suite. I was in bed, staring straight at Ahmad's brown eyes as they glinted with mischief. He removed his fingers from my face. He had been tickling it

"You were making cute noises in your sleep," he said as I sat up in bed and pulled the shirt I'd slept in.

"I had a weird dream," I scratched my hair, wiped the sides of my lips and subconsciously looked down at the pillow to make sure I hadn't been drooling.

"I could tell," he said, moving closer and leaning towards my face, that mischievous grin still on his face.

"What are you doing?" I asked, but the words were drowned by laughter as he tickled my sides, and I fell on my back again.

Ahmad got on top of me and pinned my hands to my side. "I'm giving you a morning kiss."

"What? No, no no, " I said, as I turned my head so that his lips fell to my cheeks instead. He aimed for my lips again, and I shook my head. His lips got my neck this time. "I haven't brushed my teeth," I said in between my fit of giggles.

"I don't care," he said. "I'm just happy you stayed over." I was still pinned down beneath his bare chest. He felt so warm.

"I swear this is my biggest insecurity."

"What is?" he stopped, and he raised his head to look at me.

"Smelly breath. You know how in the movies, people wake up, and they just… kiss?" I watched him nod, a half-smile on his face, "I'm always like eww – like, why don't they brush their teeth first?"

He released my hands and rolled over to his back, his head brushing mine on the pillow as we stared at the ceiling. My sides ached from the involuntary fit of laughter caused by the tickles.

"So, you don't wanna kiss me 'cos you haven't brushed your teeth?" he didn't wait for me to answer, "Okay then. But you owe me a kiss as soon as you do."

"Make me," I said. I got off the bed, leaving him with raised eyebrows as he watched me walk away like he was wondering if he should take me up on the dare. I was in the bathroom for a few minutes after brushing my teeth. I put my abaya back on and came back to the bedroom to say my morning prayers. As I folded up his praying mat afterwards, I heard Ahmad on the phone outside the room. I could tell it was with his team in Japan. I picked up my phone to check my messages then I walked out of the bedroom to find him brewing coffee in the kitchen.

"You took a shower already?" He asked me when he ended the call.

"No, I'll do that when I get back to the residence," I answered. I don't have my toiletries; I wouldn't feel clean enough using someone else's bath products. It was a Fa'iza thing. He nodded, still shirtless and bare feet. But at least he was now wearing trousers.

"Have you taken your morning dose?" I asked, tearing my eyes away from him and grabbing a mug. *He needs to find a shirt,* I thought.

"I feel much better now, don't think I need it," he said.

"You must be joking," I passed the grey mug to him and watched as the caffeinated liquid trickled slowly into the cup. I moved to the fridge and looked at the breakfast items in it – cheese, turkey sausages, eggs.

"I'm starving," I groaned. My stomach had rumbled twice already.

"I'm gonna go get us breakfast sandwiches from the café downstairs," he started walking to the room to get dressed.

The café downstairs was an owner-managed café I'd ventured into a few times – dainty and French styled."Nah," I shook my head. "I've seen their menu. Almost everything has bacon in it."

"I'll tell them to leave the bacon out," he said from the room, his voice muffled by the distance.

"It's alright, " I said as I opened the bottom cabinet and grabbed a barely used frying pan. He came back just as I was breaking eggs into a bowl, the turkey sausages turning golden brown in the frying pan.

"You... are... cooking," he pronounced each word separately with a surprised smile on his face.

"Great observation skills," I remarked sarcastically. I poured the eggs over a mix of diced tomatoes and onions. "You get an A*!"

"Haha, you've got jokes," his voice was right by my ear. "How can I help?"

"A plate would be nice," I flipped the turkey sausages over. He moved away from me and opened a cabinet, brought out two plates and set them on the counter, and was back behind me again. I busied myself with placing the omelettes on the plates, his hands around my waist as I moved.

"I'm still waiting on that morning kiss," his voice was right by my ear again.

I felt the flutter in my heart. I wanted to kiss him. I wanted to hold him. That was all I thought about all night. I switched off the burner, and I slowly turned around and looked up at him. He had a faint smile on his face, his hands still on my waist, and our thighs were pressed together with my back against the oven. His eyes glance at my lips and back to my eyes. *What harm can one little kiss do?* I thought to myself as I felt his hands moving to my arms, his fingers stroking my skin lightly. He slowly lifted my arms and put them around his neck. I wondered what his lips would feel like against mine. Without realizing it, I bit my bottom lip, and I saw a look in his eyes. I knew there was no going back. I wanted this as much as he did; I was just better at hiding my feelings.

His other hand was lightly touching my jawline now, his thumb lightly grazing my lower lip and in a heartbeat, my lips were on his. They felt so soft against mine, so unreal that I felt unsteady on my feet, and I almost forgot to breathe. His lips parted lightly, and I felt his hunger. He was trying to rein it in, but I could still feel it as his lips moved over mine. I felt his hands over my back and around my neck as he moved us closer, but it felt like it would never be enough. The closeness was still not enough. His touch was setting me on fire, and I did not mind getting consumed.

This kiss. This kiss was worth getting consumed by this fire for. But a part of me knew it wasn't just the kiss; it was the man himself – the way he touched me, the way he looked at me, the way he felt for me; it was all translated into this one kiss that had been simmering between us for such a long time now.

Our lips parted slowly, but he didn't let me go. He placed his forehead against mine as I tried to steady my breathing. My eyes were still closed, and my heartbeat was racing. "Look at me, babe," he said quietly. I could hear the smile in his voice. I slowly looked up at him and wondered if there would come a time I would stop feeling these butterflies in my stomach when I looked at him. *What is happening to me?*

"Hi," I said, feeling nervous but confident at the same time. It was all a juxtaposition of emotions.

"Hello," he laughed, then kissed me on the forehead. He looked like he wanted to kiss me again. "That was amazing."

"It was?"

"Yes, it was," he gently took his hand off my neck, his eyes never leaving mine. The smile on his face didn't look like it was going anywhere anytime soon.

"I have to get back to the residence," I said. *What I need is a cold shower, then an Islamic lecture on chastity.*

"Are you okay?" There was concern in his voice. He was still holding my hand, his fingers grazing mine lightly.

"Yeah," I lied. "I am."

We cut up some fruits from the fruit bowl and had a quiet breakfast on the kitchen island. The only sounds were from the TV in the living room behind us and the gentle crunch of the croissant we shared. We drank our coffee from the same mug, and occasionally, he would reach and wipe something from the corner of my lips. I wasn't sure if there was actually anything there or if he just wanted to touch me.

As he dropped me off, hands intertwined while he drove, we chatted about my plans for the rest of the day. He offered to pick me up from class, but I told him I had yoga after and had to study for my upcoming test. He didn't push it, and I appreciated that. Tamia's *So into you* started playing as we pulled into the visitor's parking space. It felt just right. This felt so right.

Except it wasn't.

Chapter 14

Later in the day, I was downstairs with Claire for Bikram Yoga. It was my least favorite type of yoga but the most rewarding. The darkened room seemed to have a pulse of its own as the yogi's calm voice filled the hot air with gentle instructions to hold our pose and take deep breaths. I kept holding my breath and constantly had to be reminded to exhale. It was therapeutic – the sweat and the heat. It felt like penance for everything I'd done that day; I hadn't been able to stop myself from thinking about Ahmad since I got back.

When we got to the residence, we'd stayed in his car for another fifteen minutes, talking about the most random things. He told me about this one time he lost Afreen at the Frankfurt airport when they were waiting for a connecting flight and how scared he had been, thinking she got kidnapped. He was only sixteen at the time. He helped adjust my scarf, and as he was about to finish telling his story, he held my hands, and looked at my fingers. "Why don't you wear rings?"

"I always misplace them," I answered quietly. His index fingers stroked mine as he continued with another story. Eventually, when I insisted that I had to leave, he nodded and walked me to the elevators, and we said our goodbyes as the doors closed and I started moving to my floor. I hadn't even gotten to my room when his call came in. "I'm taking you out on a date on Friday," his voice sounded like melted chocolate.

"Why are you just telling me this now?" I asked, laughing as I unlocked the door to my room.

"I just thought about it," he answered, "plus, I know Fridays are your least busy days." It was true.

The sting in my outstretched arm brought me back to the yoga class. Claire was by my left, as graceful as a swan, with her right hand stretched out in front of her and her left leg curved into the air behind her. There were not a lot of girls in the class who could hold such a pose as long as she could. Luckily, we just had to hold the pose for another second, and then everyone curled into downward dog. After a few more stretching poses, the lights came on to signal the end of the class. I grabbed my water bottle and gulped water like my life depended on it.

"Hmm, I needed that," Claire said as she twisted her head from left to right. Her face was flushed, her freckles evident in this light. We rolled up our mats and put down our names on the signup sheet for the next class. As we walked back to our room, my phone beeped a message from Niac: *Can't stop thinking about you*. I read the message over and over again, unable to find a suitable response.

"Okay, you've had that giddy look on your face since you got back. What's going on?" Claire asked, giving me a knowing look as she glanced at my phone and then my face. "Spill it," she said, pouring some water into a green St. Patrick cup.

"Oh, it's just Ahmad," I said, trying to make it less of a deal.

"Oouuu the boyfriend. Must be nice," she said in a singsong manner as she walked into her room to answer a call.

I took the opportunity to go into the restroom to remove the workout clothes off my damp body, and jump into the shower. As I closed my eyes, I remembered the feel of his lips on mine – their softness, how his hands glided down my back. I opened my eyes and could still feel his hands on my face, the way his thumb lingered on my lower lip after our kiss, the way his chest felt under my palms, and the firm yet gentle way he gripped my waist as he pulled me in closer to him. I wondered what Ahmad was doing at that moment and thought about his message: *Can't stop thinking about you.* 'Same here', I wanted to text back. 'Not a minute has passed since I got back that you haven't crossed my mind.' I shook my head as though the single gesture would help dispel my thoughts and got out of the shower. When I got in bed, I went on YouTube and searched for Islamic lectures by Mufti Menk, and listened for only about ten minutes when the topic changed to temptations. The lecture talked about how the devil tried to distract us with temptations that seemed irresistible, and my thoughts were on Ahmad the whole time.

* * *

I was with Ada and Sara discussing statutory and common law defenses when his call came in. At the same time, Sara announced that she needed to use the restroom.

I picked up. "Yeah, hello?"

"Bae?" As soon as I heard his voice, my insides started turning into jelly. *Is it possible that I'm falling even deeper for him?*

"Hey."

"You never replied to my text message. You started typing, and then you stopped," he complained.

"Yes, I've been so busy, *ne*. Sorry," It wasn't entirely true.

The silence didn't linger for much. "I understand. Are you at the rez?"

"No, study lounge," I answered carefully. I knew he wouldn't just turn up without giving me a heads-up, yet, I found myself suddenly apprehensive.

"Okay, I'll let you get back to it, then."

"Okay, bye"

"Bye, babe."

I disconnected the call and looked around the lounge. There were barely any students left. Most would rather study in the library at this time of the day.

"Is everything okay?" Ada was looking at me. She had braided her Afro into two beautiful cornrows.

"Yeah," I said. I found myself pulling the sleeves of my long-sleeved top.

"You don't sound happy," she probed. "Are you guys fighting?"

I looked around the lounge again. Sara was nowhere in sight, but still, I whispered. "I kissed him."

"*You* kissed him?" she was surprised. She blinked her eyes a few times.

"Yeah. I did." I'd thought about that morning a hundred times. He'd initiated it by closing the distance between us, but I eventually leaned in.

"I thought you guys were keeping it… what's the word?"

"*Halal*?" I supplied.

"Yeah, *halal*," she said. "So, this was your first kiss, all this while?" I nodded. "Well, how was it?" her eyes gleamed with interest as she adjusted her glasses, her voice taking on a cheery tune and dispelling the tense nature of the conversation.

I opened my mouth to speak, then closed it, my mind replaying how his hands went to the side of my neck while we kissed. "It… It was good. *Really* good, " I finally admitted, still whispering.

"Haha, that's crazy," she was about to add something when we saw Sara heading back. The conversation ended there, and we went back to studying. Now I knew for sure I'd fallen even deeper for him.

* * *

I had a busy week. Between my classes, study sessions and volunteering twice a week at *Inn From the Cold,* I barely had much time to leave campus. My phone calls with Ahmad had become shorter and shorter, and so were our text exchanges, in accordance with the strict set of instructions I had gotten from a Muslim sister's blog on avoiding temptations.

The first instruction was to pray *istighfar,* to ask God for forgiveness. Second, I needed to limit the temptation by not being around said person – so I now restrict communication. Whenever he asked to come see me, I always had an already-rehearsed excuse. Third, fasting to keep the thoughts out of my head. I continued with my Monday and Thursday fasts which were a regular thing in my father's house. Voluntary fasting was a Prophetic *sunnah* and was not hard at all. Keeping him out of my head – now *that* was the hard part. Terribly, terribly hard. Especially when he messaged me: *You've been on my mind all day* or *Hey, I'm just by that ice cream truck you like. Should I pick up your fave?* Or *Guess you are busy. Picked you a tub. It's gonna be in the freezer waiting for you.* Recently, there had been a lot of *Are you okay? You didn't sound great on the phone just now* or the one that made my heart skip a beat every time: *I miss you, babe.*

I tried to keep myself very busy by covering kitchen duties at the shelter. By the time I got there at 4 pm, there was usually a huge pile of plates from lunch that the volunteers had to run through the heavy-duty dishwashers. We would then set the table and would sometimes help serve dinner.

Inn From the Cold was a safe shelter for displaced women. Some had been displaced due to spousal abuse; they'd been kicked out of their homes and had no source of income. I'd seen some women come with luggage and some with only the clothes on their backs. Some stayed for just a night, and others stayed for weeks. Some with kids and others alone. Whatever the situation was, the shelter provided them with a safe space, meals to eat, and activities to keep them occupied. Sometimes, as I watched women come in, I imagined building a similar organization in Nigeria – how I would run it, what I would embody, and what I would do differently.

This week had been unusually busy because we were hosting a huge Thanksgiving dinner. Apart from regular volunteers like me, we also had some drop-ins for the day who would help with the work. I was looking at the schedule to see which group I would be working with when I heard Jasmeet's voice. I turned to find her in an elegant orange and black pantsuit. That's the Thanksgiving spirit! I, on the other hand, was in my regular jeans and a long-sleeved shirt, my scarf wrapped as a hijab around my head to cover my ears and neck.

"Fa'iza, thank you for showing up on time as always," she said as she smiled at me, "The kitchen is fully staffed. Could you go out front and help serve the food? We need some help there."

"Of course."

"Perfect. Grab an apron, and you can help at the coffee station," she turned on her heels. I grabbed one of the green aprons that hung on the rack by the kitchen doors and wore it, tying the belts behind me as I followed her through the double doors.

The dining hall was bustling with loud chatter and laughter. Some people were chatting like long-lost friends, others were just quietly observing or lost in their own thoughts, and kids were being kids – running around and playing, completely oblivious to whatever dire situation had brought them to the shelter tonight. Kids needed this – a sense of community at times when family units were disintegrated. I wondered yet again how this would work in Nigeria.

"This is where you'll work tonight," Jasmeet said as she led me to the coffee station at the end of the table. "You just need to place a mug here and press this button," she looked up to see if I understood, and I nodded. "We'll have someone here shortly to help you," she gestured at the second coffee station. I nodded with a smile as she walked away.

There was a lady already there. She looked as though she were in her sixties, slim build, greying hair, and the hard-to-miss Cartier love bracelet on her wrist. "Hello. Dear. I'm Amy."

"Hi, I'm Fa'iza."

"Is today your first time volunteering, too?"

"No, I've been doing this for a few weeks now."

"How wonderful! By the way, I looooove your scarf."

"Thank you," I answered with a smile. I always got compliments about my hijab, more here in Toronto than anywhere else. The news made it seem like everyone in the West thought it was a sign of oppression, but that wasn't the case with the people that I had come across.

To my right, someone was wearing an apron, his back to me, in the air was the scent of *Million* by Paco Rabanne. Brown shirt with the sleeves rolled up, dark pants and a stubble. I blinked a few times because I was pretty sure I was imagining things. "Ahmad?" my voice was barely a whisper.

"There you are!" His face was expressionless as he turned and looked at me.

"What are you doing here?"

"Volunteering," then he turned his attention towards a lady that was walking towards us. "Good evening. Coffee?"

"Yes, please," she answered timidly. She had a bruise on her face, and I stared at it, wondering if someone had hit her.

"Milk, sugar and creamers are over to your left," I said when Ahmad was done serving her.

"Thanks," she said quietly, her eyes on the floor.

As more people flowed in, Ahmad would help hand out the coffee I'd poured to the people waiting in line and direct them to sugar and everything else they needed. He was surprisingly good at this.

As it quieted down again, I looked at mothers feeding their children and instinctively turned around to look at Ahmad. I'd caught him looking at me with a hard-to-read expression as he moved closer.

"Why are you avoiding me?" his eyes fixed on mine. "And don't say you aren't because I had to volunteer at a shelter to see you." His voice was gentle. He didn't seem angry, but there was something unreadable about his expression.

I looked around. The lady by my side, Amy, was in deep conversation with a gentleman by her side. I looked back at Ahmad. "I've been busy, *ne*. Sorry."

He nodded slowly. I knew he didn't believe me. "You see, Fa'iza, we can't do this," his words were measured, deliberate. "You can't just ignore me when something bothers you."

A boy around fifteen approached us, interrupting him. "Just getting coffee for my mum," the boy said.

"Happy thanksgiving," Ahmad said, pouring him a cup. When the boy left, Ahmad moved closer to me again. With him being this close to me, all the emotions I had tried so hard to keep at bay all week came rushing back. "Was it something I said or something I did?" He was not smiling.

I shook my head.

"So, what's it then?" He was standing very close to me. We were not touching, but I was aware of how his eyes flickered down to my lips and back to my eyes. I remembered my thighs pressing against his in the kitchen that morning and how good his hands felt around my waist. I could feel my heartbeat quickening, and I took a step backwards. His eyebrows shot up, but he didn't close the distance I had put between us. He chuckled and rubbed his forehead. "It is about the kiss, isn't it?" I remained quiet, trying to dispel the memory which was vivid in my memory. "Talk to me."

I forced myself to look up at him. "It's *haram,* Ahmad. I feel guilty." My voice sounded like it would break, my whisper was loaded with uncertainty. I was scared and embarrassed at the same time.

His eyes got softer. "I'm sorry," he swallowed. "I'm sorry I pushed you to do something you weren't ready for."

I shook my head. "No, no, no. You didn't push me," I said, then adding in a whisper: "I *wanted* to."

He looked like he was going to sweep me in his arms but thought against it. He was restless with his hands and couldn't decide whether to fold them across his chest or put them in his pocket. "The past week has been torture," his voice was so low, "how was it so easy for you to just pull away?"

"It wasn't," I wanted to reassure him. "I'm just supposed to stay aw–"

"Who said?"

"Nouman Ali Khan, Omar Suleiman, and Mufti Menk," I answered, listing off all the Islamic scholars whose lectures on chastity I'd been watching all week. I started busying myself with arranging coffee cups in neat rows to avoid looking at him.

"What you feel for me – what we feel for each other – it's not going to magically disappear because you stay away," his voice was still low, and his eyes were still on me. "But baby, we can't work around it, if you keep avoiding me." I melted a bit when he called me baby. He rarely ever did, but when he did, it sounded so... *sweet.*

We were interrupted by Jasmeet, who was going around to thank the drop-in volunteers personally. "A pleasure to *finally* meet you, Mr. Ahmad," she said as she shook his hand, "thank you for your countless donations over the years."

"My pleasure," Ahmad answered.

"Oh Fa'iza, I see you have met Mr. Ahmad already," she turned towards me, "the new coding lab and all the computers in there were donated by him"

I stared at her and then at Ahmad, who was looking embarrassed. He was a regular donor at *Inn From the Cold*? He had never even mentioned it. *Ahmad Babangida, the philanthropist. Who would have thought?*

After another hour of cleaning up and putting away the garbage and recyclables, we were all exhausted. We dropped our aprons in the baskets provided and got our personal belongings from the lockers, and left at 8 pm.

"Why didn't you tell me you are affiliated with the shelter?" I asked him.

"It never came up," he shrugged. He looked at both sides of the road as we crossed. "When you mentioned how much you wanted to help women and kids, I couldn't believe how similar we were. It's one of the things I love about us."

Love. Did he just say one of the things he loved about us? "Why women and children?" I asked instead.

"The statistics show that one in three women have been subjected to violence by a partner, and only a few percent of them seek shelter elsewhere when it happens," he sighed, "I feel it's my duty to help in providing a safe space for those who do. We all owe it to them."

"I know, right?" I agreed. I thought about the happy cherub faces I saw at dinner, "and the kids."

"Yes! And the kids," we had reached the bus stop. "Imagine their mothers going back to their abusers because they had no safe place to stay. Imagine how it would affect them."

"I wanna talk to Abba about doing something like this in Abuja or Kaduna," I said.

"Really?" he turned to look at me, "That would be amazing."

"I mean, I still have to figure out the logistics," I reached into my bag to get my bus pass as we got to the bus stop right in front of the parking lot, "I'm gonna wait for the bus here."

"Can I drop you?"

"We can't be alone together."

"Let me guess, your YouTube Muftis said that?"

I nodded.

He ran his hand through his head, "I think we've done really well this evening, we managed to keep our hands off each other," his features softened as I laughed. He stared for a second too long. "Or I could come on the bus with you," he added.

"You would leave your car here?"

"I'll come back for it," he brought out his wallet and took out his card to pay for a bus ticket.

I looked up, and the bus was approaching us in the distance. It was a 45-minute bus ride to the residence. I usually liked long bus rides; I didn't think he would. "The only reason I'm coming with you is because I don't want you going back and forth."

He had a triumphant look on his face as we turned away and started walking to his car. We got in, and as I watched him shuffle his music, images of his finger on my skin flashed across my mind. I remembered how he put my arms around his neck right before we kissed, the feel of his thighs against my skin. It got harder to breathe.

"So, did your Muftis suggest the best way to handle our… situation?" he glanced at me before starting the engine, but I looked away, watching the car drive off the curb.

"Yeah, they had a couple of ideas."

"Care to share?"

"Marriage," I said.

"And what do you think about that?"

"My parents will wonder what I'm doing if – barely a year into my degree – I go back home and say I want to get married. They would think I've gone mad."

"They wouldn't oppose it, though, would they?" he probed.

"No, but I'm expected to get married after school or at the earliest, towards the end of school," I answered. No one got married early in my family. The earliest a girl was expected to get married was immediately after her first degree, but most people do years after completing their Masters.

"So, that's in what – three years?" he probed again, gently.

"Yeah, thereabouts." It seemed like enough time. A wife at twenty-one or twenty-two? Didn't sound half bad.

"Okay, so do you plan on avoiding me for the next three years, then? Or how does this work?" I hadn't thought about that. His hands rested on the steering wheel when we got to the red traffic light, and when the light turned green, his left hand moved to the gearbox and lingered close to my thigh.

"Fasting," I said, even though I wasn't sure it was helping in this case. I'd been fasting consistently that week, but I'd constantly caught my thoughts slipping back to him.

"That works," he agreed, "but you can't fast every day now, can you?"

"You have better suggestions?" We reached the residence now. He found a parking spot and pulled in.

"Don't take this the wrong way. I think getting married just to get laid is the reason marriages aren't working anymore," he looked at me. The light from the lamp posts filled the car with a yellow afterglow. "Do you understand what I'm trying to say?"

"No," I confessed.

"Okay, so you find yourself madly attracted to someone, and you get married," his voice was low but confident. "The first few months are fantastic, and you're having all this amazing sex you never even imagined in your wildest dreams. Life continues and with time, you realize sex is the only thing you enjoy together and now that it's out of your system, there isn't much to keep the relationship going. Life happens, maybe a kid or two. She's busy dealing with the changes in her body, and he doesn't know her enough in a non-sexual way to empathize with her insecurities. She's just his wife and the mother of his children and that alone cannot sustain a marriage. What they thought was love has now become a mere..." he paused for a moment as he searched for the right word, 'duty.'

"What sustains a marriage, then?"

"Security," he said without thinking as if he'd thought about it several times, "knowing that my woman will always be *my* woman, regardless of what life throws at me; that she's a friend first, then my wife."

"And for the woman?"

"I can't answer that for you, Fa'iza. You need to know what *you* need in a partner and not just on paper, but in reality too. It's easy for any man to claim to be patient, but how do you know that's for real, if you haven't seen how he treats you when things don't go his way? When he loses out on a huge contract, for instance?" he looked away, his eyes settling on the dashboard. "Any man will claim to love you, but would that love remain on the days you're difficult to love? You need an unshakable belief in him being constant. I would imagine that's what security feels like for a woman."

I thought about the married people I knew – the few times wives returned to their parents' houses due to unspoken issues, how everyone stressed patience to both parties. Is that what marriage becomes after the initial love struck feeling wears off – lifelong servitude of endurance and tolerance?

"What I feel for you, Fa'iza – it's indescribable. I want you so much it hurts."

"We can't kiss anym –"

"Are you afraid of what it might lead to?" he asked me quietly.

I nodded. *What if we get so carried away, and it doesn't stop at just kissing?*

"I respect that," he started, then he cleared his throat, "I respect what you want. We're never gonna do anything you feel uncomfortable with."

"So, what are we going to do about…" I didn't know how to articulate the tingle and the heat I felt every time he was around me.

"The feelings? We'll take it one day at a time," a smirk formed at the corner of his lips, "and lots and lots of fasting."

I started smiling, and we burst into laughter. So help me, God.

Chapter 15

Autumn got as cold as winter on some nights. In fact, the only differences between autumn and winter, I'd found, were better colors and picturesque backgrounds. As the green leaves turned orange and the brown ones covered the wet grass, every outdoor picture I took looked like something out of a magazine. It was still too early to bring out the big guns, and by that, I mean the heavy duck feather-filled winter jackets that remained locked up in the closet, so instead, the lighter warm woolen ones were all I wore.

Cashmere sweaters and artisan scarves add splashes of color to the University hallways that smelt of pumpkin spice latte and red bull.

The semester felt like it was getting progressively shorter as I found myself buried in final drafts and submission deadlines, begging for Monday not to come so quickly. After the weekend, it was like a race through time; days blurred into each other until it was Friday again.

On Friday, Ahmad and I finally went on our date. A proper date. We hadn't had one of those in a while, mostly because we hadn't been hanging out much. But we talked on the phone all the time; I knew that he was moving at my pace, and I liked it. It felt easy. But I had missed him and the simple things we did together – watching shows with him, picking up coffee and Timbits from Tim Hortons.

My phone beeped a message: *Coming up.* It was already dark outside my windows when I leaned towards the mirror in the bathroom to apply the second coat of mascara to my already darkened and curled eyelashes. There was a knock on the door. I quickly rummaged around my make-up bag until my fingers picked up a *Dior* sheer lip gloss and threw it into the black clutch I was taking. I glanced at my reflection as I walked past the mirror – the white sweater with pearl details on the wrists and neckline over the black satin slip dress I got from Hudson's Bay created a flattering silhouette.

I opened the door, and he looked up from his phone. He was wearing a white shirt and dark pants. He had gotten a haircut, and his beard had grown out a bit since the last time I saw him.

"*Um*. Why are you wearing my colors?" I smiled as I held the door open for him to come in. He was looking at me in a way that I never knew that I wanted to be looked at – like he could not stop looking at me, like he saw more than what I saw in the mirror.

"Hey, beautiful," he walked in, letting the door close behind him. He smelled good. He always smelled good.

"We're wearing co-ordinating outfits."

He nodded slowly as his eyes moved to the bracelet he got me.

"See? All this time apart, yet our minds are on the same frequency," his eyes settled on mine. I had almost forgotten this feeling, the way I felt when we were in the same space.

"I'm gonna get my things," I walked into my bedroom and heard his footsteps gently behind me. "Where did you say we were going again?" I asked when we got to the room. He was standing by my reading desk, looking at the various post-it notes with references for papers that I was researching and a phone number for a pizza delivery place cluttering my computer screen, and the textbooks that had whole pages covered in green and pink highlighters which sort of defeats the purpose of highlighting the important information, now that I thought about it.

"I never said where we were going," he answered.

"Okay. So, where are we going?"

"You'll find out soon enough, babe." A smile tug the end of his lips as he chuckled.

I sighed and knelt down in my closet to look for shoes to wear.

"This is new," he said from behind me. I turned around and saw him looking at a green and black painting that hung over my desk.

"Yeah. Remember the show the Humanities department put up? I got it there." Claire and I had joked about how it would be the greatest investment I ever made if the artist became famous in the future because I bought it for only twenty dollars.

He nodded slowly, his hands in his pocket as he studied the painting of two horses in the prairies.

"Yes, you told me you got a painting," he squinted his eyes as he tilted his head to the side. "I just didn't expect it to be this... hideous."

I turned my head around as I looked at him. He was trying hard to stop the smile tugging his lips. "Show me the last thing you painted," I grabbed my *Vince Camuto* block-heeled sandal with a high ankle strap and my *Amina Muaddi* suede pumps.

"You might not approve of it," he said. Of course, he had dabbled into painting, too, to add to his long list of talents. I turned around and raised both shoes. "Which should I wear?"

"Whatever you're comfortable in," he folded his arms and leaned back on my table. "There's valet parking so you won't be walking for too long, anyway."

I sat down on the carpet. "Which one do you think goes better with my outfit?"

He took a deep breath as he considered the question. "The crystals on that suede look..." he shrugged, "but I'm partial to open-toed sandals."

I slowly shook my head, "None of that was helpful."

"I'll have to see them on you to decide."

Before I could say anything, he knelt in front of me, picked up the *Vince Camuto* and gently tugged my leg from beneath me and placed it on his thigh. My dress gave way just a little bit as my feet rested on his thigh, my calf exposed. He was concentrating as he slipped the shoe onto my feet and took his time fastening the delicate strap. I caught a whiff of his cologne, and I held my breath. He raised his head and looked straight at me, his expression hard to read. If he had any clue that his being this close to me was taking my breath away, he showed no indication.

He looked away as he dropped my right foot gently to the carpet, then replaced it with the left and covered my toes with the shoe as he slipped it on. This one was harder to get into, so his hand went under my feet, and his index finger grazed my heel. *Four weeks,* I thought to myself. Four weeks of restraint, of intentionally not being around him, four weeks of convincing myself that I was in control of my feelings – all shattered within the first five minutes of seeing him again. What a complete and utter waste the time apart was.

"Are you okay?" his voice was almost inaudible in the quiet room.

"*Hmm,*" I answered with a slight nod.

"Is this shoe comfortable?" he asked gently.

"Yes," I nodded again.

"Can you stand up?" he stood up first and then reached for my hands and helped me up. I stood up straight despite the height difference. He was looking at my feet, his fingers absentmindedly stroking his beard.

"The pumps, for sure," he leaned back again on the table.

"Cool, thanks," I took off the sandal and wore the other pair of pumps.

"Where's Claire?" he asked as we headed out of the room.

"At a Halloween party."

As we made our way down the elevator and through the lobby decorated in pumpkins and ghouls, I knew we looked good together, not just from the way people stared as we walked past but also from the smiles we got. I tried hard not to stare at our reflection as we walked outside the residence. His car was already warmed up, so I didn't have to worry about the cold. As I sank into the plush white leather seat and wondered how long it'd been since the last time I was in the car, the familiar scent of *amr black oud* enveloped me. His phone was charging on the wireless pad, and its screen display was on his dashboard.

"Why are you being so secretive about where we're going tonight?" I asked after we got the usual out of the way—questions about Uni, his work and *Inn From the Cold.* "I just wanna make sure that I am not overdressed," I added.

"Overdressed looks great on you."

"Am I overdressed?"

"Does it matter?"

"I guess not." I really liked the outfit I was wearing and was excited to dress up for the first time in a while."Got my ticket today," I said, changing the topic. I was leaving for Abuja right after my exams.

"Excited?" His sentences were very brief this evening.

"Yeah, I am," I beamed. I was finally going home after a year and a half, and I hadn't been able to stop counting down the days.

"What have you missed most about home?" He turned into the busy downtown core, slowing down to match the posted speed limit.

I thought about everything I missed – Abba, Umma, the call to prayer five times a day from the masjid at the entrance of our house where most men on our street prayed, Eid celebrations, my brothers, unannounced visits from my cousins – I missed them everything. "My bed," I said as the car started to slow down in front of a tall building that already had Christmas lights on.

"Lucky bed," he said, his voice laced with sarcasm. As the car came to a halt, a young valet came to my door and pulled it open. I stepped out. It was a little colder than I had anticipated. My woolen coat was warm but not warm enough against the chill evening wind. I looked over the hood of the car and saw Ahmad giving his keys to the valet, his brown woolen peacoat was now buttoned up. When we locked eyes, he swiftly ended the conversation and started walking toward me.

A bellman ushered us into the lobby, and only then did I realize that we were at the Hilton. Thanks to the logo on the floor as we walked past the grand foyer, which was surprisingly not busy, and he led us towards the elevator. *Why are we going up the elevator?*

"I've missed spending time with you," he said.

"We talk every single day."

"But it's not the same."

The elevators took us to the glass-enclosed rooftop. There was a fire pit burning with oak and birchwood warming up the space. In the middle of the rooftop was an already set dinner table set for two. It had a black cast iron candle holder with three prongs holding flames burning lightly on the black and grey table runner. As we approached the table, I noticed a short bunch of pastel carnation flowers in the middle of the table. He pulled out a chair for me, and he helped with my coat. From my seat, I could see the CN Tower and its pointy needle end reaching into the dark sky. Then he removed his coat and hung it on the wrought iron standing coat rack and he sat down opposite me.

Before I could say a word, a waiter came to attend to us. I chuckled to myself as I took note of the waiter's white short-sleeved shirt, black pants and black bow tie. He filled our glasses with sparkling water and adjusted his bowtie as he addressed Ahmad: "Ready for the appetizer, sir?"

"Appetizers?" Ahmad asked me, "or should we dive into our first course?"

"Surprise me," I reached for my glass and took it to my lips, slowly taking a sip of the water as he spoke to the waiter.

"You look beautiful tonight," he said once we were alone again.

"Thank you," I smiled, "I thought we were going to a restaurant."

"Yeah, there's a restaurant on the main floor, but I wanted something more private," he looked around us, then back at me, his eyes scanning my face. " I wanted us alone and since you've made it clear that my apartment is out of bounds for –"

"I never said your apartment was *out of bounds*," I got defensive.

"Well," he leaned back into his chair, "you haven't been there in months."

"Weeks," I corrected.

He was about to say something when the waiter returned with two plates. He set one in front of me and the other in front of Ahmad. "Here you are, miss. Specially made for you, smoked salmon bites with shallot sauce and asigao cheese on crisp arugula," he had an Australian accent.

This was art – pink and orange-hued swirls of fish in a cream-colored sauce with black oil garnish. I finally understood why people took pictures of their plates in restaurants. I said thank you and looked up at Ahmad, who was unfolding his napkin and placing it on his lap. I mirrored his movements and when I was done, we looked up at each other and reached for our forks at the same time. The first bite was sweet and salty at the same time.

"How's your food?" he broke the silence.

I nodded, giving him two thumbs up as my mouth was full.

"I might have some things to do in Abuja in December," he paused a little, and I felt the little flutter in my heart start again.

"Nice," I said as our main course was being wheeled toward us by the chef.

Ahmad and he exchanged a brief nod as he set my plate in front of me. "Excuse the flames, miss," he warned, and almost immediately, my plate was set on fire as the top layer of my already cooked steak was grilled to slow perfection with a brown glaze over it.

"Okay that was a surprise," I said, watching the leaping flames.

"The flambe was achieved with sugared cubes in flavored extract, not liquor." he said reassuringly.

"And the steak is –" prompted Ahmad.

"100% halal, as you requested," the chef completed.

"Thanks, Chris," Ahmad said. The chef nodded in Ahmad's direction again and left as quickly as he'd arrived. Ah yes. *Chris Shaften* from Top Chef Canada. No wonder he looked familiar. I'd seen him on TV a few times.

So far, the evening was better than I had anticipated. It was all roses and daisies until after dessert. I was enjoying my sweetened oolong tea when the waiter returned to the table. He brought a tray with an old-fashioned glass with ice and a dark liquid in it.

"Compliments from the bar, sir," he said as he set the drink in front of Ahmad.

"No, Leo," his eyes darted quickly at me, "I won't be drinking tonight."

Leo apologized and hurriedly took the drink away, leaving an awkward silence. I tried to think back at the times we'd spent together, and nothing indicated that he drank alcohol – not his apartment, and definitely not when we ate out or ordered in. I knew he ate things that were not explicitly halal, but he never ate pork. But alcohol? There's no excuse for that. I was shocked. Appalled, even. When a Muslim drank alcohol, their prayers were not answered for 40 days. FORTY whole days!

He sighed and leaned forward towards me, while I leaned back into my chair. He noticed my movement away from him, and his eyes clouded with something I could not decipher. Pain? "You drink?" I finally asked.

"No, Fa'iza. I don't drink. Not anymore."

"Not anymore?" I asked, "so you *used* to drink alcohol?"

"Only socially. After meetings with the guys, sometimes we would hit the bar," he looked at me, and when I didn't respond, he added, "I know it's not okay."

"It's not just "not okay," it's... *haram*," I said, my voice was shaky.

"I haven't even had a drink in a year, not since I met you."

I looked away. The tattoo, the *haram* relationship with his ex, the non-*halal* meals, And now, alcohol. *What else is there? Are these all signs that he's not the one for me? What am I doing with someone who lives like the laws of our religion don't apply to him?* My head throbbed with questions.

The air was still, and all that could be heard was the crackling of the firewood in the air as yellow gusts of fire dust enveloped in the air and flew further and further away from the fireplace into the dark sky. Ahmad took his eyes off me for the first time, signaled to the stand-by waiter who walked to our side and requested he took the teacups and dessert plates away. I looked down at my fingers and clasped my hands on my thigh, willing them to stop shaking. *Why am I shaking?* A slight breeze that brushed past us took the flame off one of the candles between us. I watched as the ghost of smoke swirled upwards and wondered, like the candle, if our flame had gone away, if the relationship had now ended.

"Well, are you gonna say something?" his voice broke my thoughts, almost as if he could tell the direction my train of thought was taking.

Maybe we should take a break from this relationship, I thought as I steadied my hands and looked up at him. "I'd like to leave, please."

A forlorn look settled in his eyes, and he slowly blinked as he took in my words and the underlying meaning behind the formality of it. He chuckled sadly to himself, a dejected half-smile that didn't reach his eyes as he nodded slowly, agreeing to my request.

"Ready?" he asked, after collecting his card from the waiter, even though I was already standing up. He walked to the coat holder and was back shortly with our coats. He helped me into mine, draped his jacket over his left arm, and we walked towards the exit. He held the door open for me as we got into the empty elevator and pushed the L button for the lobby, his hands in his pockets as he leaned back. He looked up and his eyes caught mine. I looked away.

The gentle whir of the descending elevators started and I could feel his eyes piercing my skin. My eyes had run out of corners to look at and I mistakenly looked at him. The back of his head was slightly thumping on the elevator wall like he was deep in thought. Very lightly, but the thump-thump sound it made – especially without breaking eye contact –made the elevator seem too small for both of us. You were never really aware of how slow the gradual descent from floor to floor of elevators was until it was the last place you wanted to be.

"Fai'za, I..." The lights in the elevator suddenly went off. I felt a rumble shake the floor like a mini-quake, and I lost my balance. Ahmad was swiftly by my side, his hands on my waist, stopping me from falling. I felt him reach for my hands in the dark, steadying me back to my feet. "Are you okay?" His voice was just above my face.

"What – what's happening?" my voice sounded breathless in the darkness.

"Hold on," he was still holding onto me. I heard him rummage through something. His pockets, maybe? His jacket? I had no idea. The screen of his phone lit up; he'd turned on the flashlight, and the brightness was now brightening the dark elevator, casting tall shadows and adding to the already eerie feel. He hit the elevator's emergency button, and a call started ringing from our end. It felt like forever as I listened to the ringing continue. I was beginning to feel lightheaded and my head was beginning to ache with an impending migraine.

"Hello, what's your emergency?" a female voice answered.

"Hey, we're stuck in an elevator," Ahmad said.

"Would that be elevator B at the Hilton?" the voice asked.

Ahmad used the light from his phone to check the buttons on the panel; there was a letter B in yellow at the bottom. "I believe it is," he answered calmly.

"The front desk informed us just before your call came in and we've already dispatched a technician," the voice said. There was a break as static broke the conversation. "Are you alone, sir? Are there children, seniors or persons with mobility needs with you? "

"There're two of us here," he said, looking back at me then back at the speakers. "How long until the technician gets here?"

"Should be a few minutes. An hour at most to get you out –" more static, then the line went dead.

An hour? I brought out my phone from my clutch; there were zero service bars. "There's no service," I said. *How long will we be stuck here? What if we run out of oxygen*? I thought anxiously as my head began to pound.

"Hey, are you okay?" he asked. I looked up to see his eyes peering into mine, filled with concern. "You're sweating."

"I am?" I touched my forehead and my palms were immediately wet. "My head hurts," I said, as I swayed slightly. I couldn't keep my balance.

"Hey, hey…" he caught me again. "*Zauna.* Sit down," he instructed gently as he lowered me to the ground. He unbuttoned his top buttons, rolled up his sleeves and sat next to me.

"Are you claustrophobic?" he asked as he set his phone on the floor between us, the shadows that the luminescent light cast were now above us.

"What?" I asked. The elevator seemed to be spinning slightly.

"Fear of enclosed spaces," he explained. There was a concerned look on his face.

"I *know* what claustrophobic means," I snapped. I felt nauseated. "I guess this is where we find out."

"Take deep breaths. It helps," he urged. "You're still sweating." He looked down at my sweater. Underneath it, beads of sweat rolled down my neck to my chest.

"You were gonna say something before the elevator got stuck," I tried to distract myself from the burning sensation I was feeling.

His white shirt was damp now and was sticking to his skin, his biceps rippled underneath. As he unbuttoned the remaining buttons, I watched as a bead of sweat rolled down his face. He reached out and touched my head with his hand. "You're burning up."

"I think I'm gonna throw up," I could barely breathe.

"That's okay," he answered unfazed, "but you need to get out of that sweater."

"What? No way!" I panicked.

"You might pass out," he said as a matter of factly.

He was right. There was a stiffness all around me, it felt like a third person. I could barely keep my eyes open, but I couldn't take off the sweater. All I had underneath was the slip dress with its thin spaghetti straps. It showed a lot of cleavage and my bare arms. How could I keep sitting in an elevator half-naked with a man? What if the technician was male? I saw his lips moving, but I couldn't make sense of the words coming out. I shook my head like I was trying to get past the disorientation. *Ahmad, I can't breathe.* My head fell first and I felt myself falling down a bottomless pit, yet it felt like I was drowning in water with something slowly filling up my lungs. Ahmad. The last thing I saw was his face as the darkness consumed me.

* * *

The thing about dreams is that you find minor details around the peripheral that try to clue you in that the simulation is not accurate. Still, your consciousness chooses to ignore it so that you can fall deeper into slumber. "Wake up, baby," the voice came from a distance, but I knew we were in the same room. I thought it was Ahmad's room but it didn't look like it; the walls were devoid of their art, the walls were repainted to white and the interior decor was remodeled. The room was narrower than I remembered.

It was unrecognizable. As I took in the room, I felt his lips on mine. That's when I knew it had to be a dream. Wake up. Wake up.

I opened my eyes to the blinking lights – red, blue and white. They were all so bright, too bright. I closed my eyes again. What on earth was that sound? It felt like needles were piercing my eardrums repeatedly, non-stop. I opened my eyes and looked around me. My neck hurt as I moved. I was lying, moving on a stretcher. I lifted my hand and saw a blood pressure cuff around my arm. *Am I in an ambulance?* I thought as I tried to get up.

"Ma'am, I'm gonna need you to lay back down, please," a man in a dark blue uniform said, his strong hands restraining me. He was wearing medical gloves and a name tag. I squinted as hard as I could, trying to make sense of the letters, but nothing made sense. My eyes hurt. My head hurt. Everything hurt.

"Ahmad?" I groaned.

"Baby, you're awake," he was by my side. I felt someone gently hold my left hand.

"Ahmad?" I croaked again.

His right hand went over his eyes: "Fucking hell! You scared me." I had never seen him look so out of it. "How are you feeling?"

"Wha – what happened?" I asked, wincing as the ambulance went over a bump and squinting my eyes because the overhead lights were too bright. It felt like I was staring directly at the sun. He noticed, and he put his hands above my face, shielding my eyes from the bright lights. I looked at him. He looked restless like the whole world had tipped over and fallen on him.

"You passed out," he said, his fingers gently squeezing mine. I could remember now – the stalled elevator, the heat, the darkness, the migraine. He shook his head, "you were burning up, and then you just –"

"How long was I out?"

"I don't know. It felt like forever," his hands went through his hair. "You weren't responding. I –" he swallowed. "How are you feeling?"

"Well, I guess I'm claustrophobic," I managed a smile as I looked up. He smiled back.

Behind us, one of the paramedics was announcing "10-16" on the radio.

We heard static, then a muffled response from the other end. A few seconds later, the ambulance stopped.

"Can we leave now? I feel much better," I said as the doors opened.

"As soon as a doctor makes sure everything is okay," the younger paramedic answered.

"This is so unnecessary." But I was too weak to fight it.

"It's okay. I'm right here." Ahmad said as we all descended from the ambulance.

I was beginning to feel lightheaded again as I was wheeled into the hospital with Ahmad by my side. It was a busy day, and there were many voices around and over me. I heard colours and code numbers called over the intercom. And if I didn't feel so ill, I would have found it interesting. A middle-aged female nurse told Ahmad to wait behind to fill out a form, and he reassured me that he would be with me in a minute. I nodded as two other nurses transported me to a private room.

"The EMTs sent off your bloodwork, the doctor should be receiving the results soon, and she'll be with you shortly," one of them said. I nodded. Under different circumstances, I would have told her she had kind eyes, one of the most beautiful pairs I'd seen.

Ahmad walked in holding my shoes, clutch and his jacket. He dropped them on the chair and came to stand by my side. "I gave them your insurance card from your wallet and filled out a form. Do you need anything?"

I shook my head.

"Fay-zaa, am I saying that right?" That was the nurse.

"Fa'iza," Ahmad corrected.

"Thank you," she replied like she was used to being corrected over names. "I'm just going to ask you some questions," she had a tablet in her hand that she tapped as she spoke.

"Any known allergies?"

I shook my head.

"Any drug use, recreational or prescribed?"

I shook my head again, and she tapped on her screen.

"Have you had any alcohol in the last 24 hours?"

I shook my head.

"Thank you," she said as she took my blood pressure reading.

"Do you need anything?"

"I'm not hungry," I said.

"Okay, how about water, juice, tea –" he covered my legs with a blanket as he spoke, carefully tucking the edges around me. "Water, please."

"Be right back." He took his jacket and walked out of the room, turning to look at me as he closed the door.

I smiled weakly. He is caring, kind, sweet – perfect, even. But Islamically...

"We weren't able to reach your emergency contact, but we left a voicemail," I heard the nurse's cheery voice. I looked up at her.

As if on cue, I heard an unmistakable voice from the hallway – the perfect enunciation of English words and the flawless vocalization of my Arabic name. "I'm Fa'iza Mohammad's guardian. Which room is she in?" My heart paused for a fraction of a millisecond, and I had to remind myself, "I'm not doing anything wrong, I'm not doing anything wrong." The cedarwood and jasmine notes of her fragrance wafted into the room as she did and I smiled weakly; there was something about her scent that just completed her magical aura, her gait as she walked into the room. Aunty Mami.

"Fai'za *am*," she walked towards me. I tried to sit up, but she gently urged me back to the sleeping position I was so tired of, "*kwanta, kwanta*. Lay down, lay down." She briefly exchanged greetings with the nurse, before returning her attention to me. "What happened?" she touched my forehead, keeping her hands there as she recited a *dua*, prayer. This was exactly what Umma would do. "I was at the Iranian ambassadors' send forth party when I got the message and came here immediately."

I tried to speak, but my voice failed me.

She grabbed the chart at the foot of the bed and began to read. "Fainted? *SubhanAllah! Allah ya tsare*," she murmured, her face filled with worry.

The doors opened as a short woman in a doctor's coat entered the room. "How's the patient doing?" she asked. "That was a bit of a scare, ey?"

"What's going on, doctor?" Aunty Mami asked.

"The blood report just came in. Apart from the low blood pressure and the vitamin B deficiency, there's nothing to be worried about," she said.

Aunty Mami was nodding as she listened to the doctor, asking questions about what caused everything, what medications I needed to be on, if another bloodwork was necessary, how to best manage the low blood pressure. The doctor answered all her questions calmly and when she was satisfied, she thanked the doctor, who then left to sign my release forms.

We were alone for just a moment when doors opened again. Ahmad was back with a bottle of water and something else in his other hand. His jacket was back on, and he was looking at the nutrient sheet on the drink when he walked into the room, "Bae, I got you Gatorade and some wa –" his voice trailed off as he looked up and saw his mother standing next to me.

"Ahmad?" There was a surprise look on her face as his eyes moved from her face to mine.

There was no word to describe the emotion I was feeling, and if there was, it was definitely not in my vocabulary because I didn't know how to articulate it. I had never felt this way before – a weird combination of "God, please-let-the-ground-open up-and-swallow-me" and "no, this-is-not-what-you-think-it-is" but then it was what she probably thought it was.

"Mom?" Ahmad walked towards her.

The smile on her face was radiant as he kissed her on her cheek, and then he looked back at me, unsure of what to do next. He scratched his hair and dropped the Gatorade on the table next to me. "Oh, did they call you when they couldn't reach me?" she asked, watching him unscrew the cap from the bottled water.

"Who's *they*?" he asked, passing the unopened bottle of water to me. I shook my head.

"The ambulance," she explained, "I was at Yazdi's send forth and didn't hear my phone ring. You know how these events go – speeches and speeches and speeches."

"The Iranian diplomat?" he asked. "The one from the news?"

"That's him," she nodded and then turned to look at me, "Fa'iza *am*, drink some water. You need it." She took the bottle from him and helped me sit up, the hospital pillow serving as a wedge for my back. I couldn't say no, so I sat up and took a sip. She looked back at Ahmad. "Thank God they reached you when I didn't answer my phone."

I coughed. The water was too cold. I looked at Ahmad and noticed a frown forming on his forehead as he tried to make sense of his mom's confusion. "Oh no, nobody called me," he said, leaning back on the wall and folding his arms.

"Oh?" she asked, looking from me to him.

"I was, *um...*" he cleared his throat, "we were together when she – when it happened."

Is it just me, or is this hospital room cold? I thought. I could see something hover briefly over her face but couldn't quite tell what it was because her attention was now back to Ahmad.

"And where was that?" she asked quietly.

Please don't say it. Don't say the Hilton, I prayed silently. There was no way we could explain our way out of that, and I would die.

He looked at me, then back at his mom. "We were at a restaurant," he answered. *Thank God!* Not a lie. We were having dinner – that part was true. And Hilton had a restaurant, so it wasn't a lie.

"Oh," her reply seemed loaded as she looked at me and then back to him. I wondered what she thought about us having dinner together. Alone.

"Are you done?" I didn't realize Ahmad was talking to me until he added softly, "Fa'iza?" I looked up, still clutching the bottle of water in my hand. "Are you done?" he gestured toward my hands. I nodded, and he took the bottle from me, screwed the cap back on and set it on the table with the Gatorade.

She quietly observed the exchange. You could see from her face that she had a thousand and one questions running through her mind and was processing them when the door opened.

"Fa'ee?" We all looked up and there she was – a sight for sore eyes. Afreen's presence took away the awkwardness in the quiet room. She greeted her mom and then, "why is it so hard to find parking here? I got here about 5 minutes after mom called, but I kept going round and round." She squeezed me in a tight embrace, and her voice became a whisper:"what happened?" I had never been so relieved to see her.

"Low blood pressure," Aunty Mami answered. I was still finding it hard to meet her eyes because I was unsure what she thought of the... situation. But her demeanor hadn't changed; her tone and attitude were still the same as they were when she came in.

"You study too much. Don't be scaring us like this," Afreen hugged me again, then she looked up at her older brother. "How did you find parking quickly?"

"I came with the ambulance," he said.

"Oh, I see," Afreen stepped back, properly accessing the situation she had walked in on, a faint glimmer of a smile dancing around her lips and mischievous eyes.

The doctor returned with some papers, "Ah, full house. I've got your prescription here and a requisition for another bloodwork in two weeks." She was talking to me, but Ahmad took the papers from her. His mom noticed this and kept an emotionless expression as she adjusted her glasses quietly.

After a few minutes, we were all set to leave the hospital. "Fa'iza, you're coming home with me," Aunty Mami said.

"Do you need anything from the residence? I can go get it for you," Afreen offered.

"No, I left some things at the house the last time I came over. I should be fine," I answered.

"Ahmad, are you going to get the prescription?" Aunty Mami asked.

I looked up at him. I couldn't believe it, but it was hard to miss the disappointment on his face. Did he think he would be the one to drive me? Even I knew that was impossible and being alone in the car with Aunt Mami was the last thing I wanted right now, but luckily Afreen came to the rescue the second time in one night. "Mom, I'll come with you, too," she said as she threw her car keys to Ahmad, who caught them expertly. "I'm assuming you need a ride to the pharmacy since your car isn't here."

That's right. His car was still at the underground parkade of the Hilton downtown.

We went our separate ways. The ride back to the ambassadors' residence was unexpectedly quiet. Even Afreen was quiet in the car, which was a surprise. By 10:45 pm, I was tucked into Afreen's cozy bed instead of the guest room I usually stayed in.

I was already half-asleep when Aunty Mami came into the room. "Fa'iza?" she called out gently.

"She's asleep," Afreen answered from the bathroom even before I could even answer.

I heard her drop something on the bedside table next to me. "I brought *zam-zam* water for her. She should drink some." Her footsteps were going away.

"Goodnight, mummy," Afreen called out.

"*Sai da safe.* Goodnight," Aunty Mami replied as Afreen closed the bathroom door. Further away, I heard the slight jingle of keys.

"Mom?" I heard the unmistakable baritone of Ahmad's voice. They met at the door.

"Did you get them?"

"Yes," I heard the shuffle of some bags.

"She's asleep, I'll give them to her in the morning," more shuffle, then "come, we need to talk." She sounded stern, very unlike her interactions with him. The door to the room closed and the conversation continued in the hallway outside. It was hard to hear except for a few sentences here and there.

"Ahmad, what exactly is going on –" something incomprehensible, "How –?"

"Mom –" Ahmad's voice started before it was interrupted.

"You know this girl was entrusted in *my* care," she sounded worried. Not upset, not disappointed – worried. I lost the conversation for a few seconds, then: "You know I don't interfere in your life but this one –" I wish I could hear the remaining conversation. Unfortunately, the sound of Afreen's shower drowned their voices as they moved further away.

Chapter 15

The following morning, when Afreen woke me up to pray *Fajr,* the morning prayer, I saw messages from Ahmad sent after I'd gone to sleep: *I'm here if you need anything* and 27 minutes later, *Let me know how you're feeling.* After praying, I sat up in bed and read the Quran.

"*Ya jiki?* How are you feeling?" Afreen yawned from under the covers. She'd gone back to sleep after praying and was already dozing off again.

"I'm okay, alhamdulillah," I folded the hijab and got back under the covers with her. I replied to Ahmad: *I'm feeling better, thanks.*

I checked my notifications and saw that I'd missed calls from my mum, my dad and brothers. They must have heard about my little hospital visit. A reply from Ahmad came in as I was trying to figure out the time difference: *Can I come see you?*

I looked at the time. It was still very early. It might take him another 20 minutes to get here from downtown. *I should go say good morning to Aunt Mami before then,* I thought to myself as I typed: *sure.* As soon as I hit send, there was a knock on the door.

"Come in," Afreen answered, her voice was muffled by the pillow over her head.

Ahmad walked into the room in a white jallabiya and our eyes met immediately. He smiled at me as he pushed the door close. Afreen was awake now, and she sat up in bed and looked at her bedside clock as she scratched her eyes. "Good morning."

"Afreen," he walked to her vanity set and dropped her keys by her mirror. "I filled your tank, and the pressure on your front tires were off, so I pumped them."

"Thank you," she yawned. "Did you sleep here?"

"Yeah," he nodded and turned around, his eyes finding mine again.

"When last did you sleep here?" she started musing as she looked at me and then back at him, "*Hmm,* I wonder why?" she teased as she got up and went to the bathroom, making a big show of closing the door.

Ahmad moved closer to the bed, pulled out a chair and sat down. His eyes lingered on my hair and the v-neck of the fleece nightgown I was wearing. Instinctively I pulled it higher. "You look better," he observed.

"So, I looked like a mess yesterday?" Between falling unconscious, being lifted into an ambulance, and being transferred to a hospital bed, I was glad there was no mirror in sight at the hospital to etch that look in my memory.

"The prettiest mess there ever was," his eyes fell to the band-aid on my wrist from where the needle from the drip had been. He reached out as if to hold my hand, and then he stopped himself. I looked up at him and noticed that he wasn't smiling anymore.

"What is it?" There was something on his mind. Was it regarding the conversation with his mom the previous night?

"Fa'iza" he leaned closer towards me. I raised an eyebrow. "The whole alcohol thing," he stopped to gauge my expression. "I'm going to be honest with you, like I have always been. It started when I moved to the UK. It was honestly just a sip here and there."

I leaned back into the pillow, "still doesn't excuse it, though."

He nodded, "you're right. It doesn't."

The door to the bathroom opened, and Afreen walked to the bed, toothbrush in hand, to get her phone. I waited until the door closed and the faucet was turned on before I continued. "I just don't know what else to expect next."

"What's the worst thing you wouldn't accept?" he asked.

I thought about it for a moment, then replied, "honestly, I've always thought that alcohol was the deal-breaker."

His eyes pierced into mine, then I looked away. "Is there a but?" he asked.

I couldn't even look him into the eyes. I glanced up at the ceiling and sighed, "I couldn't even break up with you on the spot, like I thought I would."

He leaned closer to me, and his scent engulfed my senses. "Listen, I know this is all too much for you, okay?" He spoke slowly, "You probably hoped for an *ustaadh*, someone to teach and move you closer to religion. Then you got me instead and –"

"I never wanted an *ustaadh*." There was nothing wrong with a teacher, but it wasn't a huge criterion for me. I just wanted a normal Muslim – one who didn't touch women who weren't his *Mahram*, didn't know what alcohol tasted like and insisted that the kitchen used a different pan to make his meals at restaurants. Okay, maybe that last part was a bit too much.

"So, are we good?" The room was quiet.

I thought about it and sighed out loud for dramatics, "I don't know. I still have questions."

"Anything."

"How do I know that you're not gonna go back to these bad habits in the future?"

"You never have to worry about that," his eyes fell to my lips and back to my eyes. "I promise."

"Promise?"

"Promise."

"So, why didn't you go back downtown last night?" I asked nonchalantly.

"Because I wanted to be here when you woke up."

I'm definitely not making a mistake. He's the one, definitely the one, I thought to myself, as I felt a flutter of butterflies in my stomach.

Aunty Mami thought it was best to stay over at the house for another week, while I recuperated. Staying over at the ambassador's residence had huge perks – perks you didn't remember when you were away, like home-cooked meals, sleeping on something bigger than a twin-sized bed, breaking my Monday and Thursday fasts with something nice. With a letter from the doctor, I stayed home all week and attended lectures remotely. I received lecture notes from Ada and Sara and submitted my questions to the Professors' emails.

* * *

Afreen had been busy with her internship at the Mayor's office coming to an end, so she was out working for most of the day. When she was gone, my days started the same, with Aunt Mami asking me if I had taken my medication whenever I went upstairs to greet her. However, today was different. She was on the phone when I walked into her room. She smiled when I walked in in my pink hijab and motioned me to sit down on the bed next to her. There was a black and white picture of Afreen and Ahmad in a gold frame by her bedside and I stared at it when she spoke on the phone.

"You'll see us soon, *insha Allah*," she laughed into the phone.

They both looked so much like her. The only thing they got from their father seemed to be his height. Else, their noses, hair, complexion – it was all their mom. "She's here," Aunty Mami said into the phone, "she just came in." She handed me the phone.

"Hello?" I said into the phone.

"Hello. How are you? How are your online classes?"

"Umma, I'm fine, alhamdulillah. Everything's fine."

"When is your follow up appointment?" she asked, even though we'd spoken two or three times daily since I got home from the hospital.

"Tomorrow, insha Allah."

"Okay, let me know how that goes."

"*Insha Allah*. Talk to you later," I handed the phone back to Aunt Mami and heard them round up their phone call.

"Fa'iza, must you go back to your hostel tomorrow?" she asked afterwards.

I had to. As much as I loved staying over at the house, I was missing crucial evening study sessions and with the final exams approaching, I needed to get caught up before it was late. But I didn't say any of this; I just smiled as she spoke.

She looked at the slight bruise that the needle left on my wrist. "How's the hand?"

"It's fine, thank you," my voice sounded timid. The dynamics between us had somehow changed now that she knew that there was something between Ahmad and me.

She leaned down to open one of her bedside drawers and brought out a small box. "I got this, but the numbers on the face are too small. I won't be able to tell the time without glasses." She opened it and there was a two-toned Tissot wristwatch. "I think it would look nice on you," she passed the box to me.

"*Na gode*. Thank you, Aunty Mami," I said.

This wasn't just a gift from my mother's friend; it was a subtle stamp of approval. Our culture rarely used words to convey what actions could easily do to show approval or disapproval. She hadn't discussed Ahmad with me the entire week; she just based her actions toward me on her conversations with her son about me.

Chapter 16

I was wearing a white hoodie over black leggings, lying on Ahmad's bed, laptop propped open on a pillow. My textbook and study notes were sprawled open on the sheets as I answered multiple-choice review questions. My last exam for the semester was in less than 24 hours, and I was preparing for it by going over questions from previous exams.

"Did you do the quiz at the end of the book?" his voice broke into my thoughts. I looked up to see him taking off his black workout gloves. He was still in his gym clothes – a sleeveless black *Under Armour* shirt and black joggers. Ever since I resumed my visits to his apartment – mainly because the Wi-Fi at the Residence started going haywire – I noticed that he went to the gym a lot. A part of me believed he went there to give me privacy and not to be a distraction since I was studying for my exams.

I looked up at him. There was a damp patch of sweat on his shirt that highlighted his biceps. "Yeah, I finished it this morning." We were talking about a book Ahmad had given me earlier in the week. It was called *The Five Love Languages*. The author of the book said that everyone had a language they would prefer partners to express their love to them.

"And..?" he asked, removing his shirt and throwing it in the laundry basket with his socks. "What are your top two love languages?"

I took my eyes off his six-packs. "According to the book, Acts of Service and Gift giving." According to the quiz, I would like my partner to do things for me without my asking and to buy me gifts. Looking back at times I'd appreciated people, it usually had to do with their thoughtfulness, the little things they did to help out like Ahmad finding *Inn From the Cold* and buying that Brandon Sanderson book I'd been looking for.

"Guessed as much," he said. "But do you think it's accurate?"

"Yeah, I think so," I looked up at him. "What are yours?"

He went into the bathroom and called out, "can you guess?"

"Don't do that," I warned jokingly.

"Do what?" he poked his head around the door. He was smiling.

"Try to see what I've learnt about you."

"Okay," he said, and I heard him turn on the shower. This was the second time he was doing that – taking a shower with the door half-open. If I craned my neck hard enough, I would be able to see him in the shower – naked. I didn't, of course, although a part of me started wondering what he looked like in the shower. I focused my attention back on the ten questions I had left and had just finished calculating my final score when he came back to the room wearing a white T-shirt and grey slacks.

"Can you pass my phone?" he asked. I took the phone from under the pillow next to him and passed it to him. He quickly replied to his messages and moved two square pillows to the opposite side of the bed, and propped himself on them, putting as much space between us as possible.

"Mine are Physical Touch and Quality Time," he clasped both hands behind his head as he looked at me. *An interesting combination,* I thought to myself, wondering if gender played a role in Love languages. *Are there certain things that more men than women gravitate towards? Physical touch, maybe?*

"No comment?" he asked, ignoring the new notification on his phone.

"So, do you think it's accurate?"

"Oh, absolutely," he said. "Physical intimacy is a big thing for me, and spending time with the woman I love is a priority," he paused as he watched me take it in. "That's why I always make plans for us to hang out."

"So, you would appreciate it if I would do that for you as well? Plan things for us to do, I mean," I offered, echoing some sentiments from the book as

I closed my laptop.

"Exactly," he said. "How important do you think sex is in a relationship? Or in our case, after marriage?"

"*Um*, maybe a seven," I answered. Seven just sounded like a safe number. I started closing my books and putting them in my bag. He didn't know this, but I timed my visits; it has helped us so far.

"Out of ten?" He watched as I folded my charger. I nodded as I got off the bed.

"Interesting," he reluctantly got up, stretching as he did.

"What's your biggest fear about marriage?" I had mine, but I wanted to see where his head was at.

He exhaled as we left the room and made our way to the front door, thinking about it. "It's gotta be watching the one I love lose herself in being society's expectation of a wife, or losing herself in motherhood." As I wore my shoes, I thought about how our conversations revolved around marriage and kids these days. Three days prior he'd asked if I would prefer to live in Nigeria or Canada after marriage.

On the way back to the rez that day, we stopped at Tim Hortons for iced cappuccinos and I asked him about his conversation with his mum the night I came back from the hospital. He looked at me with a slight smile on his lips. "What do you wanna know?"

Everything. I shrugged.

"I think when it comes to you, she forgets that *I'm* her son," he took a sip from his cup. "She asked what my intentions were with you. I would expect that question from my prospective in-laws, not my mother," he paused. "Have you told your mum about us?"

I shook my head.

"So, when she asks what's going on between us, what would you say?"

I opened my mouth and closed it again. I couldn't imagine the answer I would give Umma.

We got to the rez, he parked the car, laid back in his chair and turned to give me his full attention. "I told my mom that I'm in love with you," he paused, "but you don't have a word for us for when your mom asks?"

"It's not the same." I wish I could explain it to him.

"What isn't?"

Our families, I wanted to say. Mine was more traditional, so things were done according to the culture and tradition. I tried to explain: "You and your mom are super close –" and Westernized, compared them to my family. They kissed, he took her out for brunches, and she met him for coffee at her favorite café. "Babe, it's just different."

"Then make me understand," he genuinely did not understand.

"Wait, did you really say you were in love?" I couldn't stop the grin that had formed on my face.

He shook his head like he was wondering why I would even question it. "I fast with you on Mondays and Thursdays; I resist the urge to hold you every time I see you; I respect your boundaries, even though it's the hardest thing I've ever had to do... How haven't you figured it out already?"

I smiled at him. I could kiss him. "Us not making out is the hardest thing you've done?" I teased coyly. I took a sip of my drink as his eyes narrowed.

"You don't even wanna know. On some nights, I can't sleep until I rub one out," he laughed.

"What does that mean?"

"You're joking, right?"

"No, I really don't know what you mean," I answered, and his face collapsed into a laugh.

"Goodness, I'm such a bad influence on you." He watched me bring out my phone and google the phrase. Understanding dawned on my face, highly evident with the glow of light from my phone.

"Masturbation?" I asked as I awkwardly tucked my phone back into my pocket.

"Are you gonna tell me that it's *haram?*"

I opened my mouth, but before I could say yes, he cut me short: "Pretty sure I'm not going to hell because I chose to masturbate instead of having sex."

Chapter 17

I glanced at the green and yellow LED "Arrivals" display screen at Heathrow Airport. Airports always felt the same – with airport security that tried to blend in with travelers and the ones that were visible in uniform, the cool air in the terminals, the blur of colours as people wheeled their luggage away, always in a hurry not to miss their various flights even the announcements about boarding flights in the background always felt the same.

I pulled out my phone to read the message I'd gotten from my brother, Abubakar, earlier in the day: *BA 112.* I had been tracking his flight since mine landed a few hour hours prior. I looked up at the screen and almost immediately located the flight, which was expected in 3 minutes. I paced around the terminal again, reminding myself that it would not make time go by faster. I was so excited to see him; I hadn't seen him in a long time. My phone vibrated, and I smiled at our inside joke as I picked up the call.

"Bae," the voice at the other end said. Bae had replaced hello for us when we picked each other's calls. "Has his flight arrived?"

"Yes, bae?" I answered. "No, there was a slight delay, or something. I'm already at the gate, so I'll just wait until he comes through." I had double-checked multiple times to ensure that I had the correct gate numbers. More people had begun to walk past me; it looked like the passengers from the flight had gotten off the flight.

"How many more hours till you start boarding for Abuja?" Ahmad asked.

"Two more hours," I answered. "Oh, I see him!" I shouted excitedly as I noticed Abubakar coming through the double doors, wheeling his brown hand luggage.

"Alright then, I'll call you before you guys take off," Ahmad said, excusing himself over the phone.

"Okay, talk soon," I ended the call. I started making my way towards Abubakar, giggling as I watched him scan the terminal, no doubt looking for me. I laughed as I realized he was wearing the beige *Thomas Pink* wool sweater I'd gotten him on his birthday. Abubakar was sentimental like that, and I loved him for it. We were barely five feet apart, and he was looking past me and had still not noticed me. I realized he wasn't wearing his glasses and might probably not see me if I didn't reveal myself to him. "Where are your glasses?" I called out to him.

His head whirled in the direction of my voice, and his eyes lit up. "Fa'iza!" he reached out for me, holding me at arm's length to look at me properly before we embraced. He smelled like home, like his room back in Abuja – Tom Ford's *Tobacco Vanille.*

"Have you lost weight?" he asked as he looked at me with so much fondness, the slight affection before the teasing took over. "It better be the studying." It was always a battle of wits with Abubakar, and they were sometimes brutal. I had to learn to keep up at an early age.

"Where are your glasses?" I repeated. I had never seen him without them. He looked different, his beard had also grown out since I saw him, but I knew that from his various WhatsApp display pictures over the months.

"I got LASIK over the summer," he answered as he fished out the phone from his pocket. I rolled my eyes; he was still the only member of our family who was anti-Apple products and a huge advocate for Android phones, specifically Samsungs.

"Eye surgery? It clearly didn't work because you couldn't see me," I teased, laughing.

"You still think you're funny?" he laughed as he put his phone to his ear. "I'm calling Abba to let him know I found you." Whenever we were traveling, we called home frequently to update them. In the unlikely event that we missed a connection, our dad's secretary was always quick to book us an alternate flight.

"Or I found you?" I wasn't going to stop teasing him. It was almost like that was how we expressed love among ourselves. I was closer to Abubakar than Ya Amin, who was far removed in age and character from me. Abubakar was just three years older than me, and we got along more. Well, sometimes.

"Assalamu alaikum," his voice took on a somber tone. "Abba *ina wuni*. Good evening." We stopped walking to give Abba's phone call the attention it warranted. It wasn't planned; it was a reverence that couldn't be explained. "*Alhamdulillah*," I heard him say, then "*Insha Allah*." Silence. "Amin, Abba," More silence. "*Insha Allah*." He looked at me and added: "We're together, we'll be boarding for Abuja soon, *Insha Allah*."

My phone started ringing, and I picked up immediately: "Hello, Umma."

"Fa'iza, has he arrived yet?"

"They just landed. We're together right now."

"Okay, that's good." Her relief was evident from her sigh. "Have you called Abba?"

"Abubakar is on the phone with him. When he's done, I'll talk to him." As I said goodbye, I heard her telling someone in the background, "They're already at Heathrow," before the call ended. It was probably an aunt or the cook. Days like this were usually busy in our household. With both of us returning after being away in North America for so long, the drivers were on standby for when they would be required to head to the airport, and the cooks stayed back longer than usual just in case there was a delay and plans had to be changed.

We prayed and bought a few books before our flight to Abuja. Then we talked about school and my courses as we bonded over Chai lattes and lemon poppy seed slices at Starbucks. My mind immediately went to Ahmad and our Tim Horton's drinks as I realized I hadn't had Starbucks in a while. When we were boarding, I sent him a message to inform him: *Boarding now*.

His call came in almost immediately. I glanced at my brother, who was busy on his phone. I answered as I watched Abubakar switch his American passport for his Nigerian one as we boarded.

"Bae?" It was very early morning in Toronto and he'd been up all night, tracking my flights and talking to me in-between connections.

"Hi." It was hard to talk to him with a straight face; just hearing his voice in my ear made me smile.

"Last leg?"

"Yup."

I heard him chuckle over the phone, and I was sure it was because of my monosyllabic answers. "I'm sure you are excited."

"Very," I said as I located my seat and sat down while Abubakar was putting our hand luggage in the overhead compartment.

"I'll see you in a few weeks," he said, and the flutter in my chest returned. They were coming for a visit before the New Year. It was just supposed to be his dad, Aunty Mami, and Afreen, but Ahmad decided that he had a few things to do in Abuja, so he booked a ticket to come with them. "We'll talk when you land."

"Alright, *insha Allah*."

"Have a safe flight," he said.

"Thank you," I ended the call and put the phone on airplane mode. I could feel Abubakar looking at me suspiciously as he took his seat next to me, probably wondering who I was talking to that I could barely pronounce my words out loud. I looked away from him, afraid he might be able to read the expression on my face.

* * *

It was safe to say I had finally gotten over my jet lag. I'd been back a few weeks now and in that time, I had visited to Kaduna; attended an Islamic lecture organized by some Muslim sisters I found on Instagram; went on a movie and ice cream date with my cousin, Aisha Batagarawa, who was getting married in a few months; attended two weddings and was also getting over a horrible bout of malaria. To recap, I had been quite busy in Nigeria.

In front of me, in the living room where I had spent the better part of the day, the television was playing soundlessly. It was a Netflix movie starring Genevieve Nnaji, my favorite Nigerian actress. In the movie, she was trying to save her father's company from a merger, and she traveled to Kano, the city where I was born. I had watched the movie a few times, so I was not paying much attention to it this time. I was lying down on the sofa, almost done reading a book from Ahmad's library, *Voices of Liberation* by Steve Biko, which I started three days ago. In the distance, the sound of the generator was like a soundboard for every other thing going on in the compound. I was reading with the white noise in the background when the voices of Ya Amin and Abubakar came over the loudspeakers from the masjid at the entrance of the house as they led men in prayer: *Allahu Akbar. Allahu Akbar. Sami'a Allahu liman hamidah. Rabbana wa laka al-hamd.*

Even though I was not praying, I was absentmindedly echoing their words in my mind. In Canada, no mosque used a loudspeaker that could be heard out on the street; the call to prayer was a pop-up notification from a phone app. I had missed this.

The door slowly opened as soon as the evening prayer ended with *"Assalamu alaikum warah'matullah. Assalamu alaikum warah'matullah"*. I looked up to see the maid pushing in the trolley with food warmers. She muttered salam under her breath and set the table for three with chilled bottles of water in the middle.

"Hmm," she started. I chuckled silently to myself because she didn't know how to address me since I stopped her from calling me 'Aunty Fa'iza'. I was nobody's aunt. Besides, she was about my age, maybe even older. Still, she never called me by my name. Now, whenever she had something to tell me, it started with an unsure, 'hmm.' *"Hmm,"* she said again, "Hajiya *na kiran ki*. Hajiya's calling you." She was one of the only people who referred to Umma as Hajiya and Abba as Alhaji.

"Tana daki?" I asked if she was in her room. A rhetorical question, by all

means. It was Maghrib; of course, my mother would be in her room. After the evening prayer, she would join Abba in the dining room in his section, and they would eat dinner together and then watch the news. It had been their routine for as long as I could remember. When he wasn't in town, she would eat alone in her section, and I would sometimes keep her company.

"Yes," she answered.

I got up from the position I'd been laying in for the past hour, wincing at the slight period cramp and went to the antique solid wood dining table and the aroma of dinner wafted towards me.

"Atine, what did the cook make?" I asked, even though I was already opening one of the food warmers.

She looked up from the fridge she was restocking with juice and more water, "Fried rice." The biggest warmer had fried rice, the carrots, peas and diced liver adding color to it. Left to me, there would be a strict rule against liver in fried rice but since all my attempts at enforcing that rule in my father's house had failed, I couldn't wait to enforce it in my own marital home.

"No plantain?" I asked, looking over the coleslaw.

"There's pepper soup."

I opened the next food warmer with chicken pepper soup. *That'll be my dinner*, I thought.

I wore my Aldo slippers at the door and went out of the children's living room, past the archway that connected all three sections of the main house and walked into Umma's section. The scent of *turaren wuta* burning had changed to *bakhoor*. The incense from bakhoor was richer and more fragrant than regular *turaren wuta*. I followed the light at the end of the hallway as I moved through her recently redecorated living room and pushed the door to her room open. "Assalamu alaikum," I called out. She was on her maroon praying mat in a light green hijab, her tasbeeh forming two uniform circles in front of her, untouched. She had both hands in front of her face as she supplicated.

Outside her window, I could see the cooks cleaning up the kitchen in the inner section of the house as they prepped for tomorrow morning's breakfast. *Masa,* if I could guess correctly from the number of covered containers I guessed were fermenting the rice batter. As I waited for her to acknowledge my presence, I busied myself by loosening the ties from her tasseled bedroom drapes, letting the pleats fall and block out the moonlight. I turned around to look at her just as she rubbed her hands together and rubbed her face and tapped her chest – a prayer ritual.

"*Allah shi karba,*" I offered. May your prayers be answered.

"Ameeeeeen," she dragged out the word as she stretched her legs in front of her. "Mami called me today, and we spoke for a long time."

I tried to keep my demeanor as neutral as possible even though since Ahmad and I discussed it last week, I had gone through varying emotions: excitement, panic, more excitement, uncertainty and back to excitement.

She continued, her voice soft and calm as if we were not about to discuss something as hefty as my future. "They're coming over tomorrow," she paused, "all of them – including Ahmad." She paused a little after saying Ahmad as if she was trying to read my facial expression.

I nodded. It wasn't news to me. Ahmad had told me that once his mother told his dad about our relationship, his elated father decided it was about time for both families to be bonded by something stronger than decades of friendship. It was time to finally become family, something they had joked about over the years.

"Apparently, there's an important discussion bringing them from Canada," she continued. *I'm the matter they would discuss,* I thought to myself. Our language and culture had an interesting way of putting things across – very subtly, like in everything we did. Umma's word choices in this conversation were very few, while meaning a lot. I listened very closely. "When they leave tomorrow, Abba would want to talk to you; *ya ji daga bakin ki ko kina da masaniya akan maganan da ta kawo su*; to hear from your own mouth what you think about the important matter they came to discuss."

My consent. Our religion insisted on my consent in matters like this. I nodded again.

She switched to English with uncalculated ease, "so you better have your answer ready. You know your father won't decide until he hears what you have to say."

"*Toh*, Umma. Okay," I said finally. There has always been this chasm of formality between my mother and I. Sometimes, I wondered if this unbreachable distance between us was due to the complications she'd experienced at my birth. I knew she loved me but there was a certain aloofness I felt that seemed absent in her relationship with my brothers. I used to think it was in my head, but Hajiya Uwani had noticed it too. I could still remember her high-pitched voice from a few years ago: "*Ko dan ba ita ta shayar da ke ba*? Is it because she did not breastfeed you?" and she laughed it off as a joke. It seemed like a ridiculous conclusion then because until she mentioned it, I had no idea I was not breastfed by my mother.

"Kawu Ibrahim is going to be here too," she said, "*Allah ya zabi mafi alheri*. May God choose the best outcome." Kawu Ibrahim was my uncle.

"Oh, they are back from Zaria already?" I asked to keep the conversation going.

By the time I returned to the living room in our section, my brothers were in a loud argument about football with two of my cousins. The empty plates of food on the dining table and the carpet by the sofa indicated how much energy they still had to burn. I grabbed a ladle and filled a bowl with some peppersoup. Just then, my phone started ringing, and I headed off to my room with my bowl in one hand to answer. Evening calls had become routine since I got back home. After *isha*, our nighttime calls lasted for hours before we said goodnight and went to bed. We hadn't seen each other since he took me to the airport and it had been weeks.

The next day, with less than an hour to their visiting time, I found myself checking my reflection in the mirror for the umpteenth time. None of my features had changed since I checked two minutes earlier. Yet, I checked again. Like what exactly was this visit? What would it signify? Ahmad said I was overthinking everything. In his words, everything would happen organically. *Organically?* I'd scoffed. With my parents, everything was *Qadr*. Predestined. The pink and light blue atamfa with three-quarter sleeves and a slim-fitted half-pleat skirt looked good on me. I had gone to the salon over the weekend; my hair was in a bun covered with a light blue veil. The only pieces of jewellery I wore apart from my earrings were the wristwatch Aunty Mami gave me and the Milan bracelet. Reading a book right now was impossible. The book I had started the previous night laid unattended on my bed. The television could not keep my attention long enough either. I made my way across the hallway to Abubakar's room and as soon as I closed the door behind me, he came out of his closet, fastening silver cuff links to his blue kaftan – a deviation from yesterday's jeans and a T-shirt, and it wasn't even Friday.

"Come onnnnnn," I started begging almost immediately. This conversation had been ongoing in bits and pieces since morning.

"Not happening," he shook his head. He was stubborn but I knew that if I navigated this carefully, he would come around. He took the remote from the console and scrolled through the television guide.

"I would do the same for you," I insisted.

"I would never need you to eavesdrop for me," he dropped the remote and walked towards the door.

"You don't know that, though," I stepped in front of him, blocking his way. I only needed a few seconds to make my case. "And it's not even eavesdropping. All you have to do is pick up my call and return your phone to your pocket. I'll do the rest." I could tell he was already cracking by the slight smile that was forming on his lips.

"Is this how you intend to practice law, by getting illegally sourced evidence?"

"Evidence is evidence. And if it's not being presented in court as an exhibit, there are no rules," I opened the door, and he walked through. "Besides, how good is a Samsung's microphone, really?" My tactic had now left coercion, bordering closely on reverse psychology.

"None of your business, Dean's list," his lips pulled into a smile as he referred to my honor roll status from University and I rolled my eyes.

We were in the living room now, the long drapes that hung over the windows had been pulled apart to allow sunlight in, giving us a clear view of the compound and just then, we saw two black Range Rovers pulling up into the compound. They were here. The cars pulled up slowly as they drove past the window we were looking through and parked by the house's main entrance, the one that led into Abba's living room. He normally entertained his guests and government officials who came for undocumented visits in that part of the house. A mobile police stepped out and opened the door and Ahmad and his dad came down. Ahmad was wearing a black kaftan and matching trousers, with a cap placed on his head. I held my breath as I looked. In the next car, Aunty Mami came out, and Afreen followed. I burst into a smile. They all looked regal, not that I expected any less. It was amazing how they fit right in; one wouldn't have guessed that most of their lives were spent outside Nigeria.

"Is that Afreen?" Abubakar asked. He had never met either of them.

I nodded as they all disappeared into the other side of the house as my parents welcomed them. The door to the living room opened, and we both turned around. It was Ya Amin in a white kaftan. He raised his eyebrows as he saw us by the window. He nodded to Abubakar and they walked towards Abba's section together.

"Do we have a deal?" I called out after him as a last resort, without giving away too much information, so that our other brother can remain clueless.

"Not a chance," he answered without looking back at me.

I didn't know if he was serious or not but I decided to try my luck anyway. When I could no longer see the back of their heads, I groaned and went back to my room, looked at my reflection again, then changed my veil into a pink one and made my way to Umma's living room. I wished my cousin Aisha were there to keep me company because the anxiety was nerve-wracking, but she was at a dress fitting with *Style-Temple*, and it would take hours before she arrived.

As I approached Umma's section, I could hear the quiet chatter between Aunty Mami and my mom. I parted the curtains and they both looked up. My worries disappeared immediately. After exchanging pleasantries and asking about their journey, Afreen and I left them to continue their discussions. From what I overheard, they were talking about other things, nothing to do with me.

"I love your room," Afreen stressed the word *love* as we entered my little haven. "Aww, that is soo cute," she gushed at a framed picture of her and me that we'd taken at six flags over the summer.

"Thank you."

"Are you anxious?" she asked, leaning back into the pillows and getting comfortable on my bed.

"I just don't know exactly what's going on, and I wish I did," I answered honestly. I knew that they would be with Abba until it was time to pray, then they would head out to the masjid and have lunch and when they got back. But everything would have been done by then. Whatever was happening at that moment was what was important.

"If only we could be flies on the wall," she played with a decorative pillow and then looked up to see my expression had changed. "What?"

"What if – hypothetically – we could hear what they were saying?"

Her eyes were suddenly filled with excitement as she considered the possibility and opportunity that eavesdropping could offer us. "Let's do it!" she said with a clap.

I took my phone from the dresser and joined her on the bed and she excitedly leaned closer as I dialed Abubakar's number. Afreen was quiet, and I whispered a prayer while listening as the line rang on the other end. We held our breaths.

Finally, the call was answered. We heard some shuffle and a slight thud as it got placed upside down on some hard surface. There was some static, and then my uncle's voice: " – *ita Fai'zan kenan, ko*? We're talking about Fa'iza, right?"

It worked! Afreen and I silently high-fived ourselves as we leaned closer to the phone that was on speaker, listening to the men's conversation.

"Being in school doesn't stop marriage – " my uncle again. "When the time is right –" a break in transmission, then the Ambassador completed: "It becomes a duty."

When my father spoke, his voice was the hardest to hear because he was always soft-spoken. We had to strain to hear him. I could only pick out a few words, "second year" and "after *umrah*." Then a round chorus of *Insha Allah*. We could barely make out the entirety of the exchange and it felt like forever before the call to prayer went off from the masjid, and the men dispersed to go and pray. I ended the call went back to the living room window to catch a glimpse of Ahmad, while Afreen went to perform ablution. He was walking to the masjid with Ya Amin, deep in conversation. I knew they were childhood friends who grew apart as the Ambassador's family moved from place to place on assignment, but they seem to have a lot to talk about now.

Afreen and I were eating lunch at the dining table when the door opened, and all three of them – Ya Amin, Abubakar, and Ahmad – walked in. Afreen exchanged pleasantries with my brothers and they spoke about the weather in Canada. My eyes met Ahmad's, who was deep in conversation with my brother and only acknowledged my presence with a slight nod.

They sat down in the living area and even though the television was playing loudly, no one gave any attention to it. I busied myself with my food, even though it had become tasteless to me now. My senses were now clouded by him – I stole glances at him, listened as he enthralled my brothers with European and Nigerian taxation rules for start-up businesses, and inhaled his *oud* from across the room. After they finally ate their lunch, my brothers excused themselves from the living room and left Ahmad with Afreen and me. Afreen had turned towards the television which had her complete attention, and I had Ahmad's.

Our eyes met again and he smiled. "Hi."

"Hiya," I answered awkwardly.

The change in environment made our interaction slightly different, mostly because this was my space – the house I grew up in – and here he was in it. I wondered if I ever loved him more than I did in that moment.

"Well, that went well," he said, as if he knew I was dying to know.

"Did it, really?"

"How have you been?" He nodded, never taking his eyes off mine.

I shrugged.

"I've missed you. A lot," he said. Separated by the width of the dining table with our hearts intertwined into something that couldn't be explained.

That evening, after they had left, Abba sent for me. He was having tea when I got to the covered verandah outside his library, where he sometimes read papers while watching the goings and comings of everyone in the compound.

"Assalamu alaikum," I removed my slippers and walked barefoot on the outdoor rug, settling into the cushions on the floor. "Abba, should I bring honey?" I motioned towards the tray that held tea leaves, cashew nuts and dates but not a jar of honey.

"No, I told them not to worry about it today," he spoke in Hausa as he folded up his paper and removed his glasses. He smiled fondly at me as he watched me take a date from his tray and put it in my mouth. "How's your holiday going?"

"It's already over," I answered, almost sad.

He continued smiling as I answered, and a part of me wondered what kind of tone this conversation would take. "You know why I sent for you." It wasn't a question.

I remained quiet.

"A young man was here this afternoon," he started. Abba had switched to English, which meant we were being super formal then. Got it.

"He was here with his father, a very good friend of mine: Ambassador Babangida. They came to express their interest in seeking for your hand in marriage to him – *uh,* Ahamad," I noticed that he pronounced Ahmad's name in three syllables. "You're young, just in your second year in University, and nobody is going to force you or ask you to bring a prospective suitor because it will all happen when it comes. We leave everything to God." My father spoke slowly and deliberately, dragging out his words in a way that commanded your full attention, and I nodded as I listened. "But since they've shown interest, then as your father, I have to ask. Do you like this Ahamad?"

In the distance, I could hear Abubakar's Mercedes driving in. He always went out and came back around the same time every day. I was beginning to wonder who was taking up all his time. I looked up, and Abba was waiting for my reply. I gave the slightest nod in the history of nods to indicate my interest.

"Okay," he nodded with me. "We'll start the necessary investigations. I'm sure there's nothing to worry about. I know he's a responsible young man because he was raised by exemplary parents."

Did he say investigations? What investigations? What kind of investigations? What if they found something out about Ahmad's past?

"When you come back from *Umrah* next year, they will be invited for a more formal vi–" his phone started ringing, and he glanced down briefly to see who was calling and continued talking to me, "for a more formal visit. After that, a date will be fixed – most likely in December; that way, you return back to Canada in January as a married woman." It all sounded so simple, so straightforward. We weren't being rushed, due process was being followed, but what if something came up before December? Then, what would happen?

* * *

A few weeks later, I returned to Canada. It was still winter, and I was still volunteering once a week at *Inn From the Cold* even though I had gotten the grades for the elective course from last semester. I was learning many valuable things from Jasmeet about running a Shelter, which I thought would come in handy when I created mine. I started helping her with scheduling and placing weekly orders, while still helping in the kitchen and dining rooms. I was just finishing up at the shelter one day when I got a text from Afreen asking about my bra size. I chuckled as I typed my reply and pressed send. Afreen has been in the best of moods all year. I would get a question from her regarding my preference for brands or questions about my size multiple times a week. She didn't have to tell me what it was for; I knew that they had started shopping for my *kayan lefe. Kayan lefe* were boxes of items that the groom's family took to the bride's home. Aunty Mami traveled a lot this year. She was in Europe getting some shopping done with her sister. At the end of the year, Ahmad's family would take the boxes filled with gifts for me to my family home as part of the proceedings for the wedding. It still felt strange referring to myself as a bride-to-be, and time seemed to be moving fast.

Looking back now, this was when my relationship with Ahmad started to change. It was the most subtle of changes, so gradual that I almost didn't notice. Okay, that's not true. I might have realized that our relationship was changing, but I was too excited to be bothered.

One late evening, after about three days of not seeing each other (he'd been working in California), we ended the day the usual way we did – with a video call. We talked for over an hour while he ate dinner and I brushed my teeth. Then we both made tea and as I settled into bed, he sent me links to honeymoon locations to pick out from.

"I'm leaning heavily towards Seychelles or Maldives," I said as I kicked off my fluffy slippers and tucked my legs under the covers. This year, I was in a new dormitory room with a new roommate who didn't talk much. Claire had moved out of the residence.

"Or… we could do both?" he suggested as he sent more pictures of exotic locations to look at. "Are you okay?"

"I'm just worried about the results of our bloodwork," I answered truthfully. We had gone for some tests after our return to Canada.

"The genotype test? Why are you worried about it?"

I nodded as I took a sip of my ginger tea. It needed more honey. I knew that I was AS and Ahmad said he had never needed to do such a test. But what if he was AS too? That would mean we weren't compatible. Would our parents allow us to get married?

"It doesn't matter what our genotypes are."

"Of course, it matters," I scoffed. I had a lot of cousins who were sickle cell carriers, and I had seen what patients went through – the frequent visits to the hospital, the unending pain they complained about during their crises…

"No, it doesn't. We're getting married," he spoke slowly, like he had thought about this before this conversation, "even if we're both AS."

"That'll be so irresponsible of us. Haven't you read *S is for Survivor?*"

He shook his head.

"It's a book written by a Nigerian girl about her experience with sickle cell and bone marrow transplant. SS kids go through so much."

"I'm not arguing that," he said gently, "we'll accept it as our *qadr* and adopt kids."

I looked up at him, and couldn't help but smile after seeing how serious he was.

"Do you have anything against adoption?"

I shook my head no.

"Great," he said, "it's settled then."

A few days later, on a Saturday, Jasmeet offered to drop me off after my volunteer session that evening. "How are your classes going?" she asked as we approached my destination.

"Very well. Thanks," I unfastened the seatbelt in the passenger side of her Kia.

"Thank you so much for staying on," she said. "We always appreciate all the extra hands we can get." It had been quite busy at the shelter, and sometimes people didn't show up for their shifts.

"I'm more than happy to help." I hesitated before opening the door, "I –I'm thinking of starting a smaller version of the centre back home, so this is a learning experience for me."

"Oh, that's amazing, Fa'iza! Listen, I'm here to answer any question you might have."

"That's so kind, I will. Ahm –" I stuttered, "my friend's helping me with most of the logistics. I'll reach out when we start drafting job descriptions and organizational charts."

We said our goodbyes and I made my way into Ahmad's building. The doorman gave me a brief nod as I made my way to the Penthouse. I opened the door and heard some music playing from his bedroom. "Bae?" No answer. The apartment was spotless. His room was empty, and he was not in the closet or bathroom either. I switched off the music playing from the speakers, and I dialed his number.

"Bae?" He picked up on the first ring. I could hear the splash sounds of water in the background, "Are you done? I'll be there in five."

"I'm here already," I looked at the open laptop on his bed displaying an RFP and an email about an acquisition from Edet. "Where are you?"

"At the pool downstairs. Come tell me about your day."

"Okay," I removed my coat, wore one of his slip-ons and made my way downstairs. My key gave me access to the indoor pool area, which was opposite the building's gym I'd been to a few times to watch him.

Ahmad looked up from the rippling water in the hot tub and smiled as the door closed behind me. I looked around. There were neatly folded towels on the lounge chairs next to the doors leading to the showers and changing rooms.

"How was your swim?" My voice echoed as I called out to him. I was trying hard to keep my eyes off his bare chest and keep them glued to his face. I was not so successful.

"I could only do six laps today," he said as he swam towards me, "and then I got sore."

"Uh oh, your shoulder again?" His right shoulder had been hurt during football earlier in the week.

"Yeah, it's the worst," he caught my gaze. His wet hair and the water trickling down his face made him look even hotter. He stepped out of the hot tub, the water dripping from his blue swim trunks that was stuck to his skin. The ridges and muscles on his thighs glistened as he walked towards me.

I swallowed hard. His hands went to the sides of my face as he gave me a kiss on my forehead. Then he walked past me and dived into the pool. I watched as the ripples formed around him in the blue-hued water, while the gentle hum of the now-empty hot tub died down.

"I'm supposed to alternate between hot and cold for the soreness," he explained. "Get in."

"In these clothes?" I laughed as I walked towards him to get a better look at my green peplum top and black jeans. "Sorry, I'm not dressed for the pool today."

"I've got a shirt over there, if you want." His grey T-shirt lay on the white lounge chair, "and there's a changing room just behind you."

Very tempting offer, I thought. "Nah, I'm good. I just came to watch you," I finally responded, sitting at the edge of the pool. I rolled up the legs of my trousers and dipped my legs into the cold water. My gaze went back to his body as he did another lap through the length of the pool. He looked good in clothes and somehow managed to look even better without them. I sighed as I looked away, forcing myself to read every single signage around the pool area – pool opening hours, disclaimers, directions to changing rooms.

"You okay?" he started swimming towards me. This man would be my husband in a few months. It felt surreal. Looking at him, I realized I was happy time was flying; I couldn't wait to be his wife.

"What's on your mind?" he asked. I smiled. I kind of lucked out with this one – attentive, sexy and sensitive to my needs. He was in front of me now, looking into my eyes like he would find the answer to his question in them.

"Nothing," I answered as I felt a tickle on my foot. It was his hand. He wrapped my calves around his waist as he swam to the edge, even closer to me.

"Communication, babe," he said, the deep baritone of his voice seducing me even deeper. He'd stopped tickling me now and his palms were sitting comfortably next to me. "We have talked about this."

"I promised you I would always say what was on my mind instead of bottling it up."

He stared at me. I playfully put my hand on his face to avert his gaze, and his hands held my waist as he pulled me into the pool with him.

I gasped as the water enveloped me from my neck downwards. "Ahmad!" I screamed. "Not funny." I, however couldn't stop myself from laughing after the initial shock wore off. We were in the shallow end of the pool, and he started swimming away from me.

"I'm just leveling the playing field here," he said with a wink.

"It's freezing," I complained, making my way up the pool stairs, grabbing the silver rails as I climbed. The pool was warm, but the air was cold so I got colder now that I was out of the water. I hurriedly walked to the closest pool chair and wrapped myself in a white towel. Of course, the one day I didn't wear a padded bra was the day I found myself drenched in water. I tried to hide that my nipples were hardened and visible through my top. *Well, this is embarrassing,* I sighed while I stood there shivering.

In just a few seconds, Ahmad was behind me. He pressed his chiseled chest into my back, his hands on my waist, and my stomach clenched into a fist he slowly turned me around. I felt the familiar quickening of my breath as we got closer. My already obvious nipples were getting harder by the second. *Damn lace bras*!

"Hey," he murmured, his eyes falling to my mouth and back to my eyes. I bit my lips as I looked up at him. We were wet and inches apart, and I felt his fingers gently graze mine as he took the towel from me and draped it over my shoulders. His eyes fell to my chest, and I knew he could see the hardened nipples through my top. He cleared his throat as he shifted his weight from one leg to another. He wasn't smiling anymore.

"Let's get you warm and back to the rez," he said, almost as if he was trying to convince himself. Like if he said it out loud, then he would have to follow through on it.

"Why are you sounding like a robot?"

"Because I want to kiss you so, so bad." His eyes met mine and my heartbeat quickened.

The air between us felt so heavy, and I felt weak at my knees. I wanted to kiss him so very much. "Well, then, you better get me back to the rez," I said as I started walking towards the exit. The cool air around was doing nothing to help the situation with my nipples. I heard him chuckle to himself as he followed me. In the elevators, just as the doors started to close, a black, pretty lady rushed in to join us. She smiled as she pressed the button for the 14th floor. "Nice day out, huh?" she asked us.

"Yes, it is," he answered, even though he hadn't been out all day.

"Do you guys have plans for the evening?" she asked.

Nope, I thought to myself. *Just trying very hard* not to tear the clothes *off each other when we find ourselves alone again.*

"No, nothing at all," he responded, then looked at me. I wondered if the edge I heard in his voice was just in my head.

She got off on her floor and we stood there – him behind me, our bodies against each other. When we got to the Penthouse level, he brought out his keys and opened the door, stepping aside to allow me to go in first then following behind closely. My heart was thundering in my chest and all my nerves were tingling. I watched him close the door and mustering the last ounce of my confidence, I tipped on my toes and tried to give him a quick kiss on his right cheek. At the same time, he turned his head towards me, and our lips met.

He pulled back, and my breath caught. I could tell that he was surprised by my action, even though that was maybe not what I had planned to do. He pulled me back into him, turning me around as he braced me between the door and his sculpted body. I dropped the towel as I unsteadily wrapped my hands around his neck, and his lips claimed mine. His hands cupped my face, reached for my neck, and grabbed my hands, all the while kissing me like his life depended on it. His urgency was astonishingly sensual. It was ravenous. It was breathtaking. I knew we should stop, but I couldn't. I didn't want to. I felt a tingle climbing my legs and moving upwards. His hand trailed my neck and moved downwards to my chest, and I felt his fingers trace my nipples.

I opened my eyes and stiffened. He stopped, inhaled, and he groaned into my neck. Then he pulled away. With his forehead on mine, his hands returned to my face stroking my cheekbones with his thumbs as our breathing normalized.

"I'm going to need a very cold shower," his voice was hoarse. "This is going to be the longest year of my life."

The inexplicable need for something I could not describe – a hunger, a madness. I started moving away from him. I needed water. Cold water.

"Hey, come here," he said, holding my arms and pulling me back into a hug. His strong arms held me tightly, and I softened as I leaned into him. "Don't run away like you did last time we kissed."

I sighed, then looked up at him. His eyes were searching mine while he waited for an answer. "I won't," I whispered.

"Promise?" He asked me as his hand stroked my back, drawing circles on my wet top.

I scrunched up my face at him, and he laughed. The sound in the quiet apartment reverberated around the high walls, easing the tension around us as he kissed me on my forehead. "I promise."

Chapter 18

Once Ahmad and I crossed that no-touching, no-kissing boundary that had existed for months, all prior restraint and logical thinking went out of the window. It almost felt like we had been starving, and only now did we find sustenance. It was the most natural thing in the world.

"Hello, beautiful," he said one evening as I opened the door to my dorm room. He had come to see me on his way home from the office and was holding a paper bag with a gold-colored box filled with my favorite flavors of macaroons – lavender-peach and burnt honey cheesecake. I held on to the door, and as he walked in, he leaned towards me and gave me a tiny unhurried kiss on my lips. The feeling that passed through me was almost electric. *Calm down, Fa'iza,* I said to myself. It was only a peck, an innocent one.

He went into my bathroom to perform ablution, and he prayed alone on my maroon prayer mat in my room while I munched away in the kitchenette, reading the names of the remaining flavors they had written in cursive inside the box.

When he came out, his sleeves were rolled up, and few buttons of his shirt were undone. He had come to stay for a while. He made himself at home, refilling my white kettle and plugging its cord into the wall. His dark-tailored pants and blue slim-fit shirt made him stand out in the small student dormitory.

"I'm going to make us iced tea," he said as he opened my cupboard and got a box of David's tea. He opened another and brought out two mugs.

"How was your day?" I leaned on the wall as I watched him.

"Same old," he shrugged his broad shoulders. "I was counting down hours, so I could come see you," he smiled as he looked in my direction. "Have you decided on how many families you want to start with?" he asked as the kettle started whistling. We were looking at sizing and capacity for the Shelter while brainstorming possible locations in Abuja. Ahmad has been a considerable resource; he was always pointing me in the right direction without taking over the project completely.

"Yeah, I checked. There are NGOs helping with cases I'm interested in. I was thinking of a sort of partnership with them."

"What kind of partnership?" he opened the freezer and brought out some ice, dumped them in the cups and poured the tea over.

"Since they're handling so many cases of abuse, I'll ask that they refer families – women and their babies – to the shelter for accommodation and food," his eyes burned into mine as I spoke. "And we'll stand as their legal reps and make sure the kids don't miss school."

"That's fantastic, babe." I caught his gaze as his eyes roamed down my body and back to my face, "still doesn't answer my question, though. At full capacity, how many families do you want to be able to manage? That's going to determine the size of the shelter."

"Yeah, you're right," I had thought about that, but I was still on the fence about whether I was going to do this alone or if I would have other lawyers on my team. I opened the box of macaroons and I started making my way into the room. "Rooms for about thirty families, to start with," I finally said. "Two double bunk-beds in each room, an inflatable mattress can be provided if there are more than four people in a family."

"Wi-Fi connectivity, storage space in each room…" he added as he sat down on the carpet next to my open laptop. We watched movies on the carpet when we hung out in my room.

"Dining area, kitchen area, common room, outdoor play areas for the children, security..." I was getting more excited just thinking about the possibility. I was going to start small, but I hoped to expand as time went on. I took a sip of my iced tea and noticed Ahmad looking at me with dark eyes. "What?" I asked him, sitting so close to him I could almost feel the heat from his skin.

"I can't get over how amazing you are," he said quietly. "When we're in Nigeria, we can go through the possible site options for your shelter."

I said nothing but pushed the box of macaroons towards him so it would be in the middle and took another sip of my tea. He pressed play on my laptop as I moved closer to him and got in our regular position. As we ate macaroons and drank iced tea, the plan was to finish a movie we'd started watching the previous night. We sat at the foot of my bed opposite my closet, and he leaned back into the frame of my bed with my back leaning into his chest. When the movie got boring, my mind wandered and I was reminded of our proximity – the way his fingers trailed the arms of my sweater and the goosebumps that flared on my skin as he traced invisible shapes on my hips. Even though we were half-covered with a soft blanket and I was wearing a sweater, the room still felt too cold. I shivered involuntarily. When his feet found mine under the covers, it got harder to breathe.

As the credits rolled, his hands slowly moved upwards to my shoulder. I turned around to look at him, and he kissed me on the forehead. "I couldn't stop thinking about you all day," he said quietly. It was almost a whisper. My entire body ached with desire. But what did I even desire – a kiss? A touch? Something more? I had no idea. I could still remember the taste of his lips on mine and could not stop biting my lips as I looked at him.

He leaned in very close to me and didn't stop until he was so close that our noses were almost touching. He stayed there, waiting for me to get impatient enough to close the distance between our lips. *Lord.* He waited for me to take the lead and when I didn't, he took over. All my thoughts on abstinence dissolved as his lips went over mine. He kissed me so slowly like we had all the time in the world. As I reached up for his chest, his arms lifted me, and I found myself straddling him. One of his hands went to my neck, pulling me closer to him, deepening our kiss. My hands went around his neck, and I moaned a little. I felt his hands everywhere – on my back, my thighs, and then under my sweater. His touch was slow and teasing. My heart was pounding the whole time. Maybe it was from all the sugar in the iced tea or from his intoxicating scent. Perhaps it was how gentle he was with me as he caressed my back.

He suddenly broke the kiss. Disoriented, I opened my eyes to look at him, and his had a fire within them. Without taking his gaze off mine, he started unbuttoning my sweater – slowly and steadily – and pulled me back into him, kissing me as he took it off me. Every part of my body felt like it was on fire. His mouth was on my neck now. His hands held me tightly as I arched into him. I felt his lips and tongue on my skin, our kisses no longer unhurried. He pulled me closer into him and I felt the bulge in his trousers.

His lips started moving downwards, leaving a trail of kisses from my collarbones to my chest and then the swell of my breasts. My breathing had become erratic. I felt his hands on my back as he found the clasp of my purple bra and unfastened it with a snap.

I froze. My hands went to my chest to stop the bra from falling off me, covering me. He paused, raised his head and looked at me. His lips were parted, and his breathing was rapid. He looked the exact way I felt, which was to dizzying witness, as we were both exposed and vulnerable with deep desire.

"Do you want us to stop?" he asked gently. I had never felt this way before. I had never been kissed like this, never wanted to touch someone so badly. I was going crazy, but deep down, I knew this was wrong. I nodded.

His eyes fell to my chest, and his hands went around my back as he clasped my bra back on and slowly returned the straps to my shoulder. Holding me with one arm, so that I was still straddling him, he pulled down a pillow from my bed, and he leaned back until we were both lying down on the blanket on the carpet. One of his hands went under his head, and the other held my naked waist, caressing me gently. His eyes were closed like he was lost in his thoughts.

"Are you okay?" I asked after I caught my breath. How can something that felt so right be so wrong?

"I'll be fine, babe. Are you?" I could sense the restraint in his voice.

"Aren't we moving too fast?" I asked, my hands stroking his chest as I felt his heartbeat under my palms.

"I promised you," he said as his hands went around the dip of my waist and flare of my hip. "I promise you, we're not going to do anything you're not ready for, my love." I looked at him, and all his flaws felt inconsequential at that moment. His respect for me trumped everything else. "I love you."

Nine more months, I thought. With this much desire, I wondered how much longer I could hold out after getting a taste of the pleasure that could come with us being together. I could deny it as much as I wanted, but I was slowly falling deeper into sin, and the scary thing was that I was not even fighting it anymore.

* * *

Ahmad was back in the US for two weeks. Even though at any particular time, I could tell you exactly what he was doing because we updated each other on almost everything. He became my best friend whom I trusted with my life. I told him the most mundane details about my day and he listened like it was the most fascinating thing. I missed him but I was grateful for the distance.

In the meantime, I had started reading more and more romantic stories with explicit content. They seemed to make the time go faster. I also liked being invested in other people's love stories instead of mine.

It was Friday and I was in a study room with my study group. It was almost the end of our session for that evening. Sara and Ada were in the middle of an argument about APA-styled citations. It was an endless drone in the background. The empty boxes of Thai we ordered for dinner laid on the table surrounded by textbooks and notebooks. It was already dark outside. As soon as we called it a night, I would walk back to the Rez, pray and sleep. It had been a very long day with lectures and peer-review meetings. I took a sip of coke through my straw, my phone beeped, and I almost choked as I read the message: *The things I wanna do to you...*

"Are you okay?" Ada and Sara asked in unison, startled.

"Have some water," Sara offered, pushing a bottle toward me.

I thumped my chest softly as I coughed, "I'm good, I'm good." I felt the need to over explain, "the drink was too cold and I rushed it."

Ada raised her eyebrows, "Are you sure you're okay?"

"I'm good," I cleared my throat again and plastered on a smile on my face, "are we done? I think I'm gonna get going."

"Yeah," Sara replied, scrolling through her phone. "My bus isn't coming for another 30 minutes, so I'll go into the library to get some printing done."

"Okie dokie," I said, as my phone beeped another notification, but I knew better than to open it this time. I put my laptop in my bag and started to put the empty food boxes in the recycle bin and Ada joined me, clearing out the table. We said bye to Sara and Ada and I walked out together. When she took a left to the bus stop, I took a right to the residence and brought out my phone from my pocket to check the second message: *I want to taste every bit of you.* Another one came in just then: *I want to tease you until you beg for me.*

I looked around me, flustered, embarrassed, and surprisingly slightly turned on. The automatic doors to the Residence entrance opened as I approached them, and I hurried into the elevator. As I got to my floor, the phone beeped again: *I'm crazy about you, Fa'iza.*

I walked into my room, threw my bag on my bed and read the messages over and over again. I could hear his voice; he was miles away from me, but it felt like he was whispering these words right into my ear. Another message: *Eight more months...* then: *and then I'm going to make love to you slowly...* and then another: *then fuck you hard for making me wait so long.*

My jaw fell. Excuse me?! What was that? My hand went over my mouth. That was so dirty and so raw… why was I so turned on? Am I into this? Am I enjoying it?

I looked at my reflection in the mirror, watching the rapid rise and fall of my chest, with my lips slightly parted. Yes, I was. I was definitely turned on by a man who was thousands of miles away with nothing other than words. No one should have this much power over another person.

Suddenly feeling brazen, I typed a message, read it over, and pressed send: *I think I wanna postpone the wedding.* I regretted it immediately. My first attempt at sexting, and that was the best I could come up with. It sounded so lame. That was the driest thing anyone could possibly say. Why didn't they teach stuff like this in the romance novels I read?

My phone beeped again and the blood rushed to my ear as I read the message: *Bae, don't play with me like that,* then another: *I would die.* I laughed as I read his messages. Another one came in: *I wish you were here right now.*

I was actually enjoying this. With shaky fingers, I typed back: *What would you do if I was there?* I could not keep still. I held my breath as I waited for his reply. The wait was excruciating even though it was barely seconds, but it was worth it: *I'd tell you to undress yourself ... while I watched.*

I read the message again. I wasn't expecting that. In all the novels I'd read, the man undressed the girl. Always. I could sense the authoritative tone from the messages, and I was not even turned off or repulsed. I pictured myself doing exactly what he described – undressing for him, removing my robe, taking off my lingerie while his eyes followed the thin material as it slid off my body and pooled at my feet. I knew the look I would see in his eyes. I had seen it before. And I liked it.

Wait a minute. How did I get here? *Ahmad, I'm gonna go pray Isha.* I sent the message and threw the phone on my table.

I went into the bathroom, turned on the faucet and splashed my face with cold water. *I need to delete those messages from my phone.*

Ahmad came back from the States three days earlier than scheduled. It was my birthday so I knew that he might. What I didn't anticipate was the surprise birthday dinner that was organized for me the previous evening. The thought of it had me in a great mood the morning of my actual birthday, a Monday.

"Happy birthday, beautiful," I looked up to see him – the man I was hopelessly in love with – and as usual, I could not stop the smile that had formed on my face. He leaned on his car as he waited for me in the parking lot just outside my lecture hall. He looked like he was going to be on the cover of GQ magazine with his dark pants, checkered shirt and sunglasses.

I knew for a fact that he hadn't gotten more than three hours of sleep because he called me at midnight, wanting to be the first to wish me a happy birthday and he was up at four that morning on some work-related conference call with a team in another time zone. Yet, he looked just as great as ever.

He held out his hand as I approached him, and I held it as he opened the door for me. I got in, and he walked over to his side, got in and leaned in for a kiss. It was gentle and slow.

I remembered the first time I perceived this cologne on him. It was outside Terroni last spring, before our disastrous first date. All my scarves were beginning to smell like him.

"You look great," he said quietly when I pulled away from our kiss. His hand reached for my neck and he fixed the collar of the pink blazer I wore over blue jeans. It took me forever to decide what I would wear to class today. I didn't want to overdress because it was a morning lecture and slacks were the unofficial uniforms for early morning classes. But it was my birthday and I wanted to look good, so I dressed up a bit. I even wore heels.

"As I always do?" I asked as I took the coffee he had in the cupholder for me. I took a sip and brought out my phone to reply to the few birthday messages that had piled up since I'd last checked.

"Always," he reversed out of the parking lot. Our eyes met, and he held my gaze for a second longer than usual , "So, did you decide yet?" he asked. We had been looking at townhomes for sale that were conveniently between the University and the office he'd move into after the wedding. He had his Realtor copy me on every email that had a link to properties that fit the description we were looking for.

"I thought we would go through them together?"

"Of course we will, but does any of them stand out to you? You said you wanted a backyard..."

"...and upper and lower-level balconies," I completed.

"For your plants," he remembered, even though we were both half asleep when we spoke about our dream home. I wanted a home filled with flowers and plants; I intended to be a plant mum, since we wouldn't start trying for a child till after my graduation. We were going to have two kids – a boy and a girl *insha Allah* and we would move back to Nigeria after they were born and only visit Canada in the summer. We had it all figured out.

"Bae, there's something that needs my attention real quick back at the office," he held my hands and our fingers interlocked as he spoke. "Can we stop there for a bit?"

"Of course," I answered. On my left hand was an emerald cut halo ring he had slipped on my engagement finger the evening before, after the surprise dinner with Afreen, Zafar, Edet, Tumi, Sara and Ada.

Chapter 19

His office was a modern, top-floor workplace with natural lighting from big paned windows and a monochrome waiting area. It was the workspace for about 20 people while the rest of his staff worked remotely all over the globe. As we got on his floor, the receptionist at the front desk handed him some notes, and he joined a call in the conference room.

It wasn't my first time at his office; I had been there with him on some weekends when he needed to get some things. But it was my first time watching him at work. His demeanor was so different, detached yet assertive. People scrambled around him to get spreadsheets in his view, and he leaned back into his chair when asked a question, taking his time to respond. And when he finally did, his reply would be slow, his words would be few, and his opinion trumped everyone else's.

Tired of looking in through the window of the conference room, I retired to his office, sat in his chair and started going through his desk to Google random things on his desktop to mess up the algorithm for his search engine.

"Happy birthday, Fa'iza," I looked up to find Edet by the door. "And congratulations again on the engagement."

"Hi, Edet. Thank you," I gushed. I had a love-and-hate relationship with birthdays; I hated telling people that it was my birthday, but I loved people wishing me a happy birthday. I was also in no mood to explain that Islamically, a ring was not an engagement, especially since it had become so common among our generation, so I said nothing.

"I hope you're having a good one?" he asked.

"I am, thank you," I answered. "How's Joanne?"

"She's doing great. I'm going to see her in a few weeks." He took a few steps into the office. "I just booked my flight, actually."

"Oh, right! I need to get mine too, actually," I said, mostly to myself.

"You're going to be in Abuja for the summer, right?"

"Yeah, and then Saudi with my mom." For *Umrah*.

Ahmad came into the office. The background office chatter from the rest of the staff in the outer offices and ringing phones seemed to start all at once.

"I'm just taking the client for lunch," Edet said to Ahmad, turning around to leave, "the deal should be closed before the weekend."

"Great work, man," Ahmad answered as he circled around the desk and stood next to me. "We still up for the briefing tomorrow?"

"Yup. 3 pm."

We said our goodbyes and Edet left, closing the door behind him. As soon as the door closed, it opened again, and Ahmad's personal assistant, a redhead named Brooke, came in with some documents. "I've got everything ready to go," she said to Ahmad, "Oh, hi Fa'iza. Happy birthday," she said in her high-pitched voice.

"Hey, Brooke," I said as I watched Ahmad flipping through the pages she gave him before she left us alone in the office. He laid them on the desk, grabbed a pen, and placed it in the middle of the small stack.

"They need your signature," behind him, I saw Brooke exit his office quietly.

"Who's "they"? And what for?"

He leaned in as he flipped through the pages slowly, "Company shares," he answered. I could see the yellow post-its marking where I was supposed to sign as a member of the board of directors next to his signature. He flipped again, "and funding for the shelter."

This was all a bit much. Funding for what? The shelter that was just an idea in my head? I turned to look at him."I never asked you to *fund* the shelter," I said quietly. I knew a lot of money was required to start a shelter, but I was going to figure it out somehow.

"Let's not do this whole cliché thing where I offer you something and you turn it down," he sighed and rubbed his forehead.

"We never discussed this," and that was the problem.

"We're doing it now, aren't we?"

"Discussing?" I looked up at him., grabbing the stack and flipping it open. "Really? After the funding has already been approved?" My eyes widened as I saw the amount, "And your company is ready to remit funds?" *Remit funds to whom? I don't even have a Finance department.*

He reached for my hand, and I pulled away. I stood up and tried to walk towards the window, but his hands grabbed mine, stopping me. *I really shouldn't have worn heels,* I thought to myself.

"There's no way we are fighting about this right now," he chuckled.

"It is too early for this. I don't even have a location, I just finalized the business plan…" He knew this already because he helped me with editing the document. *What if he invests in this dream of mine, and it ends up being a waste and doesn't work out? What if I'm not ready to start an NGO in Nigeria? Am I not playing above my level here? Will I even be able to put up a successful Shelter in Nigeria? What if I get too busy with life after my NYSC?*

"Okay, let's talk about this," he said, pulling me closer to him, his hands around my waist. "What is actually the matter?" He waited for me to say something as his fingers grazed mine gently. I avoided his eyes because I knew exactly how he was looking at me at this moment, and I didn't need to be distracted.

"*Daina mana*. Stop," I pulled my hand from his.

"I should have told you I wanted to fund the shelter," he said. "I just really wanted to surprise you. I know how much it means to you."

I sighed. I knew he wanted to be a part of it. I just did not expect that he would offer to pay for the whole thing and more. "I was going to find investors and reach out to family, give them a chance to be part of it," I managed to let out. It was not pretty running after people for money, but an NGO could not be supported by just one entity. It was a financial risk.

He nodded. "We can redo the numbers – And with your permission this time." His landline started ringing as he spoke and he ignored it, pulling me in closer to him. "I love you with everything I've got, Fai'za," he was serious. "You know I would never do anything to hurt you." He was looking at me that way again. He leaned towards me, gradually closing the distance between us.

There was a second knock on the door, and we broke apart. I adjusted my veil. Why wasn't the AC on? My face was flushed. *Damnit!*

The door opened, and Brooke returned. She had a tablet in her hand. As she looked from me to Ahmad, there was no way to know if she could tell we were just about to start making out in the office, like we did every time we found ourselves alone. "We might not be able to submit the second application," she said with an apologetic look on her face.

"Why not?" Ahmad's voice had become assertive, and he was back in Boss mode.

"A marriage certificate is needed," she said without looking at me. "Or a legal document showing that a civil ceremony had taken place."

Ahmad frowned, then looked up at me. I didn't know what they were talking about, but I knew it had to do with me and the papers that I was meant to sign.

"Thanks, Brooke. I'll let you know if there's anything else," he dismissed her and she made her way out. He turned to me and I raised my eyebrow at him.

"Suppose we got married at a Masjid here before our trip to Nigeria –" he started cautiously. I started shaking my head vigorously and he held my face, stopping the movement, urging me to listen to him.

I pulled away from his touch and raised my eyebrow even higher. "First of all, if Umma found out we secretly got married before the nikkah back home, she would kill me. Then somehow find a way to get me resurrected, so she could kill me again."

"She would never find out, though," he said. "The document will be locked up in my safe."

"Nope, no way," I started moving further away from him, past his desk and sat on his couch, taking the remote control and changing the channel from the Stock Market Exchange. I busied myself with news about Obamacare even though I was not paying attention to the anchor's comments.

We might have been silent for five minutes. Or more. I was not counting. He walked towards me, sat next to me on the couch and reached for my hand.

"Bae, listen to me. We'll be away for a month in the new year for our honeymoon and after that, we'll be away for *Hajj*. We might not be back to Canada until February and I need to complete all of these," he pointed to the papers on the desk, "before the end of the fiscal year, before the next audit."

I wasn't even going to be swayed into this. I had heard so many stories of these kinds of marriages ending in tears. It happened to an acquaintance of an old family friend who secretly got married to her boyfriend just for him to send her divorce papers after a month. It wouldn't have happened without the knowledge of the elders. When she saw his wedding announcements to another girl months later, she was a wreck. I looked up at him trying hard to fight his charming smile.

His fingers were grazing mine gently. "Just take a day and think about it, okay?" His gaze held mine, "and if you're still uncomfortable with it, *shikenan*. Forget I brought it up."

Chapter 20

May was here, which meant it was seven months to December. I had finished my semester exams and was at the ambassador's residence to do *sallama,* to bid them farewell. I was leaving for the airport the next day to head back to Nigeria. "Fa'ee, you have to tell me the secret. You look great!" Afreen exclaimed as soon as she saw me. She gave me a long hug and I held on tightly to her until she finally pulled back to get a better look at me. "No, seriously. You're glowing. What's the secret?"

I blushed. According to science, I could attribute the sudden glow to the love hormone – oxytocin. "*Ke dai* Afreen," I dismissed her barrage of compliments as I adjusted my veil. I was wearing a beige-colored Abaya with silver threaded embellishments on the lower half that swirled around my legs when I climbed the spiral staircase decorated with colorful pots of Begonia flowers to Aunty Mami's living room.

"Assalamu alaikum," I said, announcing my presence to her and her guest as I walked in. Aunty Mami looked up, and a smile brightened her face when she saw me. She even did a little clap.

"Wa alaikumus salam," she opened her hands and I went closer and leaned in for a hug.

"Good evening." I knew I had to stop calling her Aunty Mami soon. She wasn't just my mom's friend or my aunt anymore, she was going to become my mother-in-law.

"How are you, Fa'iza *am*?" she asked, with her hand still on my back. She turned to her guest, "This is our bride-to-be."

I exchanged salams with the pleasant-looking woman with green eyes sitting across from Aunty Mami. She looked South Asian, with olive skin and dark hair half-covered with a scarf.

"*Masha Allah, Masha Allah,*" the woman laughed. "She looks so much like you. I thought she was your daughter." Her accent was hard to place.

"Well, she *is* my daughter," Aunty Mami laughed with her.

The chatter was cut short when Ahmad came into the living room, wearing the green linen shirt I had picked out for him. There was something about the way he looked today. Even better? Maybe it was the bright light from the chandelier. "Assalamu Alaikum," the Arabic phrase heightened the deep baritone of his voice. His eyes lingered on me and a slight flush came over my face as I met his eyes. I looked away, trying to calm my nerves. He had completely changed my world, my identity and my values.

"Ahmad, you remember Mrs. Baig, don't you?" Aunty Mami saw his confused face. "From Australia." *Ah, yes! It was an Australian accent.* Those were always hard for me to place.

Recognition settled on his face as he looked at the olive-skinned woman. "Of course. They lived only three houses away." The women laughed, pleased that he remembered her.

"I told you he would remember! He was quite old when we left – about fifteen?" Aunty Mami said to her friend, then looked up at Ahmad, who nodded in agreement.

"Barely feels like that much time has passed," Mrs. Baig said with a laugh. "I hear congratulations are in order." She looked back at me and I smiled.

"Yes, Alhamdulillah," he responded. "Thank you so much." He sounded so proper like he hadn't spent that morning doing unspeakable things to me with his tongue. I felt the heat spreading on my face again, as he engaged in small talk with his mother's guest. I wondered how he could act so normal when we were around people. He seemed at ease, while I was an emotional wreck. I tried to forget what happened that morning, but I couldn't. It was on a constant loop in my head, playing over and over.

"Have you ever had a dream about me?"

"No, Ahmad, I haven't."

"Really? I dream of us all the time. I'm obsessed."

Ahmad was staying at his parent's house that night so that Afreen and he could drop me at the airport like they always did. Later that evening, after Maghrib, on my way to the living room downstairs, I got a notification reminder to check into my flight. I had just picked out a window seat when I closed the door behind me and I saw Ahmad on the sofa; he was showing Afreen something on his laptop. "Red leather interior," she was saying, "ooh, this is nice."

"What are you guys up to?" I asked as I switched on the TV, sitting on the couch away from them and crossing my legs. I scrolled through the channels looking for something that would interest me.

"Your wedding gift!" Afreen said in excitement, grinning.

"Don't you know how to keep a secret?" Ahmad raised his hands exasperatedly.

"Oops," she gestured a zipper over her mouth, then mouthed an apology to him.

Ahmad shook his head and closed the laptop. He looked towards me, but I looked at Afreen instead.

"Let me go pray," she said, picking up her phone and leaving us alone.

"Bae?"

I looked at him and my heartbeat quickened. Images of his hands on my bare skin flashed crossed my mind, and I uncrossed my legs.

"*Na'am*? Yes?" I crossed my legs again.

"Are you okay?" He sounded concerned.

No. I'm not. I have rapid heart palpitations and sweaty palms every time you look my way. "Hmm hmm," I nodded.

I could tell from the frown lines that formed on his forehead that he didn't believe me. He shook his head and leaned in towards me. "You're not a good liar," he paused. "Do you have regrets about –" he searched my face, "any regrets about this morning?"

I quivered as I remembered how his lips felt as he kissed my stomach and moved downwards. I looked around us, even though the door was closed and there was no sound in the hallway. "Ahmad, what if someone hears us?" I whispered."We can't talk about that here."

He held my gaze for three seconds then stood up, reached for my hand and pulled me up. We walked out of the living room the same time Afreen was coming out of her room. I tugged my hand out of Ahmad's, even though I doubt she noticed it in the first place.

"Are you going somewhere?" she asked us.

"Fa'iza forgot her passport at the rez," he said. I looked up at him. *I did? No, I'm pretty sure my passport is in my hand luggage in Afreen's room. It was one of the first things I packed.* "We're gonna go get it. Will be back soon."

Afreen nodded as she said goodbye and we walked past the main foyer and out of the house.

"Where are we going?" I asked.

"Get in," he said as he opened my door. When I got in, he walked to the driver's side, got in, and started driving down the street. I watched his hand move to the gearbox next to my thigh and remembered how it felt underneath my white lace panties that morning. I inhaled sharply as the car came to a halt a street away from the house.

He turned off the ignition and turned to look at me. He opened his mouth to speak but I interrupted him. "I can't explain how I feel," I said. I had tried to find an explanation to why I felt like that – why I felt jumpy around him, why I couldn't keep still. But my mind only kept replaying memories of us together that morning. I remembered his lips on mine, over my nipples and the way it felt when he kissed me down there. "Maybe I'm addicted," I said, trying be justify why it kept playing over and over in my head.

"Addicted to –?" His voice was low and sensual. His thumb grazed my lower lip and his fingers softly stroked my jaw. Those fingers… and the things he did with his tongue when his head was between my thighs.

"Everything. And it sucks because I feel…" I looked for the word that weighed heavy on my chest, "I feel like a sinner."

My mind was replaying moments of him holding my trembling body tightly in his arms. I could still hear his whispers in my ear: *"Yes baby, that's it... come for me."*

I shivered again. I needed fresh air.

His knuckles clenched the steering wheel, and his voice was barely audible. "We didn't even have sex. Because I knew that if we crossed that boundary, you would hate yourself," he paused, "and that would *kill* me."

I put my palm to my forehead. I had never imagined that I would be having a conversation like this. Then again, I had never imagined that I would ever find myself with such intense sexual feelings until I met him. Ahmad always asked if I wanted to stop whenever we made out; he always checked to make sure I was okay with whatever we were doing. I never thought my answer to his question would one day be a very breathless plea: *"No... please."*

I now understood why people got addicted to other people. This feeling was like a drug, and I wanted more of it.

"I'm going to miss you," I sighed.

"I'm counting down days until it's official," he reached for my hands. "I can come to Abuja with you, if you want."

"No," I said, a little too quickly. "We need the distance – since you obviously can't keep your hands to yourself."

A smile spread across his face. "It was so hot watching you cum," he said quietly, reminding me of my first orgasm, not that I had been able to forget.

"Oh my God, don't ever talk about that," I said, as his lips covered mine.

* * *

In June, two weeks after my cousin Aisha Batagarawa's wedding, the fibres of my reality became entangled with the webs of destiny and my little globe of a dream woven in happily-ever-after shattered into a tiny million pieces.

"How did the audit go?" I asked in a sing-song manner. This was the 3rd time we were talking today. Our calls were shorter now, but the texts were still excessive. Ahmad was consulting in the UK for the summer and we were now in the same time zone, so it was easier to communicate.

"Why would you think I was calling about that?" his voice was sensual in my ear.

"Maybe because you've been stressing about it for a week?"

"Me? Stress?" he laughed. "Nah, cool as ice. Call me the Night King."

The sound of his laughter was contagious, I joined him. "I still don't get why he was marching with his army of the dead –" My phone beeped, and I glanced at it to see Abba's call waiting. "Bae, Abba is calling me. Can I call you back?"

"Yeah, yeah, of course," he hung up, and I picked up my father's call

"Hello, Fa'iza," my father's voice came on, soft-spoken as usual.

"*Na'am,* Abba? How was your flight?"

"Alhamdulillahi. *Kina ina*? Where are you?" It was hard to hear him about the noisy background. I moved towards the window and watched as an old and battered Mercedes 190 pulled into the compound. It looked like it was white at some point but it was dusty and from a distance, it almost looked yellow. I did not recognize the car.

"I'm at home" I said, "Umma sent me to Hajiya Uwani's house; I was just about to leave."

"Okay," he said, followed by a hesitant pause. "We're on our way back"

"Abba, already? I thought you were staying for three days?" I asked. I had gone to wish him a safe trip just after the early morning prayer today; by my calculations, he arrived in Egypt with Ya Amin about two hours ago. But he was already on his way back home?

"No," he said, followed by another pause. "I'm expecting some visitors."

Visitors? I thought to myself. That was weird. Most people planned their visits to see Abba days in advance and did so around his schedule. And he didn't cut his trips short for just anyone. Who or what was he canceling this trip for? "*Toh,* Abba. Okay," I said. "*Allah ya dawo da ku lafiya.* May Allah bring you back safely."

"Ameen," he hung up.

Chapter 20

I looked at the battered whitish-yellowish Mercedes 19 parked outside and wondered who could be in it, and what could be so important. My phone beeped: *Can I call you now?* It was Ahmad. I called him back: "Sorry about that, bae."

"No, no. Don't apologize. Is everything okay?" he raised his voice above the flight announcements in the background.

"Where are you?" I asked because he wasn't supposed to be traveling back to Canada until mid-August.

"That's why I called earlier," he replied. "I'm at the Airport. My dad said something urgent came up."

"You're coming to Abuja?" I asked. Something didn't feel right.

"One minute. Just checking in," he said. I heard some chatter in the background as he got his boarding pass. I had gone to see Aunty Mami two days ago and everything seemed alright; she said they had a wedding to attend in Maiduguri. Did they want Ahmad to accompany them to the wedding? Would they actually send for him all the way from London for something like that on such short notice? "Yeah, hello?" he was back on the other end. "It might be related to that Asokoro property I told you about," he said.

Okay, that makes sense, I thought, still feeling uneasy. "*Toh,* have a safe flight," I said as I made my way to Umma's section.

"We're about to board. I'll call you once I touchdown," he paused. "When can I come and see you?"

"Abba's on his way back, too. You know I'm not allowed visitors after Maghrib."

"C'mon Fa'iza. Really?"

"Really," I answered. I still found it funny that he was surprised at how orthodox and traditional my family was; the only way he could come over was to pretend that he was here to see Ya Amin.

I parted the curtains and found Umma in her living room. She was pacing up and down while on a call. She wasn't talking much, just nodding in agreement and agreeing like one does when listening to something.

I went to Abba's section to turn on the incense burner for some oud *bakhoor* and turn on the AC to cool the living room before he got back. As I lifted the drapes to brighten up the space, I noticed that two more cars had come into the compound. I recognized one, a blue Peugeot 406, as my uncle's personal car, but the other two – a Prado Jeep and a Toyota Pathfinder – didn't look familiar. Are these the people Abba canceled his trip to see? What could this meeting be about? Could it be about… me?

I had been back to Nigeria for weeks now. A week after I got back, I started having panic attacks. I would imagine a scenario in my head and get so fixated with it that it stopped me from sleeping, gradually becoming the only thing I could think about. Sometimes, it got so bad that just thinking about it would make me hyperventilate. I would wake up drenched in my own sweat in the middle of the night. During those odd hours, the only person I could talk about them with was Ahmad.

"I understand what you mean," Ahmad said one day when I called him in the middle of the night, "but can we consider this to be a hypothetical situation?"

"Yes, but what if during the pre-wedding investigation, they find out about…" I paused, "about us?"

"How would they find out, Fa'iza?"

"I don't know," I shrugged. It was barely 3 am, and I was whispering into the phone. "What if someone that knows us saw how much time I spent in your apartment?"

"Okay. First of all, bae, you're overthinking this. Worst-case scenario, they would do the *Nikkah* immediately and host a reception in December."

I was silent.

"There's no way they know what goes on in my apartment."

I thought about it some more and realized it was kind of silly, really. Two weeks later, I had another panic attack. Mufti Menk was apt when he said, "when you commit sin, peace of mind evades you." Ahmad had to excuse himself from a meeting because I was freaking out, and he needed to calm me down. "The second genotype results came out months ago, Fa'iza. I am AA." Okay, maybe I was alarmed for nothing. Maybe he was right.

As I made my way back toward our section, I saw Hajiya Uwani coming in through the main entrance. She did not have her usual smile when she saw me, and when I greeted her, she answered with a question: "Where's Umma?"

"She's in her sitting room," I answered. She hurried to Umma's section and I started panicking again. This was about me. I could feel it in my bones. I went to my room and dialed Ahmad's number. *Please pick up*, I prayed silently.

"Bae."

"Ahmad, something's going on. Abba's coming back from Egypt, my uncles are here... Ahmad, something is wrong."

"Hey, hey, hey. Take a breath," he said. I took a deep breath and exhaled. "Okay, talk to me." His voice was calm and measured.

"I think something came up during the investigations."

"Something like what?" he asked gently.

"Maybe they found out about... about you," I finally said, knowing he would understand I was talking about the alcohol, the live-in girlfriend and other things.

There was some chatter in the background, then his voice came back on. "Babe, we're about to take off. There's no way they found out about that. Okay? *Kina ji na?* There's absolutely no way." I nodded even though he couldn't see me. "I told you the truth about my past because I didn't want there to be any secrets between us," his voice was almost a whisper. "It's not exactly common knowledge, okay?"

"Okay," I sighed. Unlike the last times he talked me out of these scenarios, I was not really convinced this time around.

"I love you, Insom," he said.

"We're back to 'Insom'?" The sound of his gentle laughter calmed me down a little. I sighed, "I love you, too."

* * *

That's the thing about panic attacks I learnt that summer, there is a stage worse than hyperventilation and breathlessness– it is when you get to a stage when you cannot physically move. After Asr, I stayed on my praying mat until Maghrib, staring at my rosary in front of me and the black glossy thread that embroidered the designs on my praying mat. Every few minutes, I would read a prayer, followed by a verse from the Qur'an. I did not have the confidence that my prayers would be answered, not after all the things I had done. Yet, I didn't relent.

Earlier on, when Abba's convoy came into the compound, I saw the expression on his face and knew for sure something was wrong. When I did not hear Ya Amin come into our section to ask after his food like he always did after a trip, I knew this could not be good. Less than an hour later, I watched through the window as Ahmad came with his father. He was picked up straight from the airport, I could tell because he had on the same clothes when we Facetimed when I woke up this morning. The black shirt I told him would go better with his tie when he raised it and a brown one. He didn't have the tie on anymore, I watched him disappear though the door into Abba's section where all of Abba's guests were waiting.

Shortly after, Umma came to my room. She did not send Atine or anyone else to ask me to come; she came all the way to my room. She opened the door and found me sitting down on my praying mat, with the back of my head leaning on the wall.

"When you're done, Abba wants to talk to you," her eyes lingered on me for a few seconds with an unreadable expression on her face and then she silently shut the door behind her. *Ya Salam.* God! I glanced at my phone. Ahmad's messages from a few hours ago were still on my screen: *Touchdown* and half an hour later: *Hey, don't panic, but I think you might be right...* Since then, his phone hadn't been reachable.

I folded up the praying mat with shaky hands and with heavy steps, headed to Abba's section, still wearing my black hijab. I walked silently and was surprised that the living room was now empty but for three people – Umma, Abba, and a woman I had never seen before. She was light-skinned and her white veil was draped over her head, almost covering her entire body. She seemed to be in her fifties.

"Assalamu alaikum," my voice was shaky. Abba looked up at me; Umma didn't. I knelt on the Persian carpet by the white leather couch in front of them.

"Wa alaikumus salam," my father answered. He exhaled loudly. "Sit down, Fa'iza."

I tried to decipher their faces, but I couldn't. We sat in silence for about thirty seconds, both my parents looking at the ground. I was filled with dread like I had never known before; maybe they found out that he used to drink. Or had they found out details about my relationship with Ahmad – the sleepovers, the make-out sessions? What else did they know? I had disappointed my parents. How would I ever face them ever again? Will they say that he is bad for me? I cannot imagine a life without Ahmad.

"The prophet Mohammed," my father started. His words were slower than usual. I looked up at him, and as he spoke, but it wasn't disappointment or anger I saw on his face; it was something else. Pity?

"*Sallallahu Alayhi Wa Sallam*," we all chorused softly, as we invoked blessings on the prophet like we always do when his name is mentioned. My mother was still looking at the ground, and the strange lady wouldn't stop looking at my face.

"The prophet Mohammed," Abba started again slowly, "advised us that in everything we do, we must have *tawakkul,*complete faith in Allah, and follow the words of Allah because He is the best of planners." I looked up at him; he seemed sad. I had never seen my father like this. "Fa'iza, this is about your marriage to Ahamad. As you know, we have been doing the necessary investigations, and something unfortunate has come up."

Oh my God. This was about his past. My stress level right now was off the charts. How do I tell them that I am willing to marry Ahmad and I didn't care about anything they found out about him.

"This is Malama Zainab," he gestured towards the light-skinned woman. "I don't think you'll remember but when we lived in Kano, she helped with the chores around the house," he paused and I nodded. "When you were born, there were some complications with your birth, and Umma had to be admitted in the hospital for about over a month," he paused again. I wondered where this story of my birth was going, but I noticed how shaken Abba was as he recounted how my mother almost died after having me. "While she was there, hanging between life and death, I was running all over the place, trying to find specialists to help with you. Finally, your aunty, Baba Asabe, – *Allah ya jikan ta.* May her soul rest in peace – along with Hajiya Uwani and Malama Zainab found someone to breastfeed you; we called her '*yar*Agadez'."

Yar Agadez. A woman from Agadez, a town in the Republic of Niger. I looked up at Malama Zainab and wondered if she was related to '*yar* Agadez. She looked like she was from Niger or Chad.

How is this the big problem everyone was summoned for? It's not a crime to pay someone else to breastfeed your child –especially around the time I was born, when baby formula was not as common, I thought. I looked up at Abba as he continued speaking.

"Malama Zainab came here to testify that this '*yar* Agadez was the same woman who breastfed Ahamad when Hajiya Mami had an accident. He was barely a year old then, and –" he was still talking, but I could not hear the words coming out of his mouth.

'Yar Agadez, the woman who breastfed me also breastfed Ahmad when he was barely a year old? The same woman? My mind was busy trying to recall the Quranic verse about wet nurses and breastfeeding: *Prohibited to you [for marriage] ...your sisters through nursing.* Suratul Nisa, the chapter about women in the Quran, yes, it states that children breastfed by the same woman are...

"Yes," Malama Zainab said, her voice bringing me back to my father's living room.

"Because of this," Abba sighed, "there cannot be a marriage between you and Ahamad," he paused, "you're like siblings and marriage between you two is not permissible."

A ringing started in my ear. I could no longer hear what was being said, but there was a loud ringing in my ear. The lights in the living room were suddenly bright, too bright. Ahmad? A milk sibling. *My* milk sibling. I had heard that term so many times. I had recited that verse many times while reading Suratul Nisa and like all the other rules in the Qur'an, I knew they were set in stone, and we had to abide by them, but I never imagined that this particular line would one day refer to me, I didn't even know that wet nurses were still a thing and could be investigated before marriage.

I looked up at Umma and she was looking at me, "Fa'iza," her voice rose above the ringing, "take this as Allah's will; He has destined it this way." My heart was beating painfully in my chest. I thought it would burst out of my chest, all I could do was nod.

"*Allah yai miki albarka* Fa'iza. May God bless you," Abba said.

If only he knew. If only my father knew what kind of trouble I had gotten into, I thought as I nodded. "Ameen, Abba." My head was throbbing, and I could not see clearly. I stood up and walked towards my room, feeling nauseated and crumbling like a bag filled with worms. Ahmad? Marriage between us is not permissible? I remembered our whispered words as we promised each other forever – how we held each other until we fell asleep. The Ahmad I had done all those things with. Ahmad, who had touched me in places I could not even say out loud. *Where do I start to undo the mistakes I've committed with him? How do I even begin?*

When I got to my room, I looked at my phone. Not one notification from him. I sat on the edge of my bed, thinking. Thinking of everything, my mind was so far away. Far far away. All I could think of was the marriage certificate locked away in his Downtown apartment. *Our* marriage certificate. The certificate that verified a marriage with the one who was forbidden for me, and the one for whom I was forbidden. *Inna Lillahi wa inna ilayhi raji'un.*

* * *

"*Ina* Fa'iza? Where's Fa'iza?" I heard Hajiya Uwani's voice from the hallway, her voice above the ringing in my ears. I wanted to call out and let her know I was in my room, but when I opened my mouth, no sound came out. I had lost my voice. The door opened and she came in. "Allah sarki," her voice was loud. Everything was too thunderous – the cars driving out of the compound, the wallclock ticking, my heartbeat... the rustle that her veil made as she sat on the bed next to me, "I wasn't happy to hear this news," she spoke mostly to herself, "take heart. He isn't the one written in your destiny, but don't worry, don't give up hope. You'll meet your husband soon *insha Allah*."

This time yesterday, I was so sure of my future. I was sure of spending the rest of my life with Ahmad. I was happy with how my life was going. All of that changed in an instant, to this irreversible misery with no end in sight.

She hissed to herself and clasped her hands on her chest. "We're lucky we found out when we did. If we'd found out after –" her voice trailed off. She could not bring herself to voice out the thought.

My hands got clammy, and my vision started blurring. I didn't know what to deal with – the loss of the love of my life, or the unspeakable secret I was now harboring? I laid back on the bed and remained still. All I could hear was the loud beats of my heart and Hajiya Uwani's continuous monologue on faith and destiny.

After she left, Ya Amin came into the room. Unlike Abubakar, he was not a man of many words. He sat on the bed next to me quietly as I tried to block all the thoughts that were threatening to flood my mind. *"Allah ya sa haka shi ne mafi alheri*. May this be for the best outcome," he finally said as the athan for Isha was called. "Stand up and pray." He left and closed the door to my room quietly.

I stood up to go perform ablution, but as soon as I caught my reflection in the mirror, I crumbled to the cold floor. I could not bear to look at myself and the tears wouldn't stop. I closed my eyes and saw Ahmad's face, heard his voice, felt his touch. And every time I did, I died a little inside.

My father's voice kept playing over and over in my head: *you're like siblings and marriage between you two is not permissible.* It went on like a broken record on a loop. I was suffocating in the knowledge that the bridge to redemption had been burned. I remained curled up on the cold floor in a corner. I could not get up; I did not have the willpower to. I was in intense physical pain. My limbs felt like I had been beaten severely and my chest – oh my chest – there was an excruciating pain that dug deeper every time I took a breath. I was short of breath as the sobs raged uncontrollably out of me. I had a migraine and knew I had to seek forgiveness. I needed to pray Isha then repent for my sins. But as hard as I tried, I could not physically get up from the floor. I had no will to live.

The call for *subh* met me on the floor by the toilet sink, still curled up with my knees to my chest. I had not even realized that the whole night had passed. I had not heard from Ahmad since he left our house. His silence was loud. I went searching for my phone and realized it had run out of battery and was now dead. It had probably been dead all night. I put my phone to charge, performed wudhu, and spent more time than I had ever done crying on my praying mat.

Beep beep. Beep beep. Beep beep. Multiple messages came flooding as my phone came back on. I hurriedly went to check. It was Ahmad. First, *Pick up your phone* then *Please say something. We need to talk.* There were also missed calls from him, Afreen, and Aunty Mami before the phone died.

I prayed, and I crawled up to my bed, going under the covers and hugging myself. I felt too heavy to move or do anything else, and the weight of the ring on my finger was crushing me. For the first time since he put it on me, I removed it, placed it on my bedside table, and my hand fell limply on the bed next to me.

There was a knock on the door and my brother poked his head through, "Fa'iza?"

"Ya Amin," I said, mustering the will to get up and look alive. I wondered if he'd heard me crying all through the night. I hoped not.

"*Kin tashi*? Are you awake?" he mumbled quietly. Our language and its rhetorical questions. I nodded and watched him struggle with what to say next. If Abubakar were here, he would have given me a hug or said something to make me smile. "Come," he cleared his throat, "Ahmad is in the living room." It felt like something in my chest had cracked. Ahmad?

Here? I wondered if I could face him. "You should come before Abba comes this way."

As soon as I stood up, I felt a wave of dizziness over me and it took all the strength I had to stand straight. I took the black hijab I prayed in, put it on and followed my brother out of my room.

I walked into the living room, and in the dimly lit room, the first rays of morning sunlight gently filtered through the curtains, casting a bittersweet glow upon the scene. Ahmad was pacing back and forth a few feet from the door; his movements reflected the turmoil within him. His fingers ran through his disheveled hair as if trying to grasp onto any semblance of hope. It felt like my heart stopped when he looked my way with his eyes red-rimmed. He was still wearing what he wore the previous day when I watched him come with his dad through the window: black trousers and the black shirt, now rumbled with creases all over.

Ya Amin, on the dining table, was constantly glancing up to look at us covertly behind an open laptop at the other end of the room. I looked back at Ahmad. He looked down at his feet and back to my face.

"Why are you here?" I asked quietly. The quiver in my voice betrayed the sadness that enveloped me.

"I tried calling and texting, but – but you –" he swallowed, "I didn't know if you were okay. I had to –" his shoulders were slightly hunched upwards.

"It's 6 am…" I whispered softly; my voice sounded distant and tired.

He hesitated, and then, "I prayed subh here," he confessed. *How? Why?* Off the top of my head, I could count about four mosques between our house and theirs in Maitama. "Are you okay?" he asked slowly while his eyes searched my face.

Do I look okay to you? I thought to myself, fighting back the feeling to slump to the floor and wail. I shrugged. There were no words. He must know exactly how I was feeling; it was a pain that refused to be described. The fact that we could not be together for something we never saw coming was unbearable. Just thinking about yesterday evening's discovery made the tears start again, and I couldn't stop them. His hands started reaching for me, and I took a step back. "Please don't," I whispered.

He looked at the ceiling and exhaled. I could see how hard he was trying to keep it together. He looked behind him, and Ya Amin looked away, pretending to focus on his laptop. "I can't bear to see you cry," he said quietly as he shook his head slowly. He looked so devastated, and he kept shifting his weight from one foot to another like he was unsure of what to do. "I cannot fathom a life without you. The thought of waking up each morning, knowing that we are separated by... by this, is a torment I never imagined I would face."

I fight back my own tears, the pain cutting through me like a thousand sharp blades. I held onto my composure because it was the only thing I had left, but even when I spoke, my voice was filled with a mixture of sadness and determination.

"You know we can't see each other anymore," I said, my heart pounding with each syllable. I was dying inside.

"I'm *not* giving up on us." He chokes out, his voice thick with emotion.

"Why?" This was bigger than us; we didn't stand a chance. We were not destined for each other and were too blind to see it. I hoped that he could see what I wasn't saying in my eyes, the words I didn't have the strength to voice out.

"You know why," he said, his eyes piercing into mine, forcing me to remember the private vows and whispered promises we made to each other. I thought about us and the year we spent together; those were the happiest moments in my life. But he was not the one written in my destiny and we needed to find a way to undo our error before anyone found out. "I am *not* giving up on us. You hear me? You're mine, Fa'iza," his eyes pierced mine with such intensity that I had to look away. "There has to be a mistake somewhere." I shook my head, wondering if he had gone mad. *How is he going to fight this? How can he fight scripture?* As if he could hear the thoughts in my head, Ahmad continued: "I'm going to Kano today. Zainab is going to lead me to the wet nurse," he paused, trying to read the impression on my face, while ignoring the phone that had started vibrating in his pocket. "I have some questions."

"Malama Zainab?" I asked. I doubted that there was a mistake. I doubted that anyone would bring false evidence to Abba, especially regarding something as important as his daughter's marriage. My father was known for painstakingly reviewing and scrutinizing witnesses for the cases he handled.

"Yes. I tracked her down last night, and we are going back to Kano together." I nodded, not sure what he hoped to find in Kano. "There's a lot we don't know. We don't know the number of feeds necessary to establish the milk-kinship, to begin wi–"

"Once is enough," I cut him off. Anyone who went to Islammiyah knew this.

"It's heavily debated, though. Some say it's five, or ten –"

"Ahmad…" I was a complete wreck. It broke my heart to see him this, grasping at straws.

"Will you pick when I call?" his eyes were pleading. "When I call from Kano to update you?"

"Ahmad, maybe we should just accept this brother -sist –" His sharp inhale stopped me.

"I would rather *die* than I call you my sis –" he swallowed the word back like it was pungent, like it was an insult to him.

With those words, I took a step back, my heart heavy with the weight of our reality. As the morning light grew stronger, it cast a melancholic glow upon the living room, and we shared one final, longing gaze. It is a gaze that speaks volumes, expressing the love and ache that intertwined our fates.

Tears were streaming down my face now. I turned around and with each step taking me further from Ahmad, my heart shattered into a thousand pieces, forever marked by the pain of a love that could never be. As soon as I got into my room, I fell to the bed, praying to God to take this pain away. If not for anything, but for our sanity.

II

Part Two

If one day you wake up and I am gone
Will you forgive me for losing to the void?
For leaving you with nothing but an absence so present,
Will you miss the sinner or the saint in me?
Will you ever forgive me for time lost - pain bought?

Chapter 21

Toronto, January 2011

"Where's the blonde? Or are you bored already?" Edet asked as he nodded at the bartender who dropped his usual in front of him. The bar itself stretched along one side of the room, crafted in chrome and gleaming brass accents. Rows of crystal-clear glassware, shimmering bottles of premium spirits, and an array of meticulously arranged bar tools faced them.

Ahmad dropped the short tumbler with some whiskey sour in it on the polished mahogany table. "I'm done with university girls, man," he said over Edet's laughter ringing out of the confines of the private cubicle of the bar reserved for VIP clients. "No, for real. Check this out," he raised his hand to illustrate his point. "I took her out on Thursday, we had a good time and started chatting over text, then –"

"Were there nudes?" Edet interjected.

"I didn't ask her, but sent a few anyway," Ahmad replied. He knew the effect he had on women. He never had to try hard for their attention because most of it came unsolicited; all he had to do was show up, and things fell in place for him. "Anyway, we would chat and," he shrugged, "I knew it just wasn't going to work."

"Bastard!" Edet roared as he laughed at the familiar story. It was always the same with Ahmad – he lost interest when he got things easily.

"No, we were just not on the same wavelength. She follows all the Kardashians, man," he took a sip of his drink again.

"Why is that such a bad thing?" Edet mused out loud. At some point, he would have to tell his friend that his need for a challenge in every scenario might require a sit down with a therapist. As well as his fear of commitment. When Ezgi, whom Ahmad had been dating for years, started talking about settling down, he ended the relationship.

"It's not a bad thing. I just don't know why she needed to tell me. You should have seen her the day one of them liked her picture. She was over the moon. Like, how is that the single greatest highlight of your adult life?"

"So, you dumped her because she was bragging about her Kardashian-approved picture on Instagram?" Edet was enjoying this exchange, as he did most of Ahmad's girl-related stories. Being in a committed relationship meant he had to live vicariously through the shenanigans his single friends experienced.

"I was tryna let her down easy."

"Mister let her down easy," he laughed, "You haven't changed at all!"

"Tell me why she texted me two days later, talking 'bout "what are we"?"

"We? Oui? Oh, you teach French now? That reminds me, the update in French didn't go through. The conversation casually changed to business. Both of them had been working together since their university days, even though they had been friends for over a decade prior to that.

A few weeks later, on Ahmad's birthday, they were at an Italian restaurant with some potential business partners when she walked in with two other girls. They were all good-looking in their own right, but she stood out. He recalled the way she walked, with grace and poise, her eyes: large and soulful, full of depth and expressiveness. Her dark hair was pulled into a sleek high ponytail partly covered with a floral patterned scarf delicately wrapped around her head. There was something about how unassuming she was and how she carried herself. It was almost as if she was unaware of just how much her smile illuminated the room she was in, how her eyes that sparkled with a hint of curiosity completely closed for a whole second every time she giggled. Amidst the clinking of cutlery and murmurs of conversations, he found himself constantly glancing in her direction, wondering why she took forever to decide which meal to order. She must have gone over the menu about five times before she eventually decided on the first item on the menu: Seafood pasta.

She laughed easily, and her eyes didn't wander. If they did, she would have noticed him staring. When they got up to leave, he knew he shouldn't go after her, but couldn't deny the burgeoning desire to talk to her again.

"Excuse me," he said to the ladies and to Edet, "I'm just gonna go say hi to someone I know."

"Those are university girls," Edet reminded him teasingly.

"No, it's not like that," he tried to ignore the knowing look on Edet's face. "That's Afreen's friend. I'm just gonna say hi." He wore his blazer, picked up his keys and phone from the table and headed for the door. "Fai'za," he called as he stepped out of the restaurant and towards the slim silhouette a few meters away.

Abuja, August 2012

Ahmad had not shaved in weeks. He sat on the secluded table, barely listening to the Burna boy song playing in the background. He called the number again and listened to it until it rang out. No answer.

The past five weeks in Kano had proved to be more challenging than finding a needle in a haystack. The last known address for *'yar* Agadez was Minjibir. There, they were told that she had moved to Bichi. When they found her house in Bichi, the landlord said she got a job at the Government Girls Secondary School in Sharada and was living on campus. When they got to the school, they received a black-and-white passport picture from a dusty old file that came out after a couple of bribes. It was a picture, Zainab was there to confirm it as well.

Finally, he had a face to blame. The longer he stared at the picture, the more disconnected he felt to the woman looking back at him, which is why he hated the importance that such tiny detail of his life was playing today. It was over twenty years ago, for fucks sake. Why should it matter?

The process of securing *'yar* Agadez's picture had taken about three weeks. His driver had interviewed people who knew the old city of Kano well and that was how he met Audu, a primary school teacher who freelanced as government research projects. When he heard the monthly salary being offered to whoever found this woman, he quit both jobs.

Ahmad worked most nights from one of his father's houses in Kano to code a mainframe for an aging app. His developers in Toronto finalized it and the programmers in Beirut worked on developing an image of what the woman in the photograph would look like presently. Armed with both pictures, the three of them scouted for anyone who knew anything about her, from Kurmi market all the way to Gidan Makama. Audu often took the lead as he knew the butchers in the markets, the *alhazai,* the policemen and the *hisbah,* Islamic law enforcers.

After the fifth week, Ahmad stopped accompanying his driver and Audu on the search; he stayed at the hotel instead, redialing Fa'iza's number obsessively.

The more he hung out with her, the more captivated he was by her. Most men would be; she was kind, innocent, and never turned down a challenge. After a few weeks of playing tug and pull with Fa'iza, he realized that her walls were higher than most girls he had encountered and that fascinated him. He knew she had a crush on him and he decided it was worth exploring. So, he turned on his charm and left no stone unturned.

"Ahmad, you know I don't interfere in your personal matter," his mother had said the night they returned from the General Hospital. He knew that she was aware of some aspects of his lifestyle even though she never brought it up. *"Amma wannan kam,* I have to ask you to leave this girl, if you don't have intentions that you can look me in the eye and say."

He had fallen in love with her. She fit right into his family and with her, imagining a future was easy. They had the same passions and aspirations.

A couple of days later, he waited for his mom to turn up for their usual coffee date on Thursdays at Balzac's Coffeehouse. It was a tradition they did whenever they were both in town. Between his back and forth to the US and her frequent trips out of town, sometimes they only met once a month. They usually met at noon, but he liked to go a few minutes early just to see the joy on her face when she saw him waiting. She usually met him there with both their orders on the table but this time, she found him sitting on an empty table, playing on his phone. When the barista brought her regular order, she asked why he wasn't eating.

"I'm fasting," he answered, "it's Thursday."

When he told her that he had been doing it consistently for over a month, she said, "*she's* really good for you."

He knew that already. She was probably even too good for him. At the beginning of the year, probably because of their upcoming wedding, she had lowered her guard around him, and he saw no harm in it. He loved her, and he was clear about it.

So, when he was expected to stop loving her based on a stranger's attestation, Ahmad knew that they did not comprehend how much. When he could not reach her on that day, he drove to her father's house at 2:30 am. He had thoughts that drove him blind with rage, thinking up the worst possible scenarios.

He dialed her number all night, but it was unreachable. Security patrol in the area tried to approach the vehicle he was in, but they backed off when they noticed the number plate. He waited until he heard the call for prayer, and he followed the few neighbors who came out of their houses to go pray in her father's masjid. When the morning prayer finished, he was able to get Amin's attention after her father went back to the section. Ahmad would have found the look of surprise on Amin's face funny if he were in a different situation.

"You know that's not possible," Amin said when he told him he wanted to see his sister.

"When last did you see her?" he asked.

"Last night," he answered. "Just before Isha."

"And how was she?" he asked. He couldn't believe that they were not checking up on her consistently.

"A little sad, but nothing serious," Amin answered and that was when Ahmad knew that they did not know how well Fa'iza masked her emotions. Did they even know her at all? As well as he did? He wondered.

"I have to see her," he said, "I'm not leaving until I do." He meant it.

The two men stared at each other until Amin sighed. He knew a determined man when he saw one. So he took him into the house and warned him that if she was still asleep, there was nothing he could do about that.

His phone rang. It was an unsaved number. *Is Fai'za calling from a different phone?* He thought as he answered. Disappointment clouded his face when he realized that it was Audu calling him from Kano. He was still on the trail. Ahmad wondered if they had reached another dead end.

"*Ranka ya dade,* we interviewed former teachers from the school she worked at and found that she moved back to Dag Manet in Niger. I have an address with me," he paused, "it seems fate has a sense of humor, afterall because *'Yar* Agadez is back in Agadez."

Ahmad smiled for the first time in weeks. That should have been the first place they checked. "Okay, get ready," he said as he stood up, leaving the booth and getting the keys to his car. "We're leaving for Agadez in the morning." As he ended the call, he looked at the picture of Fa'iza on his phone screen. It was a picture he had taken of her at the Caribana festival the previous summer in Toronto. That was how he wanted to remember her – full of life and laughter.

"I'm gonna fix this," he said to himself as he drove back home to Maitama.

Back in the club, the bartender wondered why the shot of vodka laid untouched.

Chapter 22

The wedding vendors no longer brought samples to our house and the wedding planner had stopped her search for a wedding hashtag. All my appointments with stylists and trials with make-up artists were canceled. What started as a busy year for Umma and my aunts became just another regular one year until someone else's wedding came up, and all of them busied themselves again.

Afreen and Aunty Mami came by the house almost immediately. It was one of those days I was laying in bed, crying quietly, when I heard the knock. I started to wipe away my tears and when she opened the door and saw me, her face fell. "Fa'iza *am*," she whispered, "oh Ya Allah!"

I sat up on the bed as she joined me and engulfed me in a hug. Afreen was behind her with teary eyes and seeing her, I started crying uncontrollably again.

"Ki yi hakuri. Be patient," she shushed me, rubbing my back. "You'll always be my daughter. You know I'm always going to be here for you." Her presence was calming and familiar, even though I had never felt so disconnected from her as I did in that moment.

The best thing about Aunty Mami's visit was that she didn't quote the Qur'an to me. That was what everyone else did – from Aisha to my uncles, unknowingly adding to my intense guilt and increasing anxiety.

Afreen joined me on the bed with her mum and they just held space with me, our silence punctuated by my loud sniffles. Even when it was just Afreen and me alone in my room, I couldn't bring myself to ask about Ahmad. I wondered if he had really gone to Kano, but I didn't want to even cling to a glimmer of hope because I wasn't sure I could survive another disappointment if his trip ended up yielding no good news for us.

The worst thing about facing my family was that I had to be cloaked by the cover of pretense every waking moment. Sure enough, my family was being sensitive to my plight. I realized that when Atine knocked on my door with breakfast, which was something that never happened, not under Umma's watch; None of the maids brought food into mine or my brothers' rooms. It happened again at lunch and at dinner time. I knew that if I didn't want to raise suspicions about the true nature of my relationship with Ahmad, I had to mask the hurt I was going through. It was terribly hard because I was already drowning in the weight of my own helplessness. So for days, before Atine came back for the plates, I would go and dump half of my breakfast in the wastebasket in my toilet. I didn't have the energy to take a bath, but I changed my abaya after zuhr to look like I did.

In her own way, Umma showed me extra love around that period. Whenever she grilled Abba's special chicken that even the kitchen staff didn't have the recipe to, she would send some to me. The cooks were always asking me if I wanted something different from what everyone else was eating; I knew they were following her instructions. I had no appetite, and I was still tossing most of my food in the garbage. On the weekends, I kept myself busy by going to Umma's room to help organize her closet, she would always 'find' some jewelry or perfume she would tell me to keep. Without fail, I would always pretend to be elated, even though I was dying inside; the pain had refused to stop. My mental health was deteriorating because I could not sleep at night. Every time I closed my eyes, I saw Ahmad; I felt his touch on my skin; I heard his voice in the hallway even though I knew he was not there. My next breakdown was always around the corner. Today, it was triggered by the scent of his oud on one of my scarves.

I was very relieved to leave the house for *Umrah* with Umma because

Ya Amin had become quite suspicious since Ahmad's impromptu visit to the house. I caught him staring at me a few times with an expression I could not read. He also listened closely to my phone calls and insisted on dropping me everywhere, even when I was just going to the store to pick up a prayer book. I kept acting like I was only disappointed and sad that I couldn't get married. It was exhausting because I was battling major panic attacks with no one to talk to.

I could not talk to the one person who could help me. After a week of letting Ahmad's calls ring out and go straight to voicemail, I switched off my phone. Hearing his voice would break me entirely, and I was barely hanging onto the thread of whatever was left of my sanity. I tried to delete our texts and pictures, but every time I started reading and deleting them, I would see something that sent me back to the edge of depression. Sometimes, it was as innocent as a picture of a book he was reading, or a picture of us together at an outdoor event with a crowd of people in the background. Those were happier times.

The evening before we left for Mecca, Hajiya Uwani was on one of her exhausting tirades of unwanted advice. We were sitting in Umma's parlour and the television was playing an Indian drama about unrequited love. Umma was watching the show and eating her fruits silently. "This is not a loss; just look at it this way, you've gained another big brother," Hajiya Uwani managed to make me feel worse every single day she came here.

I looked at Umma to bail me out, but she just stared at me quietly. My eyes filled with tears as I remembered the way Ahmad would plant tiny little kisses on the nape of my neck every time he walked up behind me. I remembered his hands going around my waist and pulling me closer to him. How could I think of him as a brother after everything we had done? The thought alone left me nauseated.

"With time, you'll forget him," Hajiya Uwani continued.

I nodded. Everybody went about minimizing the situation and it was not their fault; they could never have imagined what was between Ahmad and me in their wildest imagination. No one ever thought their daughter would engage in a haram relationship or a secret marriage. We were brought up to know better.

In Abuja, I gave out alms, I fasted. In Mecca, I completely surrendered myself; I cried and prayed to God for forgiveness with my forehead to the ground in *sajda*. I prayed to God to take away the feelings I had for Ahmad, my sadness about how my relationship with him turned out, and my shame about the acts I had committed that I couldn't talk about.

The Holy City brought about honest reflections. On days I didn't find myself surrounded by people, my mind would wander, and I would think about how I brought all this upon myself. This was the reason the Qur'an warned us against engaging in sin – especially premarital affairs and fornication. Now I was saddled with memories I couldn't erase, memories with a man who would never be mine. *If only I had been patient,* I thought. *If we had continued our halal relationship, maybe I wouldn't be in this much pain.*

Two days before I went back to Canada in September, Abba called me to go on a drive. We talked about the courses I was registered for in the upcoming semester. When the car finally came to a halt, he asked me to come down. I looked out of the window and realized we were now on the outskirts of Abuja. I opened the door, my black abaya flowing in the humid evening breeze. The sun was almost setting. We walked to an incomplete two-storey building.

He walked in front and I followed behind slowly. On the way, he saw a shovel by the steps in a dangerous position, bent down and changed its position away from the entrance. "Look where the workers left this – very dangerous." That was imbibed in him, a part of who he was.

"What do you think?" he asked, as we walked around the incomplete building. "For your Shelter?"

I widened my eyes in surprise. I had emailed him my business plan when I was in school and he'd reviewed it and made suggestions, which I implemented in the final document. But since I'd been back, we hadn't really spoken about it. I'd assumed he forgot. "Abba…?" my eyes welled with tears as I gave him a big hug, unable to come up with more words.

"I'm proud of your initiative, Fa'iza," he said as he patted my back. "The construction should be completed by your graduation, *insha Allah*, and you can start running it immediately."

On the plane to Canada for the Fall semester, I finally restored my phone to factory settings to erase all the content. With the reset, I was starting afresh; all the texts, pictures, videos and voice notes were gone. At the university, I buried myself in my studies. My study sessions with Ada and Sara continued, and we were even busier than usual; most of our sessions ended around 5 pm, and I always went back to the residence immediately.

Imagine my surprise, one chilly evening, when I returned to the rez, went through the sliding doors and found Ahmad in the quiet lobby. He looked at me silently as I stood rooted by the entrance.

Chapter 23

Ahmad had always been an analytical thinker. Logic and reason guided his actions; he questioned everything. Whenever the answers were vague or rooted in some timeworn tradition, he simply refused to ascribe by it. These traits influenced every aspect of his life, down to his career choice.

Ahmad did not let the shackle of being seen as a disappointment to his father hold him back from pursuing what he really wanted to study, UX design. Mid-semester in his second year in Law school, he informed his parents of his decision to drop out and move to the UK to start a new program. Years after his graduation – now a successful entrepreneur – he anonymously donated to numerous charities. When he found gaps in service delivery and healthcare teleconferencing, he built apps to solve those problems and to make lives easier for people. Islam, in his understanding, was also about charity and kindness, making life easy for people, and helping the needy.

He'd thought he was making his and Fa'iza's lives easier when he suggested that they got married late spring in Toronto. The marriage was a safety net, as he didn't want Fa'iza to be guilt-ridden every time they crossed one of her boundaries. He knew that the regret that came after the shame would drive her away from him forever, the shame that women had been conditioned by society into facing whenever they gave in to their desires outside marriage. Their marriage was officiated in the presence of an Imam at Eman Mosque with two Muslim witnesses and dowry – all the components needed for an Islamic marriage to be valid.

"Wifey," he'd said later that evening, raising his glass to Fa'iza during the small dinner they hosted in his apartment.

"Is that supposed to be a toast? I read that making a toast with water is bad luck," she'd joked, and he'd laughed. Together they looked picture-perfect. Both were blessed with great looks and a quiet kind of self-assurance that came with multi-generational privilege. She had a way of putting a smile across his face so effortlessly.

But for a while now, since he received news about the wet nurse, he had not been able to smile. When he returned from Agadez, Ahmad was faced with an unbearable truth, that he might lose Fa'iza. Several weeks in the Sahara with no progress had diminished his optimism of fixing the situation; yet, he held on, never giving up because there was so much at stake.

Logic just required him to start from the baseline, to make sure that all contingencies were accounted for. The first question was simple: Were they sure that it was the same woman?

He placed the enlarged black-and-white photograph on the table in front of his mother as she ate dinner. She sighed and adjusted her glasses as she studied the picture before meeting her son's gaze. "*Ita ce*. It's her."

"Can you please ask Fa'i' –" he paused. That was the first time he tried saying her name to someone else in weeks, "can you please ask Umma if this is the same person who worked for them?" He brought out another black-and-white picture of a random Fulani woman he had gotten from a Google search and placed it next to *'yar* Agadez's picture. "Actually, could you please ask her to pick which of these women worked for her?"

"Why do you think this matter hasn't been properly looked into?"

"Mum," his voice was strained. "Please do this for me."

Two weeks after their discreet wedding, Fa'iza and Ahmad were laying on his bed in Toronto. She laid on his chest, reviewing past exam question papers, while he read the final chapter of a book she'd recommended to him, *The Handmaid's Tale* with his head buried in the pillows. His fingers tugged her soft hair absentmindedly when she suddenly looked up at him and smiled.

"*Meye ne*? What is it?" he smiled down at her.

"I love you."

"I love you *forever*," he said, kissing her forehead.

On the last day of her exams, they got back to the residence late; they had gone to watch a late-night movie and then stopped for a midnight snack at one of the restaurants downtown that serve all-day breakfast.

"What time should I come pick you up tomorrow?" he asked. He was dropping her at his parent's house the following day, so she could spend the night before leaving for Nigeria. "Or... do you want to spend the night downtown?"

They started binge-watching a show when they got back to his place. It was dark but for the brightness of the television. As they shared a tub of ice cream – her head on his chest, listening to his heartbeat – the silent realization that they wouldn't see each other for a few months made them sleepless. They started kissing gently at first, and it got heated and passionate within minutes. He had never wanted someone as much as he did in that moment, and he wondered if he could physically stop himself this time as he had done over the months because the pressure of his hard-on was unbearable. His hand went over hers and slowly placed it on him. Her eyes widened as she looked down between them, but she did not take her hand off.

"Look at me," he said as his hand lifted her chin and his other hand went over hers, slowly guiding her as she stroked his length. He groaned as he pulled her into him and parted her lips with his. In one swift move, his hands went around her possessively and carried her into the bedroom.

They found themselves in a frenzy of intense need, with a forwardness heightened by legally being man and wife. His mouth went over her body, memorizing the taste of her skin and the softness of her curves. He pushed her to the brink and pulled back every time she got to the edge, and the sounds she made drove him wild.

"Do you want me to stop?" he looked down at her half-lidded eyes, her mouth slightly open, and her hair fanned out over his white sheets. All she had on was her white underwear and him, his black boxers. They had never made it this far.

"No… please…" her voice was laced with desire.

He took his time, stretching the night into what felt like forever as he learnt what made her moan. He pleasured her in ways she didn't know, and when her back arched and soft whimpers escaped her lips, he caught her trembling body in his arms, and his fingers continued from where his mouth stopped, moving with the urgency he knew she needed. "Yes, baby… that's it. Come for me," he said into her ear. And she came undone.

He held her through it all; he felt a fierce need to protect her. He knew he was the only one in the whole world to ever see her this vulnerable and so beautiful. He kissed her neck and her bare shoulders slowly. She moved and buried her face in his neck as she caught her breath, her fingers digging weakly into his skin. In that moment, Ahmad knew that he could never feel this way for anyone else but his wife.

"Are you okay, babe?"

"I don't think I'm ready to go all the way. I want to, but –" She looked up at him with her eyes slightly moist, the only light coming into the dark room was from a crack in the drapes allowing the moonlight in.

"That's okay, babe," he said as he pulled the duvet over their bodies, their arms still wrapped around each other. He kissed the tips of her fingers as she reached up to stroke his face gently. "This was perfect." It was – breathtakingly so.

"I love you," she said.

"I love you forever, Fa'iza," he kissed her forehead gently.

* * *

As the distance between them closed in the busy lobby of the residence, it took a lot of willpower for him not to grab her, hold her tightly, and never let her go. She had lost some weight since he last saw her in Abuja; it had been three months. Her neck seemed longer, her cheekbones were more prominent, and her figure was much thinner in the puffy black jacket she wore over baggy black jeans.

"Hey," he said. A moment of silence passed between them as they looked at each other. "You've been hard to reach." When her phone number rang endlessly and when it went to voicemail, he told himself she was still processing her thoughts and maybe she needed time. When her number became invalid, he concentrated on combing through Audu's daily reports from Agadez and finding possible solutions for them. But something happened the previous evening. When he got back from the office, there was a package waiting for him and he recognized her writing on the address label.

"Hi," she said. She wouldn't meet his eyes; she looked everywhere but at him.

"Do you mind if we sit for a minute?" his voice carefully measured as he pointed to the chairs by the fireplace in the lobby.

"I need to g–"

"Just one minute," he interrupted. He had expected her to come up with an excuse.

She sighed and walked slowly to the chair and sat down. She was fidgeting – pulling the sleeves of her jacket to cover her wrists, adjusting the ends of her scarf.

"How have you been?" He was worried about her.

She shrugged. "Why are you here?" Her eyes unable to meet Ahmad's gaze. The air crackled with unresolved tension from the raw emotion that made him want to close the distance between them. As if searching for an escape route from the overwhelming emotions that threatened to consume him, he exhaled as he answered with a question.

"What's this?" He raised the small box that came in the mail the previous evening and pushed it toward her.

"You know what it is."

"Why would you return it?" his voice was gentle, "it belongs to you."

"Ahmad, I can't wear your ring anymore."

"Give it to charity, then. Or throw it in the garbage," he said, glancing at the box and then looking back at her. The ring he had proposed with was in the small Tiffany box, and the bracelet he had bought her in Italy was in a velvet Chanel pouch. "Damn it," he shook his head slowly, "I can't believe you would give up on us so easily."

"Staying away is the right thing to do."

"We've been here before," his voice was rising, and he had to mentally recalibrate to bring it down. "These feelings won't disappear because we're staying away from each other." She looked down at her fingers, saying nothing. "C'mon. Tell me you don't think about us." He was talking about the last few weeks they had spent together; he could not get her out of his mind. He knew that it had to be the same for her.

"Let's just pretend that – that it never happened." She looked uncomfortable at the subtle mention of their intimacy.

A muscle in his jaw clenched, and he chuckled bitterly, "but it happened. You can't undo that."

A veil of silence descended upon them, the weight of unspoken words hanging heavily in the air. Their eyes locked for a fleeting moment, an ocean of shared memories and unfulfilled desires passing through them. Pain clouded her eyes, and he watched as tears formed.

"Bye, Ahmad," her voice was strained and fragile as she stood up and tightened her scarf over her head just as the first tear fell.

"Fa'iza – listen." He said, his tone a mixture of resignation and longing. His words had hurt her, and he felt like complete and utter shit.

She started walking away, and before he could stop himself, he stood up and grabbed her left hand. She turned around and looked at him. "Ahmad, get your –"

He didn't allow her to finish her sentence. He leaned down and covered her lips with his. *Heavens be damned, you are mine.* That was the only thought in his head as he pulled her closer. All logic and sense of reason deserted him.

Chapter 24

December was hard. The panic attacks have been in full swing since the last time I saw Ahmad and the dreams started immediately after. Most nights, I woke up at odd hours drenched in my own sweat, unable to breathe and my heart thumped like it would burst out of my chest.

As I scrambled into an upright position, I frantically tried to recite all the prayers I could recall: *a'udhubika min sharri ma sana'tu. La ilaha illa anta subhanaka inni kuntu minaz-zalimin. La hawla wala quwwata illa billahil aliyyil* azim. I clutched my chest in the darkness, muttering the shahada over and over until it subsided.

The dreams always started the same way, and they felt real; so real that I often thought Ahmad was there with me. Like most of my memories about him, they were in dorm room or on his bed and the pleasure I could feel was familiar. But when I woke up, I would be alone, aroused and wet. It was like my body remembered and craved his touch. I felt like an addict getting nightly reminders to get a fix from him.

It started the day he returned the jewelry. As I sat next to him in the lobby, listening to him speak, I could not keep calm. I could feel the familiar tightening in my chest and the quickening of my breath. My mind kept wandering to now-deleted filthy texts, stolen kisses when we thought no one was watching... but he was my milk brother. My brother.

Has God forsaken me? Why are my prayers not answered? God, please since he is forbidden for me, take all the feelings I have for him away from my heart. Why do I still feel the same for him, after everything I've done during the summer to ensure that this feeling was removed from my heart?

I couldn't bear looking into the pain in his eyes. He looked at me the same way he did during our stolen moments of passion when he made me feel things I'd never experienced before. But now, his eyes carried only hurt.

I tried to leave, before he could see the effect he was having on me, because he always knew but his hand stopped me. Before I knew what was happening, he was kissing me. Two seconds of his lips on mine – that was all it took to send me down this rabbit hole. The little progress I thought I'd made all washed away as his cologne overwhelmed me. "Ahmad!" I screamed as I pushed him off me. I looked around the almost empty lobby, hoping nobody saw. I felt my eyes moistening up and tears began rushing down my face. "Are you mad?"

"Fa'iza, wait. I'm sorry," his hands went over his mouth. "It has been so long, I – I lost control."

If he truly loved me, he wouldn't be here. This was not something we could change, no matter how desperately we wanted to. It was something written in the Qur'an. Who was he to fight that? What was he trying to rekindle? Was I supposed to become his *haram* girlfriend now, and then his mistress in the future? What exactly was he hoping to accomplish by coming here?

"I'm so sorry," his eyes were now reddened, "I wasn't think –"

I put my hands together in front of my face. "*Dan girman Allah, ka rabu da ni*. For the love of God, stay away from me." I begged, my voice shaking. I was falling apart day by day and all he came to do was kiss me. That was all he was thinking of? I walked away angrily, moving past the elevator and going up the stairs, trying very hard not to look back at him.

The next day, I couldn't make it to my lectures or for the study session. Ada came by the rez to find me when she couldn't reach my phone. My roommate must have opened the door for her because she came straight to my room and found me sitting down on the floor in my pajamas, blowing into a brown paper bag trying to calm down.

"Jesus! Fa'iza?" she dropped her bag and rushed to me, lifting me up to help me sit on the bed. She opened the window behind my bed and started opening my drawers frantically. "Where's your inhaler?"

I struggled to catch my breath. "I am not asthmatic," I gasped.

She stared at me. I'd told her I was struggling with the cancellation of my engagement, but I didn't give her details. I'd been acting like I was okay all semester, so she was visibly shocked to find me in that state.

"You have to see a therapist." Without waiting for a reply, she took out her phone and started dialing the University's counseling services.

"I don't need therapy," I managed to say, trying to steady my breath.

"Have you seen yourself?" she asked. I glanced up at the mirror and to be honest, I wouldn't recognize myself too – dark circles around my eyes and stress acne all over my face. I was also a size smaller; I hadn't gone to shop for new clothes this semester, but I'd used safety pins on my skirts and belts for my trousers.

Two days later, the counseling services referred me to a therapist's clinic after my initial assessment. As I looked through their website, I saw someone in a hijab. She was the only non-Caucasian therapist on the list, so I decided to reach out to her to book an appointment.

"Hello Fa'iza. I'm Dr. Na'ima," she said, offering the couch opposite her for me to seat. "Before we start, I want to let you know that everything we discuss here is confidential and guided by the Canadian doctor-patient privacy laws." I nodded. "So, what brings you here today?" she asked, opening her notebook.

It took four sessions for me to bring up Ahmad. I talked about everything else – my insomnia, the loss of my appetite, and the panic attacks. She made notes and asked questions. She must have known that something was connecting all my problems together, but she didn't push.

"I was supposed to get married this month," I blurted out on our last session before I went back home for the Christmas break.

She didn't look surprised. "Why didn't you?" she asked as she wrote in her book.

I looked at her black hijab – something that made me feel like a fraud whenever I wore it nowadays.

"Dr. Na'ima, where are you from?" I asked. I had always wanted to know.

She made some notes again, dropped her pen and glanced at me. "My parents moved here from Somalia when I was five," she removed her glasses, "Fa'iza, why do you use avoidance as a coping mechanism?"

"I wasn't avoiding. I've always wanted to ask," I answered.

She looked through her notes, "You keep talking about this marriage, you don't say who he is, or what happened and when I ask, you change the subject. Why do you think that is?"

I didn't tell her the truth until the second session of the new semester, after I'd come back from Nigeria. "I think I'm being punished for my sins," I said. As I used my fingers to smooth the fabric of my long skirt.

She didn't write anything in her notebook. "Who's punishing you?" she asked gently.

"Allah."

"And why are you being punished, Fa'iza?"

I chose a Muslim therapist because she would understand. From her profile, I had read that she was an Islamic therapist who mostly worked with Muslims, so I knew I didn't have to explain the tenets of my *deen* to her, since I was paranoid about going with a Nigerian therapist, scared that they might know someone who knew my family and I was scared of this aspect of my life finding it's way to my family. Dr. Na'ima here would understand the different levels of my error. For me to heal, I had to accept everything that had happened with me and Ahmad and talk about it with someone who could help because clearly, bottling it up was not helping. "Because I committed Zina," I said as the tears filled my eyes.

Dr. Na'ima must be in her forties and maybe she had a daughter who was my age or close to my age. When I finally said out loud what had been eating me up for months, I waited for the judgment, for the you-should-have-known-better, you-should-have-abided-by-the-Qur'an look. A year ago, that was what I would have done. She did none of that.

"Well, Allah is *At-Tawwab,* the acceptor of repentance. Do you believe that?"

I nodded yes and broke down completely in the white-walled office on the 3rd floor of the building. Only then did I begin to heal.

Chapter 25

While time normally moved for everyone else, it seemed to crawl for Ahmad – hours dragged into days and then into weeks and new months came and went without reprise. There were only so many ways a man could bury himself in work while fighting against his better judgment. He had to consciously stop himself from reaching out to her. Ahmad was a man with pride. Maybe it was a Hausa thing – perhaps it was a masculine one – and although he would never admit it, he had an ego. He had canceled business ventures in the past just because he felt that someone on his team was being disrespected. He could never tolerate it when people treat people around him with lesser respect than they accorded him. Yet, he found himself multiple times resisting the urge to remind Fa'iza that he was not giving up on them, that he was still searching for the wet nurse

He spent sleepless nights going through the documents Audu sent him from Agadez whose search had taken him to Niamey. Every time he read the transcripts of interviews with people who claimed to know her, he wanted to reach out to Fa'iza to tell her that they were getting closer. But they weren't getting closer; it had been many months of disappointments. It was like chasing a mirage; the harder they chased, the further she got.

Without fail, he showed up at the office at 7 am every day, earlier than everyone. On the day that marked their first anniversary, he found himself more and more agitated. He was opening an email when he heard a shuffle at his door. He looked up as Brooke came in.

"Would you like me to cancel the Ritz Maldives reservation?" she asked, looking up from her tablet.

"No, don't worry about it." They were supposed to start their honeymoon with ten days in the Maldives before immersing themselves in the wonders of Bali. He looked back at his computer screen and let out a deep sigh.

The past year had been the most difficult in his life thus far. It had started on a high and, despite all his efforts, snowballed into a colossal loss. Like a phone call right around the time the snow started falling over Yonge-Dundas Square, covering the city he thought he would call home for the next few years in a blanket of white. Like everything he had feared, he faced the phone call head-on. Clearing his throat to mask his hesitation.

"Ahmad?" It was his mother. "Did you see my text?"

"Yes, I did."

"I'm sorry, Ahmad. Umma confirmed *'yar* Agadez's picture. It's the same woman."

Well, it is official. She does exist, he thought. "That's okay, mum. I just wanted to be sure."

* * *

For the seventh time since the new year started, Ahmad sat down at Toronto Pearson's business lounge, waiting for his flight. He was distractedly scrolling through her pictures – too quickly to linger on any, just a mindless scrolling that indicated that his mind was elsewhere. Truth be told, he even knew the exact order that they came in. There was one he took of her right before summer; she was covering her face with a green scarf on the football field as she laughed. Another of her wearing his black hoodie and petting a kitten at the zoo in Mississauga. He scrolled faster. She'd sent this to him on one of his work trips to the US; she was in the library, posing with a Tim Horton's cup. The next one was of both of them together at a Basketball match when he got them front row tickets to the Raptors game, another kissy-face picture she sent him.

He exhaled loudly as he returned to his home screen. he did this multiple times a day, like he was trying to alter his memory of their last interaction – her words, the tears in her eyes, how was it that he was the cause of that much pain? Why would she beg him to leave her alone? Did she really mean that?

As his flight to Ireland was announced, Ahmad returned his phone to his pocket and dragged his hand luggage to the waiting airport staff to board. His passport had such varied recent stamps for countries he had visited for the same purpose. While he was in Nigeria, he went to Minna, then Sokoto. When he didn't get favorable answers to his questions, he left for Sudan. Two weeks later, he was in Riyadh, then Malaysia. It was safe to say he was following scholars that he remembered her listening to, scholars whose words she kept close to her heart.

In between flights, he would go through his emails for replies to his questions. It always started the same way: *As-salamu alaikum, esteemed brother in Islam. We thank you for your generous donation to our institute. After discussion with the Ulamas, we regret to inform you that –*

After the fifth letter of regret, Ahmad stopped reading the emails past the first paragraph. Not even the impressive dividends from his company's financial records could get him in a better mood. Yet every time, he reached a roadblock. He insisted to himself that he must have missed something. His gut would just not allow him to accept what everyone was telling him. He started paying more attention to religious texts and publications. When he had questions for the sheikhs, he would attend their lectures, join them in congregational prayers and then reach out to them with his question. Nothing changed. Eventually, he was at the end of her list. It was June and her favorite scholar was holding a lecture in Ireland. Ahmad booked a flight as soon as the opportunity presented itself. An old classmate of his from university happened to be the organizer of the Muslim event and had reached out for donations. He gladly obliged and then pulled some strings for a one-on-one with the Scholar.

As Ahmad sat in the air-conditioned waiting room of the hotel suite, his right leg was restless, and he could not stop hitting the heel of his shoe on the carpet. The seven-hour flight was a drag, but the lecture was very informative, and he stayed for all three sessions of it.

When the door opened and the bearded man walked in wearing a white robe, Ahmad found himself on his feet. "As-salamu Alaikum wa rahmatullahi wa barakatuh," he said as he walked into the room, his voice carrying an air of authority as Ahmad had expected. It was a face he recognized; Fai'za used to send him short video clips of the mufti's lectures on Fridays and since their separation, he often found himself rewatching the videos to fill the void her absence.

"Wa alaikumus-salam rahmatullahi wa barakatuh," Ahmad answered as they shook hands.

"Sit down, brother," he motioned for Ahmad to sit on the plush chair. He took a seat behind the glossy white table and looked down at the paper he was holding; Ahmad knew it was the letter he had written to him. The room was quiet as the mufti read, the only sound was Ahmad's foot hitting the ground restlessly. Eventually, the scholar finished reading.

"Brother," he started. "My attention was already brought to your question a few months ago by another Alim you reached out to some months back," he paused and looked Ahmad straight in the eye, "I can't tell you anything different from what they've all told you; marriage between this couple is not permissible in Islam."

Ahmad leaned forward. "No, I completely understand that." It had taken him a while, but he now understood the implications and limitations of why it was that way what brought him all the way here was something different.

"As I said in the letter, I wonder if something can be done," he paused as the scholar watched him with steady eyes, "My point is, when you mistakenly kill someone – an accident or something – you pay *diyah*, right?"

"Yes, financial compensation to the family of the victim," the scholar responded, adding, "if it was a real mistake." He raised his hand to emphasize his point.

"Exactly. And there's *Fidyah* and *Kaffara* for people who can't fast or have to break their fast," Ahmad said and the older man nodded. *Fidyah* was made for fasts missed out of necessity, when someone couldn't make up for the fast due to ill health or pregnancy. "So, you have to do *Kaffara* when you intentionally break your fast during Ramadan – you either fast for 60 days straight, or you feed 60 poor people. Yes?" The scholar nodded, and Ahmad continued: "My question is, in this situation, can the people involved feed – let's say 1000 people for 1000 days – as atonement?" He was grasping at straws now, but he had to. He owed it to her.

Ahmad could feel the Mufti's stare as he read the situation of Ahmad's crisis through the words he didn't say and the ones between the lines of his letter. He sighed as he leaned back into his chair. "Brother, I'm going to ask you this and you don't have to answer, if you don't want to. Have you – in any way – transgressed the boundaries that Allah imposed upon you regarding what is *haram* and what is *halal*?"

Ahmad remained quiet. He sighed, then clasped his hands together and looked at the floor. *Which of the boundaries?* He thought to himself. The ones they thought of as minor before they got married, or the one that they crossed by getting married. There was also a third one they crossed because they had gotten married. A marriage he had initiated so that she would not feel guilty about getting physical with him – only to find that the marriage was never valid in the first place. The relationship they shared had no name, which made everything they had done worse than just *fornication*. Until recently, he didn't think of it as a big deal, but this was not just that; this was incest. The thought of that alone was enough to make the strongest of men go mad, enough to make a man in love deranged.

"From your silence," the Mufti continued silently, "I may know your answer."

When Ahmad raised his head again, his eyes were moist. The Mufti said a few more things, but everything he heard made his head pound. All his efforts had been a waste. They were impossible right from the beginning.

When Ahmad got up to leave, the weight in his heart was heavier than it was when he came in.

"Brother Ahmad?" the Mufti called. Ahmad turned around to see the Mufti looking at him with eyes filled with sympathy. "Where are you from, if you don't mind me asking?"

Ahmad cleared his throat, "Nigeria."

The Mufti nodded. "I guessed as much from your last name. I've been there a few times – wonderful people, mashaAllah," he said. "You look like you're from a good family." He allowed his words to sink into Ahmad's mind for a minute."If you have the means to feed 1000 people in need for 1000 days, do it *fisabilillah,* for the sake of Allah. Allah is the best of planners."

Ahmad nodded.

"May Allah make us stronger than our desires," the Mufti said.

"Ameen," Ahmad reached for the doorknob and repeated the prayer back to himself in Hausa: *Allah ka sa mu fi karfin zuciyan mu.*

Chapter 26

I wasn't sleeping well. I always woke up around 2 am or 3 am, no matter how late I went to bed. I did some *nafila* (voluntary prayers), studied before fajr and talked to my parents in Abuja before the sun came up. I also started going for yoga more frequently, and I looked so much better than I did around this time last year. I had been having so much free time since deactivating my Instagram; everyone was suddenly into "couple goals," and I got tired of liking pre-wedding pictures. The shelter in Abuja was almost complete. Most of the primary donors were extended family members and people who wanted to impress Abba since he never accepted their gifts; they always seemed extra eager to dig deep into their pockets whenever I dropped by with my business proposal. But there was still a staffing problem. I was putting out job ads and going through multiple resumes and when Abubakar noticed how overwhelming it was, he suggested a staffing company. With that came dealing with carpenters, electricians and plumbers. I had lost my vocal cords trying to coordinate logistics in three weeks I spent in Nigeria while I was on Christmas break, so when the time came to leave the supervision to the caretaker, I was elated.

Back in Canada, the ambassador and Aunty Mami were still kind and gracious when I visited them, which was now only twice or thrice in a semester. I was very busy with school – at least, that was my excuse for not visiting as often as I used to. Towards the end of the semester, Afreen and I were at their dining table talking about a mutual friend's divorce, which was a big surprise because she got married about two years prior.

"She told me that he just changed overnight," Afreen said as she painted her nails with black *halal* nail polish. "You know they only dated for a month, so she never really got to know him."

"Well, sometimes, courting for shorter periods is the best. *Ya fi lada*; it has more blessings." If not for anything, short courtships didn't allow you to succumb to sexual tension and engage in sin like I did.

"Not always. People just aren't honest about who they are in general. They don't show who they really are and short courtships don't give you much time to figure it out."

I noticed movement outside the window, and the smile slowly disappeared from my face as Ahmad's white SUV pulled up into the driveway. I had not seen him since that day he came by the residence and it had been nine months, two weeks and five days. If I had known that he was coming to see his parents today, I would have postponed my visit.

We heard him come into the house and listened to his footsteps as he went upstairs to Aunty Mami's living room.

"Are you okay?" Afreen asked as she watched my face, "we can go watch something in my room if you want."

I was tired of running from him. I never slept over in the house anymore because of him; the only reason I dropped by was that it was an election year in Nigeria and the ambassador's tenure was coming to an end. They were leaving for Nigeria in less than a week, and I came to wish them a safe trip back.

"No, it's okay," I said as I added some grilled fish to my plate and heaped a spoonful of *yaji* pepper. I needed to numb my senses, and the heat from the chili pepper usually did the trick by making me focus on my burning tongue.

"I didn't know he was back from Ireland; I would have told you," she said apologetically. Afreen knew how hard the breakup was for me. My messages were filled with texts of her checking on me. Ahmad, on the other hand, was always traveling – not that I was keeping tabs on him. I just heard it in conversations the few times I visited. He was in Riyadh, somewhere in Malaysia, and now Ireland. *It must be nice,* I thought to myself. *He's busy globetrotting and chasing his paper, building his company every other day. For him, life just continued easily.*

"Nah, I'm good actually," I said as I put a heavily-peppered piece of fish in my mouth. She turned around as the door opened. I could perceive his cologne even before he walked in and I didn't want to look up, but I did. He was on the phone and our eyes met. He held my gaze for a second before he looked away. He didn't say anything to either of us; he just mumbled something to the person at the other end and left the sitting room, quietly closing the door behind him. A few seconds later, we heard a bang down the hallway as he shut the door to his room. I flinched at the sound and I drank the iced zobo to drown the pain. My heart had not stopped beating wildly and the goosebumps on my skin didn't look like they were subsiding anytime soon.

"You know what?" Afreen broke the silence. "I don't like this color. How about we go out for a real mani-pedi?" She tried to keep her voice light and cheery, but her eyes looked sad. Somehow, I knew they were a reflection of my own eyes and I was happy to leave the house for some fresh air.

My sessions with Dr. Na'ima continued. They ranged from a varying degree of emotions – sometimes indignation, sometimes anger. "Why does he still send me flowers on my birthday, yet he could not even say salam when he saw me?" I stood behind the couch in Dr. Na'ima's office as I paced the carpeted floors.

She barely made notes these days. Our sessions felt like conversations with a really wise sage.

"Let's hold onto that thought for a minute," she said calmly, "and let's examine how that made you feel."

"I don't know," I replied. "How would getting flowers on your birthday from your ex make you feel?"

"Did you want him to say salam?"

Not really. I didn't want to be reminded of what his voice sounded like. But instead, I said: "Yeah, it would've made the whole situation less awkward."

"How did you know he sent the flowers?"

Flowers got delivered to me on the morning of my birthday – two dozen red roses. I honestly didn't care for flowers and what having them entailed – finding a vase, watering them and trying to keep them alive for as long as possible even though they would eventually wither.

"It came with a handwritten scribble," I said, sitting down on the chair and putting a throw pillow on my legs. "It said: "Happy birthday, Insom."

"He was the only person who called you that. That's his nickname for you," she said quietly, and I nodded.

Dr. Na'ima somehow managed to remember all the details about my relationship with Ahmad. I had been candid with her – telling her all about how we met, how I fell for him and how it ended. Sometimes our sessions were like chatting with an old friend but other times, it was painful, like around the anniversary of our mistake of a "marriage" That day, I sat down with bloodshot eyes on her couch with a box of tissues and the bin next to me, bawling shamelessly.

"I just feel like I'm a bad person," I blew my nose, "I know that I'm not supposed to, but I still have feelings for him." I still loved him.

"Fa'iza, that doesn't make you a bad person," she said.

"No but, like, a bad Muslim. How do you have feelings for someone that's like your –" I struggled to call him brother. My heart just refused to accept the idea, even though my mind had made peace with it.

"Well, love isn't a tap you can just turn off instantly," she said. I looked at her in her nice warm blazer and her teal-colored hijab that matched her inner blouse. "Liking him and being forbidden to him are two truths that can exist together. The fact that you're not acting on those feelings is commendable, Fai'za; and you need to remember your affirmations," she smiled softly, "use kinder words to yourself."

I blew a raspberry, exhaling loudly. I felt so tiny, like a child even. "Can I lie down?" I asked, arranging the pillows at the end of the couch without waiting for her reply.

"Of course," she replied, "get comfortable."

I laid on the couch staring at the ceiling until her voice broke into my thoughts, "you know what? How about we do an exercise?" She brought out her notebook for the first time in today's session. "I call it the 3-1 balance."

I liked learning new things, so whenever I heard something I knew nothing about, my curious mind forgot about my other problems and latched onto that immediately.

"It's about humanizing people we place on a pedestal. I want you to tell me three things that drew you to Ahmad and then one thing you dislike about him."

I sighed. I had to make a conscious effort not to think of the things we did when we were alone. Those things only brought back my panic attacks. I could never forget the way he smiled, the way he held his coffee mug with his left hand, the way he always inhaled and exhaled whenever we hugged, the tiny pecks on my lips after we kiss, the forehead kisses, the way he knew about changes to my flights before I did. "I like how he treats his mum and his sister," I said slowly and honestly. Ahmad's relationship with his mom was so beautiful, he revered and loved her, and his mannerisms around her showed just that. I loved their relationship and even though he and Afreen were constantly bickering, I knew how much he cared for her. I saw how hard he fought for her happiness with Zafar. He was practically the only one in the family on her side. The only one she felt comfortable enough to come clean to, in the hopes that he would persuade her parents on her behalf.

"Okay, that's one. You're doing great. What else?"

"I like that he built his own thing from scratch instead of relying on his father's wealth, like most guys I know would." She nodded at me as I spoke; I had told her months before about how Ahmad lived by his own rules.

She nodded, waiting for me to continue.

"I don't have a third reason," I said. It was a lie.

"I'm sure if you dig a little deeper, you would find something."

This was the reason I fell as hard as I did. "I liked how he made me a priority," I sniffed, "like nothing else mattered when I was with him. He made me feel good about myself and –" *I know his love is genuine.* I couldn't complete my sentence. The tears choked me.

She gave me a minute to reach for the box of tissues. The room was once again filled with the sound of me blowing my nose.

"Thanks for sharing," she said, as if to encourage me to trust her with my deepest secrets. "Just so you know, having feelings for a man like this doesn't make you a bad person, Fa'iza. He sounds like someone anyone would fall for. You're not weak for doing so."

I sighed, relieved. I needed to hear that. It was okay that I still had feelings for him because I was sure that with time, they would slowly fade. It was a brutal truth but, with the much-needed compassion.

"In our earlier sessions we talked about how being the youngest and only daughter in cultures like ours can make one feel unseen," she reminded me, "and when we find someone who sees us for the first time, it is like a serotonin and dopamine high."

My sessions got better, and so did I. As I started looking for internship positions in November, my sessions had dropped from weekly to once in three weeks after my follow-up assessment. I was shopping again, I even went on a road trip with Ada and Sara to Niagara Falls. My first time there was with Ahmad and Afreen the previous year.

The year had come to an end and the week the snow started again, I excitedly walked into Dr. Nai'ma's office. I dropped my bag on the couch and made myself some tea. "You know, I've been thinking," I said as I stirred some honey into my cup. "When you asked, I didn't have anything I disliked about Ahmad, but I finally got one." I sat down on the couch, pleased with myself. "He's actually very manipulative," I said. I was literally shaking with excitement at the idea. Ahmad might actually be the villain in my story, and I had a damn good reason to give him that title.

"You seem very happy with this epiphany,' she said as she watched me take a sip of my tea. "How did you arrive at this?"

I dropped the teacup on the saucer, placed it on the wooden coaster on the side table, leaned back into the couch and crossed my leg. "He has this way of making you do what he wants in a way that makes you feel like it was your idea." I spoke fast, with animated hands, excited to share this information with her.

"Can you give me more clarity on that?" she said, unmoved.

"So, for example, when he's talking to anyone – his assistant maybe – he would not say, 'Brooke, bring me x-y-z', if he wanted a file; he would say, 'do you wanna send me that file we talked about?'" I did an awful imitation of his British accent.

"Okay?" she did not get it. Why else was she not celebrating this incredible moment? I had finally found what I could use to hate Ahmad forever, what would help me get over him. And she wasn't excited.

"Okay, so while we were dating, he would not say, 'I want this', or 'let's do this'," I spoke slowly so that she wouldn't miss a word I was saying, "He would ask, 'what do *you* want? 'or 'whatever *you* want',"

"So, he always wanted your input?"

"As a way to convince me into thinking it was my idea."

She was silent for a while, like she was wondering how I came to such a conclusion. Finally, she asked, "so you think he was persuasive?"

"Yes," I clapped as I exclaimed. Manipulative sounds better in my head but sure, I'd take this.

"Okay, good job completing the 3 -1. Always remember not to get fixated on anyone else. Take responsibility for your actions. Therapy is about you, not the people who you believe have wronged you." Our 1-hour session seemed to breeze by these days. This time last year, they were such a drag.

Chapter 27

It was past midnight in Vegas, and Ahmad was wide awake. Surrounded by loud music and flashing lights. Scantily dressed hosts in fishnet stockings and leather corsets holding liquor bottles were walking around the VIP section. Edet's bachelor party was just beginning to get into full swing and he was already looking for a way out. He wondered when Vegas stopped being fun for him, when *he* stopped being fun. The old Ahmad was always the life of the party but this version of Ahmad hid in the shadows, away from the partying as he could possibly get.

He brought out his phone, checked his email and made up his mind to put the townhome he purchased back on the market. It was Fa'iza's and his dream home – a backyard, double master bedrooms with a jacuzzi. It would have been the perfect home and he had held onto it long enough, like he held onto pieces of her.

Edet danced towards him. Bobbing his head and throwing his hands up, he had done a very good job of ignoring all the ladies trying to give him a happy sent forth into married life. Edet was fiercely loyal; Ahmad knew that they didn't stand a chance. Joanne had this on lock and key. "You sure you don't want a beer?" Edet asked Ahmad for the umpteenth time, as he ordered himself another one. He was staying off the hard stuff; a passed-out groom was never a good look.

"Nah, I'm good, man," Ahmad replied, pulling his bottle of water closer to him.

Edet was slightly buzzed. He took a selfie and sent it to his wife-to-be, who was also out with her girlfriends.

"Still not drinking?" Edet asked. Even though he knew Ahmad had never been much of a drinker, he knew his friend to never reject a sip.

"Kinda lost my taste for it," he said as he drank some water. He had not had a drink in years, not since he met Fa'iza. He went through a slump where he would just order shots, but he could not bring himself to drink them because of a promise he had made to her.

A lady trying to catch Ahmad's eye all night started making her way toward them. He took the opportunity to go outside for some air and found himself critical of women who were just being friendly. They tried too hard, and they laughed at things that weren't funny. Most importantly, they were not *her*.

As he walked back to his hotel room, he called Audu and told him to retrace his steps one more time from the beginning to see if they had missed something.

Back In Toronto, Ahmad spent most of the day working and half of the night doing the same. He thought about times he used to go to the gym whenever she was around him because it was hard being in the same room and not being able to touch her. Now he went to the gym to keep her thoughts out of his head, and he was there a lot. He couldn't stay for long hours in his room either because her scent was wrapped up in everything – his sheets, his pillows, his shirts. He eventually told the cleaners to toss out the extra toothbrush in his washroom and her gym shoes.

Every morning, when Ahmad walked to the Tim Horton's downstairs, the baristas would start brewing his usual two cups of French Vanilla to go. He tipped well and knew most of them by their first names, so they remembered his regular order. Even though the person he usually got the second cup for wanted nothing to do with him, he couldn't bring himself to tell the baristas that he only wanted one cup, so he always took both and drank them. The caffeine high kept him productive for most of the day.

On some days, Ahmad would find himself driving towards the residence.

He would park far from the building, but close enough to see people as they entered and exited the building. On Tuesdays and Thursdays, she had early morning classes and at 7:46 am, she would come out of the sliding doors hiding in oversized sweaters or puffy jackets, always in a hurry. She didn't drink coffee anymore; she drank from a clear water bottle with lemon or cucumber slices instead. Two days every week, if he was not out of town, Ahmad found himself watching her for about 40 seconds as she walked past the trees, crossed the road and walked further away until she disappeared into the University building. Then he would drive to work for his meetings.

During one of those meetings, Edet noticed a man who had been coming to the office every month for a year. He was not on the payroll for the company, but he noticed that Ahmad always paid him in cash. The man wore a baseball hat, ducked his head around corners, as if he were hiding and carried a black briefcase. One morning, as they discussed the in-house ratings and an upcoming pilot-testing for their most recently launched software, Edet looked at the man through the glass pane outside the meeting room, wondering what business he had with Ahmad. It was peculiar that Ahmad had the receptionist usher him in without waiting every time he stopped by.

Ahmad's gaze followed Edet's and when he realized that the man was waiting, he cut the RFP bids short and requested for a break. "Why don't we circle back to this after lunch?" he looked at his phone as everyone got up to leave the conference room, except Edet.

"Are you in some kind of trouble?" Edet gestured to the man outside the window, who was pacing up and down the hallway with his head ducked.

"What do you mean?"

Edet lowered his voice. "Is it drugs? Money laundering?" He had known Ahmad longer than everyone in the building and knew that his friend was not the kind of man to indulge in shady business of any kind. However, he had watched Ahmad become more and more of a brooding recluse this past year. This was not the man he knew.

"Drugs?" Ahmad started laughing, and Edet joined him, relieved.

"Well, you never talk to me anymore, since –" Edet started but couldn't bring himself to finish the sentence. He looked towards Ahmad's phone, knowing Fa'iza's picture was still set as his screensaver.

Ahmad looked up at him, and when their eyes met, Edet knew that the conversation was over. Whenever Fa'iza was mentioned, even without words, Ahmad always found a way to end the conversation.

"Let's talk about *Project Feed-A-Child* when you have a minute," Edet said as he left the room and headed downstairs to run a facial recognition analysis on the stranger.

"You said if anything suspicious came up, I should contact you," the man with the baseball hat said in an unmistakable French accent as he came into the conference room.

Ahmad found Pierre on a cold winter day a few months prior huddled outside a café on St. Laurent Boulevard, Montreal's busiest street. He gave him a hundred-dollar bill to get out of the cold and get something to eat and the man said, "I just want someone to talk to." They walked into a café and ordered sandwiches and coffee. Ahmad listened to the man talk about conspiracy theories and government surveillance. He had been a computer science major who dropped out due to "an event" he claimed he could be killed for talking about. Ahmad could tell the man was intelligent from the way he spoke; when he refused to get professional help, Ahmad started giving him little assignments to keep him off the street. The little assignments like background checks eventually evolved into bigger projects.

As Pierre typed a 30-character password into his computer, Ahmad watched as the man opened multiple tabs and showed Ahmad several wire transfers to a corporation. Some ranged from five figures to six, except the last one, which was higher than the rest; An 8 figure donation which when converted to USD was roughly about $250,000.

"It's an upcoming NGO," Ahmad said as he leaned back into his chair. "Donations of this amount aren't a problem."

The man typed some more and pulled up several tabs on his computer. "Yes, but then I rerouted this offshore account and was able to track it to an exiled former senator." Ahmad's eyes narrowed with interest as he moved closer. "Shortly after, this email exchange happened."

Ahmad leaned closer to read the email, first was hers in response to his request for a bank account. She ended the email with gratitude: *Thank you very much for your support, uncle Sheriff. Jazakallahu Khairan. Fa'iza* and then a reply: *I'm in Toronto in transit. It would be good to see you in person. A.A Sheriff.*

Ahmad's muscles tensed as he read the exchange. *That bastard. He picked the wrong girl this time,* he thought.

After Pierre left, Ahmad and Edet discussed the *Project Feed-A-Child* West African project Ahmad wanted to fund as a separate entity from his corporation.

"Just so you know, I did a police check on the guy that came earlier."

"I'm surprised it took you so long to do that," Ahmad chuckled. He would have done the same thing if a stranger had suddenly started coming to the office to disrupt meetings without an explanation. It was an unwritten code of business and friendship. "And?"

"Well, nothing came up. It's like he doesn't exist."

"No kidding."

"So, that confirmed my suspicions."

"What suspicions?" The two men stared at each other and Ahmad could tell that Edet already knew.

"What do you need a hacker for?"

"Just some things I can't be too involved with, but I need to monitor."

"Is this about her?" Edet asked. Ahmad looked at him and even without saying a word, Edet found the answer to his question. "You've gotta let her go, man," he sighed in resignation.

She's not an easy person to forget, Ahmad thought to himself as he picked up a stress ball from his desk and squeezed it, his mind going to the email exchange between Fa'iza and Senator Sheriff. Later that evening, he busied himself with a newspaper as he sat in an armchair in the busy lobby of a 5-star hotel. He tried to remain discreet while monitoring the entrance of the lobby behind a basketball hat. Moments later, he watched as Fa'iza dropped from a taxi, went through the revolving doors and made her way up the elevators. He looked from the left and right, waited by the overhead display to see what floor the elevator stopped on and then he followed her up.

Chapter 28

Cheques bounced. People went back on their promises for donations. It was frustrating, but I was beginning to understand that it's part of running an N.G.O. and dealing with people.

With less than three months to our official opening date, things were beginning to get hectic, especially with getting ready for graduation. So when an old family friend, Alhaji Sheriff, finally replied to my business plan asking for my account details, I was elated. I sent the details and was very grateful when a substantial amount was wired to the account.

With the money Kaltume's dad sent, I would be able to pay the staff we hired for the first three months and the outstanding balance for the standby generator will also be taken care of. Naturally, I was very appreciative. He also happened to be in Toronto on his way to the U.S. for a medical check-up and with the change in government that was about to happen, he might be granted clemency and finally get to rejoin his family back in Abuja. Right now, he was lodged in a suite at the Fairmont Royal York and had asked to see me so I came. But being here – with him sitting too close to me for comfort on the couch in a heavy black and gold Versace robe and Hermes slippers, and his request that his personal assistant leave us alone – was beginning to seem like a wrong idea.

"How are your studies?" he asked in Hausa, looking more at my chest than my face.

"It's fine, uncle, Alhamdulillah. Thank you so much for your contribution to the shelter, uncle." I shifted in my seat, repeating uncle a few times to remind him.

He reached out and patted my back, "no problem, my dear. Running a Charity like yours is very expensive, you know that, right?" he smiled cunningly and I nodded. "Eat." It was not a request.

I nodded again, ignoring the platter of sushi, sashimi and the sparkling water he'd ordered before my arrival.

"There's no support whatsoever from the Nigerian government. You'll be left running after all these small donors for petty change," he shook his head as he switched to English, his hand still on my back. I laughed at the situation in my mind – that I was receiving charity from a man who was in trouble for embezzling government funds, the same government he was now criticizing for lack of support for the same charity. I looked up to find him licking his lips as he looked at me. I opened my mouth to speak and felt my dinner climbing up my throat and closed it up again. "It's beneath someone of your status, *hmm*, Fa'iza?" he was leaning closer, his hands caressing my thigh, "a beauty like yourself?"

I jolted up the seat like I had been shocked by electricity.

"*Haba*, don't act like a child," he laughed. "Let me be your sponsor. You'll never run into any financial problem," he said, pouring some orange juice into a glass. Pronouncing his Fs as Ps. He was a walking embodiment of every negative Arewa stereotype.

I could not believe my ears. This was Kaltume's father. I played with his kids while growing up. We attended each other's birthday parties. Even though we were not related, I called him Uncle. He always gave us obscene amounts of dollars –not even naira – when we visited him during sallah. His praises used to be played regularly on the radio because of his huge donations to religious institutions. *'A righteous man - son of the soil.'* the jingles said.

"Not just Abuja, I can open shelters for you in as many states as you want." he interrupted my thoughts.

"Uncle, you're misreading this situation," I said in the most indignant voice I could muster as I started backing away from him. Then I started panicking.

"This isn't my first rodeo, Fa'iza. State your price and I'll fulfill all your wishes," he smiled at me, revealing a toothy grin; it reminded me of a rabbit. He drank his juice and burped loudly. There were stacks of cash placed strategically next to his mobile phones. "Nobody has to know, *hmm*?" he watched me with hungry eyes. "All the girls running things in Abuja – you think they're doing it by themselves?" he laughed. "Do you understand what I'm saying? We can come to an understanding, can't we? Because if we can't..." he left the sentence incomplete, but the implication was loud; he would cancel the donation to the shelter if I refused.

I was confident that there were girls in Abuja doing things without so-called help from nonreligious men like him. I looked up at him, and despite myself, I started laughing in his face. Looking at his bald head and pot belly, looking so out of place in what he was wearing. At his big age, he was out here trying to lure young girls with money. It was all he had to offer - money. I might have had a need for the money, but definitely not at this price. It was laughable that he would think he stood a chance. Maybe with other girls. But with me? "I don't want your money!" I spat at him. "You vile, disgustin –" There was a loud banging on the door and a scuffle, followed by a concerned voice: "Fa'iza? Fa'iza?" *Is that Ahmad's voice?*

"Ahmad," I shouted as I ran towards the door. It was not a question.

"Fa'iza, open the door," and the banging continued.

I rattled the doorknob from the inside. It was locked. "I can't. It's locked from outside."

Alhaji Sherriff stood up, apprehension and fear spreading all over his face. His voice was now a panicked whisper. "Who did you bring?" He brought out his phone and started dialing frantically.

"Fa'iza, the police are on their way," Ahmad's voice came through again.

"The police are on their way," I repeated loudly, in case the old man next to me had missed Ahmad's warning. I watched as his body shook and blood drained from his face.

"No, no. Please don't involve the police. Let's – let's settle this between us, *dan Allah*. Please." He dared to bring God's name into this after his dirty proposal minutes ago.

"Open the door right now," I commanded, looking into his eyes as I watched him quiver like a rat.

He reached into his robe, got out the key card to his room and with his hand shaking, he passed it to me. I rushed to the door and opened it.

Ahmad stormed in with his sleeves rolled up and top buttons unbuttoned. He quickly scanned my body, and his eyes went to my face, searching my eyes. "Did the bastard touch you?" he thundered. I had never seen him so angry.

"No, but he tried to," I said. I was so happy to see Ahmad. I wondered what would have happened if he hadn't shown up.

In a split second, Ahmad grabbed Alhaji Sherriff by the collar and punched him in the face. There was blood all over his broken nose and on the white singlet inside his robe. The man fell backwards as he held his face, trying to stop the bleeding.

"You dared to touch *her*?" Ahmad looked dangerous, standing over the man begging on the floor. As the older man attempted to sit up, Ahmad kicked him down again.

"Ahmad!" I screamed as I ran towards him, "leave him alone." I didn't want him to waste his breath on the lowly scum of the earth. "Let's go." The Canadian police would see his action as assault and I was worried about him having a criminal record. We left the room and hurried towards the elevators, I pressed the button for the ground floor and turned around to see Ahmad breathing hard and he was shaking with so much anger, he wouldn't even look at me.

"Thank you," I finally said to him as the elevator started to descend.

He still wouldn't look at me, he slowly put his hands in his pocket. The elevator stopped, the door opened and someone — from the name tag on her chest, she was hotel staff, walked in. She pressed a button as the door closed. He exhaled and finally looked at me, my heartbeat quickening as our eyes met.

"Are you okay?" Ahmad asked quietly. I had forgotten how his voice sounded when he was next to me. The way his voice made the words he spoke sound like they were made for me alone.

I nodded.

As we made our way out of the lobby, the cold air engulfed me and I shivered. "How did you know that I was here?" I managed to say.

He kept quiet for so long that I was sure that he wouldn't answer. "*Um*, I was having dinner with a friend when I saw you come in. I knew he was staying here and I wondered if he was the one you were here to see."

Oh. A friend, huh? Or maybe a girlfriend? I glanced at my feet. *Why do I care? He's free to do as he pleases.*

He continued, "some years ago, a friend of mine in the University of Abuja needed some help from him. He pretended like he was going to help, spiked her drink and took advantage of her." My jaw dropped open. "There was nothing we could do because he was in power then, and nobody believed her. But I did and I've hated him since then."

Oh, so that's what he meant when he said you can't choose family when he didn't want to fly to Milan for Kaltume's wedding, I figured. Even Afreen had told me that he didn't like this particular uncle, but he missed me so much that he came anyway. I remembered our time together that summer. My finger absentmindedly scratched the wrist I used to have the bracelet on.

"Do you want a ride back to the residence?" he asked, watching me shiver. The cool evening breeze around us and the little space between us was a reminder of everything that could have been. We hadn't been this close to each other in years. I remembered what Dr. Na'ima always told me about healing and being honest with my feelings.

"I have to tell you, Ahmad," my voice cracked as I spoke, "it hasn't been easy for me at all." His jaw clenched as his hands went back into his pocket, his eyes still holding mine. "Everything that happened with us," I felt the tears form, "It broke me," I said as I looked away, willing myself not to cry. I thought about us a lot – more than I cared to admit. I wished things had turned out differently. "No, I think I'm just gonna take an Uber," I finally said.

Ahmad was quiet even though for a split second, his eyes looked sad. He looked like he was about to share something with me but instead, he said: "I'll wait with you until your ride gets here."

The next time I saw Ahmad was three months later, during Afreen's wedding in Abuja. That wedding was pretty much the highlight of my year; seeing Zafar and Afreen's love finally getting such a happy ending was something I was truly happy to witness. They had held onto each other through every stumbling block.

At the wedding reception, I looked up from the picture I had taken of the bride and groom to find Sakina, Hajiya Uwani's youngest daughter, pouting and fluttering her lashes as she walked up to Ahmad, "Ahmad!" she called out in her shrill voice, "*Ba ka nema na.* You don't even look for me." Her turban was tied unnecessarily high and she was struggling to walk properly in her jewel-encrusted heels. She had been hovering around him at every opportunity throughout the wedding that most times, I had to physically remove myself from their vicinity. My dislike for her had nothing to do with Ahmad; her shrill voice was just quite irritating.

After my internship, my family flew in for my graduation. My parents arrived first, and I had just confirmed the gate my parents will be coming through after going through immigration from the flight board in the Arrivals terminal when I started making my way towards gate 8, looking down the empty walkway before looking at my wristwatch. There were a few people waiting and I excitedly kept glancing at my watch and the empty hallway behind gate 8.

"They should be out in a minute," a deep baritone said.

I turned around to see Ahmad scrolling through his phone and leaning on the barricaded wall that had a white Telus communication banner.

"You don't have to do this."

"Do what?" He looked up at me as he slid his phone into his pocket.

"This. Picking my parents up, I am very capable of getting them, I have a cab waiting outside."

"Me picking them up has nothing to do with your capabilities. You would have known not to bother with a cab if you had picked up my calls or read my message." His face suddenly broke into a smile, one that didn't reach his eyes as he looked up and walked towards the gate as my parents came through. Abba was pushing a trolley with their luggage and next to him Umma's eyes searched the crowd and her eyes lit up as they met mine.

"I told Mami not to bother you about picking us up," Umma said to Ahmad as I gave her a hug, after we had exchanged greetings.

"No, I am very happy to do this; I hope there were no issues with your flight." Ahmad asked as he subtly maneuvered himself to push the trolley my father had been pushing.

"Alhamdulillah, it was a very long flight." I heard Abba say as he and Ahmad walked ahead of my mother and me. I held onto her hands with one hand and her handbag with my other. She peered into my eyes as she listened to me go on about all the places I wanted them to visit on their short trip, if she had a question, she never voiced it out.

My brothers arrived the following day and they all stayed for five days, and during that time, I moved into the hotel with them. On the morning of the ceremony, as I was getting ready, a hotel staff came to deliver a bouquet of two dozen red roses in an elaborate flower vase. I came out of my room in the connecting suites we shared and saw Ya Amin inspecting the bouquet on the dining table, with Abubakar eating breakfast next to him.

"So, who got you flowers?" Abubakar asked as he ate from a bowl of fruits. He picked up the card and read it out, while Ya Amin looked at me quietly. "The sky is the limit. Congratulations. Niac," Abubakar read. "Who's N.I.A.C.?" He looked up at me as he spelt out the nickname I'd given Ahmad years ago. There was another sealed envelope at the bottom of the bouquet. I hurriedly grabbed it before my brothers did.

"Oh, just someone I know," I mumbled dismissively as I folded my scarf in two unequal halves.

"Did you cut your hair?" Abubakar asked as he watched me comb my hair and tie it into a bun.

"Just a little," I answered as I wrapped my hijab, inserting pins to secure it in place.

The joy on my parents' faces as I walked onto the stage when my name was called out at the top of the honor list was an image I wanted to be imprinted in my memory forever. We took a lot of pictures and had lunch at my favorite restaurant. As usual, Ya Amin was quiet, and Abubakar and I were chatty as we caught up. I told him about what I would miss about Canada – my favorite libraries and galleries, the food and sounds of summer festivals, ice sculptures in the winter, the fireworks in spring, road trips with Ada and Sara to Rideau Canal and the parliament buildings in Ottawa in Autumn and all the shopping malls I went to with Afreen. Everything except the long hours in Ramadan, fasting from 3 am until 9 pm, was a feat on its own.

Later in the evening, with less than 30 hours to my flight back to Nigeria for good, I brought out the envelope that came with the flowers and opened it. When I saw what it was, I excused myself to make a call to his office.

Chapter 29

Toronto, June 2015

Ahmad had just commissioned *Project Feed-A-Child,* which provided three meals a day to *Almajiri* children and the less fortunate in 10 states in northern Nigeria. In 12 months, he hoped to cover the country, and by the 36th month, he planned on spreading out to major cities in other West Africa like Dakar, Accra, and Bamako. He made an undertaking to feed 1000 people, but he intended to do more than that as *sadaqah,* goodwill for them both. On Friday evenings, he usually stopped at the Mosque before heading home. This Friday was different; he had never imagined that he would not be standing next to her on the day she eventually graduated. He left the office early to catch a game at his place. As he watched the basketball match in his living room, his sister called him; she had just gotten back from her honeymoon.

"Somebody's wife," he said as he picked up. Ignoring the multiple unread messages from Sakina, the daughter of a family friend he met during Afreen's wedding.

She laughed, "thank you for the wedding gift." She knew that she didn't have to thank him, but this was her excuse to check up on him. "You doing okay?"

"Why wouldn't I be?" he continued watching the game.

"Well, for one, you're moving to Nigeria."

"Yeah, temporarily. I'm just gonna be there for like three months to kickstart a project." He had no intention of telling anyone in his family about *Project Feed-A-Child*; that was between him and Allah.

His sister remained quiet on the phone, then she asked, "sure it has nothing to do with her?"

"Nope," he answered a little too quickly.

"Because you didn't decide to leave Canada until she graduated, and –"

"Afreen, don't you have a husband to bother?" he laughed.

"It's just that she has finally healed. Your timing is really awful."

"Okay, noted. I'm just gonna suspend everything until it's convenient for you both." His doorbell rang; it was the dinner he'd ordered on his way back. "I gotta go. Thanks for checking in."

"Ahm –"

Ahmad ended the call, pulled on a shirt and opened his wallet to find a bill generous enough to cover the tip. When he opened the door, he was surprised to see Fa'iza. She was wearing a black dress and a black veil, her eyes were lined in kohl, and her lips were covered in red lipstick. She was not smiling.

"I called your office and they said you'd left," she spoke quickly and angrily as she held up an envelope, "I didn't wanna come here, but what the heck?"

"Wa alaikumus salam to you too," he said dryly as he stepped to the side to allow her in, "you can come in."

She walked past him and into the apartment, not stopping to take off her shoes. Now standing in the sitting room, she turned around to face him and started tapping her feet impatiently; she was wearing open-toed stilettos, and her toes were painted red. "What's this?" she asked. It suddenly crossed Ahmad's mind that she'd shied away from confrontations, but that seemed to have changed. She looked beautiful when she was angry, and he had no idea what she was angry about. The scent of her perfume made it harder to think; it had been so long since she was in his apartment, yet now that she was here, it was like she never left.

"What's what, Fa'iza?" Ahmad asked as he made his way to the kitchen to grab a bottle of water. He almost wished he had alcohol because his mind was suddenly agitated. He wondered how much of a stress-buster nicotine was, and maybe it was time for him to pick up smoking as a habit. As he drank the water from the bottle, he turned around to see that she had opened the envelope and was waving him a cheque.

"I don't need your charity."

Ahmad thought about how stubborn she was and how much he loved that about her. "It's not charity. The money is yours," he said, distracting himself from her presence by drinking more water." There was more than enough for her to run the Shelter for five years at least without her worrying about donors, especially men who would want to take advantage of her.

"Your money is not mine! And we have sufficient donors. I don't need you."

That was not true. Pierre updated him on her NGO financial and transaction records every few months and the expenses were more than the donations. By his projections, they would barely make it into the first quarter before they became bankrupt. He scoffed and shook his head, "It's your dividends from your shares over the years," he looked at his wristwatch, wondering where his dinner was.

Her phone beeped and she ignored it. "What dividends?"

"Dividends from the company shares," he replied, wondering who was texting her, and if she was seeing someone.

"Spousal shares?"

He nodded gently.

"Why are the spousal shares still in my name? When the marriage was voided, they should have automatically gone back to you."

Ahmad knew she read the contract before she signed it but he must have underestimated how meticulous she was to remember this one clause. He scratched his forehead as he looked at the floor.

"You annulled the marriage when you got back, didn't you?" she was staring at him, unblinking.

He didn't answer.

"Ahmad!"

All that was going through his mind was how beautiful she looked in that dress and the way she called his name. "Yeah, about that…." he started.

"You did not annul the marriage?" she whispered like she was scared someone would hear her and slowly sat on the chair by the dining table, muttering the *shahada* over and over.

"You weren't picking my calls and they needed both parties at City Hall to sign the divorce documents," he shrugged, picked up the remote and started changing channels. "It's not my fault."

"That's not true," she shook her head as she spoke. "If the marriage is less than three months, one person can file for dissolution." She buried her head in her hands and continued saying the *shahada*.

Oh yeah, that's right, he thought to himself. *She's a Canadian lawyer now.* Their Islamic marriage might be void, but the documents he submitted in the court still had them listed as husband and wife.

"I'm leaving tomorrow, so this needs to be taken care of now," she said as she stood up.

"What's the hurry? *Aure za ki yi, ne?* Are you getting married?" he chuckled bitterly as he gulped down the rest of his water and squeezed the empty bottle into a flattened mess. He watched as her eyes glance down at his unbuttoned shirt and back to his face; he knew that, like him, she remembered everything that had happened within these walls. As she adjusted her veil over her head, he remembered running his hands through her hair and the floral scent of her shampoo from the many nights they spent together with his face buried in her hair. *Oh boy.*

He walked away from her and back into the kitchen. This would be a good time for the food to arrive, Ahmad thought as he glanced at his watch again.

"I can see you're expecting someone. I'll leave you to it," she left the cheque on the chair and angrily walked towards the door.

"I'm waiting for my food."

"Whatever. I'll start the proceedings for what you should have done years ago. I also won't be expecting any more dividends. Thank you." She opened the door and let herself out, banging the door shut.

Ahmad sat on his couch, rubbing his temples and thinking of the marriage certificate he still had in his safe after all these years. In the beginning, he had held onto it because he knew he could fix the situation and there would be no need to annul the marriage or relinquish her stake in his company as his spouse. Unfortunately, as it became apparent that Fa'iza was not going to be his in this lifetime – with all the slow leads for the wet nurse's location going cold – he still could not bring himself to do what was needed.

There was finally a knock on the door and Ahmad was relieved his food was here at last. He got up, picked up his wallet again and went to open the door. It was Amin. The look of surprise on his face was a clear contrast to Amin's unsmiling face and stiff demeanor. Ahmad knew that her brothers were in town for her graduation, but he was not expecting a visit from them.

"Aminu," he called out playfully to his old friend. He held the door open for him and Amin quietly walked into the apartment, looking around as he did. As Ahmad closed the door, he asked him how he had been and invited him to stay for dinner. "Amin, *lafiya*? Is everything okay?" Ahmad asked, noticing Amin was still not smiling.

"How long has this been going on?" Amin asked quietly, chuckling as he walked further into the living room."There's no need to pretend; I followed her here."

Her! Ahmad laughed in his head. *Of course, this was about Fa'iza.*

"Oh no, she just came to clear up a little misunderstanding," Ahmad said, careful not to go into details. He knew that Fai'za wouldn't want her brothers to know about their secret.

"A friend of mine saw you two leaving a hotel a few months ago." It was not a question.

"What? Me and Fa'iza? Must have been a mistake."

" Fairmont Royal York," Amin was certain.

Ah, damn it! Ahmad thought. That was the day he followed her downtown with the donor fiasco. He sat down on the chair and started rubbing his temples.

Chapter 29

"You betrayed me," Amin's voice was hoarse as he looked at Ahmad with anger and disgust. "She's my sister, for God's sake."

"It's not what you think," Ahmad tried to explain, but Amin raised his voice even higher. *"Ba ka tsoron Allah,ne?* You're not even afraid of Allah?"

Here came Amin with the righteousness, Ahmad thought, remembering the reason they had drifted apart as teenagers. Everything was black and white in Amin's world, a blatant refusal to see reason sometimes.

"Why do you insist on being in a relationship with someone forbidden for you?"

"We're definitely not in a relationship," Ahmad spoke slowly, trying to talk over Amin to get his words across.

"Yaudaran ta kake yi; you're deceiving her. That's the conclusion I've come to. If she insists on being stupid, why won't you be the responsible one and do what's right?"

Ahmad remained still as he listened to Amin's words. *This could end really badly,* he thought. But this was Fa'iza's brother, and that meant something to him. Ahmad chose to reason with him. "If you knew her well, you'd know that she's not that type of girl; she's responsible. And it's been years since she cut me out of her life."

"I've had my suspicions since that morning you showed up at the house, you know."

"For the last time, Aminu. *Wallahi tallahi ba komai tsakanin mu*; I swear there's nothing between us."

"Then prove it," Amin said smugly.

"Prove what?"

"Prove it. Find a wife and get married. I imagine that wouldn't be a difficult task for someone like you; there're always women falling at your feet," he had a wicked smile on his face as he stared at Ahmad. "My sister may be stupid, but she's got our mother's pride; she won't continue with whatever you two are doing, if you have a wife."

"You can't force me to get married. What are we, kids?" It infuriated Ahmad how Amin talked about Fa'iza, but he knew he couldn't defend her. He walked to the kitchen to get another bottle of water.

"I'm not going to watch you ruin her life. Get married and leave my sister alone," Amin followed him and placed a photocopied piece of paper on the kitchen island. "Or I'm going to show Abba this."

Ahmad closed the fridge and looked down at the piece of paper Amin had pushed toward him. The unopened bottle of water fell on the white marble top almost on its own accord as he looked at the copy of the marriage certificate on the kitchen island.

"Where – where did you get that?" Ahmad knew how bad this looked to someone on the outside; it looked like they had disregarded the stipulations forbidding them to be together and continued a clandestine affair over the years.

"It is almost too easy to access public records in this country," he smirked as he watched the blood drain from Ahmad's face.

"It's not what you think," was all Ahmad could manage to say.

"She's forbidden for you but – as usual – you found a way around the word of Allah."

As he stared at the marriage certificate, all Ahmad could think about was Fa'iza. His heart crumbled at the thought of her being devastated again and having tears in her eyes again. This was her worst nightmare coming true – her family finding out about what they did years ago. If her father or Umma ever saw this, it would kill her; she would be forced to relive the pain all over again, and they might not even believe her. It would be her word against Amin's, and right now, Amin made a compelling argument on paper, even though the reality couldn't be further than his assumptions. His head was pounding. He had no plans to get married, not anytime soon. However, the secret marriage and not annulling the marriage were on him. This was all his fault, and if getting married was the only way to be held accountable and to hide the secret from the rest of her family, it seemed a small price to pay. "Please don't show Abba that," he finally said.

"Get married, and this secret is safe with me." Amin repeated.

Chapter 30

Abuja, September 2016

I had been handling all cases pro-bono cases for months now. Sometimes Ada came down from Lagos to fight a case or two and even though I could now afford to pay her, she took up the cases like she did from the beginning – as favors. Apart from us, all the lawyers on the team were on a yearly contract, as per donor stipulations. We had three main donors : *Pocket of Hope, Al-Yusra Islamic Foundation* and *The Cain Mosni Foundation* funding the shelter, along with occasional donations from citizens.

My office was on the ground floor along with the other offices, the kitchen, storage, sick-bay and living area that also doubled up as a dining area. Upstairs, the rooms housed displaced women and kids. Sometimes, the husbands came and tried to win their families back after realizing their mistakes, and the women would go back. Other times, the women would stand their ground, insisting that they wanted out of the marriage. In some cases, the men never even came to look for their wives or children. My job was to ensure that the children never suffered the effects of parents at war by providing a safe space, regular meals, and tuition for all the kids in need.

"We need to include the audit reports along with this year's balance sheets to the donor," I said to Zee, the finance director, as she sat across me in my office. "It's crucial to ensure donors know that their money was allocated correctly and well spent."

"Yes, I cc'd you in an email this morning. CMF already approved next year's funding with a 25% increase," Zee responded.

"Are you serious?" I was shocked. I looked through my email, filtering through them until I got to hers. Most foundations had to go through a rigorous process to continue getting sponsorship and monetary aid, but ours was sailing through. It was not even the fourth quarter yet and one of our donors, *The Cain Mosni Foundation,* had sent funding for the following year. We cleared a few more financial details and as I rounded up the meeting, I got a phone call from Afreen. "Afreen mama, how are you?" I excitedly asked her. Afreen was in her second trimester. She was due to give birth in a few months.

"Fa'ee, how are you doing?" she said quietly, not at all her usual cheery self. I stopped typing on my computer to give the call my full attention.

"I'm fine. How did the ultrasound go?"

"Alhamdulillah, everything went well," she hesitated, "I just wanted to check up on you."

"Aww, that's sweet of you. I'll come over this evening." I had a box of Turkish delights in my car that I had gotten for her as she was always craving something sweet.

But I never made it to her place that day. As I was having my lunch and scrolling through Instagram, I saw that one of the blogs I followed announced Ahmad's wedding to Sakina. The food in my mouth lost its taste and I found myself staring at his face. It was a black-and-white picture from his website since Ahmad was not active on social media and Sakina's picture was next to it; it was from one of her recent posts. I scrolled through the app and found that other accounts had reposted the picture too. It was already being talked about as 'the wedding of the year.'

I pushed my plate away. *I knew this day would come, so why do I feel like I've been sucker-punched right in my guts?* I thought angrily. I think what angered me was the fact that he still sent flowers to me on my birthday after all these years. Actually, no. That was a lie. What angered me was that he had truly moved on. I chuckled to myself, overwhelmed by the extreme sadness and the deep sense of loss I felt. What eventually broke me down and sent me down the deep end was the following day when he dropped by our house on the pretense of seeing my brother. He stopped me in the hallway on my way to the dining room to get milk for my tea and asked if I wanted to talk about it. I was heading out to work later than usual as I'd had a rough night, and he looked even better than I had ever seen him in my entire life in a brown kaftan and matching trousers. But his eyes looked sad. Or maybe that was a lie I told myself to cope. A part of me wished that he was not happy, that we were both unhappy. Misery did love company.

Once every few months, I checked in with Dr. Na'ima over video call sessions. I never took the sessions at home or in my office; I always had them in my car. Today, I called her without a pre-scheduled appointment. She was with a patient, but as soon as she finished, she called me back, and she listened to me cry over Ahmad for the first time in a while.

"We've talked about this moment for years, Fai'za," she spoke gently.

I nodded. I knew that we would eventually marry other people, and I had been preparing myself for that. "Still doesn't numb the pain," I said. Over the years, I had watched him become a better Muslim, more like someone I prayed for when I was a teen and now, years later, he was officially going to be someone else's. Forever.

"Would you have preferred it if you heard it from him first?" she asked.

I thought about it. I didn't pick up his calls or reply to his messages for years. Besides, hearing it from him first wouldn't change how I felt. It wouldn't change the fact that someone else gets to wake up next to him every morning, that someone else gets to hold him, to touch him, to love him openly. It didn't change the fact that I was not destined to be that person.

"No. What's the point? In a weird and twisted way, I'm kinda happy that he has moved on. He's a good person," I started crying again. I was just a chapter in his life story, and he had found his forever person.

"That is an interesting choice of words. Moved on. Do you feel like you've been left behind?"

"Yes," I covered my eyes with my hands as I sobbed, grateful for the car's tinted windows.

"How are you and Umar doing?" she asked quietly after I'd finished crying and calmed down. "Has anything changed?"

For lack of a better phrase, Umar was someone my friends and cousins thought was perfect for me. We had mutual friends, but we never actually met until one day at *Bleu Cafe* in Abuja when we were set up by said mutual friends.

"Nothing has changed." I answered. I still felt nothing for him. It was easy to be in a halal relationship this time around because I was not even attracted to him. When Aisha told me that was okay – that the attraction comes after marriage – I knew that was not true; the attraction between Ahmad and I was instant and constant. Even through the years we were not talking, the few times we ran into each other, I was reminded of how much I still cared for him. I used to look up and catch him stealing glances at me, and I would feel… seen. It was not the same with Umar and I could never quite picture him as my husband. I never really imagined myself getting married. I knew I would eventually, but I was not exactly racing to get to that point. To be honest, I get repulsed thinking of what will happen if I married Umar and he tried to touch me. I shuddered at the thought.

"You have to give yourself a chance at happiness," Dr. Na'ima's voice came through the speakers. "Umar has shown you in many ways that he cares about you. You should stop turning down his requests to get the families involved."

"He deserves someone who loves him, though," I said, sniffing. Not someone still pining over her ex. He deserved better.

"That's a decision only you can make. What kind of wife are you going to be to whomever you marry? Are you going to be the one he deserves?"

I wasn't listening anymore; my mind was far away. Ahmad Babangida. My whole world and more at one point in time; I remembered the first time I ever saw him: the day I bumped into him at the airport, the day I mistakenly walked into his room, waking him from his slumber, the football matches we used to go to, the books we shared, staying up late talking about everything, the plans we made for our future. *It still hurt.* I nodded as I wiped away my tears. It was time to stop being faithful to the wounds of my past.

After the longer-than-usual session, I stopped at Zainab's cubicle when I got to work. "Zee, where are our updated donor files? I want to make a PowerPoint for *Cain Mosni* highlighting our wins for the past year."

"Is everything okay? Your eyes are puffy," she sounded concerned as she reached for the cabinets behind her and started looking for the files for me.

"*Ba komai,* it's nothing. Just allergies," I shook my head as I sniffed, I went down the hallway into my office and started drowning myself in work. At least this aspect of my life was going well.

Chapter 31

Ahmad had just finished lunch with his mom on a day that seemed like a regular Thursday. He was sitting at the dining table and had just gotten off a call with Anas Madaki, the *Feed-A-Child* program coordinator in Sokoto. when his mother joined him. As she pulled out a chair, she handed him her phone, scrolling down the screen displaying the *Selfridges* website. "These bags are from the spring collection. What do you think?"

Ahmad had no interest in the handbags or the sets of luxury boxes she wanted his opinion on a few days prior. He scrolled for a few seconds to not hurt her feelings and handed her back her phone with a smile. "They look alright, mum."

"Just alright? Do you think she would like them?"

"I have no idea what she likes." He couldn't remember which bags Sakina had carried the few times he had met her. If these were for Fa'iza, he wouldn't take a minute to pick out crossbody bags with long straps and oversized totes for the days we went out with her laptop, study notes, and a novel or two. Three days ago, when he was at her house, he had noticed *Americanah* by Chimamanda Adichie sticking out of her leather tote on the counter in the kitchen. He wanted to ask her what she thought of the book, about the nickname Ifemelu called Obinze; he wondered if the word 'ceiling' made her roll her eyes in jest like she always did when he called her

'Insom.' Now she wouldn't roll her eyes at him; she wouldn't even look at him. There was an air of indifference every time they were alone together, and that hurt even more.

His mother sighed and removed her glasses as she dropped her phone on the table. "Ahmad, are you sure about this?"

"Sure about what, mom?" Ahmad smiled at her as the help cleared the table. He knew she was talking about his general disinterest in the *kayan lefe* – the gift boxes for Sakina that were being put together.

"The last time we were doing this, you were so invested. You had opinions and specific choices you wanted us to include, you –" her voice trailed off.

Ahmad thought about how his mom and sister teased him every time he dropped by with extra items he'd picked out to add to Fa'iza's *kayan lefe*. That felt like a lifetime ago.

"This time around, you don't care how it's going. You haven't even asked about any of the wedding preparations."

"I know that you have it all under control, mum. And thank you – I know how busy all this has kept you."

"You don't feel like you're rushing into this?" she asked for the first time since the discussion about his marriage to Sakina arose. She had seen him and Sakina talk a few times during Afreen's wedding, but knowing her son, she knew he was not at all interested in her at all. Maybe it was Mother's instinct, but despite him never bringing up Fa'iza, she knew he was still in love with her. So, his decision to get married felt sudden and unexpected.

"You think it's rushed? I've known her for about the same time as I knew Fa'iza before our wedding was fixed," he laughed as he answered.

His mother sighed as she leaned into her chair, "this is different. I could see how much you cared for Fa'iza. But this –" her voice trailed off again as she thought fondly of Fa'iza.

His phone started ringing, and he let it go to voicemail; he never allowed work to interrupt conversations with his mother. When he was finally alone after lunch, Ahmad prayed Asr and played the voicemail from Audu.

"Sir," he started, his voice high with excitement, so much so that he was stuttering. "I was in a cybercafé by the University campus when the owner of the cafe recognized *'yar* Agadez's picture. He said that her daughter was his course mate here in Kano –" the message was abruptly cut off, and Ahmad played the next one. "He showed me her daughter's Facebook profile, and it was her! I sent you pictures from her profile. We've found her! We've found *'yar* Agadez!"

Ahmad hurriedly opened the attachments Audu had sent to his Whatsapp. There were multiple pictures of a computer screen in a cyber café, displaying a Facebook account. The picture was hard to see, but it looked like a picture of a mother and daughter, both wearing brown hijabs in the background of trees. He scrolled to the next image; it was a picture of the older woman wearing *atamfa,* patterned fabric, and a scarf from the same material was tied around her head. She was sitting on a mat on the floor surrounded by decorated calabashes and dried gourds filled with milk, while holding a newborn baby in her hands, with the caption *'My mother and son.'* When the pixelated image was enlarged into a less blurry image, he could make out her features – her angular-shaped face, prominent forehead, and the bridge of her nose. He scrolled back to the previous picture, to the daughter. She looked around Ahmad's age. He scrolled to the picture of the woman and the baby again, paying particular attention to her face. It was very close to the one his aging app had designed. It was her. it was *'yar* Agadez.

Ahmad called Audu immediately, who picked up on the first ring. *"Ranka ya da* –" Audu started.

"Where does she stay?" Ahmad cut the salutations short.

Audu explained that Halime, the daughter, was married and based in France and a few years prior, she relocated her mother to live with her. As Audu spoke, Ahmad searched the Facebook account on his laptop and went through Halime's pictures. She looked very much like her mother – tall-boned and slim. She was married to a Moroccan she met in Niamey and with whom she was raising three kids. They – the family of five and *'Yar* Agadez – currently lived in Saint-Malo, France.

When Ahmad spoke, his voice had a slight tremor to it: "Do you have a valid passport?"

"Yes."

"We're going to Saint-Malo," Ahmad said, already googling the requirements for an expedited work visa application to France from Nigeria for the private investigator.

Two days later, Ahmad's driver took him to the international airport in Abuja, where Audu – who had arrived from Kano earlier that day – was waiting for him. He was checking into his flight on his phone when Sakina's call came in.

"When did you get back, love?"

"I've been in Abuja for a week," he answered distractedly. He wanted to ask her why she sent their pictures to the blogs when the wedding was still months away. When his friends started calling to congratulate him a week prior, they told him that it was all over social media. That was not how he wanted Fa'iza to find out. But he was not in the mood to hear her deny it.

"Are you ready for tomorrow?" she didn't wait for him to answer, "you never replied to my texts. So for your second outfit change, are you wearing blue or white? My friends are here to help me decide which gown will complement your color." He could hear someone talking to her in the background; she was always around people when she called him. Her voice came through again, telling him about event planners, decorators, makeup artists, and background colors.

"What's happening tomorrow?" he finally asked to shut her up.

"Babyyyyy," she softened her voice even further and dragged out the syllable longer than necessary. Ahmad thought about telling her that baby talk made her seem even more unattractive, but he decided against it. "Tomorrow's the photoshoot, remember?"

He had completely forgotten about the photoshoot – not that he was looking forward to it. He remained quiet on the phone as he thought of his reply and after a few minutes, she sighed dramatically to get his attention back to the call. "I'm afraid that's not gonna work," he finally said. "I'm flying out to France in a few hours."

Her silence would have been uncomfortable if Ahmad did not have a thousand things running through his mind – the hotel bookings he was yet to make, how they were going to locate *'yar* Agadez, if she would be willing to talk to them and able to answer his questions...

When Sakina spoke, her background was quiet, like she had moved into another room or her friends had stopped chattering. "I – I don't understand," she said quietly. When are you coming back?"

"No idea," he answered truthfully as he got down from the car at the airport. Ahmad intended to stay in France for as long as he needed.

"It was so hard to get photoshoot dates with George because of your busy schedule and we were meant to do the couple's interview right after," she raised her voice as she spoke. "You don't tell me when you're in town; I only hear about it from people who see you around town. I don't know when you leave Abuja –"

Ahmad zoned out as she spoke, his headphones allowing him to scroll through his phone to select the car he would be picking up from the airport car rental for the duration of their stay in France. As he waited in the Flying Blue lounge, he watched as Audu proudly showed his business class ticket to the door attendant and walked toward him. The investigator looked out of place in the black winter jacket he was wearing over a red turtle-neck sweater in Abuja's humid heat.

Sakina was still going on about the makeup artists that she now had to cancel and what her friends would think, what people would say about her family, the humiliation it would cause. Ahmad sighed. There was no way this marriage was going to work. Theirs was already an unhealthy relationship – with him being emotionally unavailable and her willingness to turn a blind eye to how much he avoided spending time with her or even attempting to get to know her. The relationship would only worsen after marriage, especially since he intended to keep her in Abuja, while spending most of his time in the US away from her. She said she was okay living apart as long as he visited Abuja every month. He did not commit to visiting every month, but he suggested trips to destinations she wanted to visit. The whole arrangement was unfair to her, even if she was too carried away by the quick proposal and wedding preparations to realize it.

Amin's words were now beginning to ring in his ear: *"If she insists on being stupid, why won't you be the responsible one and do what's right?"* Ahmad knew that as big a threat Amin made back in Canada, he couldn't be bullied into this marriage. He knew, for the first time in a while, that he had to be the responsible one; and that meant ending whatever this charade was. "Listen, Fa'iza. We need to ta –"

"What did you just call me?" It sounded like she was going to cry.

"Sakina," he corrected. "We need to talk."

* * *

Ahmad was sitting in an almost empty café, waiting for an old friend who worked in health insurance. While he waited, the coffee he'd ordered remained untouched. He stared at an old couple outside by the waterfront feeding the ducks through the windowpane. Audu was also outside taking pictures of birds perched on lampposts and mailboxes. Every few seconds, his hands would reach up, holding up his phone to take a selfie, always sure to include a few white people in the background. He went on to post the pictures on his Facebook account with some caption about it being just a regular day. As he watched Audu, Ahmad noticed some people coming into the café and searched for a familiar face among the crowd.

"Zehra," he said, standing up and waving at her. He had a big smile on his face and when she finally approached him, he slipped his hands into his pockets as they exchanged pleasantries. He didn't hug or shake women's hands anymore. It had been years since he saw her at the gallery in Toronto and when he reached out to her with his request, she sounded surprised to hear from him, if not disturbed by his request. Whatever the case, he was happy she arrived at their meeting place with a thick file. "Can I order you something – a latte, an espresso?"

"No, it's a fifteen-minute drive back. I need to get going." She was a little apprehensive, and she kept looking over her shoulder as she spoke.

He nodded gently, knowing that she was trying to avoid being seen with him. That was why they had agreed to meet in this secluded café away from the city center and away from where she worked or anyone who knew her. "Listen," she said in English, "I'm doing this for you for old times' sake."

"You have my word. It'll never be traced back to you."

"*Bonne chance,*" she whispered as she handed him the red file and left as quietly as she came. She knew she could trust him.

When she turned towards the parking lot, Audu returned indoors and sat opposite Ahmad. Ahmad braced himself as he opened the file. It was all there – her immunization records, her current address, emergency contact information and a colored passport photograph at the bottom. Ahmad stared at the picture; the face looked the same and yet different from the one he had seen in the photograph in Kano. A face once young – pretty even – was now lined with age and the wisdom of a woman who has struggled in life. He glanced at the date of birth and right above it was her full name: Hussaina Amadou. Something didn't feel right. He had gone through the files from Kano and Agadez so many times that he knew every detail in those files by heart.

"Give me the Sharada file," he asked Audu and waited as the investigator checked through all the neatly organized paperwork in his backpack for the white office file. Ahmad took the file and began searching through the papers they brought from Nigeria with the compulsion of a man who could feel that he was on the brink of a realization that might indicate a light at the end of the tunnel. Ahmad found the black and white picture of *'yar* Agadez from GGSS Sharada and he turned it around and read the name scribbled behind. The name on the back of the black and white passport was Hassana Amadou.

Twins. It all made sense now – why it seemed like she had lived in so many parts of Kano within a single decade. It explained why they never narrowed down where to find her easily. They had unknowingly been on the trail of two different women - identical twins, it seemed.

Chapter 32

On some days, when Zee's car had problems, I would offer to pick her up on my way to work, despite the extra five minutes to my drive-time. She was one of the first people we hired and she stuck with us through uncertain times. Today, we were stuck in traffic; the food truck nearby was causing a minor commotion by the roundabout. This was a sight I was used to in Ramadan, but not just out of the blue.

"Please, what is causing this hold up?" I asked out loud, but mostly to myself.

"I think it's the vendors for that *Feed a Child o*," Zee said. Looking out of the window, I could see children and teens being handed wrapped food and water packages by some women in aprons and hijabs.

"Oh, they're also in Abuja?" I asked. A few months before, when I was in Kaduna for a wedding. I escorted my aunt's driver to go pick up my cousins from Zamani College. Opposite Dalema was one of these food trucks and the driver told me that they handed out meals to the less privileged three times a day. He said that it had been ongoing for months.

"That's impressive. Affluent people are finally beginning to use their wealth for worthy causes," I'd replied. It was awe-inspiring – if not surprising and suspicious – that someone would dedicate so many resources to children when it was not tied to votes or campaign season.

The driver laughed at my comment about the rich people in northern

Nigeria and repeated the phrase *"masu kudin Arewa"* for himself, as if he were whispering a silent prayer to one day be referred to as such. Those people – *masu kudin Arewa* – were often men, who had more money than their wives and children could spend.

I buried myself in work for the next few days while working on the PowerPoint presentation I intended to present to our donors. The statement of cash flow, balance sheet and audit reports were updated and filed away in one folder on my desktop. This was the first time I worked alone on donor documents. Whenever I needed more information, I would reach out to Zee, who knew every little detail about the foundations that sponsored us in the past years. So, I asked her to find other NGOs our donors financed; I needed to know who we were competing against so that I can ensure that our shelter is in an advantageous position, due to the number of Ts I was crossing, and I's I was dotting, I barely had any idle time.

Idle time led to a social media binge. These days, I could not scroll more than three posts without seeing a repost of Ahmad's wedding announcement from random blogs; so I took home as many reports as possible. Thanks to the algorithm that accelerated the downward spiral of self-esteem, idle time became something I could no longer afford, for my own sanity. So, naturally, I did what I knew how to do best: touching other people's lives and ensuring that I would continue to do so well into the future. However, to do so, I needed to secure our spot in the competitive NGO stratosphere, especially here in Abuja.

One evening, I was in Abba's library, printing some documents after work when Abubakar came in. Abba and Umma were in their living room having tea; I could hear the voice of the newscaster faintly coming in through the open door. Of both my brothers, Abubakar was the one who showed that he cared about my work although, to be fair, it was Ya Amin's personality to be indifferent unless it had to do with business and real estate. Sometimes, Abubakar would drop by the shelter to ask how he could be of help and when he was out of the country, we would talk about specific issues I was facing with management and how to mitigate them.

"Are you still working on the presentation?" he asked now, as he came around to look at the double monitors with excel spreadsheets and PowerPoint slides. I looked at him in his tailored maroon kaftan and noticed that he was smiling at a text message.

I opened my mouth to ask who the new girl was, but instead, I replied: "I just need it to be perfect, that's all." With all other donation streams thinning every year, I didn't want our most significant donor to cut their funding.

"Are you presenting it by yourself, or will one of your staff do it?" he peered through the images of outdoor children's activities that we organized weekly.

"I feel like this is too important to be delegated," I paused. "But we're still not able to set up an appointment with their outreach department for me to make the presentation. And when I asked Zee to find our original application so that I could reach out to the contact person, we realized that we never actually submitted a request or application to them – so we have no idea how to contact them. But we've applied to foundations abroad –"

"*Haba*, don't worry about those ones; their waiting lists are long. But I'm sure they'll get back to you soon," he laughed at my obvious inexperience.

I nodded. It was a busy time in the year; most foundations were reviewing their contracts, dropping the NGOs that underperformed and looking to fund credible ones. Mine was a credible one. Abubakar was right; they would get back to me. I just hoped they would soon enough because days at the shelter were becoming gloomy – people were coming in more regularly, kitchen staff was busy every day of the week, cases were piling up, and we were running out of funds quicker than I could have imagined.

"Maybe they probably just found your NGO on some database and picked it at random."

"That was what I thought. But we were only a year old when they gave us the green light. We weren't even that established. So, how did they find us?" I reviewed my presentation one final time and saved the most recent copy while Abubakar googled the foundation's name. Apart from standard websites with basic information and a head office in Palestine, there wasn't much to go with.

"It could be a shell company, so they probably don't really exist."

I stood up to leave, tidying the desk and making sure I left it the way it was when I came in a few hours ago. Abba was very particular about where everything on his desk was placed.

"Maybe you could start with the name. Jumble the letters and see if it spells something else – perhaps the name of a popular company; it could be an anagram," Abubakar said, switching the light off, as we left Abba's section.

When I got back to my room, as I prayed Isha and arranged all the documents in my folder, I found a copy of the first letter they'd sent us. The glossy white sheet had an embossed letterhead that spelt out *The Cain Mosni Foundation* in big blue letters. I flipped the paper around and the word "CAIN" stuck out to me backwards. I froze. *Wait a minute. No way.*Backwards, the word spelt N-I-A-C. NIAC. *Ahmad?* It couldn't be. There was no way this was what I thought it was, but I kept spelling backwards. MOSNI was I-N-S-O-M. *"Insom + Niac,"* his words started playing in my head. *"Together, we make sense."* Ahmad had been our biggest sponsor all this time? Since the beginning? All this time? Oh my God.

I remember how bad things had gotten with funds drying up and staff not getting their salaries. We reached out to The Bill and Melinda Gates Foundation, Change Exchange, Danjuma Foundation and many more and unfortunately, had no luck; all we got were letters of regret. I remembered spending nights awake praying *Tahajjud* when we received the news that our NGO had been approved for sponsorship by this The Cain Mosni foundation. It was the first big win for us – a much-needed one; and our morale was boosted.

I held the paper, unable to move. My mind raced back to the days Ahmad and I drew up plans for what I wanted the shelter to look like and our multiple business plans. I remembered how I used to show him the organizational chart for staff and the suggestions he offered. M y mind went to my birthday when we were at his office and he showed me the documents he wanted me to sign, saying his company would fund the shelter. I remembered turning him down. I could hear his voice now: *I know how much this shelter means to you.* I also turned him down when he wrote me a cheque during my graduation – the cheque I left at his apartment years ago. But he still wanted to help me achieve my dream – even if it meant he had to stay in the shadows while I did so.

Ahmad. He had always been my biggest supporter – even now, when we have no chance of being together. In that moment, my heart was filled with so much happiness at the realization that Ahmad would always have my back; but at the same time, filled with an equal amount of despair. Fate definitely had favorites, and Sakina is high up on that list; she was truly blessed.

Later that night, after reciting my Qur'an and turning out my lights, my phone beeped. It was a message from Umar, a forwarded broadcast about the health benefits of garlic. I sighed as I put my phone back to charge. My thoughts went back to my conversation with Dr. Na'ima about my future. Umar was safe – unexciting, but safe. If I had not met Ahmad, I wouldn't feel like I was missing something. But I did – I met Ahmad. The memories of our shared moments reminded me. But he had moved on now and as painful as that fact was for me, I knew it was for the best. I knew I should too. I stayed awake for a few more hours, listening as the whole house quietened down until I was awakened by the morning call to prayer.

When I got to work that morning, Zee met me in the kitchen where I was deep in conversation with the head chef, discussing the inventory of food items for the month.

"Here's the document you asked for," she said as she almost tripped on the stairs that led down to the entrance of the kitchen. For an accountant with great attention to detail, Zee was clumsy with her steps.

"Watch your step," I called out to her as I instinctively reached for her.

"We were able to find the other NGOs that *The Cain Mosni Foundation* is sponsoring," she handed me a piece of paper. *The Insomniac Foundation,* I thought to myself. "There was just one name on the sheet. The *Feed-A-Child* project," she continued.

I looked up at her, surprised. So, Ahmad was the person behind *Feed-*

A-Child? I chuckled sadly. He was and he still remained the man of my dreams. I mumbled thank you as I stared at the sheet of paper with a deep sigh. If only 'yar Agadez never existed, if only my mother never fell ill after having me, if only Aunty Mami never had the accident on her way to Bauchi. If only… But too many variables had to be changed for my dream to be realized. So, that was all he and I would ever be – a dream.

Chapter 33

At *Le Grand Hotel des Thermes,* Ahmad and Audu spent all their time brainstorming on their line of action. Ahmad's priority was ensuring that no questions were raised about how they got Malama Husseina's address because Zehra could easily be persecuted if the authorities found out. She had broken about three different clauses in her government contract regarding privacy laws by giving him the file containing sensitive information on a resident.

For days, they monitored the two women's routines. Halime's husband, who drove a grey Subaru, left the house first with the youngest kid. A few minutes after, the mother or grandmother would walk the two older children to the bus stop and watch as they got on the school bus. Later in the day, the women would walk to the store to get groceries.

One Friday in the grocery store, after Jumaah prayer, Audu bumped into the older woman as she picked out vegetables. He turned to face her and started apologizing profusely in English, even offering to hold her shopping cart for her.

"*Bai ji miki ciwo ba, ko*? Hope he didn't injure you?" It was Halime.

"*Ku Hausawa ne?* You're Hausa?" Audu's eyeballs almost popped out of their pockets as he feigned surprise. He looked towards Ahmad, who was picking out plums – or more accurately, pretending to – and beckoned him over. "*Zo ku gaisa*; come and say hello. They speak Hausa."

Ahmad walked towards them and the group exchanged pleasantries. They asked about each other's countries of origin and what they were doing in Saint-Malo. At first, Halime was uneasy about divulging any information about her mother due to immigration concerns, Ahmad figured. But when he explained that they were working on a project and researching older Africans in the diaspora, she seemed a bit more relaxed. He even showed her the falsified identification cards he and Audu hung around their necks.

Three days later, they were at Halime's house to interview Malama Husseina for their project. They spent an hour listening to *'yar* Agadez narrate why she and her twin sister fled their hometown in the middle of the night. Ahmad thought about how remarkable human memory was – to be able to remember vivid details from decades ago due to trauma. Her face was lined with the ordeals of time. She told them about how her husband had stayed back to cover their tracks so that they could cross over to the other side safely. He'd promised to meet her in Kano and he waited for him for years, but he never found her.

Ahmad remembered a migration book he read while in University. Economic situations, violence and political devastation in the 1990s led a lot of Fulani, Tuareg and Hausa citizens from Niger to migrate to neighboring African countries. Most of them went to Nigeria through porous borders without proper identification; they blended in well due to some semblance in religion and language. The men found menial jobs working as security guards for northern households, and many of the women went into trade. Some women eventually married into northern families and got absorbed into what was now known as the Hausa-Fulani tribe in modern-day *Arewa*.

"How did you enter Nigeria?" Audu pretended to read from the research questionnaire that made up part of their cover.

Ahmad was sitting opposite them. According to his ID card, he was a radio program producer. Between them was a voice recorder recording the conversation, which was primarily in Hausa.

"We came in through Gumel," her dialect of Hausa was different from what Ahmad was used to. "We walked until we boarded a commercial bus carrying rams in Ringim and it took us to Wudil. I was heavily pregnant at the time." She had a faint smile as she reminisced.

As she spoke, Ahmad could not stop looking at her; this was a woman he had never seen before, yet he felt inexplicable compassion towards her for a reason that defied logic. He almost wanted to ask where she got the scar on her left hand; he'd noticed it earlier when she rubbed her face after reciting the opening prayer to start the interview session.

"Wudil," Audu repeated as he scribbled on his paper. "So, how many years did you spend in Kano?"

"I was born in Wudil," Halime answered, walking into the room with a silver tray and small glass cups. "*Ga shayi*," she said, offering Ahmad a cup of tea.

He smiled and accepted it without explaining that he was observing a six-day fast for the month of *Shawwal*. He watched as she poured the hot liquid into another cup for Audu. "We lived in Kano until I graduated from BUK. I studied Mass communication." Audu kept the feigned look of surprise, even though he already knew all this information.

Halime looked at Ahmad as she sat opposite him, the similarity between both women was even more obvious now that he was seeing them in person. "You said this interview was for BBC Hausa?" she asked.

"Yes, and the Voice of America."

Halime seemed pleased with the answer and as Ahmad watched her movements, he had the most tremendous urge to ask if she had a younger sibling around Fa'iza's age. If it turned out that Malama Husseina was the one who suckled them both, they would leave the women alone without them ever knowing what really brought them here. But he knew they had to stick to the script; they was no need asking such a question right now.

"What kind of jobs did you do in Kano?" He looked at the questionnaire. "Earlier you said that you didn't go to school." Ahmad listened to her talk about the menial jobs she took up to sustain herself and her infant daughter. Some of them matched information that they found about her while they were in Kano. Even though she did not state the years, she remembered the governors of Kano at various times.

"After that, I got a job in Tarauni in the household of the state's Permanent

Secretary at the time," she finally said.

Ahmad cleared his throat, the signal he and Audu had agreed upon to indicate when something about his parents came up. Audu looked up at Ahmad and immediately knew they had hit the spot.

"Okay, so this Perm Sec," Audu probed, "do you remember his name?"

"I honestly can't remember his name. I never met him. I only worked closely with his wife whose name was Hauwa, but everyone called her Mami. She was an exceptionally kind woman who treated me well."

Audu looked up at Ahmad, who nodded in agreement; that was his mother. It took all his willpower to sit calmly in the living room.

"What was your job in their house?"

"I breastfed their first son, Ahmadu," she paused. "It was just before the elections. I was a cleaner at the hospital when I heard the nurses saying that the family of a patient was looking for a Muslim with a suckling child to help feed a young child. I had a baby of my own at the time and the payment multiplied my salary as a cleaner about four or five times."

To Malama Husseina's surprise, Audu handed her an old sepia-toned picture. Ahmad, a toddler, was being held by his mother, who was sitting on a chair; his father was next to her, his arms around her. She recognized her former employers immediately and asked the two gentlemen how they got the picture. Before he answered, Audu brought out another picture Ahmad found in one of his mother's old albums; it was one with Fa'iza's parents. Audu asked her if she knew the couple in the picture. She took longer to respond this time, taking the photograph from him and squinting as she raised it to the light. "I think I know her," she said, pointing at Umma.

"Did you ever work for her?" Audu asked.

Ahmad held his breath. The only sound that could be heard was the ticking of the clock. The hand on the wall clock above the door ticked slowly; it was as if time itself paused to witness this moment. As he looked at Malama Husseina, who was still studying the picture, he wondered if fate had brought him this far and lured him in with the possibility of what could be only to find out that the same woman was hired by both families at different times of her life to breastfeed both of them.

"Did you ever work for her?" Audu asked again.

She looked up at him slowly and shook her head.

"Did you breastfeed any other child, after the Perm Sec boy?"

She shook her head again. "No," she replied. "I stayed in their house for over two years, helping them raise the child. I couldn't breastfeed another child even if I wanted to because I was not blessed with another child after Halime." With the remuneration from the Perm Sec's house, she bought a house in a low-cost area and started a business selling jewelry, patterned textiles and mixed perfumes in Kano GRA. In no time, she was no longer referred to as *'yar* Agadez; all her customers called her *Dillaliya*, the trader.

The room was quiet for a moment, even the clock seemed to have read the tone of the room. Halime's expression had now turned from welcoming to confusing, as though she were wondering if her previous reservations were right. Her mother was also confused, but only because she couldn't quite figure out the connection between these two women and a BBC broadcast. *Are they in some kind of trouble*? She asked herself. *Have I said too much*? She looked up to meet Ahmad's gaze and as their eyes met for the first time since their meeting. He looked away immediately and headed towards the door.

Outside, he paced up and down the front yard, trying to wrap his head around the information he'd just gained. He would start typing Fa'iza's number but could not bring himself to dial. The only thing more painful than not being able to speak to her at that moment was the knowledge that she did not want to hear from him. But he needed to tell her. He needed to tell her that their marriage in Toronto was valid, that she was his wife. She was still his wife. He needed to see her. He needed to tell her that what they had – that night she couldn't forgive herself for – was never haram. They were never forbidden from each other.

When Audu came out of the house, he found Ahmad pacing the outside porch, staring into nothingness with his phone in his hand. "Malama Husseina just confirmed that her sister worked as a wet nurse for another wealthy family. The pict –" he started.

"Where does her sister live now?" Ahmad asked as they boarded their flight back to Nigeria.

"Suleja."

Ahmad could not stop himself from laughing as he looked outside the cabin window. The answer they had been looking for was just an hour and a half from his parent's house in Abuja. On a good day, he could get to Suleja in 50 minutes; yet it had taken them years – and thousands of miles – to get there.

* * *

Back in his parents' house in Abuja, Ahmad watched as his mother looked at the picture of the twin sisters that Halime had given them. After he and Audu explained who he really was and the journey that had taken them to Saint-Malo, both women were moved to tears. Halime said that her mother spoke fondly of how well his family had treated her, but when she went back to their house in Tarauni decades later, she was informed that they had left Kano. Ahmad promised that he would be back to visit. From the files Zehra provided, he's seen that Malama Husseina was on a long wait list for a corrective knee surgery and he planned to take them to Canada to accelerate the process. That was the least he could do for the woman who saved him. Twice.

The shock on his mother's face was evident as she stared at the picture of the twins for a whole minute before handing it to Ahmad's father. Next to her, Afreen looked confused; she looked like she wanted to laugh and cry at the same time. Unlike her usual self, she had remained quiet as Ahmad narrated the story – starting from how he met Audu to meeting Malama Husseina in France. When he ended his story, he requested for his parents to accompany him to Fa'iza's house to speak to her parents in light of the new information. Afreen, still quiet, rubbed her protruding stomach as she met her mother's gaze.

"God is great," his father said, unable to take his eyes off the picture. He was lost for words and looked at his wife for some sort of help. She moved her gaze from her son's excited expression to her husband's unreadable expression to her daughter's confusion.

"I thought you hadn't spoken to Fa'iza in years?" she asked Ahmad when she returned her gaze to him.

Ahmad wondered why she was bringing that up. The reason his wife cut herself out of his life was because of this misunderstanding. Now that it had been corrected, they could resume their relationship. "Yes – which is why we need to let them know right away. I have all the evidence they could possibly ask for."

The room was quiet for what seemed like forever until Afreen finally spoke: "But it's been so lon –"

"What has that got to do with anything?"

"What if she has finally moved on? Did you stop to think about that? I – I just don't want you to put yourself out there and – and get rejected," her eyes were moistening up and tears were beginning to form.

"But she hasn't," he said as-a-matter-of-factly. He never moved on, and neither did she. He knew her well enough to know that just as he never stopped loving her, she still loved him. This was why she avoided being around him and why she practically made herself invisible during Afreen's wedding, even though he could tell she was looking for him every time she entered a room. Her eyes would keep searching until they found him, and then she would avoid that area for the rest of the night.

The sound of Afreen blowing her nose brought him back. He looked up to find his sister burying her face in her mother's lap in tears.

"Ahmad, you know there's nothing that would make me happier than bringing Fa'iza to this house as your bride," his mother started, shaking her head slowly. "I didn't know how to tell you this, but last week... last week Umma came by. She came by and... she came by with – with an invitation to Fa'iza's wedding."

"I know Justice Mohammed. He would never go back on a promise he made – especially about something like this," his father chirped in. "It's not done. It would make him a man with no honor. And that's not the Justice Moham –"

Ahmad was watching his father's lips move but was unable to make sense of the words coming out of them.

Chapter 34

These days, it's getting harder and harder for me to get out of bed; my body just refuses to do anything that requires much movement. I spend half my weekends in bed, drowning in a book or listening to a podcast. It was a strange kind of fatigue that I blamed on how busy we'd been these past weeks spent in court. I also blamed it on giving up yoga. I'd tried to stay consistent since I moved back home; I downloaded aerobic and meditative yoga videos on my laptop and for a few months, I had a routine that I stuck to religiously. After *subh,* I would unroll my lime-green workout mat which had pink letters that read: "Om is where the heart is"; and spend thirty minutes in various poses and stretches before I took my shower. Gradually, my daily workouts reduced from daily to twice a week, then once a week. Now, I can't even remember the last time I unrolled the mat. I didn't know if my exhaustion was why I stopped working out or if I was always so exhausted because I stopped working out regularly. Or maybe it was because I didn't take vitamins. Afreen always recommends holistic supplements and multivitamins because, as she says, everybody needed them. But the hard-to-swallow big green pills she gave me months ago were still unopened and tucked away in the bathroom cabinet.

My mind went to the text message I'd received from Afreen when my wedding invitations and *asoebi* were sent to her and Aunty Mami: *Allah ya sanya alheri, Fa'ee am*; May Allah bless your Union. An uneasy knot formed at the back of my throat when I thought about my upcoming wedding to Umar. From the first visit his parents made to our house for *gaisuwa,* introduction, when I met his father for the first time to the one when his aunties and stepmother came last week with the *kayan lefe,* it had all been a big blur. It felt like a mistake. Every passing day made it feel real. I was going to marry Umar and I could not explain what it was exactly, but I felt like I was being unfaithful. But unfaithful to whom? Unfaithful to the one from my past, the one who had moved on, the one who was forbidden for me? Or unfaithful to the one I was marrying, as I replayed memories I shared with someone else every night? All the sleepless nights were probably why I was exhausted in the morning.

An hour later, after I finished the one episode of *I said what I said* that I had on my podcast queue all week, I decided to make some tea and check on Umma. On my way to her section, I met Atine carrying some incense in a clay burner with balls and sticks of oiled incense and collected it from her. When I entered her room, I found Umma sitting in front of her *cabbasa,* a brown woven raffia basket we use to put incense on clothes by placing the burner under it and clothes are draped over. As I placed the burner under the *cabbasa,* I wondered about the engulfing the white swirls that could not escape from the enclosure, leaving the clothes fragrant. That was what I felt like sometimes, like I wanted to escape from this upcoming union, but I felt trapped after agreeing to it. I had drafted multiple text messages telling Umar that I thought we should wait a little longer, but all the messages were erased halfway.

"Hmm," Umma's voice broke into my thoughts as she showed me the newest batch of *khumrah,* liquid body incense. I watched as she selected two bottles – one tinged in yellow and gold specks and the other, milky white – and used the droppers to place a little on her wrist, she screwed them back shut and used her fingers to rub the blend into her skin. She inhaled appreciatively, undoubtedly pleased with her order, "come and smell this."

I walked towards her outstretched arm, sniffing the aromatic blend of myrrh, musk and sandalwood. It was rich and unique, like the hard-to-place scent I had grown to associate with Umma, yet I could never replicate.

"I love this, Umma." I inhaled again, this time longer than I did earlier.

She laughed as she closed the box containing about two dozen bottles. "Glad to hear that. They're all yours. You should start using them from today. After every ablution, apply a little, like I just did." She showed me different combinations for more potent scents and a green one I was supposed to use only in the evenings.

"*Nagode* Umma; thank you," I leaned in to give her a hug – an act that was once strange and unfamiliar between her and me. However, since my moving back to Nigeria, I found myself spending more time with her, even more so now that the clock was ticking on my permanent leave from my father's house, from seeing her daily. I would be moving into a house that Umar's father had gifted him; it was a three-bedroom apartment in an estate in Apo, which was a thirty-minute drive from my parent's house on the other side of Abuja. My aunts had been busy coordinating all the furniture deliveries to the house and sending Umma pictures of my kitchen, bedroom, and living room. Pictures of the place I would spend the rest of my life in. It still felt like a dream and not the good kind; it felt like I was living someone else's dream. I was just happy I didn't have to move to Kaduna like Umar originally wanted us to. I told him I couldn't not leave Abuja because I was worried about the shelter and how it would thrive without me overseeing the daily operations.

"I need to go to the office," I said, draping Umma's veil over the *cabassa*.

"Isn't it Saturday?"

"I just need to pick up a file for a case. We were supposed to go to court at the end of the month, but the defendant had the case moved up to this week, so I need to prepare."

"Didn't Magajiya tell you to avoid going out when the sun is so high up in the sky?"

Magajiya was the woman who did my *gyaran jiki*, local spa treatments. For weeks leading up to my wedding, I was scheduled to treatments that would scrub, pluck, and prune me to perfection. I started a weekly treatment two weeks prior, but the regularity would eventually increase to daily during the week of my wedding. During my first session, I was waxed entirely from neck to toe with *halawa*, a sticky sugar and lemon mix, and massaged with *kurkum* paste. The yellow tinge from the turmeric made my skin unnaturally bright, and throughout the next day, my palms and feet left annoying stains on my white bathroom tiles. My next appointment had me sweating in a steam room, wearing nothing but a wrapper tied at my chest. I sat on a wooden stool that had a hole, and the steam and smoke from the burning pot below filled with aromatic herbs steamed my vagina. Our culture and tradition said a bride had to be perfect for her husband. I refused to have my hair buried in *chebe* mix that I was supposed to carry without washing for two days; that was where I drew the line. It made my head feel heavy, and I hated not being able to feel my pillow. I washed it all off in just over an hour. Everything about *gyaran jiki* felt so intrusive and time-consuming, and I wish I could just be left to dedicate my time to the case files at the shelter instead.

"Just a quick stop. I won't be long."

"Alright then. Drive safe."

As I got into my car, it occurred to me that Umma hardly went to Hajiya Uwani's house anymore. In fact, Hajiya Uwani had not visited our house in a while; perhaps she was even busier than Umma with Sakina's wedding preparations. I never allowed my mind to think about their wedding. When I finally started scrolling through social media a few days ago, I was not barraged with announcements of the 'wedding of the year'; I looked through Sakina's profile and saw that her account had been deactivated. I couldn't blame her; the thousands of notifications she got hourly must have made it hard to use her phone. I could only imagine how stressed she must have been. Anytime my mind drifted off to Ahmad – as it often did – I drowned out those thoughts by listening to the radio. Today, Davido was singing '*30 billion for my account o*', and I sang along with him.

As I was leaving the office, I got a call from Umar asking if he could come drop a brochure for our pre-wedding counseling sessions. I told him to meet me outside the shelter and while I waited for him, I went through the file, memorizing the names of the couple's children and dates of the assaults reported. Layla, a woman in her 30, and her children: 10 year old Mamman, 8 year old Maryam and a toddler, Isa. Her husband, one Alhaji Sani had married a teenage girl and he beat Layla his first wife to pulp after she locked the door to the house and hid the key insisting that the man would not go to spend the night with his new bride. I flipped the pages and read her written statement from the police complaint. A few minutes later, Umar pulled up and came out of his car. I did the same.

"Hajiya Fa'iza," he crossed the quiet road between our cars and stood by mine, peering into my vehicle. I honestly wished he would stop calling me that.

"*Na'am?*" I answered. Our interactions were polite at best.

He started telling me about a burst pipe that had to be fixed in the apartment in Apo, saying that he had to go meet the plumber before the man left for the day. He gave me the paperwork from the counseling workshop we signed up for, which had a PIN number I was meant to use to log into a website to watch the recorded videos and take the personality quizzes. Our wedding was going to be a low-key one, I told him I would prefer it that way. I wanted a few, quiet events: *saukan Qur'ani,* Quranic recitations, the *nikkah* and *kai amarya,* conveyance of the bride. I was not trying to compete with the other lovebirds; if what I read on social media was true, they were to have a week-long line-up of events from Kano to Abuja. Umar and I also had no plans for a honeymoon; we never even discussed it. We were both heading back to work the first Monday after getting married.

As Umar got into his car and left, I noticed a white Range Rover parked a few meters away from me. I looked its way and the door opened. To my surprise, Ahmad stepped out, wearing a white kaftan, a Hausa cap and brown Hermes slippers. As he slowly closed the distance between us, his scent engulfed me. I wondered if he had been driving this way and stopped to say hello when he saw me outside the shelter. The previous month, after I decoded Cain Mosni, Zee brought the final package that was going to be mailed out to them for my final review. I brought out the cover letter, scratched over the "Dear Cain Mosni Foundation," and used my black pen to write his name. When it read "Dear Ahmad Babangida," I sealed the envelope that contained our letter of gratitude and financial records and she sent it to their forwarding address. He never acknowledged it.

"Assalamu alaikum," I managed a smile. I hadn't seen him since the day he came by the house after his wedding announcement. I didn't even give him my attention then, and now I felt bad. Maybe we would have remained friendly if he hadn't kissed me that day at the residence, knowing we were... knowing that we were... knowing about *'yar* Agadez. Could I ever really be just friends with someone I was madly in love with? Maybe in a few years, we could be cordial; we had to be. If we were all going to be in Abuja, we would always run into each other at events and weddings of family and friends. I wondered what seeing him and Sakina would feel like. I wondered what their kids would look like. *No, I don't want to think about that,* I thought. *I hope we never run into each other again.* Maybe moving to Kaduna with Umar was not such a bad idea, after all.

"Who was that in the Honda?" There was something off about his voice. "One of your staff?" His hands slowly went into his pocket.

"Staff *kuma*?" I chuckled as I adjusted my veil, suddenly conscious of my bare face and the simple black Abaya that I was wearing. I didn't care when Umar saw me like this but there I was, wishing I was wearing something better for Ahmad. I looked up to meet his gaze. "That's – That's Umar."

He was quiet for a moment, then replied: " Congratulations."

"Thank you," I dragged out the last word, trying to sound as happy as I possibly could. If only I could tell him that my marriage to Umar was just to stop me from thinking about him, another woman's husband, that this was an attempt at moving on, at forgetting about him.

His eyes fell to my lips and back to my eyes. He looked behind us and back to my face, "so, do you love this Umar guy? Are you in love with him?"

Was there a tiny chance that he felt the same desperation I did? Especially now that the cords of our separation were going to be cut finally? Officially? I looked away. Ahmad could always read me and if I wanted to sound convincing, I needed to avoid his eyes. I thought about how bland everything was with Umar and how much I pined for Ahmad. But what use was that? Our fate was sealed even before we met each other.

"Yes. Yes, I do," I smiled, mustering all the strength I had in me for that lie. I looked up at him and noticed for the first time how glazed his eyes seemed.

He chuckled sadly, took his eyes off mine and looked at the ground, nodding slowly. "I just wanted to let you know that I'm heading back in a few days," he exhaled. Was that pain I could see in his eyes? "I closed the Canadian office and moved the headquarters to the States."

I nodded. I still saw articles about him in *Business Insider,* about how his company had grown exponentially. It seemed like both our dreams came true, career-wise. "Oh okay. And then you'll be back for…" I swallowed, "the wedding?" It hurt to say that out loud.

"Actually, that has been called off."

Oh. I didn't know that. That explains Sakina's absence on social media, I thought. Out loud, I say "sorry to hear that." I was not really sorry; It just seemed like the right thing to say.

"Well, I'm not. There was nothing between her and me. It was just a means to…" he hesitated, "I guess it doesn't even matter anymore."

My phone started ringing and I looked down to see Umma's picture on the screen. I had been out for longer than I said and the sun was beginning to peek from behind the clouds. I excused myself, wishing him a safe trip and got into my car, willing myself not to look into my rearview mirror as I struggled hard to keep the tears away.

Monday morning came with a different kind of struggle. It was only a few hours to lunch, and I had three doctor's reports on battered women. The latest one was of Anita, who came to the shelter after her husband of six years beat her when she found messages of lewd chats between him and different women and picture evidence of him cheating on her. When she confronted him, he beat her black and blue until she managed to run out of the house, stop a taxi and found her way to the shelter. The security guards at the gate paid for her taxi and brought her indoors; she was transferred to the clinic later that night, where she remained heavily sedated due to the pain. I stood up and made my way downstairs to the finance office to give Zee a copy of the hospital bill.

"I am going to check on her at the hospital after work," I said to Zee as I left her office, she was right behind me, I guessed she was going to fill her water bottle from the water dispenser in the reception.

"Who? The Anita woman?" When I nodded, she added, "I'll come with you."

"Assalamu alaikum."

I looked up to see a man in his late thirties walk in, wearing a blue polo shirt and blue jeans. He was dark-skinned and robust with a solemn look on his face and fan-shaped tribal markings at the corners of his mouth. He was carrying a black laptop bag.

"Wa alaikumus salam," Zee and I answered as he stepped into the reception. I kept my eyes on him as he moved closer, wondering if he was the husband to the battered lady whose x-rays were displayed on my screen upstairs.

"I'm looking for someone," he brought out a piece of paper from his pocket and read from it. "Her name is Fa'iza Mohammed."

"And who's asking?" I cleared my throat. With the recent bomb blast attacks in Abuja, one could not be too careful anymore.

He smiled as he looked at me, raising his hands as if to show that he was harmless. "Just me, Hajiya. I need a favor." He looked earnest, and I wondered how I could help him.

"I hope it's something I can do." Maybe he had a relative who needed our help. Sometimes women in helpless situations didn't leave such situations until relatives, friends or neighbors nudged them to. And as sympathetic as the situation was, our hands were tied if the woman didn't come in by choice; we couldn't just go into houses to take abused women, even though part of me wished that we could.

The man brought out a white office file from the laptop bag and he moved towards me. " My name is Audu," he said in Hausa. "Hajiya, I don't know you, but I've been fortunate enough to work for someone who does and he has gone through a lot of trouble for the information in here." He handed the white file to me. He reached into the black bag again and brought out a tape recorder and handed it to me too. "Please listen to this, too." He turned to leave.

"Excuse me, who do you work for, and what are all these?"

"He doesn't know that I'm here, but all the answers you're looking for are in the file. Please read it," he pleaded and with a slight nod, he was gone.

I looked at Zee, who shrugged in confusion. I started making my way to my office from the reception to read it properly. When I opened the file, printouts of receipts from hotels in Kano from years ago fell out, with flight ticket stubs to France and hotel receipts from Niamey. As I knelt down to pick everything up, I saw a picture; it was Ahmad. But I barely recognized him; he looked much thinner and had a full beard, wearing a dark T-shirt and black jeans. It didn't look like he knew the picture was being taken; he seemed lost in thought as he stared away from the camera. He was sitting on a wooden bench under a tree outside a mosque, a signpost behind him read Minjibir.

Minjibir, Kano? When was Ahmad in Kano and what was he doing in Minjibir? I scowled as I hurried to my office and opened the file on my table. *What was this about?* I thought to myself as I turned the picture and saw the date at the back: July, 2012. That was the year Ahmad and I were supposed to get married. I sat down and saw more pictures of the man I just met, Audu, in different places at different times through the years; months and years were scribbled in blue ink at the back of all the pictures. I started flipping through the pages and they had screenshots of emails and daily reports from a search. The daily reports then became weekly reports, then monthly. For years, for so many years. My finger moved to the message recipient line and saw that all the reports were sent to Ahmad's personal email and the subject was always '*yar* Agadez'.

My jaw dropped. *Ahmad has been looking for her all these years*? My head started spinning. I found an envelope with a black-and-white picture of a young woman in a hijab. I turned it around, and all it said was Hassana Amadou. I flipped the page and saw another picture of two older women, who could have been in their forties or fifties – it was hard to tell –but I could tell that they were sisters from the resemblance.

Wait. I glanced back at the black-and-white picture. Could *this* be '*yar*

Agadez? There were two of them? My heart was pounding. I flipped the next page, but all it had was a hurriedly scribbled note from a handwriting that I didn't recognize. "Please listen to the recording," it read.

I pressed play on the tape recorder Audu had given me. It was only static for a few seconds and then I could hear voices – a woman's voice and a man's. It was an interview. I listened as the male voice asked the woman how life in France was for her and her grandkids. And as I listened, I went through the flight ticket stubs; there were two from Abuja to France. One was for Ahmad, and the other was for Audu. Wait, Ahmad went to France? I looked at the dates on the ticket stubs and they were just two months old – right about the time he came by the house. All these years? Ahmad never stopped looking? My palms were getting sweaty, and my throat was parched. The recording continued and I listened with rapt attention. It was her; it was *'yar* Agadez. She talked about working for Ahmad's family in Kano. My heart skipped a beat when she said she never suckled anyone after him. Nobody. Tears started falling down my face. *Nobody? Does this mean...wait? We were not... we were not breastfed by the same woman? Does that mean... Then how... If it means...* I could not think straight. Ahmad knew this when he saw me over the weekend and he didn't tell me?

The interview continued and I heard her say that her twin sister worked for another family. Two different women – sisters – breastfed us. I started to feel faint. I needed to call Abba and Umma. I had to find Ahmad. I stood up and made for the door and was halfway down the stairs when I remembered that I didn't take my car keys. I rushed back to the desk, got my bag, packed up the file and ran out of the office. Didn't Ahmad say he was leaving for the States today? What if he'd gone already? I glanced at my wristwatch, wondering what Abuja traffic would be like at lunchtime because it was an odd hour for me to leave the office. I heard Zee asking if everything was okay, but I could not form a coherent answer because I rushed into my car and threw everything I was holding in the passenger seat, my hands shaking and my head spinning as I pressed the ignition button.

Ahmad. My Ahmad. Where would I even find him? Oh my God. We

were never forbidden for each other. It was never haram. I started driving to his parent's house in Maitama, as I called Afreen. It didn't go through. *Ah damnit!* She was on her way to Dubai to shop for the baby. How would I even reach him? I never saved his numbers when he called and I always deleted his texts once I realized it was him. *I've been so stupid!* I thought. I swerved as I almost got hit by a green cab and narrowly made it through a red light but eventually, I made it to their street. My hands were still shaking when I left Dr. Na'ima a voice message asking to be scheduled for an urgent appointment.

The guards opened the gates of the ambassador's private residence and I drove through. When I parked, one of the security guards wearing a blue uniform told me that only the staff were around.

"Where's aunty Mami?" I asked, trying to keep my composure as I looked around the white-painted exterior walls of the sprawling mansion flanked by a beautifully landscaped garden, lush green grass, tall palm trees and a water fountain.

"They're in Minna, but they're supposed to be coming back today."

"What about Ahmad?" It felt strange saying his name out loud after many years. His name was always on the tip of my tongue, but I never uttered it; I never had a reason to.

"I don't know if he is around," the security man said. "But let me call the house to ask if –"

"Don't worry," I said, running into the house. *Please be around. Please don't be gone.* "Assalamu alaikum," I called out as I walked past the grand entrance through the hallway leading into the living area.

Silence echoed back.

I went to the stairs and called out again. Silence. There was no sound from the television, no clatter of pans from the kitchen and no vacuum going off somewhere. It was so quiet and so clean, as though nobody lived there. *This was a stupid idea,* I thought. If Aunty Mami traveled and there was no one home, she probably gave most of her domestic staff the day off and Ahmad wouldn't be here. He told me that he was going to the US and I started crying because I didn't even have a valid visa to the US anymore.

And I needed to see him. I need to talk to him. I must tell him that I knew, that I knew what he had been doing all these years. Oh, Lord. All these years, he had been looking for her? That was why he asked me if I loved Umar – and I said yes! Shit, I said yes. *I am so stupid,* I thought to myself. *I can't marry Umar. I have to find Ahmad.*

I came out of the main house, walked around the circular driveway and went towards the guest chalets. It was also empty. How could such a big house be left completely empty? I slumped to the ground, holding my head in my hands and sobbing helplessly.

"Fa'iza?"

Chapter 35

Ahmad's bedroom in his parent's house seemed to be the only place where the walls did not move closer on their own accord. He stared at the intricate paneling on the white ceiling, his migraine getting worse by the minute; the familiar pressure was building at his temples and concentrating at the center of his forehead. The sleepless nights in France, the jetlag and the turbulent flight back to Abuja must be the reasons why the migraine seemed to spread quicker today than it usually did, not to forget that he hadn't had a proper meal in over forty-eight hours; now that he was thinking about it, all that was punctuating his fasts were hurriedly-eaten fruit and granola bars. Apart from his sister's voice, the only sound in the room was the Quranic recitation that was playing through the ceiling speakers connected to his phone.

"It has been so long; it's unfair to expect her to keep waiting. She didn't even know you were still searching for *'yar* Agadez. Nobody…none of us knew."

Ahmad remained quiet as Afreen moved further into the room, passing the dent that his phone left on the flat-screen television on the wall. She sat on the bed and looked up at him; his face was expressionless, and his eyes were closed, covered by one folded arm.

"Nobody expected it to turn out like this," she continued. "Not even me – and I'm your biggest cheerleader."Afreen watched as her brother's chest heaved heavily and she tried to pull his arms away from his face. "Ahmad?" she called out softly, her voice breaking. "I know this is painful but *ka rungume kaddaran Allah*; please accept it as fate."

Ahmad sat up and rubbed his face at the mention of fate. Fate brought them here. And it was more complicated than everyone realized. It was not about him just finding the truth; it was about his relationship with Fa'iza. He looked at his sister. Her eyes were beginning to redden as she looked at him, one hand cradling her belly, as though she were comforting her unborn child.

He opened his mouth to tell her the truth about his relationship with Fa'iza, but thought about the preterm labor complications she'd experienced in her earlier trimesters, the fluctuating blood pressure and her 'high-risk' pregnancy, and he decided not to burden her. "I need to see her, Afreen. I need to tell her." That was all he could say.

"No, you're right," Afreen sighed. Although in her mind, she wondered if that was going to change anything. The five years they'd spent apart were more than the time they had shared as a couple.

After Afreen left, Ahmad spent more time than he cared to admit finding out about the man Fa'iza would be marrying in the following days. Umar Tasallah.

Two days later, when Ahmad eventually made it to the street her parents' house was located, he sat in his car, contemplating if he should drive into her father's house. He was still undecided when he saw the black cast iron gates roll open and her car – the black Hyundai Elantra slowly drove past him. He followed her, allowing a vehicle or two in between them. When they got to the shelter, he parked a few meters behind her and watched as she alighted from her car and dashed inside. He waited in the car, holding the *'yar* Agadez file, wondering if he should follow her.

She came out a few minutes later with a folder tucked under her arm, as she spoke on the phone. She used her free hand to shield the sun from her face and got into her car. Ahmad waited for her to start moving and when she didn't, he guessed she was waiting for someone. He was right. Within minutes, a black Honda pulled up on the other side of the road across them.

Chapter 35

Ahmad recognized the man the minute he saw him. He thought about how the man looked even less impressive in person than the picture he saw on the souvenir packages brought to his mother, he had a medium build, a broad forehead and a posture that leaned forward like he was pulled by an invisible thread. Almost out of sync with the rhythm of the world around him.

What kind of man keeps someone like her waiting for over ten minutes? Ahmad chuckled bitterly to himself as he watched them talking. Well, the man was talking, and she was listening. Even from a distance, Ahmad could see that her body was slightly turned away from the man throughout the interaction and she never looked at him directly. *She looks uncomfortable,* he thought.

After the brief interaction, the man left. *What kind of man doesn't wait for a lady to drive away first?* Ahmad thought. *Isn't that basic etiquette?* Ahmad glanced at the file that was now on the passenger's seat. He knew he had to ask her. He had to ask if she was happy and if she had truly moved on. If she was, there would be no need to give her the file; he would have to let her go. But he had to ask. He had to know. He came down from his car and moved towards her.

Later that evening, as he sat by the drained pool at the back of the house, Ahmad read the confirmation email for his flight to America. He scrolled through his gallery, aware that his battery was on seven percent. He sighed. *When it eventually runs out,* Ahmad thought, *I won't charge this phone again.* He was going to lock it up in his safe, along with everything else that reminded him of her. He stopped scrolling when he got to a picture he had taken of her years ago, after their nikkah. That day was still etched in his memory – the white dress she wore, the silk hijab that framed her face perfectly and the biggest smile on her face.

III

Part Three

Broken into fragments,
Heartbeats - counted, limited.
Yet, I'd give all the beats I have left
To hear my name escape your lips, again
Ours is a togetherness that honors the beauty of our solitude.

Chapter 36

Ahmad just canceled his flight to America when he hears a voice downstairs. He stands still because it sounds like Fa'iza, but he knows that it can't be possible. His mind is playing tricks on him again like the days he would reach for her in bed and remember that she wasn't there. He hears the voice again now, saying *Assalamu alaikum.* It is faint, but it is unmistakably her. He makes his way downstairs and checks both living rooms, but they are empty. Ahmad turns back around to go back upstairs when he notices her car in the driveway. He opens the main doors and walks out of the house, peering into the tinted glasses to check if there's anyone inside. It is empty.

"*Oga*, she just went into the Boys Quarters," Mark, the head of security, walks towards him.

It is her. She is here, Ahmad thinks to himself as he goes through the white iron gates that lead to the inner section of the house. He walks past the staff quarters and is about to turn around when he hears a sob coming from around the corner. He follows the sound, walks past the unoccupied guest chalet, and finds Fa'iza on the green carpet grass, sobbing with her hands buried in her face and her brown veil slipping off her head as her body shakes with the quiet sobs. "Fa'iza?"

The sobbing stops, and he watches her stiffen. She looks up at him in shock and covers her face with her hands again. Ahmad can't stop himself; he walks toward her and crouches next to her. "Hey, look at me," he says. *What happened to her? What's making her cry?* His mind goes to Umar. *Did he touch her? Did he hurt her? I swear I'll kill him.*"Fa'iza," It is hard keeping his voice leveled as she cries next to him. "Talk to me."

Her hands fall to her sides, and she reaches for something next to her. He sees Audu's file on *'Yar* Agadez on the floor next to her. *How did she get the file?* Fa'iza looks up at him. Her eyes are reddened and her cheeks are damp with tears, but she looks just as beautiful as the first day he saw her when she bumped into him at the airport.

"Were you just going to leave without telling me?" her voice is a pained whisper.

Ahmad opens his mouth to tell her that he canceled his flight, that he can't relocate knowing she's here, that he wants to be wherever she is. But the words won't form and he closes it again. Now that he is next to her, admitting he so much as entertained the thought of leaving the country feels like a crime. He can't take his eyes off of her as she picks up the file and opens it towards him like he didn't know the contents.

"All this time, Ahmad? You've been searching for her *all* this time?" She flips through the pages, looking up to catch his gaze.

"I told you I wasn't gonna give up on us," he swallows as he holds her gaze, "I – I love you, Fa'iza."

She looks at him like she cannot believe the words he's saying and starts crying again. But this time, she does not cover her face, like she's finally pulling off the facade of strength she used as a mask all these years. She holds herself and starts rocking herself back and forth. "I never stopped loving you. I couldn't –" her voice trails off as the sobs take over.

Ahmad tries to regulate his emotions. It is all too much – the pain of separation all these years and the joy at this unexpected glimmer at a chance at happiness.

"I can't marry anyone else," she finally says.

Ahmad has imagined this moment for years. He has stayed awake for many nights, praying that this day will come. He played different variations of this scenario in his sleeplessness, imagining how he will kiss her, hold her tightly against him, the words he will use to tell her how much she hurt him by giving up on them without a fight. Now that the moment has come, he is powerless, almost speechless; he can't do any of those things. At this moment, he realizes that when Fa'iza removed herself from his life, it was an act of love; it was love for the sake of Allah. Right now, he wants nothing more than to hold her, but he can't bring himself to for the same reason – for fear of Allah.

He spent all night reading up on the status of their marriage – whether they are still married or not. He can't bring himself to touch her until he knows for sure that he can.

She wipes away tears from her face and exhales: "We need a plan. Abba's not going to believe a recording."

Ahmad nods. His father often shares stories of how hers remains unswayed in Nigerian politics by standing for what is just and right, regardless of the people involved or their relationship to him.

"Can you get them? Can you get the sisters to testify to him in person?" she searches his eyes.

"Of course," he nods. "What else?" He'll do anything to make it happen, whatever she asks for.

Ahmad spends the next half hour making phone calls and the next half booking flights and arranging both sisters' transportation from Saint-Malo and Suleja to Abuja.

When he finds Fa'iza again, she's by the drained pool typing on his laptop and looking serious, as she did back in Toronto when working on a school report. Every few minutes, he'll look up and asks, "what can I help you with?" and for a few seconds, she stares at him like she still can't believe what's happening, then she'll smile and shake her head. After a few hours, she tells him that she needs to use some books from Abba's library and as he sees her off, holding the driver's door open for her, she looks up at him. "You're gonna have to tell your parents everything," she says. "*Everything.*"

He pulls his eyes from her lips and back to her eyes. "Alright," he nods. "Are you sure you don't want me to drop you?" he asks, as if the twelve-minute drive to her house is what he needs to prolong their time together.

"No, I have to stop by the shelter," she explains. "There's this domestic abuse case I need to follow up on."

He smiles at her in awe. Even with everything happening in her personal life, she still remembers the case waiting for her in the office. It is that kindness, compassion and tenacity that makes a woman like her hard to forget.

He watches as she slowly drives through the gates, a million thoughts going through his mind. He doesn't want her to leave; she does not want to leave either. But they both know that this second chance is one they have to fight to earn.

Later that night, as he waits outside his mother's suite, he hears her talking to Afreen on the phone. The doctor is suggesting induction or cesarean section for the baby and her due date is in less than a month. When she hangs up, he walks through the frosted glass double doors and the bedroom was empty. "Mom?" he calls out, his voice strained.

"I'm in here," she answers. She is in her walk-in closet, already in her white night robe, her hair uncovered in a loose bun and her glasses down the straight bridge of her nose.

"How's Afreen?"

His mother sighs, rubbing her forehead. "She's worried about a possible CS, but I told her it's nothing to worry about. She's in safe hands."

"Everything will be fine, Insha Allah."

"Insha Allah," she smiles, putting a green abaya on a hanger.

He remains quiet.

She looks up at his face for the first time since he walked in – at the worry lines etched between his eyebrows. "What is it?" she asks quietly.

Ahmad swallows as he moves closer to her, rubbing his beard, "I have to tell you something."

"You're scaring me, Ahmad," she replies, still holding the green abaya on a hanger.

"Mom," he starts. He knows he can't beat around the bush or gently ease her into this. He has to be direct. "Fai'za and I are married."

Chapter 36

The room is quiet, the only sound coming from it is from the air conditioner. Although in the distance, they can hear the security team doing their rounds around the house.

"I – I don't understand. Wh – wh – what do you – what do you mean?" his mother speaks quietly, not taking her eyes off him.

He rubs his eyes, and he looks down at the soft grey carpet on the tiled floor. "It was about two months before we found out that –" he couldn't bring himself to complete it. "It was my idea. I needed to put her on the board in my comp –"

"What?" The green abaya falls to the floor. "You got married where?"

Ahmad clears his throat before he answers. "Umm – Eman Masjid."

She frowns, "in Toronto?"

He nods.

Her mouth drops open and her eyes widen in bewilderment. She looks like she's going to faint and when he sees her falling to the ground, Ahmad hurriedly pulls out the white tufted ottoman tucked under the vanity and puts it behind her. "You got married without telling us?" she puts her hands to her chest as she sits down, looking at his face with equal amounts of shock and disbelief on hers.

"Mom –" he begins, even though he doesn't know what to say.

"You mean this whole time – *this whole time* – you kept a secret this big from me? A whole marriage, Ahmad? What were you thinking?" She covers her mouth with her hands.

Ahmad's voice lowers to match hers as he slowly explains that it was all his fault, that he thought he was doing the right thing then.

Hajiya Mami stands up from the chair and walks into her room. She sighs loudly as she sits on her bed while Ahmad remains by the chaise next to her, watching her as he stares blankly into a picture frame of their family, taken on his graduation day from Cambridge. He follows her gaze as it lands on the invitation cards, *asoebi,* and some treats that were delivered to the house as part of Fai'za and Umar's wedding invitation. "Is it even still valid?" she finally asks.

"I never uttered a divorce. We just assumed the whole *'yar* Agadez thing nullified it."

"So, this marriage, was – was it consummated?" she looks straight into his eyes.

Ahmad read up on that last night. While there is a misconception that an Islamic marriage can only be consummated with penetrative sex, it turns out that any kind of sexual intimacy between a married couple is enough to consummate the marriage – as long as both of them are okay with delaying sex. In other words, what happened that morning in his penthouse before she left for Nigeria validates their marriage. He looks up to find his mum still looking up at him, waiting for an answer. He exhales. "She's – she's my wife, mom."

His mom closes her mouth and looks away.

Saying it out loud brings some relief. This isn't just between him and Fa'iza anymore; this is real. She is his wife, and he's her husband.

After a few minutes and without saying a word, his mother stands up and makes her way out of the suite towards the living room to find her husband. Ahmad follows her through the brightly lit hallway with high ceilings, white walls, and large family portraits framed with dark wood panels.

When they find the ambassador, he is reading a newspaper with a frown on his face. Ahmad watches as his mother sits next to his father on the brown leather sectional and he sits on a sofa opposite them, looking at the floor. He listens as his mother explains everything he told her to his father. When she was done, his father looks up at him and removes his glasses. "Is this true?" The disbelief and disappointment in his voice are very hard to miss.

Ahmad meets his father's eyes and nods slowly.

Chapter 37

By the time I get home from the shelter, it's almost Maghrib. I dash into Abba's library, while he's in his living room with some guests and spend a few minutes looking for his most comprehensive texts on *Shari'ah* and laws governing Islamic marriages and Divorce. I go back to my room with three textbooks that measure half my weight and four smaller publications and spend the next few hours reading, outlining, writing and tearing up pages from my notes in frustration.

Growing up, I was lucky to see the kind of lawyer that my father was. In primary school, I spent after-school hours in his library doing assignments and studying for common entrance exams into secondary school, on the same spot in the later years. During those times, I heard him discuss cases over the phone. A few years later, while I was in Junior Secondary School, he got a contractor to break the back wall and extend it to create more room for an office and more bookshelves, and after the renovation, I almost relocated to the office. When I got to Senior Secondary School, my evening visits to his library reduced until they completely stopped when I went to the university. I watched how my father never pulled up citations from just one source during those days; he would always have multiple texts in front of him. I can't remember what year it was – I must have been fifteen or sixteen –some law students from ABU interned with him for a few months and they were always in the library helping doing research for his cases. I remember that he always told them to anticipate the other side's defense. It was not enough to just know your case; you should think about all the possible ways your claim could be refuted and build your supporting disquisition around that.

My phone beeps. It is a message from an unsaved number: *Are you awake?*

I find myself smiling as I text back: *Yes.*

Another message came in: *Can I call you?*

As soon as I send another *Yes*, his call comes in.

"Hey," he says as soon as he picks up.

"Heyyy."

"Why are you still awake?"

I smile at how familiar his voice sounds in my ear. It has not changed one bit. I can't believe that I get to hear this voice again after so many years.

"Why are you still awake?" I ask him back as I look at the wall clock, surprised to see that it's almost midnight.

He let out a deep sigh. "I can't sleep."

"I can't either." I am laying on my side in bed, looking around at all the books I was surrounded by in my room. I can't believe how many years it has been since we spoke on the phone, yet, talking to him right now feels like there hasn't been a gap at all. My mind goes to the last phone call we had; he was talking me out of a panic attack. It was the day I saw my uncle's car in the driveway, the day Abba came back from Egypt, the day I met Malama Zainab. My eyes start tearing up as I remember the events of that day and everything that followed.

"I can't sleep. I'm afraid that if I go to sleep, I'll wake up to find that this was all a dream," he pauses, "I don't think I can survive that."

I chuckle silently. It feels like a dream to me, too. Everything has been a slow haze since I found out.

"You there?" he asks after a while.

"Why didn't you tell me that you were still looking?"

"I tried to tell you a few times, but you wouldn't pick up my calls."

"I cried every time I disconnected those calls, and deleted the messages without reading," I confessed.

He is quiet for a while, then his voice drops: "*Um* – I told my parents."

My heart skips a beat. A feeling that was like shame but not entirely it overcame me, shame at what I had done in secret. What I had done with Ahmad. What do they think of me now? Of us getting married secretly? I know this is just the first hurdle; if anything, it's the easiest hurdle. "What did they say?"

Ahmad tells me how it went with his parents and I know I have to do the same – to tell my parents the truth, too. The thought of it almost makes me hope for the world to end right now.

"My dad is calling yours tomorrow," he shuffles some papers, "and by the end of the week, we'll be coming to see him."

I sigh as I think of all the implications. If only I waited a few more weeks before saying yes to Umar, this would be easier. Now, I'm not just breaking up with him; I'm breaking up with his family.

"I know this is sudden," he says. It almost feels like he was next to me. "How are you feeling about all of this?"

I scratch my forehead, looking for the right word. "Scared…?" I finally said, even though it came out like a question.

His voice is hoarse when he speaks. "I'll be by your side every step of the way, okay? Put the blame on me; it was my idea. It was all my fault."

"No, it's not." It felt like the right decision then – brilliant even; we were going to keep our Canadian marriage a secret for a few months and then get married in front of our family and friends in December with no sins committed. But now the day of reckoning is finally here. Right behind it is the gate to redemption and if Ahmad and I want to get through the gates and be together, this is the price to pay. For Ahmad, I will pay it with interest.

The following day, after concluding a meeting I chaired with the legal team on our cases for the week, the receptionist comes in to tell me that someone wants to see me urgently; she is waiting in my office. I have an open-door policy because I realized that some people didn't want to wait in the reception for fear of being followed or meeting people who know them. Keeping up with appearances in this part of the world is a big thing.

I nod to her, excuse myself and go toward my office. To my surprise, I find Aunty Mami sitting at my desk. My heart starts pounding, my mouth gets dry and I feel faint.

"Goo – good morning," my voice comes out as a whisper. I want to melt to the floor and completely evaporate. I can't look at her; all I can think about is: *She knows. She knows of what Ahmad and I did when we were alone. What does she think of me? What does she think of the secret we hid all these years?*

"Ahmad said I would find you here," The last time she was here was at the opening ceremony; she came with the Ambassador and other dignitaries to support the initiative. I remember how she hugged me that day as she told me how proud she was of me. But looking at her now, I wonder if she would say the same today. She gestures at the chair next to her and I sit. We are now facing each other, but I'm looking down at the lines on my palms. "Fa'iza," she finally says." Look at me."

I drag my eyes from my hands and look into hers. She looks at me the same way she always did – with kindness and tears begin to fill my eyes.

"Umma needs to hear about this from you," she says, standing up. "I called to let her know that I'm on my way to see her about something important, but she needs to hear it from you. So, come. Let's go."

I nod. The day of reckoning. I might not even make it till the day the trumpet blows. Today might just be my last day on Earth because Umma will surely kill me. But I know that if anyone knows how to get through to her, it's Aunty Mami. She's her oldest friend and even though they spent a lot of time apart, they have always been there for each other when it mattered.

The car ride is quiet, even the radio is silent. Forty-five minutes later, I'm sitting on the carpet in Umma's living room sobbing uncontrollably, my blazer soaked with tears I didn't know I still had left in me. What is killing me was my mother's silence – the way she's covering her face with her hands, her slow movement as she shakes her head. I want to run out of the house and never return. *Why isn't she screaming at me? Why isn't she insulting me? Why isn't she telling she's disappointed?* I cover my face with my hands, too.

"She's sorry," Aunty Mami leans towards my mom and speaks in hushed tones – the kind reserved for confidential matters that start with telling none of the domestic helps to come into a particular section of the house until they were called in. You would be surprised to know how often this happened in conservative Northern households. "They were young and stupid; they didn't know better." Umma is still quiet. "Ahmad's father is coming over in two days to talk to Abba about this situation," she says to Umma, who is cradling her cheek in her palm and staring into the distance. "We have to put our heads together, so that the outcome will be in the children's best interest."

"We have to know exactly what to say to Umar's family so that it doesn't bring shame upon us," she finally says. "If people find out –" she can't bring herself to finish the thought. She shakes her head and lowers it to the ground.

Later that night, I look up from my father's *Shariah* book to find my phone ringing. It is Ahmad. When he asks, I start to tell him how everything went and start crying as I tell him Umma has still not eaten dinner. I tell him about how she cried because of me, how she didn't look up at me when I went into her room after Isha, and how I'm not sure she'll ever forgive me.

"Fa'iza, I'm so sorry," he says quietly, crying with me.

"It's not like you forced me. I agreed to it," I sniff. "I agreed to it, without thinking. I didn't think about the shame it would br –"

"You were innocent in all of this," he insists. "I should never have brought it up."

"Did you print the documents?" I finally ask him, as I lay in bed. With his parents backing us up and hopefully Umma forgiving me, we might actually have a credible case to present to Abba. When that time comes, we need to be well-prepared.

"Yes, everything."

I open my mouth to reply but am interrupted by the sound of my phone beeping. Umar is forwarding me something about the health benefits of drinking lime water before bed, another generic message. I sigh.

"Are you okay?" Ahmad asks. Even after all these years, he can still tell when there's something on my mind.

"It's Umar."

"Are you worried your dad might not accept our marriage?" Ahmad asks, like he knows what I was thinking. I know exactly how my dad thinks and in this case, it's going to be a blessing for us.

The two *'yar* Agadez sisters are already in Abuja and in Ahmad's parents' guest house. They're going to be part of the entourage coming to see Abba. After Subh, I go over the drafts I wrote on presenting my case to Abba. It is absolutely perfect. It's as if the decisions we made while being apart all through the years led up to this moment and it finally seems like there's a chance of me getting my Happily Ever After, after all.

Chapter 38

When Malama Hassana sees Fa'iza's mother for the first time in over two decades, their reunion is colored with chants of '*Allahu Akbar,* God is great', as the ladies close the distance between them with an embrace amidst teary eyes.

"*Ashe da rabon zan sake ganin ki eh,* so it had been destined that I would use my eyes to see you again before my death, Hajiya."

"Is this your face I am seeing?" Fa'iza's mother asks in disbelief, she holds her face in her hands before she hugs her again; they exchange pleasantries with her sister Mallama Husseina, whose limp has gotten even more noticeable due to the long flight into Nigeria, and Halime before they make their way to the Ambassador's section.

Justice Mohammed's house in Abuja is traditionally designed and divided into separate sections. The man's affairs and businesses are kept separate from the area that housed his wife and children. Today, however, all members of the Mohammed family -all the siblings are going to be present. Apart from the Mohammed family, there were eleven other people in the room: two of Fa'iza's uncles, Ahmad, two of his uncles, the Ambassador and his wife, and the '*yar* Agadez twins – one is here with her husband and the other who came from Saint-Malo with her daughter Halime.

This is the third time Ahmad has been in this living room. The first time was when he came with his parents to ask for Fa'iza's hand in marriage; the second time he was within these walls, his life unexpectedly fell apart. It's been five years and the white paneled walls, which are separated by floor-length white drapes, still look the same to him, as well as the three-tiered crystal chandelier hanging from the ceiling.

Ahmad finds himself staring as Fa'iza walks into the living room in a black abaya and scarf wrapped over her head, covering her neck and shoulders. She gently sits on the floor next to his mother and Umma. This is the first time Ahmad is seeing her since the day she came looking for him after receiving the file, and he can tell that she has been crying. When she settles, she looks up slightly, her eyes searching the room until their eyes meet. Ahmad gives her a reassuring smile, and he watches as she reciprocates the gesture for just the length of a heartbeat.

A few feet away from her, Justice Mohammed listens to both women with rapt attention. They speak about their jobs for both families back in the 1990s, their claims supported by their companions – a husband and a daughter. When they finish, Fa'iza's father places the picture of the sisters back in the file he's now holding. *"Allahu Akbar,"* he says, and everyone echoes his words.

Justice Mohammed is a very soft-spoken man. He pronounces his words slowly and carefully, conscious of every utterance he makes, as though he believes he will one day have to account for everything he has said. He slowly looks around the room, then speaks: "In this very room, we were led to believe that Ahamad and Fa'iza could not get married as they were suckled by the same woman. Now, evidence has been adequately provided that that was a misunderstanding. It was not done out of malice or with any sinister intention; Malama Zainab made an honest mistake – one I'm sure we can all forgive her for," he takes a long pause before continuing. "In the Quran, Allah *subhana wa ta'ala* says: *Wa iz yamkuru bikal lazeena kafaroo liyusbitooka aw yaqtulooka aw yukhrijook* –"

"Wa yamkuroona wa yamkurul laahu wallaahu khairul maakireen," Ahmad completes the verse quietly with him.

Justice Mohammed translates the end of the verse. "They plan, and Allah plans; but Indeed, Allah is the best of planners." He looks at Fa'iza as he speaks, "everything that happens is all part of Allah's plan." He stays silent for a few seconds, then he speaks again, his eyes meeting Ahmads. "I believe in this case, Allah has planned for Fa'iza to marry Umar."

A murmur spreads across the room as the other men speak among themselves. Justice Mohammed waits for the slight chatter to die down with the patience of a man used to saying uncomfortable truths to courtrooms. This particular living room is well air-conditioned, but Fa'iza starts fanning her face with her hands. As Ahmad watches, his mom discreetly holds Fa'iza's hand and steadies it on her lap, squeezing her fingers gently as if to reassure her. Ahmad looks away and his eyes meet Amin's, who doesn't look away until Abba's voice continues.

"I believe that if Ahmad and Fa'iza were meant to be together, this would have been revealed – this information would have come to light – before we gave our word to Umar's family."

One of Fa'iza's uncles nods his head vigorously in agreement. Ahmad looks at Fa'iza's, and he sees her hand shaking, her eyes are downcast and even though he can't see the expression on her face, he can hear her tiny sniffles before they are drowned by the athan for Asr as it rings out loud and clear from the Masjid in the compound.

"I hear there's a matter you would like to present before me?" he directs his question to his daughter. Umma looks at Fa'iza for the first time and the young girl nods. Fa'iza never thought there would come a day when she would be on the opposite end of his counsel, trying to appeal his verdict.

"Okay," he smiles at her. "Let's table that till after we pray."

The men stand up, filing out slowly to go and pray in the Masjid and the women do the same, taking the doors that lead back into the house. When they return, the group is considerably smaller, the twins from Agadez and their companion are having lunch at the other section of the house and all the uncles and her brother are in Abba's dining area. In the living room, Justice Mohammed is on his brown leather couch, now holding the Holy Qur'an. To his right on the white leather couch are Ahmad's father and Ahmad, and to the Justice's left on the white leather sectional are Umma and Aunty Mami. Fa'iza sits on the floor next to them.

"What do we have here?" Justice Mohammad asks as the Ambassador hands him a piece of paper. He squints at the paper, then wears his reading glasses and listens as the former ambassador tells him everything he knows about Fa'iza and Ahmad. To their sides, both mothers watched quietly, Fa'iza's hands are still shaking.

Justice Mohammed looks up at his daughter. He is blinking rapidly, as though nothing could have ever prepared him for this day. Fa'iza looks down, refusing to meet his gaze. He readjusts his falling glasses and looks at the title of the document. It is a marriage certificate. He takes his time to read every word on the piece of paper: the name of the Mosque, the location, the names of the bride and groom, the date and time the marriage of officiated, the name of the Imam, the names of the witnesses and the amount was paid as *mahr*. After going through the certificate three times, he removes his glasses and looks at Ahmad.

"Ahamad," he speaks in Hausa, "What's this? What's this document?"

It takes a few seconds before Ahmad finds his voice. "It's – It's a –" he clears his throat, "it's a marriage certificate, Abba."

The Justice's eyebrows shoot up as he turns to Fa'iza again, as though he is waiting for her to say something, to say that it isn't true. When she can't meet his gaze, he sighs and returns his glasses to reread the document. This time, even slower than he did the first time.

"Fa'iza, what *madhhab* – what school of thoughts of Islamic jurisprudence – do we follow in this house?" he bellows at her. Still looking at the certificate.

"Ma –Maliki." Her voice is almost inaudible.

"So, Fa'iza, who gave you away in marriage?" He looks at her with his features pulled into a worried frown. "I don't see the name or signature of your *Wali*. So, who served as your guardian during this marriage? Who gave you away during this Nikkah?"

Ahmad's father looks at the girl shaking next to her mother. She opens her mouth a few times, but no words come out. Even though he knows that the Justice already knows, he explains that the Mosque Fa'iza and Ahmad got married at was a Hanafi Mosque. Unlike their *madhhab* requirements, a *Wali* is not required, as a woman acts on her own behalf.

The Justice has a few more questions and seeks clarification from Ahmad and Fa'iza directly. When he asks questions about each of the witnesses and dowry, Ahmad answers him clearly, speaking with no ounce of uncertainty. When he asks his daughter if they lived under the same roof at any time after they got married, Fa'iza's head remains bowed and she can't form her words between tears; her mother responds based on her conversation with Fa'iza earlier that morning.

"You knew about this?" He asks Umma with surprise.

"She confessed to me just yesterday." She answers.

Abba's eyes trail towards Fa'iza and then at the crumbled tissue paper she holds in her hands as she dabs her eyes every few seconds, and with a resigned sigh, he leans back into his chair. He clasps his hands with both his index fingers touching his lip, uneasiness written all over his features. He remains silent for a very long time, except for when he utters verses from the Qur'an to himself while praying for patience because he knows that this is also a test for him. He picks up the marriage certificate again and goes through it one final time. "If this is truly the case, then this marriage is valid; all conditions seem to have been met," he says as he puts the marriage certificate back down. "We're now looking at a case of separation."

Ahmad steals a glance at Fa'iza, recalling she told him that her father would come to this conclusion.

"Now, there are stipulations regarding separation in marriage," he reached for a book next to him and starts flipping slowly. "If the couple has no knowledge of each other, then four to six months is the longest they can be separated for." Meaning if they have not been intimate, six months is the longest a couple can go without seeing each other before their marriage has to be dissolved, according to Islamic law. Otherwise, the separation can be years, if it is something they both agree to, but under two conditions," he flips the pages of the book and looks up at Ahmad. "The husband must provide financial support to his wife during the time of separation, and two, the wife must remain faithful during the time of their separation." Justice Mohammed removes his glasses and looks from Ahmad to Fa'iza and back to Ahmad. "If these two conditions have been met, you're still married to each other."

Fa'iza nods without looking at her father as though answering a question he hasn't asked. Ahmad brings out the papers she asked him to print out and his father passes them to her father. They all watch as Justice Mohammed goes through highlighted transactions on Ahmad's bank statements. The statements show money being transferred from his personal bank account to a trust he set up for that sole purpose and the remittance of the funds to Fa'iza's account for her NGO. It went on for years. When Ahmad set up the automatic monthly payments to The Cain Mosni Foundation years ago, he was only doing it to support her dream; he had no idea Allah was guiding his actions and that one day, this would be the string by which his marriage to Fa'iza would be held.

Ahmad thinks of all the choices he made that brought them to this moment – his impatience to wait for less than a year until Allah tested them to wait for years. He almost laughs at the irony as he realizes that he's a patient man. In the past, he only respected her boundaries because they mattered to her, he respected them to gain her trust. Yet a few days ago, before he knew that their marriage was still intact, he could not touch her because of *Taqwa,* the fear of Allah. There was a huge difference. His love for her transcends his feelings; he would never do anything that will cause her *Rabb* to be displeased with her.

Chapter 39

When I was a teen, I prayed for a husband who feared Allah, who never drank alcohol or touched women who were not his *mahram*. And that is exactly who I'm now married to. But the journey here has not been so easy. Ahmad once asked me, *"Any man can love you. But will that love remain on the days you're difficult to love?"* I didn't understand it in its entirety then, but today I do. In all the time we were apart, while I tried to bury my love for him, he held on for the both of us. This is what security feels like – knowing that he will love me even on days I'm difficult to love.

The fallout from the canceled engagement with Umar was a lot. As soon as the boxes brought as *kayan lefe* were returned to his family, people gossiped about us in hushed tones at weddings, naming ceremonies, and death condolences. A blog that was known for its gossip about Abuja residents, in its blind item about me, said that 'I weaseled my way back into my ex's life and snatched him from his loving fiancee weeks before their wedding.' Umma and Hajiya Uwani didn't remain as close afterward.

We didn't want a huge ceremony. What's the point after all of these years? I just want to spend all my time with my husband and away from prying eyes. But a few months later, our mothers said they had a thousand reasons to celebrate, so they went all out. The wedding reception hashtag was – you guessed right – #InsomNiac. When our younger relatives or random strangers comment on our pictures on social media, they write the usual things like 'couple goals,' and sometimes, they will wish for something like what we had for themselves. I always pray that may only the best of this be theirs – because our story has got dark parts, ugly parts, and really painful parts. But people don't see our story when they see our pictures all over social media; we don't wear our scars from years of being broken. I was in therapy for years for the anxiety the separation brought. Nobody talks about that except me. I am and will always be an advocate for therapy. I made mistakes, and Ahmad's mistakes finally caught up with him, but Allah is *Al Hadi* and *Ar-Rasheed,* The Guide and The Infallible Teacher. He brought us closer to him in the process. He wanted to test our patience and faith in Him, and if we had defied Him and continued meeting secretly, we would never have ended up together because Ahmad would not have searched for *'yar* Agadez as hard as he did, and our families would have never found out the truth.

As I watch Afreen, Joanne and Ada dancing with family and friends on the dance floor at our wedding dinner, Ahmad leans towards me and whispers in my ear. "How much longer is this supposed to go on for?"

"Next on the agenda is our 'Vote of thanks', and then its open dance floor for all."

"There's a car parked out front and the driver's waiting. How about we just ditch this and go continue from where we left off?" He bites down on his lower lip as he smiles.

"You are soo bad, Ahmad." I look at him and laugh.

"You weren't complaining last night."

I open my mouth as I gasp in mock shock, although flashes of us together didn't allow me to keep a straight face. I am in love with how he loves me and how tender he is when he touches me.

"I wanna hear you say it," his husky voice filled my ear the previous night as his weight pressed into me on the bed while I was naked beneath him.

I hesitated as I glanced up at him and felt his thumb graze my lips. Even in the dark, I could see that his eyes never left mine. "Don't make me beg…" My breathing was ragged as I got impatient.

"Say it," he dared teasingly.

"I want you." It was a confession, almost a plea. A look I knew all too well crossed his face as he reached down between us. I gasped as I felt his fullness in me. He was torturously slow and groaned softly into my ear as his grip tightened on my thigh.

"Oh, fuuck," his mouth covered mine as he silenced my cry.

* * *

A few days after the wedding reception, the sun pours through the curtains in the private chalet overlooking the white sands and deep blue water of the Maldives. Our legs are intertwined, and we are both wrapped in the white sheets on the king-sized bed. When I rub my eyes and raise my head from his chest, my husband opens his bedside drawer and places a small black box wrapped with a red bow between us.

"What's this?" I sit up, wrapping the sheets around my naked body. He smiles as he opens the box, and in it are my ring from years ago and the Milan bracelet. I can't believe that he held onto them all these years. "Babe... ?" My mouth remains open. I didn't think he would still have them after all this time.

"I love you, Insom," he smiles at me as my tears begin to form.

"I missed you so much."

"I know. We're together now. Nothing's gonna ever tear us apart again."

"Insha Allah," I say.

"Insha Allah," he laughs as he wipes the tears from my eyes and kisses my forehead. "Do you still want to see the coral reef today, or do you want to come back tomorrow?"

"I wanna see baby sea-turtles, Mr Cain Mosni." I say, still leaning on his chest as I listen to his heartbeat and the sound of waves outside our chalet.

Sitting with him on this bed now, I can still remember years ago when he said all he wanted was someone who was completely his. *"Whatever life throws at me, I wanna know that my woman will always be my woman,"* he said. Today, without any doubt, I can say that's who I am. I am his. I belong to him – heart, soul, body and mind. Always and forever.

"I'll love you forever," I say as he places the ring on my finger and return the bracelet back to my wrist. I kiss him on the lips, savoring the feel of his arms as they wrap around me.

This is home.

About the Author

Fatima Bala is a lecturer, poet, and writer who lives in Canada with her family. Her books have received starred reviews from *The Los Angeles Tribune, London Post,* and *New York Weekly*. She is the award-winning author of an Afro-futuristic speculative fiction book, Before the Origin, to which she hopes to one day complete the sequel.

She can be reached on Instagram at @aka.fatima.bala

Also by Fatima Bala

Hafsatu Bebi

A story of two women, unconnected yet related. Birthed in the same society, they struggle to balance ugly truths and well-intentioned sins while facing different realities. When it all comes crashing down, leading to loss of self and identity crises, truths they fought so hard to hide become revealed. Can they recognize themselves now that the masks are off?

Hafsatu thinks she has it all figured out until destiny starts to pull out pieces of her picture-worthy life apart, secret after secret. Sadiq is a man with a dark past and darker humor. When complexities bring a whirlpool of love that can't be tamed into his life, fate vows to pull them apart. Can they stand strong against the tides of destiny and sins of the past?

"If everything is preordained, then aren't the choices we make daily just setting the stones into the grand stage of our fated destinies? Is free will not part of an already written script that we unknowingly act out even in our rebellion?"

Available in paperback and ebook on Amazon and Kindle.

Made in the USA
Middletown, DE
11 September 2024